Born in 1893, **Anthony Berkele**
novelist. A founding member (
one of crime fiction's greatest innovators, being one of the first to predict the development of the 'psychological' crime novel. He sometimes wrote under the pseudonym of Francis Iles. He wrote twenty-four novels, ten of which feature his amateur detective, Roger Sheringham. His best-known Roger Sheringham mystery is *The Poisoned Chocolates Case*. Anthony Berkeley died in 1971.

BY THE SAME AUTHOR
ALL PUBLISHED BY HOUSE OF STRATUS

Death in the House
Jumping Jenny
The Layton Court Mystery
Murder in the Basement
Not to Be Taken
The Piccadilly Murder
The Poisoned Chocolates Case
The Second Shot
The Silk Stocking Murders
Top Storey Murder
Trial and Error

PANIC PARTY

ANTHONY BERKELEY

HOUSE OF STRATUS

This edition published in 2001 by House of Stratus, an imprint of House of Stratus Ltd, Thirsk Industrial Park, York Road, Thirsk, North Yorkshire, YO7 3BX, UK.
Also at: House of Stratus Inc., 2 Neptune Road, Poughkeepsie, NY 12601, USA.

www.houseofstratus.com

Typeset, printed and bound by House of Stratus.

A catalogue record for this book is available from the British Library and the Library of Congress.

ISBN 0-7551-0210-X

TO
MILWARD KENNEDY

MY DEAR MILWARD KENNEDY, –

You once challenged me, in public print, to write a book in which the only interest should be the detection. I have no hesitation in refusing to do anything so tedious, and instead take the greatest pleasure in dedicating to you a book which is precisely the opposite, which breaks every rule of the austere Club to which we both belong, and which will probably earn my expulsion from its membership. On the other hand, this story, in somewhat shorter form, was rejected by a leading popular magazine as 'lacking sufficient human interest.' As a lady remarks on a late page: 'Life is very, very difficult.'

ANTHONY BERKELEY.

chapter one

Roger Sheringham, choosing papers at the bookstall, heard a voice at his elbow.

'Hullo, Roger, my sweet. I thought I'd see you. Can you find me a corner seat opposite yours?'

'Hullo, Crystal. I haven't got my own yet, but I expect we can find two. The train doesn't look as if it's going to be crowded. Are we all going down on it?'

'Oh, no. The others have been told the two-seventeen. You and I are going down alone.'

'That will be very delightful,' said Roger politely.

'Baa!' said Mrs Vane. 'Buy me a *Vogue*, Roger, there's a pet. There's a new one out today.'

Roger bought a *Vogue*, and a *London Mercury* for himself, and signed to the two porters who were standing by with the luggage.

'First or third?' he asked his companion.

'My sweetest, need you ask? Need you really? Of course, I know my contributions to the world's gossip columns are worth untold millions, but unfortunately it isn't untold millions that they pay me.'

'Well, I'm travelling first. Goodbye, Crystal. I'll see you at Poole.'

'I always disliked you, Roger,' said Mrs Vane with equanimity, settling the fur on her shoulders with a Reynier-gloved hand. 'I'm travelling first too, with you; and if the inspector catches me, you're going to pay the difference.'

'If you can afford silver-fox furs and French hats, to say nothing of clean gloves at any hour of the day, you can afford not to cheat the railway company, Crystal,' said Roger virtuously.

'But it's so terribly exciting,' Mrs Vane pleaded. 'And what an eye for detail the man has. No wonder the women in his books are so marvellous. You really are a terribly good novelist, Roger, aren't you?'

'Yes,' said Roger.

'I mean, even though you are a best-seller too,' added Mrs Vane pensively.

'That will do, Crystal,' Roger said sourly. 'If I'm going to be travelling about the world for the next month with you, it's just as well that I am a best-seller; so you needn't try out any more of your Irish blarney on me.'

'I've *always* said you were a lamb, Roger, ' said Mrs Vane fondly.

An empty carriage was found without difficulty, and Crystal Vane set about making herself comfortable in her corner. From the care with which she did so, arranging this and that on the rack, and that and this on the seat beside her, and fussing with rugs, coats, handbags and papers, one would have said that she was settling herself for a journey of several days, instead of only two hours.

Roger watched her with amusement. It was so like Crystal.

Crystal Vane had, in fact, created for herself something of a character. She lived in an expensive little flat in Carlton Gardens, she was always charmingly and correctly dressed, she was always seen at the right places; and how she did it, Roger could not fathom. He knew as much of her history as anyone else did, which was a fair amount, for Mrs Vane was not a reticent person. He knew, for instance, that, married in Ireland as quite a young girl, she had been left by her very Irish husband without a penny at the age of twenty-four. She had managed to get somehow to London, and from that point, without money, influence or connections, had gone straight ahead.

Journalism, of the more obscure kind, had been her line: fashion articles, paragraphs for the gossip columns, a little reviewing, reading for a publisher, articles in the women's magazines, interviewing, anything to which she could turn her witty pen or nimble mind. Now, somewhere in the early thirties, she was something of a figure in journalistic London; one met her at all the big literary parties, she was to be seen at any important first night (probably writing up the frocks for some paper), she had the freedom of more than one London restaurant. And she was popular. Not exactly pretty, she had an attractive face and a trim figure, and her conversation was uncensored and amusing; she frankly loved gossip and said so, and those who wanted their secrets to be spread about as rapidly and efficiently as possible, told them to Crystal Vane. Roger both liked and admired her. There was plenty of good, solid stuff under Crystal's normal effervescence.

When the train was at last underway, she looked at him with a quizzical smile. Characteristically, she had pulled off her hat, and her neatly waved hair was already a little ruffled by the wind from the half-open window.

Roger returned the smile. He was quite sure that Crystal had something to say to him, that was the only explanation of the deliberate encounter at the station, and the orders he had had to catch the 1.10 instead of travelling down with the others on the 2.17; but he was not going to angle.

'Well, Crystal?'

Well, Roger?'

Roger returned to his paper.

'Roger, my sweet.' Crystal called everyone she knew at all well her sweet, or her pet.

'Yes?' Roger came out of his paper again.

'I expect you've been wondering about this yachting cruise of Guy's?'

'No, I haven't. Why should I? When a man invites me for a cruise on his new yacht, I don't wonder; I accept. But I'll admit that I do wonder how Mr G B Pidgeon, MA, Fellow of St Mary's College, Oxon., late Classical Tutor to the said College, Reader in Greek to the University and sometime Proctor of the same, comes to be known to you as "Guy."'

'Guy's a lamb,' observed Mrs Vane, with some irrelevance.

'No doubt. But...?'

'Oh, I wrote him up when he came into all that money. Naturally I saw a bit of him. Do you realise, Roger,' added Mrs Vane with some awe, 'that Guy's one of the richest men in England?'

'I understood it was a packet that he came into so unexpectedly.'

'It was. And it hasn't spoilt him a bit. In fact, he's just like a child with it. Hardly a child. A baby.'

'Is he?' said Roger with interest. He remembered vividly an occasion when he was an undergraduate of St Mary's and Mr Guy Pidgeon had been its Dean, on which Mr Pidgeon had behaved not at all like a child and still less like a baby. Nor could Roger, try as he might, see the lean and black and angular Mr Pidgeon at all in the role of child or baby. But women look on these things differently.

'Yes. This yacht was one of the first things he bought, and this will be its first real cruise.'

'I was most surprised to get his invitation. I hadn't seen him since I went down, in 1914, and I didn't know that he even remembered me.'

'Oh, yes, he did. In fact, you were his suggestion.'

'His suggestion?' Roger looked surprised, and felt a shade uneasy. 'Am I to understand then, Crystal, that you and Mr Pidgeon planned this party between you?'

'Of course we did. And do stop calling him "Mr Pidgeon." I told you, Guy's a lamb. Yes – well, I wanted to have a word with you about that, Roger.'

'I'll believe you did,' said Roger, with some severity. A party of Crystal's choosing, which would probably consist of stage and literary folk, was not at all to Roger's taste; he saw too many of both in London, without having to cruise with them too. 'Your lamb only wrote that he was getting one or two interesting people together.'

'Well, and so he has, with my help.' Mrs Vane said defiantly. 'That's to say, they *will* be interesting together, though they might not be apart.'

'Would you mind,' Roger said patiently, 'explaining exactly who is coming, and why.'

'That's just what I'm trying to do, my pet, if you'll only let me speak,' smiled Mrs Vane. 'Well, Valentine Combe, for one.'

Roger bounded in his seat. 'Oh, *no!*' he wailed. 'Not Valentine Combe!'

'Why not?'

'Why not? Because he'll be wanting to commit suicide all the time, and I couldn't bear being shut up on a yacht for a month with a man who wants to commit suicide. I might help him.'

'Valentine's a poet,' explained Mrs Vane tolerantly.

'He says he is,' Roger retorted. 'Personally, I don't believe him. And in any case, I can't stand the fellow.'

'Well, anyhow, he's coming. And so is Angela St Thomas. You'll like her.'

'Shall I?' said Roger sceptically. 'I've never met her, but her books are tripe.'

'Oh, she's not bad. Her father's Lord Beechwood.'

'Oh, I know that. There must be some reason for the reviews she gets, of course.'

'Now, now, don't be cynical, darling. Anyhow, she's bringing an aunt, so perhaps she'll behave herself nicely.'

'Why is she bringing an aunt?'

'Because Guy asked her. How stupid you're being, my pet.'

'Does he know them?'

'Of course not. But I've met her.'

'You've met her, so her aunt accepts an invitation for a month's cruise from Mr Pidgeon. Is that it?'

'Well, I don't know. I suppose it is,' admitted Mrs Vane. 'But then I always think aunts might be capable of anything, don't you?'

'I'm not interested in bright young things, or their aunts. Go on.'

'Well, you probably won't know any of the others. There's a couple called Bray – he's a bucket-shop keeper, or whatever it's called; I mean, they won't have him on the Stock Exchange. Then there's a cousin of Guy's, and his wife; and the daughter of another don, called Vincent; and Stella Crosspatrick, the organiser; and – '

'Never heard of her. What does she organise?'

'Oh, I don't know. Things. And Captain Twyford, the explorer. You've heard of him, of course.'

'Yes, vaguely. Captain Reginald Twyford. Where does he explore?'

'Africa, I think, doesn't he? Anyhow, some place where there are films. He's rather a lamb. Elephants, you know,' added Mrs Vane somewhat vaguely. 'Or is it gorillas?'

'Oh, yes, of course. I remember now.' A vision had come to Roger of a large, virile man, slightly sunburned like other handsome men, in a white topee and shorts, smiling in rather a languid way over the corpses of various animals: different animals, but always the same deprecatingly bored and faintly superior smile. 'Yes. A lamb, is he?'

'Well, perhaps not a lamb,' admitted Mrs Vane reflectively. 'But *rather* a pet, for all that. Let's see, is that all? One, two, three, four...oh, yes – Sir John Birch.'

'Never heard of him, either. What's his line?'

'Whisky, my sweet. I don't know of any other.'

'And is he a lamb too?'

Mrs Vane considered. 'Well, I suppose really all men are lambs, in a way, aren't they?'

'Am I a lamb?' Roger asked, with some interest.

'You? Darling! You're the sweetest lamb that ever bleated.'

'Well, it's lucky I can bleat, if I'm to get a word in sideways with you on the same boat, Crystal,' said Roger rudely. 'Is that all?'

'That's the main bunch.' Mrs Vane smoothed down the growing wildness of her waves and looked at Roger expectantly.

'Well?' said Roger.

'Well? Haven't you anything to say?'

'Only that you and your Guy-lamb seem to me completely mad. I've never heard of a more ridiculous mixture in my life.'

Mrs Vane laughed gleefully. 'I knew you'd see it, given time. Of course it's a ridiculous mixture. It's the most ridiculous mixture we could think of. My love, we spent simply *hours* compounding it.'

'But what's the idea of it?'

'Why, to see what will happen, by the end of a four-weeks' cruise. It's like making a haggis. Have you ever made a haggis, pet? They say you take a nice big bag and throw into it all the most awful things you can think of; then you put it on to simmer, and hope for the worst. I think we ought to be quite a nice haggis by the time we've been simmering for four weeks, don't you?'

'Then you and I are both part of the haggis, are we?' asked Roger coldly.

'Oh, I'm not. For one thing, I'm one of the cooks. But apart from that, I shall be there in a perfectly professional capacity. In fact,' said Mrs Vane with pride, 'I've got a commission for it, from the *Daily Distress*. You know – Millionaire Don's Novel Cruise; Famous Poet Saved from Suicide by Intrepid Explorer; Noted Author Advises *Sicco* for Sea Voyage – "I am never without it for more than a few moments," says Roger Sheringham, leaning over the binnacle. A thousand words twice a week, my angel, and on my own terms too.'

'Am I to understand,' said Roger, still more coldly, 'that you propose to write *me* up, as well as the rest of the haggis?'

Mrs Vane laughed delightedly. 'Well, we are letting you in on the joke, anyhow, my lamb. I wouldn't steal a march on any fellow-writer. And I tell you what you can do, Roger. You can write *me* up.'

'Do you mind reading your *Vogue* now, Crystal?' said Roger. 'I want to look at the *London Mercury*.'

2

Mr Guy Pidgeon had taken a reception room in the Hotel Magnificent, where his guests were to gather and have tea before going on board. Roger and Mrs Vane, however, had time to pay a visit to the yacht first, in its own motor-launch, to choose their staterooms for the cruise.

Mr Pidgeon was waiting for them on board, lean and tall and stringy as any don, but grinning wickedly as no don grins. Roger wondered that Mr Pidgeon had not forgotten to grin so wickedly during the thirty years of his don-ship. In spite of the chilliness of the April day, Mr Pidgeon was the complete summer yachtsman, in cap and jacket and white duck trousers.

'Hullo, Sheringham,' grinned Mr Pidgeon.

'Hullo,' said Roger, a little ill at ease as a man still is before the preceptors of his youth. 'Very good of you to ask me.'

'Wasn't it?' Mr Pidgeon agreed. 'But I hope that a great deal of the pleasure will be mine. And no doubt it will be, unless you've changed very much, Sheringham; and I don't think you have.'

'Nor have you,' Roger returned politely.

The wickedness of Mr Pidgeon's grin deepened. 'I haven't, eh? That's very penetrating of you, Sheringham. You can't have been such an empty-headed young nincompoop as I thought. So I haven't changed, eh?'

'Well, perhaps I should have said, not in appearance.'

Mr Pidgeon cackled.

'Cut out the reminiscences you two,' interposed Mrs Vane. 'Guy, my sweet, do you know you haven't kissed me yet? No, I don't care if the sailors are watching.'

'My dear Crystal, neither do I,' said Mr Pidgeon gallantly, and pecked like a gaunt crow at the cheek offered him.

Roger did not know whether to grin or to gape. Was this really the sarcastic, terrifying, doom-bearing creature who had had Roger so ferociously on the carpet for entertaining an unauthorised lady-friend to tea in his rooms all those twenty years ago?

Well, well, well, thought Roger.

'Come on,' said Crystal. 'We haven't got much time, and if you want to look round the yacht before it's infested, Roger, you'd better get Guy to take you now.'

The tour of the yacht was duly made. Roger was astonished at her size and luxury. She was almost a small liner, of at least 1,250 tons, and would accommodate the large party with ease. Mr Pidgeon, professing to know nothing whatever about her, was yet able to offer the information that her total length was 270 feet, and breadth 33.

There were three decks: the main deck, with the dining-saloon and staterooms; the promenade deck, with the smoking-room, main saloon, and so on; and the boat-deck, about half the length of the other two and formed from the roofs of the rooms on the deck below, and containing the wheel-house and the Captain's cabin, just in front of the single funnel. In addition to the owner's suite, there were no less than sixteen staterooms, small but beautifully fitted with everything that luxury or ingenuity could suggest; while on the promenade deck there were, in addition to the main rooms, a small card-room just big enough for two tables, and even a tiny cocktail-bar.

'Well, I'm blessed,' said Roger, with considerable awe. 'She must have cost a fortune; and not a small one either.'

'Oh, she did,' nonchalantly agreed Mrs Vane, who seldom felt awe. With altruistic pride she went on to inform Roger that it took twelve hands to work the yacht, to say nothing of the Captain and two officers, and the engineers and greasers. She carried, moreover, half a dozen stewards and stewardesses, three cooks, a pantryman, and heaven only knew whom else as well.

'So she costs a fortune to run, too,' Crystal told Roger, when Mr Pidgeon had gone off to speak to the captain. 'But as Guy says, he's too old to hoard now, and he doesn't see why he shouldn't throw his money about while he's still alive to enjoy it. I agree with him. After all, it isn't as if he had any children to leave it to.'

'He's a lucky devil,' Roger said, with frank envy. 'Who is his next-of-kin, then?'

'I believe his cousin. The one who's coming on the cruise. In fact, the only one he's got; and only a second cousin at that. Guy and I are the only people we know who aren't bothered with relations.'

'Humph!' said Roger. 'If I were your Guy, I'd think twice before I took my second cousin and heir on a lonely cruise through shark-infested seas and what-not. It seems to me to be asking for trouble.'

'Now, Roger, my pet, don't get on that hobby-horse of yours. You're going to have a rest from murder while you're with us. Willie Fayre (that's the cousin's name) isn't Guy's heir. Guy doesn't think much of Willie, and he can't stand his wife. He says he'd rather give his money to the nation than let Enid Fayre spend it on herself; so that's what he's done.'

'What?'

'Left it all to the nation for the reduction of debt. Every penny. And he sent Willie Fayre a copy of the will, so that he shouldn't have any illusions or expectations. I don't know – I think sometimes Guy has rather a cruel streak in him. But perhaps,' said Crystal brightly, 'that's what makes me love the poor lamb so.'

3

Spurred on by Mrs Vane, the trio reached the hotel before the train was due to arrive in Poole Station, but even so two of the guests were already waiting for them in the sham Louis Quinze room which had been put at Mr Pidgeon's disposal. Valentine Combe and Sir John Birch, neither of whom had been coming from London, were eyeing each other with suspicion as they engaged, from opposite corners of the room, in stilted conversation – a conversation which had consisted for Sir John's part almost entirely of reluctant grunts.

Valentine Combe was a black-avised young man with brown eyes and very dark hair, which he wore a little wild; although tolerably kempt, he yet managed to present an unkempt suggestion. All his movements were rapid and jerky. Young women were known to liken him to a wild thing of the woods; but Roger, who knew him slightly and disliked him heartily, considered that he must have heard about this and been not displeased. He was extremely poor, and lived with a wife and two children in a cottage somewhere in Hampshire, where he wrote his nature poems. Roger did not approve of his habit of accepting invitations, like the present one, in which that wife had not been included.

'Hullo, Sheringham,' he said in his high, rather excitable tones, after he had greeted Crystal and been introduced to his host. 'How are you? I don't seem to have seen you for a long time. But then I don't seem to see anyone. The wild life is all very well, but one can have too much of it. This month is just about going to save my reason.'

'How is your wife?' said Roger, who did not consider that Mr Combe had very much reason to save.

'Oh, she's all right, thanks,' returned Mr Combe indifferently. His restless eyes darted about the room. 'I say, who's in the party? Do you know? Crystal wrote something about Angela St Thomas. Do you know her?'

'No.'

'Nor do I. But, of course, I don't know anyone. My God, I wish I could afford to live in London. Lucky devils you are, you novelists. I say, who's that old cormorant over there? Sir John Birch? He hadn't got the manners to introduce himself before you people came. Sir John Birch, is it? Well, I've never heard of him. But then, I don't suppose he's heard of me either, so that evens it up. Have you ever thought, Sheringham, how few people really do hear of one, till one's dead?'

'It's a distressing thought, ' agreed Roger solemnly, his right toe itching. It was all very well for the fellow to think himself a genius; probably he couldn't work without that comfort. But such thoughts should be private. One should not take it for granted that other people agree in the estimate. Besides, Roger did not agree. Valentine Combe's stuff was very well, but it was only second-rate.

By the window Roger could hear Sir John Birch robustly refusing tea, his heavy red jowls quivering with aversion. 'Eh? No, no. Never drink the stuff. Leave that to the ladies. Wishy-washy. What? Yes, a whisky-and-soda's more in my line. Thanks. Yes.' Sir John had a curiously high-pitched wheezy grunt of a voice, that seemed to be squeezed in jerks from his short but massive frame, as if he were a huge, india-rubber doll. Much fox-hunting, much whisky, and much wooden-pated ancestry had gone to the making of Sir John; and at a first glance Roger privately considered that the result had not been worth the expense.

He caught Crystal's eye and exchanged smiles.

Then the party from the train began to arrive, the room filled, and Roger found himself involved in a swirl of introductions, with Crystal winking at him wickedly between each.

None of the new arrivals knew each other, so that they had travelled down separately, and made their own way to the hotel from the station. The first to arrive were the couple called Bray, a large, florid man with an unmistakably Cockney accent, who at once filled the whole room with the pervasion of his mere presence, and a buxom woman, with exceedingly tight gloves on her podgy hands, who spoke with such overwhelming gentility out of the round little mouth underneath her parrot nose, that Roger was seized with an insane urge to say 'lavatory-paper' to her just once, and then catch the heavens as they fell.

'Such a long time since I travelled by train,' confided Mrs Bray to Roger, as she took a cup of tea from the waiter's tray. 'Not that it wasn't very comfortable, I'm sure, but one can't help missing the car, can one, Mr Sheringham?'

'That's very true,' agreed Roger, who had never possessed a car and never intended to do so. 'You usually travel by car, then, Mrs Bray?'

'Oh, yes. I wanted to come down in it today, but Mr Bray thought it might not be safe to trust the showffer to go straight back to Town again. Such a nuisance servants are. I often say to Mr Bray I do believe we were better off when we didn't have so many of them.'

Lavatory-paper! thought Roger – and said politely: 'You must find it a great strain, looking after them.'

'Oh, *I* don't look after them,' bridled Mrs Bray. 'I mean to say, well, the housekeeper does that, you know, Mr Sheringham.'

Oh, lavatory-paper! thought Roger.

'What's that?' demanded Mr Bray from the other side of the room in a rollicking roar. 'Mrs Bray talking servants to you already, Mr Sheringham? That means she's taken a fancy to you, that's what it means. Eh, Gladys?' He strolled towards them.

'Well, really, Harry!' protested Mrs Bray in ladylike tones.

Mr Bray proceeded to take Roger in hand himself, and Gladys faded out of the picture. Roger felt, with an unusual prick of compassion, that life for Gladys must have meant a ceaseless procession of fade-outs.

'You're the Roger Sheringham that writes books, aren't you? Never read novels myself, but Mrs Bray'll know all about them. Eh, Gladys? You've read Mr Sheringham's books, I'll bet? Yes, Mrs Bray's the one for culture in our family. Now you might think it funny, Mr Sheringham, but I'd only be interested in books to know what the author made out of 'em. I wouldn't mind betting now that you make a pretty good thing out of yours, eh?'

'Probably not what you'd call a good thing, Mr Bray,' Roger murmured.

'Well, really, Harry,' fluted Mrs Bray, 'you oughtn't to ask questions like that. I don't know what Mr Sheringham will be thinking of you, I'm sure. Really, Mr Sheringham, sometimes I don't know what he'll say next.'

'Oh, come off it, Gladys,' riposted Mr Bray jovially. 'Mr Sheringham won't take offence so easily as that. I'm a plain man, Mr Sheringham, and I say what I think. And after all money's my business, same as book-writing's yours. Company promoter that's what I am, and not ashamed of it either; though to hear Mrs Bray talk sometimes, you'd think that every company that's promoted must be a shady one. Why, I've promoted hundreds in my time. Hundreds! And I don't suppose above nine-tenths of 'em have been wound up to this day. Not such a bad record, eh?'

'It sounds very good,' said Roger, who was finding himself a little swamped.

'That's right. Everyone knows Harry Bray's companies are on the level all right. But look here, Mr Sheringham, I want to ask you a favour. It's a bit of a short acquaintance for asking favours, I'll admit, but I'm a plain man, and when I've got a favour to ask, I ask it. See here, you know our worthy host pretty well, don't you? Yes, of course you do,' affirmed Mr Bray, trampling on Roger's incipient doubts. 'So I want you to ask him something for me. It's like this: he gave Mrs Bray and me the invite for this cruise, but he didn't say anything about my secretary. Well, you can see for yourself, Mr Sheringham, a busy man like me can't afford to take a whole month off without keeping in touch, slack though things may be just now, and I happen to know there's a wireless on board – well, I'm a plain man, and I'll say at once that I couldn't have come at all without there'd been a wireless, because – '

'You want me to ask Mr Pidgeon if you can bring your secretary with you on the voyage?' Roger interposed at last. 'Yes, of course I will. Where is your secretary now?'

'He's waiting outside this blessed room,' said Mr Bray, with manly simplicity. 'Mr Pidgeon has only got to say the word, and we'll both of us stay behind; but if I'm to come, I must have Harold with me, and that's the truth of it.'

Roger made his way over to his host to break this news.

Mr Pidgeon was in the act of greeting a tall, slim, extremely elegant lady, very pretty in the fair-hair-and-blue-eyes style, who had just entered the room followed by a small, nondescript man who looked smaller still through sheer negativeness, just as his perfectly ordinary walk appeared like an uncouth shuffle beside the lady's gliding grace.

'Ah, Sheringham,' observed Mr Pidgeon, espying him. 'Let me introduce you to my cousin and his wife – Mr and Mrs Fayre. Enid and Willie, this is Mr Roger Sheringham, whose books have given you so much pleasure.'

The lady gave Roger her hand, and a brilliant smile. 'This is *delightful*, Mr Sheringham. I can see already that the cruise is going to be a success.'

'Just what I was going to say myself,' said Roger, not to be outdone in floweriness.

He exchanged the usual shamefaced grin and half-nod with Fayre, and turned to Mr Pidgeon, to whom he delivered Mr Bray's petition.

'I expect we can squeeze him in, can't we, Crystal?' said Mr Pidgeon to Mrs Vane, who had joined the group while Roger was speaking.

Crystal looked doubtful. 'Well, there isn't a – '

'Oh, of *course* we can squeeze him in, Guy,' interposed Mrs Fayre gently. I'm sure it would upset all your arrangements if Mr Bray couldn't come. Do please bring the poor young man in, Mr Sheringham, won't you? And Guy, you must go and tell Mr Bray at once that we'll manage somehow.'

With a positively vulpine grin at Roger, Mr Pidgeon went. As Roger went too, he also smiled. From the very beginning there was going to be no doubt at all who was to act as hostess on Mrs Fayre's second-cousin-in-law's yacht. Roger hoped that Crystal appreciated the incident too.

In the passage was a weedy and somewhat pimply young man in a blue serge suit and stiff collar, loitering palely.

'Are you Harold?' asked Roger superfluously.

The weedy young man swayed eagerly towards him, as drowning men sway towards straws. 'My name's Harold Parker.'

'Then come inside.'

The young man swallowed a gulp. 'Er – pardon me…you don't happen to know?… Am I – are we going?'

'On the cruise? Yes, you are. Got your luggage here?'

The young man nodded in silence. For the second time in five minutes Roger felt touched. The young man was momentarily speechless, through sheer, pious gratitude; he swallowed several gulps in quick succession; every pimple on his face shone with a brighter lustre.

'Come inside and have some tea,' said Roger kindly.

The young man looked at him as if he would have liked to lick his hand and, wagging a metaphorical tail, preceded him into the room as if he were walking straight up the golden stairs.

Well, someone's going to enjoy the cruise at any rate, thought Roger, preparing to follow.

'I beg your pardon: is this Mr Guy Pidgeon's party?' asked a voice behind him – a curious voice, quiet and languid and yet conveying an impression of confident efficiency: exactly like a vocal parallel of the velvet glove on the iron hand, thought Roger, turning about.

Towards him there was advancing on the thick carpet of the passage a stocky young woman (or young as women go today, which is to say about thirty-two years old), who wore tortoiseshell glasses and what are known as 'sensible' shoes. Beside her bounced along a girl with the large physique and very chubby cheeks which distinguish a certain type of modern maidenhood, and make their inadequate hats look even sillier than usual.

'This is Mr Pidgeon's party, yes,' said Roger.

'Thank you.' The stocky young woman looked at him. 'You're Roger Sheringham,' she drawlingly accused.

'And you,' said Roger boldly, 'are Miss Crosspatrick.'

'I am,' admitted Miss Crosspatrick, with a tolerant little smile. 'And this is...'

'I'm Unity Vincent,' pronounced the bouncing girl. 'I heard Miss Crosspatrick asking the porter, and tagged on.'

'Mr Pidgeon is in here,' Roger smiled politely.

He followed the two into the room. Miss Crosspatrick walked, firmly and unhurriedly, straight towards Mr Pidgeon, who was maliciously engaged at the moment in introducing a shrinking Mr Valentine Combe to Mr Bray, who was only too obviously trying to create the impression that he really did look on poets as human beings. Miss Vincent, coming suddenly into the chatter and smoke and press, hesitated uncertainly.

Dash it, thought Roger, she's very young.

He looked round. Crystal was occupied, everyone was occupied; only young Mr Parker, nervously balancing his cup of tea somewhere by a wall, was disengaged. Roger caught his eye and beckoned him over.

'Do you think you could get Miss Vincent a cup of tea, Parker? She's only just arrived, and doesn't know anyone. Mr Parker, Miss Vincent.'

He saw the look of relief which passed rapidly across both faces, and knew he had done the right thing. The two youngest members of the party were bound to gravitate together sooner or later, and better sooner.

4

For three of Mr Pidgeon's guests the tea *séance* was held in vain. Neither Captain Twyford, nor the Honourable Angela St Thomas, nor Lady Darracott put in an appearance. In order to allow the rest of the party time to get unpacked before dinner, the launch had to leave without them.

Actually, the missing trio turned up just seven minutes before dinner was due to be served. Roger, sipping a cocktail in the smoking-room with Valentine Combe and Fayre, heard their arrival.

'Are you Mr Pidgeon?' came the sound of a rather strident female voice. 'I say, so terribly sorry we couldn't make the Magnificent. It was all Reggie's fault. He drove us down, you see, and he was two hours late collecting us. Yes, you were, Reggie, so you'd better own up like a man to Mr Pidgeon. By the way, I don't think you've ever actually met my aunt, have you? I mean, not to say met. And this, of course, is Reggie. I say, what a marvellous boat. Do you think we could have a wash, or something? I'm rather musty.'

'I'll show you your cabins,' came Mr Pidgeon's courteous tones. 'The steward will bring your luggage down at once. Dinner will be in – let me see, yes, six minutes.'

'Then,' said the strident voice, 'we look like being a trifle late for it.'

'I'll have yours kept hot for you,' Roger heard Mr Pidgeon promising politely, as they passed out of earshot.

Roger laughed.

'That was Angela St Thomas,' observed Mr Combe, not without respect.

'Better late than never,' muttered Mr Fayre.

'A woman,' remarked Roger happily, 'would have kept dinner waiting for them; a don, even an ex-don, would keep dinner waiting for no man, or woman. How right dons are.'

'And serve them right,' said Mr Combe violently. 'People like that deserve that kind of thing. My God, Sheringham, living in the country like I do, never seeing anyone but the peasants, sweating and grinding their lives away without purpose, joy, or even comfort – well, it makes one something of a Socialist. I'm a Socialist, and I'm not ashamed to say so.'

'Bravo,' said Roger.

'There's a lot to be said for Socialism,' murmured Mr Fayre.

5

The Hon. Angela St Thomas was very tall, and rather gawky, and had a nose that was too large; her photographs, and there were very, very many of them, flattered her. Crystal Vane had told Roger that she was twenty-four, but she had already published three smartly precocious novels which had been received with lyrical raptures by certain critics. She was now engaged in talking kindly to Roger, as author to author.

'Of course *I*,' said Miss St Thomas, 'am only experimenting. You've found your methods of expression, but I'm still looking for mine. And I feel there's scope, even in such an outworn medium as the novel, for a little originality. New forms, a little more subtle way of approach, a rather different means of presentation. You do agree, don't you?'

'I'm afraid I must strike you as very old-fashioned,' said Roger, hugging himself.

'Oh, it isn't that, exactly,' conceded Miss St Thomas, in her odd pinched Cockney drawl of today's Mayfair. 'I just believe it's a mistake to get set in one's forms. Probably I shall always experiment a little, even after I've decided what medium suits my own material best. I do think if one's doing creative work, one should try to remain fluid, don't you?'

'Fluid, but not gaseous,' Roger agreed solemnly. Good lord, he thought, she really does take her tripe seriously. It was Roger's sad experience that almost all authors except himself took their tripe seriously. 'Not, in fact, Gertrude Stein,' he added.

'Oh, well, Gertrude Stein's really terribly dated now, don't you think?' said Miss St Thomas, a little absently.

All the time she was talking to him, Miss St Thomas' eyes had been wandering round and round the saloon, alighting now on one man, now on another; over the women it passed apparently without seeing them. When it happened that her glance found one of the pairs of male eyes fixed on herself, Miss St Thomas seemed to experience a flicker of pleasure. Roger watched the phenomenon with interest.

Dinner had been over about ten minutes, and coffee was being served in the saloon. The newcomers had been made known to the rest when they first made their appearance, but so far they had not made very good mixers. Captain Twyford, massive, broad-shouldered, and very patently bored, lounged aloofly against a pillar near Lady Darracott's chair; little Mr Fayre, trying bravely to open a conversation, had been languidly snubbed for his pains, and retired with red cheeks. Only Miss St Thomas, leaving her aunt to the high-pitched grunts which served Sir John Birch for conversation, had so far appeared to recognise the existence of anyone outside her own circle. To Mr Valentine Combe she had spoken a few well-chosen words; on Mr Fayre she had smiled tolerantly; to Mr Bray's heavy-footed badinage she had replied with a positively provocative vivaciousness; and now she was doing her duty by Roger. But the women of the party might not have existed at all for all the notice that Miss St Thomas took of them; except for Mrs Vane, whom she already knew and who contributed paragraphs to the gossip columns and was therefore valuable, she had not spoken a word to any of them.

Roger glanced round the room. Sir John Birch, only too obviously relieved at finding someone he knew in this herd of barbarians, still remained in the chair into which he had plumped himself beside Lady Darracott. At the other end of the age scale, Mr Harold Parker and Miss Unity Vincent still clung to each other, subdued and round-eyed, in the most unobtrusive corner. Scarcely less alarmed, though concealing it valiantly, Mrs Bray was being engaged in gracious conversation by willowy Mrs Fayre, really beautiful in ice-blue satin and obviously taking pains not to be in the least condescending. Not far away Miss Crosspatrick appeared to be giving Mr Bray some hints on the organisation of public companies within the meaning of the act; and Mr Valentine Combe and Mr Fayre stood together, eyeing the assembly with suspicion and, on Mr Fayre's part at any rate, dismay. Mr Pidgeon and Mrs Vane moved from little group to little group, on their own purposes bent.

But if they're sanguine enough to imagine that they're going to make all these incompatibles coalesce, thought Roger, I don't.

Scraps of conversation reached his ears, as he stood pretending to listen to Miss St Thomas' theories on her art.

'Yes, I don't know whether you've ever heard, Mrs Fayre, but a cousin of mine married a nephew of Lord Felix.'

'Really, Mrs Bray? How very interesting…'

'Of course, mind you, I waited for an interim dividend on the ordinaries, but the preference I'd been badly had over. Seven per cent wasn't much good to me, Miss Crosspatrick, I can tell you. So when I saw they weren't being bulled at all, I made up my mind pretty quick, and – '

'Yes. By the way, Mr Bray, perhaps you can tell me something I've always wanted to know. I dislike ignorance, on any subject. What *is* a Contango?'…

'Have you *any* idea where we're going, Sir John?'

'Don't ask me.'

'Well, I suppose we must just smile and bear it. But it's very odd, I do think. Haven't *you* any idea, Captain Twyford?'

'None, I'm afraid, Lady Darracott.'

'What, hasn't he even taken your advice, young feller?'

'I've got an idea it may be east.'

'Ah! East's east and west's west. Eh? How does it go?...'

Roger found himself abandoned by Miss St Thomas, and strolled over towards his host.

'Well, Pidgeon?' It still cost him an effort, although by Mr Pidgeon's own urgent command, to drop the prefix. 'Are you satisfied?'

Mr Pidgeon's eyes seemed to veil over with cunning as he uttered a gentle cackle. 'Eminently, eminently.'

'You think we're all going to amuse you enough to warrant this ridiculous idea of yours?'

'I think so. Don't you?'

'I? If you ask me, I think murder will be done on this boat of yours before the month's out.'

Mr Pidgeon's shoulders shook. 'That is more than even I could hope for, Sheringham.'

Across the saloon floated Miss St Thomas' corncrake voice.

'I say, Reggie, this is pretty dim, don't you think? Let's go ashore and try the Magnificent. I believe there's quite a respectable band there. I happen to know there's a motor-launch we could borrow. Could you manage her?'

'Oke,' said Captain Twyford languidly.

They went.

Mr Pidgeon grinned at Roger. His grin was wicked and malicious, and seemed to promise all sorts of things.

chapter two

Mr Pidgeon draped his long, spare frame over the rail and watched the tumbling green water as it swirled past the yacht's side. In his white ducks, which managed to look so out of place beneath his sharp-nosed, academic face, and with his habitually hunched shoulders, he looked not like a pigeon at all but like a huge crow, monstrously white instead of black.

Beside him leaned Roger Sheringham.

It had taken Roger the last four days to get accustomed to the idea that the great steam-yacht really did belong to Mr Pidgeon. Now he was wondering idly why he should have the feeling that the ocean which stretched out all round them, probably belonged to Mr Pidgeon too. He decided that it was a sensation which one does get in the presence of very rich men. When Roger had been an undergraduate at St Mary's and Mr Pidgeon its junior dean, it had never occurred to Roger that Mr Pidgeon ought to own an ocean. But Mr Pidgeon had not then been a very rich man.

'And to think,' murmured Mr Pidgeon appositely, 'that less than six months ago I was still lecturing to idiot youths on Juvenal.'

'To think!' Roger agreed. He added: 'I've often wondered what I should do if I suddenly came into an enormous fortune. Everyone does. Had you?'

'Of course, my dear fellow. There was no reason to suppose I ever might; but just in case, I'd decided that if I did, the first think I'd do would be to shock the Senior Common Room really thoroughly, and then buy a desert island and a large yacht. And within a fortnight,' said Mr Pidgeon, with a sudden crow, 'I'd accomplished all three.'

'Well, well,' said Roger, refusing to admire. 'And how did you shock the Senior Common Room?'

Mr Pidgeon had the grace to look slightly guilty. 'That, I think had better remain a secret between the Senior Common Room and myself.'

Roger laughed.

Secretly, he did rather admire. A desert island is a criterion. To possess one is youth's earliest longing. So long as a desert island holds its lure, the mind is still young. Not until one discovers that a bathroom h. and c. is definitely preferable to a shark-infested lagoon, and central heating to a tropical sun on a palm-thatch, can one be said to be grown-up. It must have been a shock to the Senior Common Room when Mr Pidgeon announced to it, as he probably did, that he proposed to exchange it for an uninhabited island, and the society of small monkeys for that of his colleagues. Apparently not even endless glasses of college port, and the irksome company of young men pretending to be old and old men pretending to be boys, had been able to quench the spark of real youth that had persisted in fifty-year-old Mr Pidgeon's bony bosom.

Roger definitely did admire.

Then it occurred to him that this was the first time he had heard anything about a desert island.

'Where is this island of yours?' he asked.

Mr Pidgeon waved a vague hand towards the west. 'Somewhere over there, I fancy. Miles away. Miles and miles.'

'Have you ever seen it?'

'Oh, yes. That was the first trip I made in this boat.'

'What's it like?'

'Well, more or less like any other island, I suppose. To tell you the truth, Sheringham,' confided Mr Pidgeon, 'I was rather disappointed in it. There are no lagoons and no land-crabs. I did want some lagoons, and I've always wondered what a land-crab can be. Do you happen to know what a land-crab is?'

Roger looked at his host suspiciously. 'Are we heading for this island of yours now?'

'My dear Sheringham,' protested Mr Pidgeon, 'what can have put such an idea into your head?'

'Simply because you refuse to tell anyone where we are going. We've been four days at sea now, and still no one has the least idea what place we're making for. And you won't say. Why,' asked Roger, still more suspiciously, 'won't you say?'

Mr Pidgeon's shoulders began silently to shake. Except for an occasional cackle, it was Mr Pidgeon's habit to laugh more heartily with his shoulders than with his vocal chords. This produced not only a disconcerting but at times a quite sinister effect. It was as if the crow had changed into a wicked old vulture, gloating horribly. Yet, as Roger was beginning to know, Mr Pidgeon's sense of humour was not in the least sinister; though it could be, from other people's point of view, misplaced.

'My dear fellow,' said Mr Pidgeon now controlling his shoulders with difficulty, 'because I don't know. I've told you all that you're to choose your own cruise. When you've decided where you want to go, I shall have great pleasure in asking the Captain to take you there.'

'And until then, I suppose we just steam straight ahead?'

Mr Pidgeon looked helpless. 'Well…'

'While you know perfectly well that this extraordinary mixture of people you've gathered together never would agree on anything under the sun.'

Mr Pidgeon uttered a sudden cackle. 'Extraordinary? My dear Sheringham, they're the exact reverse of extraordinary. Each one of them is the most typically ordinary example of his or her particular genus that could be discovered. A more absolutely ordinary collection of people can never have been gathered in a confined space before.'

'Sez you.'

'I beg your pardon?'

'Nothing,' Roger said hastily. 'An American expression, meaning "Well, really." You were saying?'

Mr Pidgeon turned himself about and with his back against the rail surveyed the deck. A large awning protected the centre portion from the brilliant sun which was streaming down. Under the awning sat a little group consisting of Sir John Birch, Captain Twyford, Miss St Thomas, and Lady Darracott, the last with a folded rug across her knees in spite of the warmth of the day; Lady Darracott, with her white hair and tall but fragile figure, was understood to be something of an invalid, though combating with well-bred fortitude the impertinences of nature. On rugs spread in the bows reclined Miss Vincent and Mr Parker, in the full glare of the sun; both were in bathing suits, with bottles of coconut oil handy to their greasy grasp, and they were talking very earnestly. Under the awning on the other side of the deck, hidden behind the deck-houses, was known to be Miss Crosspatrick, with a book that was strongly suspected of being serious.

Mr Pidgeon's eye lingered on the large group, which fortunately was just out of earshot.

'Perhaps one or two of the types are to some extent duplicated,' he mumbled argumentatively. 'You may for instance complain that it was a mistake to have included two professional aristocrats, but I don't know. There are always interesting subdivisions of the same genus.'

'You call Sir John Birch a professional aristocrat?'

'Perhaps "aristocrat" was too strong a term,' murmured Mr Pidgeon reflectively. 'A professional gentleman, shall we say? It's an interesting type: the man whose birth is his only asset. That, I think, is a pity about the world of today, that there is no place in it for the Sir John Birches. They were designed for yesterday's world, and a very useful part they played in it. One might almost say that they held the countryside together – the natural keystones of the rural arch. But the times have outgrown their squirearchy. Generations of beef-eating, hard-riding, agricultural ancestors, shoulder the moral as well as the material responsibility for their own districts because it never occurred to them to do anything else, completely brainless because body and not brain was demanded of them – these still produce the type, but we don't want it any longer. So what happens to them? Crushed out of their lands by taxation, forced to sell their horses and their houses, unable for the most part to compete in making a living with the descendants of those who had to live by their wits instead of by their physique, what can they do? Soak up unlimited free whisky and accept invitations from total strangers for their board and lodging. Offer Sir John a fee to perform an action repugnant to him, and he'd refuse without hesitation; but he finds nothing degrading in taking free food and drink from a stranger in exchange for the prestige of his company: for he really does consider that his company confers honour.'

'Well, well,' said Roger.

'But he, after all, isn't so bad as the real professional aristocrats,' continued Mr Pidgeon, now warming up nicely. 'What are we to say, for instance, of the men who sell their titles to the proprietors of newspapers, to adorn the head of some column of rubbish? – as though tomfoolery purporting to be written by a titled tout were any better than tomfoolery written by anyone else! Or of the girls who sell their titles to the proprietors of face creams, for use in the advertisement columns of the muck press?

'You may say that the girls who go on the stage under assumed names, or try to write novels, or do any other job of work, are honestly doing their best to pull their weight in a world which has refused to carry noble passengers. But are they? Doesn't the girl on the stage make very sure of the fact becoming known, with photographs, that the name is an assumed one and that she is really the sister of Lord So-and-so? And doesn't the young novel-writer count on a similar blazoning of the fact that she is really the daughter of the Earl of This-and-that, and therefore it is rather wonderful that she should have had the intelligence to write a novel at all?

'Yes, my dear Sheringham, the time was when our aristocracy really was rather a fine thing. It produced a type that could not be duplicated in any other country, and it played a big part in the making of the civilisation which is now destroying it. There are still representatives of it left. But the section which is vulgarising it is growing every day: the professional aristocrat who looks on his title not as a responsibility, but as a means either to publicity or money.

Let us, however, console ourselves with the reflection that the section of the fool-public which still believes that there is any virtue in a title, merely *qua* title, must be correspondingly dwindling.'

'From all of which,' said Roger, 'I deduce that you are another of these moneyed socialists?'

Mr Pidgeon looked at him with disgust. 'I thought I'd been telling you for the last ten minutes that I'm a hide-bound conservative.'

'I beg your pardon. Of course you are. The trouble is that the two things are nowadays practically the same. By the way,' said Roger, with a glance at the figure of Lady Darracott leaning back in her chair, with odds and ends of scarves blowing in the breeze and her general air of resigned fortitude. 'By the way, I suppose Lady Darracott is your example of the old type of aristocrat as opposed to the new professional ones? Or after all, as you didn't know her before this cruise, is she a feminine counterpart of Sir John Birch?'

'Neither,' said Mr Pidgeon, with a subdued cackle. 'She's an example of the honestly commercial aristocrat.'

'Commercial?' Roger repeated, puzzled.

'Didn't you know,' said Mr Pidgeon, with assumed surprise, 'that Lady Darracott is a professional chaperon? Certainly.'

'But you're not...?'

'Indeed I am. A very substantial fee, I assure you, my dear Sheringham. To lend a cachet to our little gathering. Crystal arranged it.'

'Well, I'm blessed,' said Roger.

'And I really think,' said Mr Pidgeon, in a complaining tone, 'that she isn't earning her salary. I engaged her after all to lend us all tone, not merely to her own niece and the gallant Captain. Do you feel you have imbibed tone from Lady Darracott, Sheringham? Does Mr Harold Parker? Does Mrs Bray? Do even I? I shall have to ask Crystal to instruct her to distribute tone a little more evenly.' Roger had no doubt that if the whim took Mr Pidgeon to make such a request, he would undoubtedly do so.

'What,' he asked hastily, 'do you make of Captain Twyford?'

'What,' asked Mr Pidgeon cautiously, 'do you?'

'Well, we all know what he's done. He's a fine man, and physically, too. But I do wonder why he hangs round Angela St Thomas all the time. After all, he doesn't really belong to that lot.'

Mr Pidgeon's shoulders began to twitch. 'Doesn't, no. But perhaps he'd like to? After all, they have one large bond in common, haven't they?'

'Have they? Which?'

'Well,' said Mr Pidgeon, in a deprecating voice, 'they really are experts in publicity, both of them, aren't they?'

'I suppose they are.' It was a new idea to Roger. Angela St Thomas had, of course, the usual craving of her kidney for publicity, a craving to which the more vapid illustrated papers pander so obligingly. But it had never occurred to Roger that Captain Twyford might indulge in the same vice. He was a very famous explorer, and a brave man; but after all, how did Roger know with such certainty that he was these things? Yes, the Captain's methods might be subtler, but undoubtedly he quite understood the uses of advertisement.

'Well, anyhow,' Roger said, with some distaste, 'to go back a few minutes: I didn't say your individuals were extraordinary. I said your mixture of them was.'

Mr Pidgeon's shoulders gave another twitch or two. 'Perhaps it is, perhaps it is. A little oleaginous-and-aqueous, you think? But they'll mix by the end of four weeks. They'll mix.'

'Humph!'

'And after all,' said Mr Pidgeon in hurt tones, 'you shouldn't complain, seeing that the whole thing was arranged especially for your benefit.'

'Mine?'

'Certainly. You're a novelist. You like to see specimens of different types reacting on one another, don't you? My dear Sheringham,' said Mr Pidgeon, grinning wickedly, 'I had you in mind all the time. Didn't Crystal make that clear?'

'Nonsense,' Roger laughed. 'You had yourself in mind, and no one else, as you very well know. You meant to coop these unfortunate people up on these miserable few square yards of boat, and watch them drive each other mad, while you stood by and rubbed your hands. You're positively inhuman. You ought to have been lecturing on Morbid Psychology, not anything so human as Juvenal.'

'There's no chair of Morbid Psychology at Oxford,' said Mr Pidgeon, with regret.

They watched the swirling water for a few moments.

'Anyhow, where are we going? Roger asked.

'There seems to be a divergence of opinion about that,' murmured Mr Pidgeon, with humility.

'Do you know what I think?' Roger said suspiciously. 'I don't believe you intend to touch land at all. I don't believe you mean these wretched people to have a single chance of getting away from each other.'

'I intend? But my dear Sheringham, I keep telling you that the matter is entirely in their own hands.'

'Well, I'm quite sure you've got something up your sleeve.'

'How you do distrust me,' sighed Mr Pidgeon. 'And misjudge me.'

'Rats!' Roger said rudely.

Mr Pidgeon's shoulders began to twitch once more.

2

Roger paused on his stroll round the deck and looked benevolently down on Miss Vincent and Mr Parker. There was no doubt that whatever social antics were being performed by their elders, these two young persons were mightily enjoying themselves.

Mr Parker's duties had proved to be light; except for looking after the wireless messages which kept arriving for his employer, and concocting certain mysterious reports and tables of figures, Mr Parker had most of his time to himself – for which Roger put a good mark against the name of Mr Bray. As for Unity Vincent, with the adaptability of twenty-one she had very soon shaken off her first shyness and bounced her way more or less into the position of ship's pet, tolerantly smiled upon even by the St Thomas contingent. A life-long acquaintance with the *genus* undergraduate had given her powers of aplomb and repartee which had quickly asserted themselves, but she still seemed to find herself more at home with Mr Parker than anyone else; and Roger had been amused at the mixture of conscious *savoir faire*, unconsciously predatory eagerness, and undisguised condescension with which she had instantly taken that young man under her wing.

'Well?' said Roger. 'No sunburn yet?'

'Oh, no, I've told Harold how careful he's got to be,' said Miss Vincent, somewhat absently.

'Am I interrupting?'

'Not at all, Mr Sheringham, I assure you,' said Mr Parker, rising politely.

'Don't get up, for goodness' sake.'

'Mr Sheringham,' said Miss Vincent earnestly, 'are you busy for a minute? We want to ask you about something.'

'No, Unity,' implored Mr Parker in high alarm. 'You promised you wouldn't say anything to anyone.'

'But Mr Sheringham may be able to help you; and you've got to learn, Harold,' said Miss Vincent, that experienced girl of the world, 'that one has to make use of people's help when one can. Harold has an idea for a film scenario, Mr Sheringham. He's terribly keen on films. He says their possibilities have never been properly exploited.'

'Ah!' said Roger.

'Unity!' groaned Mr Parker.

'We've been talking about it a lot, and really it's a terribly good idea. I think he ought to go on with it, don't you? He says he doesn't know how to begin it, but that's all rot; he's just too lazy. You see, he doesn't want to go on living in Golders Green all his life, and being secretary to shady financiers; so – '

'Unity!' gasped Mr Parker, horrified.

'You told me yourself he was. You must learn to be honest, Harold,' said Miss Vincent inexorably. 'Anyhow, Mr Sheringham, Harold's really quite clever, but he just hasn't got enough experience yet to know how to make use of it. I keep telling him he ought to talk to you about it, but he's frightened to ask you, I believe.'

'Anything I can do, of course, I will,' Roger smiled. 'But I'm not a scenario-writer, you know, and I'm not really up in the technique.'

'Wouldn't think of troubling you, Mr Sheringham,' gulped Mr Parker. 'Miss Vincent never ought...'

'So if he writes it down, more or less like it would be in the film, will you criticise it for him and help him put it right? Because it really is a marvellous idea, Mr Sheringham, and Harold will be an idiot if he doesn't do something with it.'

'Of course,' Roger promised. 'Just jot it down, Parker, with some notes on the characters and their scenes and so on, and I'll be very pleased to tell you what I think, if that would be the least use to you.'

'Very kind of you, I'm sure,' mumbled Mr Parker fierily. 'Deeply grateful...invaluable advice...must forgive Miss Vincent...very much obliged...'

'That's enough, Harold,' said Miss Vincent critically. 'I've told you before not to overdo the thanks.'

3

'Guy – Mr Sheringham! Surely, *surely* I see land over there. Don't disappoint me. Isn't that Madeira?'

The eyes of both men followed the direction of the slim finger. The owner of the finger waited with a quizzical expression on her lovely face, as if smiling indulgently at her own eagerness. Neither the group a little forward, nor the pair in the bows, distracted her vision ahead.

'Right as usual, Enid,' nodded Mr Pidgeon. 'That's Madeira.'

'Oh!' breathed Mrs Fayre. 'Madeira!' She dropped her hand to her side and gazed at the indistinct blur, her lips just parted.

Roger studied her profile. It was a good profile. Roger had mentioned to Mrs Fayre how good it was only the previous evening, on this same deck after dinner. It was kind of her to present him with this opportunity of studying it afresh. It did not escape Roger that from the angle at which Mrs Fayre's head was turned, Captain Twyford was in a position to study the profile too, should he care to do so.

'Where's Willie?' prosaically asked Mr Pidgeon, who cared nothing for profiles; certainly not for the profiles of his cousins by marriage.

Mrs Fayre very slowly withdrew her gaze from Madeira, and focussed it, apparently with some difficulty, on Mr Pidgeon. It seemed that although her ears had received the question, her mind, still wrapped round Madeira, had not properly grasped it, for it had to be repeated before Mrs Fayre appeared to understand it.

'Willie? Oh, he's in the smoking-room. Playing bridge.' Mrs Fayre smiled brightly at Roger. 'On a day like this. And with Madeira waiting over there.'

'You've been on the promenade deck, then, Enid?' asked Mr Pidgeon, not without malice. 'That's funny. I didn't see you.'

'I? Oh, no; I've only just come up. I've been in my stateroom. You know, I always have a siesta after lunch. When one's off the coast of Spain I think that's the least one can do, don't you, Mr Sheringham? And then, of course, I had to change my frock, and powder my nose, and – oh, all sorts of things that wouldn't interest *you*, Guy, in the least.' But another smile at Roger hinted that perhaps he at any rate might not be such a dry stick as to have been uninterested.

'On a day like this? Mr Pidgeon grinned wickedly. 'With Madeira waiting over there?'

'You're a great tease, Guy, aren't you?' smiled Mrs Fayre tolerantly.

'Who made up the bridge four?' Roger asked idly. 'Bray wanted me, but I really couldn't.'

'Let me see, there's Willie, Mr Bray, Mrs Vane, and I think, yes, Sir John.'

'Oh?' said Roger. For a fleeting moment he regretted not having been into the smoking-room to watch; the table sounded interesting. 'Not Combe, then?' Unkindly he had suggested Valentine Combe as a substitute for himself: unkindly because Mr Combe was the worst bridge-player in the five continents, and appeared to be too pleased with the fact to abandon the game.

'Mr Combe? Oh, no. I happen to know he's in his own stateroom, reading his own poems, because he left the door open and I saw him when I passed.' Mrs Fayre's laugh tinkled out like little bells. 'Well, Guy, when do we reach Madeira?'

'Madeira?' Mr Pidgeon looked innocently surprised. 'I didn't know we were putting in there?'

'Not putting in at Madeira?' Mrs Fayre wailed. 'But Guy, you promised...'

'I don't think so, Enid. No, I really don't think so. Why, do you want to put in at Madeira?'

'Of *course* I do! Don't you realise, Guy, that I've never been out of Europe before? Never! Of course, it's difficult for you to realise, now; but when one's as hard up as Willie and I,' said Mrs Fayre, with a brave little laugh, 'it means a great deal to one to get out of Europe.'

'Well, you're not out of Europe,' returned Mr Pidgeon, wilfully literal. 'Madeira's in Europe.'

'Oh, you know what I mean.'

'I'm not sure that I do. But really, this is rather awkward, Enid. You see, I happen to know that Miss Crosspatrick, for instance, doesn't want to put in at Madeira. She's been there already.'

'Miss Crosspatrick!' observed Mrs Fayre, with as near an approach to a snort as such a delicate lady might permit herself.

'I've undertaken to bow to the wishes of the majority,' Mr Pidgeon murmured mildly – so mildly that Roger looked at him with renewed suspicion.

'But the majority *does* want to stop at Madeira. Really, Guy!'

'Oh, I see, I didn't know. Does Willie?'

'Of course he does. Everyone does.' Mrs Fayre turned her sweetest smile on Roger. 'I'm sure you do, Mr Sheringham, don't you? And – and Captain Twyford. Captain Twyford! do back me up, please. You'll vote for putting in at Madeira, won't you?'

'Do you want to, Mrs Fayre?'

'I'm simply dying to.'

'Then of course I will,' said Captain Twyford, with his lazy smile.

Mrs Fayre flashed one look at Miss St Thomas, which Roger had some pleasure in interpreting, but did not canvass that young woman's opinion. She turned back in triumph to Mr Pidgeon.

'There you are, you see, Guy. Everyone wants to stop at Madeira. How absurd you are.'

'I must be,' agreed Mr Pidgeon humbly. 'Ah, here comes Miss Crosspatrick herself. We'll put it to her.'

Miss Crosspatrick had come into sight round the angle of the Captain's cabin. She still wore her tortoiseshell spectacles, and carried her book in her hand; her short, stocky figure swayed competently to the motion of the boat. Like Mrs Fayre she was dressed in white, and no doubt quite as correctly; but Roger wondered why Stella Crosspatrick looked so wrong beside the other lady's slender, silken elegance. And yet Roger well knew that Mrs Fayre's high-heeled white buckskin shoes were not at all correct on a yacht, whereas Miss Crosspatrick's low-heeled canvas ones were. So much for correctitude as against the picturesque.

Miss Crosspatrick marched up to her host. 'The book you lent me,' she said, putting it into his hands. 'Thank you. Or would you like me to put it in the ship's library?'

'No, thank you; I'll take it. You've been very quick over it.'

'I'm a quick reader.' Miss Crosspatrick enunciated this fact without pride, or very much interest. It was just a fact.

'Oh, *Murder in the Attic*,' Mrs Fayre chimed in. 'I made sure it must be a serious book you were reading, Miss Crosspatrick.'

'Did you?' said Miss Crosspatrick coolly.

'Yes,' said Mrs Fayre, a little dashed. 'Very good, isn't it? I enjoyed it so much. I'm sure you didn't guess it.'

'On the contrary,' stated Miss Crosspatrick. 'I guessed the solution on page 47. The average detective story,' she added to Roger, 'is really pathetically ingenuous, don't you think?'

She sauntered to the rail, and glanced efficiently at the sea.

Mrs Fayre flushed delicately. 'She looked at the end,' she whispered to Roger.

Avoiding his cousin-in-law's eye, Mr Pidgeon called Miss Crosspatrick back. 'I'm told there's a general wish to put in at Madeira for a day or two,' he said to her blandly. 'You won't mind, I'm sure?'

'Mind?' echoed Miss Crosspatrick, turning round with a kind smile. 'I don't think it's a question of "minding," is it? As you've been so kind as to offer us our own choice for the cruise, it's obviously a case for majority decision, isn't it?'

'But which way would you vote?'

'I? Oh, I should vote against Madeira,' said Miss Crosspatrick in her gentle drawl. 'I've been there before.'

'You see, Enid,' said Mr Pidgeon, with an effect of helplessness.

Mrs Fayre swallowed. 'If Miss Crosspatrick is against it,' she said nobly, 'of course, we won't put in there.'

Mr Pidgeon looked, to Roger's eye, a trifle disappointed by this altruism.

'Not at all,' said Miss Crosspatrick sweetly. 'I'm quite prepared to do whatever the majority wishes.'

'Well, what would be your own idea for an alternative vote, Miss Crosspatrick?' Roger asked humbly.

'As I told you. To get off the beaten track. Visit some of the islands to which the tourist doesn't flock.'

'My island, for instance,' Mr Pidgeon said, rather wistfully.

'I think not,' smiled Miss Crosspatrick. 'I'm interested in human beings, not monkeys.'

'There aren't really any monkeys there,' pleaded Mr Pidgeon. 'I only said that to annoy the Senior Common Room. It's uninhabited.'

'Then of course we don't want to go there, Guy, you silly old thing,' remarked Mrs Fayre girlishly. 'I *quite* agree with Miss Crosspatrick. We want to see people, not monkeys. People, and lights, and civilisation, and – and things.'

Miss Crosspatrick smiled, but said nothing to this unexpected interpretation of her wishes.

'Well, in that case,' Mr Pidgeon said, with patience, 'we must decide where to find these things. Now what about Madeira?'

'Of course we must put in at Madeira, if Mrs Fayre wishes, and the majority agrees,' said Miss Crosspatrick briskly.

'Oh, no,' fluted Mrs Fayre. 'I couldn't possibly drag people there who don't want to go. Though of course,' she added in a deprecatory voice, 'quite a lot of people do, I know.'

'Then that will be quite simple,' agreed Miss Crosspatrick. 'Who does, for instance?'

'Well, there's Mr Sheringham,' said Mrs Fayre, with an intent little frown, checking the names off on her fingers, 'and – '

'Honestly, I don't mind whether I do or not,' put in Roger, thereby earning a grateful look from his host, which he ignored.

'Oh, I am so sorry, Mr Sheringham. I really thought you said you did. Well, I must begin again. There's Captain Twyford, then, and – '

'Oh, I don't care a rap, if people don't want to,' languidly interrupted that gentleman; and Roger hoped for her own sake that Mrs Fayre had not received the look which this time it had been Miss St Thomas' turn to toss across.

'Don't you? Oh, I am stupid. I quite thought...well, never mind, I must begin again. There's – there's Mr Bray,' said Mrs Fayre, so desperately that Roger was sorry for her. After all, why shouldn't she have a look at Madeira if she was so keen on it? 'Mr Bray, and – and – Mr Parker – ' said Mrs Fayre eagerly, clutching at this straw in passing, 'Mr Parker, you'd like to see Madeira, wouldn't you?'

'I should be delighted,' said Mr Parker, in the awed tones with which he paid tribute to Mrs Fayre's beauty: a tribute which for all his terrified respect for them, he did not offer to either Lady Darracott or Sir John Birch. He paused uncertainly for a moment, then discovered that the goddess who had snatched him up had dropped him just as swiftly, and passed on his coconut-oily way.

'There, you see,' said Mrs Fayre, rallying. 'Mr Parker, you see. And – and Mr Bray, and – oh, lots of us. But of course, it doesn't matter a bit,' added Mrs Fayre nobly, 'if Miss Crosspatrick and the others don't want to.'

'On the contrary,' smiled Miss Crosspatrick, 'no one will mind in the least, if it will be a disappointment to you not to stop there.'

'What about you, Angela?' suggested Mr Pidgeon diffidently.

'Oh, I'm like Reggie; it's oke with me either way.'

'Lady Darracott?'

'Really, Mr Pidgeon. So kind of you. I'll leave it to the others to decide. I should not land in any case, you see,' said Lady Darracott, with her fluttering smile, and smoothed a lock of white hair under her hat with a fragile hand. 'The exertion…'

'Quite, of course,' agreed Mr Pidgeon, with unctuous understanding. 'And you, Sir John?'

'Matter of indifference to me.'

'Dear me,' murmured Mr Pidgeon, 'we don't seem to be getting on much, do we?' He walked over to the stairway and called down cooingly to the promenade deck below for Mr Bray.

Miss Crosspatrick and Mrs Fayre continued to assure each other, just as cooingly, that she who wished to put in at Madeira would not for an instant contemplate anything of the kind, and she who did not was determined that the ship should do so.

4

Mr Pidgeon drew Roger a little aside.

'Just like a suburban tennis-party, isn't it?' he confided happily. '"Oh, no, I wouldn't dream of playing this set; let someone else."' Mr Pidgeon's imitation of a suburban lady, who appeared to possess a strangely squeaky voice, was very humorous.

Roger frowned, unamused.

'But wait,' prophesied Mr Pidgeon darkly, 'till they've been at sea a little more than four days. Perhaps we shan't all be so grovellingly polite to each other then.'

'I take it,' Roger said, not without malice, 'that one of your nasty little plans has gone wrong. You hoped to set everyone by the ears over this Madeira business, and all they're doing is to show how unselfish they can be. It must be most disappointing for you. The truth is, of course, that this is a very decent collection of people; and they're behaving, just as anyone but you would expect them to behave, in a very decent way. And what's more, they'll continue to do so, until the cruise ends.'

'Oh, yes?' said Mr Pidgeon.

He paused.

'Enid, of course,' continued Mr Pidgeon, with candour, 'is a very ill-bred woman. She doesn't know when to stop. To know instinctively where to draw the line, and then not to draw it, is one of the first marks of breeding. Enid doesn't know. But then neither, apparently, does Miss Crosspatrick. And I will not disguise from you, my dear Sheringham, my recognition of the truth which you are even now pondering: that I am a very ill-bred man. I'm glad to say that I am; for that, you see, allows me to enjoy ill-breeding in others, instead of feeling that something ought to be done about it.

'Yes,' went on Mr Pidgeon with some pleasure. 'Yes, on shore I pass, strange though it may seem to you, Sheringham, for quite a passably bred man, just as Enid passes for a passably bred woman. It takes a sea voyage to bring out one's innate commonness. I had an idea that it would. This must be extremely interesting to you, as a novelist, my dear fellow. – But dear me,' added Mr Pidgeon, with concern, 'why does Bray not come?'

He called again.

There was a short pause. Lady Darracott, being a well-bred woman, addressed an observation to Captain Twyford regarding the League of Nations and Japan. Her niece, having the advantage of ill-breeding, awaited the arrival of Mr Bray with a faint grin.

'Mr Bray's playing bridge in the smoking-room' replied a feminine voice from the promenade deck. 'Is it anything I could do?'

'Oh, thank you, Mrs Bray. Yes. Could you come up here for a moment? We're just having a little discussion about plans.'

Mrs Bray appeared, surmounting the little staircase with a difficulty which her efforts to hide made only the more apparent. Mrs Bray, too, was dressed in white, but everything about her seemed a little too tight: her white stockinette jumper, her buckskin shoes, her too-small white hat, the white gloves which she was not wearing but somehow should have been. And why? Because Mrs Bray was too stout inside them, and would not believe it.

'Have you had a nice siesta, Mrs Bray?' Mr Pidgeon asked solicitously.

Mrs Bray hesitated for a moment. 'Oh, quate.'

'I'm so glad,' said Mrs Fayre graciously. 'I thought of taking forty winks myself, and then it seemed a shame to waste such a glorious day.'

'Oh, I haven't been to sleep, you know. I've been sitting on the deck – reading,' Mrs Bray added firmly.

Miss St Thomas slouched towards the group, writing something in the little black notebook which was always with her.

'How dim for you,' she said, eyeing Mrs Bray with the air of detached interest in an unusual specimen with which she was wont to contemplate all those outside her own little circle. 'Weren't there any chairs?' She made a further note in the little book.

Mrs Bray laughed, in a somewhat constrained way, and turned to Mr Pidgeon. 'Mr Bray says they're just finishing the rubber. He'll be up in a minute, he says.'

'It seems a pity to disturb him,' Mr Pidgeon replied gently. 'It was only a question of whether we should put in at Madeira for a day or two, or not. We were wondering what he would like to do. Do you happen to know, Mrs Bray?'

Mrs Bray seemed uneasy, as she obviously wondered what she was wanted to say. Gaining no enlightenment, she fell back on the truth. 'Well, I don't know whether Mr Bray mightn't rather go on somewhere else, if you left it to him,' she said doubtfully. 'We've been to Madeira, you see.'

Enid Fayre looked just a little taken aback. 'Oh, but he – ' She rallied. 'In that case,' she said, with great warmth, 'of *course* we mustn't put in there.'

Mrs Bray, still not quite sure whether she had said the right thing or not, but hoping very much that she had, glanced round with relief. 'Well, here comes Mr Bray,' she said.

Unmistakably it was Mr Bray's large red face which had just emerged above the level of the deck, like a rising sun to warn the shepherds. Mr Bray's double-breasted blue coat, his white trousers, and his white buckskin shoes with brown straps followed the sun, as a gent's natty yachting cap had preceded it.

'Wanting me, old man?' boomed Mr Bray, in a voice so hearty that one expected the rather brittle-looking Mr Pidgeon to shiver into pieces before it like a glass vase before the blast of a trumpet. Roger had learned by now that Mr Bray was Mr Pidgeon's financial adviser. He had also learned that the election to that post had been the unaided work of Mr Bray himself. Nevertheless, Mr Pidgeon had confided to Roger that Mr Bray's tips were really wonderful. By consistently doing the opposite from what Mr Bray advised, and never allowing Mr Bray to handle the transaction himself, Mr Pidgeon had already made considerable sums of money.

'Eh?' puffed Mr Bray, gaining the deck. 'What's the trouble, old man?'

'Oh, nothing at all important,' Mr Pidgeon said diffidently. 'We were just talking about putting in at Madeira, and wondering whether you would like to or not.'

'Madeira? Not for yours truly. Seen the place. Overrated, if you ask me. Nothing but old crocks in Bath chairs. Reminded me of Bournemouth. Take it from me, we don't want to waste our time there.'

'That's just what I told Mr Pidgeon, Harry,' said Mrs Bray, with complacence.

'Then that seems to settle it,' said Mr Pidgeon. 'I'm sorry, Enid, but...'

'Oh, of *course*, Guy.' Mrs Fayre, her smile a trifle strained, gave her parasol a twirl.

'Eh?' said Mr Bray. 'What's that?'

'I'm afraid I owe you an apology, Mr Bray.' Mrs Fayre's voice was sweetly wistful. 'I quite thought you told me yesterday that you'd like to stop at Madeira. Really, I can't understand how I can have been so stupid.'

'Did I?' Mr Bray sounded puzzled. Then he winked largely. 'Why, of course I did. I remember now. Funny, I'd clean forgotten all about it. You want to see Madeira, Mrs Fayre?'

'Oh, no, that doesn't matter at all. Not a tiny bit. We must do what the majority wants. After all,' added Mrs Fayre in a confidential undertone, smiling gently, 'after all, a hostess is expected to sacrifice herself.'

'Not a bit of it,' riposted Mr Bray robustly. 'No need for anything like that. I'll fix it for you. 'Sides,' added Mr Bray, with an ingratiating ogle, 'must please the ladies, mustn't we? Eh, Fayre? You agree to that, I take it?'

Mr Fayre, who had just arrived on deck, looked up with an apologetic smile at the large man towering genially above him.

'I beg your pardon? I didn't quite catch...' Mr Fayre often did not quite catch things. It was as if Mr Fayre, completely bewildered at catching his exquisite wife, had never managed to catch anything since.

'Mrs Fayre wants to put in a day or two at Madeira. You've no objection, I take it?'

'Oh, none, none,' agreed Mr Fayre at once. 'An excellent plan. Certainly.'

'Oh, thank you, Willie, dear,' fluted Mrs Fayre. 'So sweet of you. But it's quite unimportant, and I don't think some of the others want to stop there.'

'It's oke with me either way,' drawled Miss St Thomas.

'I assure you, I don't mind at all,' repeated Miss Crosspatrick.

'Nor do I really,' affirmed Roger.

'Madeira?' said Mr Combe with much gloom. 'Well, I suppose we'd better now we're here, hadn't we?'

'Madeira?' repeated Unity Vincent, who had arrived, too, to see what all the fuss was about. 'Oh, do let's. That would be marvellous.'

'Then that's settled,' pronounced Mr Bray loudly. 'We stop at Madeira, old man, since you've been so sporting as to say we can stop where we like. Everyone agreed?'

'No, I really mustn't drag people there who don't want to go,' almost wailed Mrs Fayre.

'Very well, Enid,' said Mr Pidgeon. 'We'll put it to the vote.'

'Yes. And I shall vote against it, because I know lots of people don't really want to stop there a bit.'

'Then I shall vote in favour, to neutralise your vote,' smiled Miss Crosspatrick, not to be outdone in generosity.

'But I don't mind at all...'

'But neither do I...'

'But really...'

'I assure you...'

The discussion proceeded. Everyone who wanted to go to Madeira insisted that they did not really want to go there at all; everybody who did want to go there assured the company that Madeira was the last place they really wanted to visit; everyone else proclaimed their earnest anxiety to fall in with anyone else's wishes rather than express a preference of their own.

A storm of altruism raged.

Mr Pidgeon intercepted a silent person with a beard who was passing the group on his way to the wheel-house. 'Oh, Captain Soames, we're having a discussion...' Mr Pidgeon put the problem.

The taciturn one forced himself to Scots speech.

'Madeira? Weel, I never haird anything aboot putting in there. And by noo we're richt oot o' the coorse.'

There was a profound silence.

'Well,' said Mr Pidgeon, apparently with acute regret, 'that seems to settle it, I'm afraid.'

But for a single twitch of his left shoulder, one might have thought Mr Pidgeon really upset.

chapter three

'Oh, Guy, it *is* a nice little island,' exclaimed Crystal Vane with enthusiasm.

'Quite a nice little island,' agreed Mr Pidgeon.

The whole ship's party were leaning on the rail, watching the island as it drew gradually closer. It was two days now since the Madeira discussion, and Mr Pidgeon, taking decisions into his own hands, had sailed unimpeded for his own island.

'And it's really all yours, Guy?' asked Mrs Fayre.

'Every uncomfortable rock of it, Enid.'

'How wonderful,' Mrs Fayre sighed. 'It's always been my dream to have an island of my own, all to myself. Always. Hasn't it, Willie?'

'Always, dear.'

'She'd never thought of such a thing before in her life,' Roger heard Mr Pidgeon confide to Crystal, not very *sotto voce*.

'What did you give for it, Pidgeon, old man?'

'Harry, you mustn't ask such things,' expostulated Mrs Bray mechanically.

'I paid the Portuguese government the equivalent of three thousand and seventy-two pounds, eighteen and fourpence,' replied Mr Pidgeon equably.

'Then you got a bargain. Care to take three thousand, two hundred and fifty, for a quick deal?'

'Well, really, Harry.'

'I'll take fifty thousand,' replied Mr Pidgeon gently.

'Meaning, it's not for sale?'

'Not at all. Meaning, that's what I consider it's worth. There are nearly forty acres of almost level ground above these cliffs. As an emergency landing-place for the transcontinental air service of a few years hence, I find it worth quite fifty thousand pounds. I think the Portuguese government overlooked that. It's the only island between Madeira and the Bahamas, and it's only a hundred miles away from the regular Gibraltar–Panama Canal shipping track, as Twyford will assure you.'

'Eh?' observed Captain Twyford. 'Where are we? About 33 West 27 North, I suppose. Almost due South of the Azores. Yes, it would be. But of course, shipping will take care to give it a wide berth, you know.'

'Still, there it is. Do you care to clinch the bargain, Bray?'

'Not me. I'll give you what I said, to let Gladys have a chance of browning her back without a beach inspector getting hot and bothered over her, but no more.'

'Well, really, Harry, I don't know what you'll say next.'

'I'm afraid I must stick to my figure,' said Mr Pidgeon, with regret.

'He's a cute 'un, the old man, I can tell you,' remarked Mr Bray in stentorian admiration to the company in general. 'Hear that, Lady Darracott? A transcontinental air-service landing-place, if you please. Yes, he's a cute 'un all right. You wouldn't think it to look at him, would you? But he is.' Mr Bray's tone was that of the gratified owner of a performing animal which has just completed an unexpectedly intelligent trick.

The island was now only a few hundred yards away, and its features and formation were plain. It was very small, not much more than fifty acres in all, with steep rocky sides against which the sea rolled lazily, as if too much affected by the heat to break properly and throw up the correct clouds of spray. Only straight ahead of them a tiny sandy cove, scooped grudgingly out of the unwilling cliff, ran back a few dozen yards into the grim circle. From this cove the rock rose at a less precipitous angle, forming a steep but easily negotiable ascent to the plateau, invisible at the moment, which lay three or four hundred feet above. Two sheer bluffs of rock, running a little way out into the sea, guarded either side of the cove and still further discouraged the lazy waves from advancing on it in any force.

'Nice little landing-place,' commented Captain Twyford with knowledge. 'Any fresh water, Pidgeon?'

'Oh, yes. There's a spring just on the left there which never seems to run quite dry; though how it manages not to do so with such a small rainfall, I really can't say.'

'Ah!' Captain Twyford somehow conveyed the impression that he understood all about that, but preferred not to say in the presence of ladies.

'Oh, look!' squeaked Miss Vincent. 'There's a canary! Lots of canaries! You'll be able to write some lovely poems about this island, Mr Combe.'

'Huh,' replied Mr Combe shortly.

'Canaries!' repeated Mrs Bray. 'Well, fancy!'

'It's not really very surprising,' Mr Pidgeon said mildly. 'Considering we're only a few hundred miles from the islands which are named after that bird.'

'Well, fancy,' said Mrs Bray.

'Actually, of course,' Miss Crosspatrick informed her, with a tolerant little smile, 'it is the birds which are named after the islands, you know; not *vice versa*.'

'Well, fancy,' said Mrs Bray.

'Water laid on, eh?' remarked Mr Bray jovially. 'All modern conveniences, I suppose. You'll be telling me next you've got central heating and indoor – hi! what's up?'

A nasty jarring noise had interrupted Mr Bray's geniality. The yacht's smooth progress had been violently interrupted; she seemed to hesitate for a moment, quivering and vibrating, and then began to move slowly backwards.

'Run aground,' remarked Captain Twyford expertly, and stifled the inevitable yawn.

Mrs Fayre clasped her slender hands. 'Guy – Captain Twyford! Oh, dear, there's no danger, is there?'

'Shouldn't imagine so,' Captain Twyford replied, just a shade too languidly.

'Of course there's no danger,' pronounced Mr Bray in a loud voice. 'That's all right, Mrs Fayre. No need to be alarmed, Lady Darracott, I assure you.'

'Thank you,' said Lady Darracott, with the air of faint bewilderment which Mr Bray invariably seemed to induce in her.

'I'll go and ask the Captain what's happened,' murmured Mr Pidgeon, and went.

The others eyed each other with a certain uneasiness, more or less successfully concealed behind smiles of incredulous amusement.

It transpired, however, that there was no danger. Mr Pidgeon reported that the starboard propeller appeared to have fouled a submerged rock; and though it was impossible to say yet whether any damage had been done, there was certainly no danger.

'Told you so,' said Mr Bray, gratified.

The yacht, successfully avoiding any other mishaps, drew a little closer to the shore and dropped anchor; and Mr Pidgeon proceeded deprecatingly to usher the first batch into the dinghy for the short trip to the land, where the party was to lunch.

As soon as everyone was safely landed, he proceeded to do its honours.

Lady Darracott, who had been persuaded to land only with difficulty, remained on the beach, obviously shaken after her ordeal of crossing a wobbly plank from the dinghy to the shore with only the shoulder of a rough sailorman to lean on, but just as obviously concealing the fact like a noblewoman. Miss St Thomas announced that she would remain to support her aunt, and informed Captain Twyford that he would do the same. Captain Twyford agreed. So did Sir John Birch. Chairs were brought, and the rest were shooed up the steep little path that led to the high ground above, with Mr Pidgeon clucking anxiously at their heels like an elderly hen.

The vegetation of the plateau, as it appeared to the heated gaze of the visitors, was sparse. It consisted chiefly of a rough coarse grass, which was all that would grow on the three or four inches of soil which covered the greater part of the rock. Rather unexpectedly, however, there was, on the farther side, in a little dip in the ground, a small group of trees, which presently showed themselves to be those of the orange and lemon, with a few banana-palms among them.

The plateau itself was, as Mr Pidgeon had said, fairly level; but at the sides, where the scanty soil petered out, the top of the cliffs was cut up into deep ravines and fantastic shapes, and split into knife-edges so sharp that to climb down among them to the sea would be not only a difficult but a dangerous activity. Among these spiky black edges there grew a strange kind of cactus, which Mr Pidgeon referred to familiarly as the candle-cactus or *euphorbia*.

'I am,' he explained, in somewhat pedagogic tones, 'extremely lucky in this island, as those of you who know Madeira and the Canaries will readily see. The rock of which this one is composed, is of course volcanic, and of the same nature as that of those groups. It must, however, be of considerably more ancient origin, for it is much better weathered. The succession of razor-edges which those islands afford are here blunted by the kindly hand of time to mere butter-knife sharpness. The unusual depth of soil covering a pocket on the rock on the north-east corner of the plateau, which has enabled the trees you see there to exist and even to flourish, is due to the same cause; and so, too, is the existence of a sandy beach; so rare in the other – '

'My – did you see that?' demanded Mrs Bray excitedly. 'It was a lizard. Honest it – I mean, rahlly it was. A lizard, as large as life. Ran behind one of those rocks it did. A lizard! Well, there.'

'The fauna,' continued Mr Pidgeon instantly, 'consists largely of lizards, and similar reptiles. At least one sort of turtle, too, may be found occasionally on the beach. I caused one to be procured the last time I was here, and it proved excellent eating.'

'He makes me feel like the Swiss family Robinson,' Roger remarked to Crystal.

'It's nothing to what kind of a family Robinson he's going to make us feel soon,' Crystal grinned back.

Roger frowned in a pained kind of way. All through the voyage Crystal had been dropping this kind of hint to him, coupled sometimes with a plea that Roger should be a lamb and not pass it on to any other member of the party. Roger had pretended to take no interest, but secretly he was uneasy. Something was brewing between that pair, he was sure; and knowing both of them, Roger felt his uneasiness would be justified.

'In addition to tortoises and lizards,' Mr Pidgeon was continuing serenely, 'the sea in these parts of the globe may be said to teem with fish. I succeeded in catching several, and they proved excellent eating. No one, therefore, who has the misfortune to be cast away on this island need ever suffer the pangs of starvation. Unfortunately the flora – '

'I say, isn't that a sort of stone hut over there, among the trees?' broke in Miss Vincent, shading her eyes against the glare of the sun. 'See, Harold? Oh, sorry to interrupt.'

'Not at all,' returned Mr Pidgeon politely. 'What you see is, actually, not a stone hut but an iron one, which I had erected when I was last here to house certain stores which I felt it would be useful to have on the spot. There is, however, on the other side of the grove, though you cannot possibly see it from here, the remains of just such a stone hut such as you describe, Unity.'

'I must have second sight,' observed Miss Vincent with satisfaction.

'I sincerely hope you have nothing of the sort, in *that* connection,' returned Mr Pidgeon, with great gravity.

'The island's been inhabited, then?' asked Mr Combe, in his high-pitched tone. 'Some poor devil of a fisherman, I suppose?'

'Well – inhabited,' Mr Pidgeon said doubtfully. 'Yes, I suppose you might call it that.'

'Oh, Guy, there's a mystery, and you're keeping it from us,' Mrs Fayre cried. 'Do tell us.'

Mr Pidgeon looked troubled, and his obvious reluctance increased as other voices supported the request. At the sight of a sailor approaching from the beach his relief was plain.

'Beg pardon, sir, the Cap'n's on the beach and would like a word with you, if you can spare a minute.'

'Certainly,' said Mr Pidgeon, with alacrity.

'Oh, but Guy – the mystery!'

'Later, Enid, later,' said Mr Pidgeon, and disappeared.

Roger happened to glance at Crystal. Her face was as innocently eager as anyone's, but Roger could have sworn that there was a wicked twinkle in her limpid eyes.

2

'No, no, not serious,' Mr Pidgeon assured the company. 'Nothing serious, I assure you. The Captain just thinks it would be advisable for us to spend the night ashore, that's all.'

'Eh? What's that?' grunted Sir John Birch. 'No beds. Not going to sleep on the bare ground, I can tell you. Eh, Laura?'

'I'm sure Mr Pidgeon doesn't expect us to do anything like that,' said Lady Darracott, with a long-suffering smile.

'Of course not, Lady Darracott. As a matter of fact there are tents and beds, and all that sort of thing, already stored here. The stewards will get them up this afternoon, and I'll have all your things brought ashore. I needn't say how grieved I am to inconvenience you all to any extent, but I assure you the inconvenience shall be as small as I can make it.'

'That's all right, old man,' Mr Bray assured his host. 'Captain's orders. We understand. You'll be as right as two pins, Lady Darracott, take it from me. You won't mind a night ashore at all. Not a bit of it.'

'Shan't I?' said Lady Darracott helplessly.

By ones and twos the plateau party had trailed back to the beach, as Mr Pidgeon's confabulation with the Captain showed no signs of ending. Sitting now among the rocks and sand, they were sipping iced cocktails before lunch as they listened to Mr Pidgeon's apologies. Mr Pidgeon continued to assure them that the yacht had met with no serious damage; but the more he did so, the more did a suspicion percolate between his words that perhaps all might not be quite so well as he asserted. There was, however, nothing that anyone could do, so that the suspicion had to remain a suspicion and nothing more.

While two of the stewards served the picnic meal, the rest of the staff, and most of the crew, engaged in an endless procession from the yacht to the plateau above with bags and trunks, bales, cases, and packages.

'Really, Guy,' protested Mrs Fayre gently, 'aren't you giving the poor men a great deal of unnecessary trouble? We surely can't want so much luggage just for one night. I can't think why you wouldn't let us go back to the yacht and pack a little case each for ourselves.'

'No, no,' Mr Pidgeon said smugly. 'The stewards and the stewardess can see to all that. If I have got to upset our arrangements, I certainly won't have any more inconvenience than can be helped. Certainly not.'

Everyone murmured what an admirable host their host was.

Only Roger looked at that worthy man askance. Roger had a suspicious nature, and did not trust many people. Least of all people in the world just then did he trust Mr Guy Pidgeon. And yet, indubitably, the yacht had met with a mishap; and surely not even Mr Pidgeon in pursuit of a whim would run a forty-thousand-pound yacht aground.

The afternoon passed in lazy ease. Some of the company dozed openly in the shade, undisturbed by the faint sounds of hammering which came down from the plateau above; the younger contingent made use of the bathing-dresses and towels which Mr Pidgeon, that man of power, had commanded to appear for them. Tea was served on the beach, nor was Sir John deprived of the iced stimulant which he preferred in the place of that poor-spirited fluid. As Mr Pidgeon had hinted, if inconvenience there must be, that inconvenience should indeed be as little in evidence as money could make it.

Shortly after tea was over, the head steward approached Mr Pidgeon and, as the police reports say, made a communication to him. Mr Pidgeon thereupon rose to his feet and announced to his guests that the little camp was completed, and perhaps they might like to see their tents and make sure that everything was satisfactory before dinner, though, of course, all their things were already unpacked. With noble fortitude Lady Darracott, smiling bravely, agreed that she would make a supreme effort to struggle to the uplands. Much gratified, Mr Pidgeon insisted on taking her arm and heading the procession with her, at a pace of about half a mile an hour, with many deferential requests to her to put all her weight on his bony arm and spare her valuable person to the fullest extent.

When at last the top was reached, those who had seen it that same morning uttered moos of surprise. On the level ground in the south-east corner of the plateau had arisen a little canvas village. Flanked by two big white marquees, more than a dozen green tents lay in two exactly straight lines, about twenty feet apart from each other. They were not of the bell type or anything so inconvenient, but of the cottage pattern, with a ridge-pole and plenty of head-room; their size, as Mr Pidgeon informed Captain Twyford, was twelve feet by eight, and there was one apiece for everybody. Pinned by the doorway of each was a neat piece of cardboard, with the name of the occupant upon it.

'Pretty good show, Pidgeon,' commented Captain Twyford, with unprecedented praise.

Amid squeaks of excitement the party set about finding their allotted homes; and the squeaks were intensified as the interiors were revealed, each with its spring bed, collapsible but very serviceable dressing-table, ingenious chest of drawers which (as Mr Pidgeon again informed Captain Twyford) would take to pieces and fold up quite flat, folding table, canvas armchair, and, supreme cause of pleasure, real wardrobe, of green canvas on a wooden frame; and already the belongings of each person were adorning the dressing-table, filling the chest of drawers, and hanging up in the wardrobe.

'Guy, it's *too* marvellous,' crooned Mrs Fayre. 'Just *too* marvellous. Isn't it, Willie?'

'It's a great effort, Guy. Very successful indeed.'

From all sides congratulations streamed over the gratified and smirking Mr Pidgeon, and even Miss St Thomas pronounced the result to be glamorous. Only did the face of Roger wear a gloomy look. As the sinewy form of his host wriggled through the doorway of his tent, Roger turned from a suspicious examination of its fittings and remarked, with sour ingratitude:

'This is a hell of a lot of trouble to take for a single night, isn't it?'

'Ah,' said Mr Pidgeon, and grinned naughtily.

3

It was at twenty minutes past five that Mr Pidgeon had begun to display his model camp. At seventeen minutes to six Miss Crosspatrick remarked:

'I see that Captain Soames is taking no more risks. He must be going to anchor nearly a mile out.'

Miss Crosspatrick uttered these words as she made her way into one of the marquees which, furnished with collapsible canvas chairs and tables, was obviously the lounge, or drawing-room, of the camp. There were three or four other people in the marquee at the moment, including Mr Pidgeon. The way in which that gentleman received the piece of news struck everyone. He sprang to his feet, fixed on Miss Crosspatrick a look of horror, and bounded into the open. There he stood for a moment, staring at the distant and tiny silhouette of the yacht, and the horror on his face deepened.

'Guy! Whatever is the matter?' asked Crystal Vane from inside the marquee.

Without answering, Mr Pidgeon proceeded to leap headlong down the path to the shore, uttering shrill cries and flapping his arms like a buzzard.

'Has he gone mad?' queried Miss Crosspatrick, watching her host with gentle interest.

'It must be something to do with the yacht,' murmured Mrs Vane, and her tones were plainly apprehensive.

Attracted by the strange cries, other people were now coming out of their tents, and soon a dozen pairs of eyes were fastened on Mr Pidgeon's headlong descent. They saw him begin to rush across the little beach, and then bring up sharply. Peering over the edge, they could make out that he had come a halt in front of a stick standing upright in the sand. From the top of the stick Mr Pidgeon took something white, which he appeared to unfold, study, and ponder over for some moments. Then, with hanging head and dejection in every line of his drooping figure, he slowly made his way up the path again.

A chorus of questions greeted him at the top, and he looked at his interrogators exactly as if he were about to burst into tears.

'Guy, what *is* the matter?' cried Mrs Fayre urgently. 'Do tell us. Has something dreadful happened?'

'Something appalling,' groaned Mr Pidgeon.

'What? Tell us quickly.'

Mr Pidgeon cast a hunted look round him, as if he feared that his news would cause the party to tear him at once in small pieces and throw the remnants over the cliff.

'What? *What*, Guy?'

'I fear,' gulped Mr Pidgeon, 'I very much fear that we are – what is the technical word? – marooned here – yes, marooned. The stewards have gone on strike, and gone back to port with the ship.'

chapter four

It had taken some time for everyone to understand the exact circumstances of the catastrophe. Mr Pidgeon admitted freely that although prompted by the best intentions he had been unwise, and hardly anyone failed to agree with him; many indeed went further, and by implication at any rate, if not directly, called Mr Pidgeon considerably worse things than just unwise.

According, then, to Mr Pidgeon's story, what had happened was this:

The injury to the yacht's propeller might be very much more serious than had been given out. In the Captain's opinion it was essential that she return at once to port and be docked for examination and repair. To make the journey with the full load of passengers, was, the Captain considered, highly inadvisable for a number of reasons. Fortunately, however, here they were, safely landed on a charming little island, on which tents, stores, and all necessities were already waiting, and to set up a temporary camp was a matter of ease. A temporary camp had therefore been set up. No word had been spoken to Mr Pidgeon's guests of the arrangement in order to prevent unnecessary alarm, and also to avoid acrimony and difficulty; for whereas it might have been possible to take back to port one or two passengers, seven or eight might want to go; it had therefore been decided that, to prevent inequity, all had better remain. The yacht was to slip quietly away, and Mr Pidgeon break the news as best he might when it became inevitable.

So far, so bad. And what Mr Pidgeon had to divulge next was worse still. For it had been naturally part of his plan that the steward, the cook, and the stewardess should remain on the island to minister to his guests. It appeared, however, that these gentry did not see things in that way. The note which had been left for Mr Pidgeon on the beach made that only too clear.

> DEAR SIR [ran the note],
> On behalf of my mates, I am requested to inform you that we were engaged for a sea trip, and not for service on land. We have to tell you that we do not care about serving on land, and that is why we engaged ourselves for a sea trip, so we regret that we are not able to comply with your request to stay behind and serve on land, as we were engaged to serve at sea only. So we are sticking to the ship and will serve the captain and other officers, because that is what we engaged ourselves for, to serve at sea. Trusting that this will not cause you any inconvenience.
>
> Yours respectfully,
>
> ALFRED JIMBLE
> (*Head Steward*).

Mr Pidgeon, having read out this doleful communication, gazed unhappily round. 'I – I really am exceedingly sorry,' he stammered. 'Really exceedingly so.'

A hoarse roar, as of a bull in distress, alarmed the canaries for furlongs round.

'The wireless!' it said. 'Have you brought the wireless ashore? Is the operator here?'

Mr Pidgeon's crest fell still further. 'Why – no. I'm afraid – tut, tut, tut, I quite forgot. My dear Bray, I really am exceedingly…dear me.'

Mr Bray stared at him, while his large red face grew slowly purple. 'I'm ruined, then!' he shouted. 'Do you understand? Ruined! Good God, man, didn't I *tell* you…'

'I really am exceedingly sorry,' repeated Mr Pidgeon helplessly. 'Very sorry indeed.'

'Ah, to hell,' barked Mr Bray, and marched away.

Mr Pidgeon glanced round again, as if imploring a kind word from someone.

'I – I'm afraid we may be here a fortnight,' he said, with a ghastly kind of smile.

There was a dead little silence.

'Good!' said Miss Vincent briskly. 'I think it's a marvellous place for a holiday, Mr Pidgeon. And I adore camping. A fortnight won't be any too long. Will it, Harold?'

Harold was far too crushed by the anger of his Jove to do anything but smile in a feebly non-committal way; but Mr Pidgeon looked as if he were ready to frisk round Miss Vincent's rather large feet for this kind speech.

2

'I don't believe a word of it, Pidgeon,' Roger said sourly, looking up from the potato he was peeling.

Dinner looked like being late. The stewards had made no preparations for it at all, beyond filling the little kitchen-tent behind the second marquee with a stock of provisions. With an alacrity that Roger had viewed with the greatest suspicion, Crystal Vane had taken charge of affairs while Mr Pidgeon was still looking too crushed to do anything, Enid Fayre was wringing her white hands, and everyone else appeared quite helpless. Calling on a reluctant Captain Twyford to assist her, she had organised a kitchen squad, a parlour-maid squad, and a squad to look after the tents. Miss Vincent had proved a ready lieutenant and, after a moment's consideration and observation, during which she had no doubt noticed Mrs Fayre wringing her pretty hands, Mrs Bray trying to look aggrieved on behalf of her husband, and Lady Darracott presenting a picture of inefficient despair, Miss Crosspatrick had stepped forward briskly, too.

Everyone (except, of course, Lady Darracott) had now been allotted to one or the other of the three squads, pending a reorganisation of the personnel the next morning; and though it cannot be said that Sir John Birch, who had been put in charge of the drinks, had as yet done very much beyond console himself with them, most people were already resigned to doing their best towards a bad job. Indeed, Miss St Thomas was surprisingly proving quite a useful asset to the parlour-maid squad, and was now assisting busily to lay the long trestle-table in the farther marquee.

'It's a crashing bore,' as she had remarked 'to think of those dim cads knocking us for six like this, but I suppose it's no use getting strenuous about it, is it, Reggie?'

'Oke, angelface,' Captain Twyford had agreed.

So Roger had found himself allotted to the potatoes, by a grinning Crystal, and had taken his pail and pan away to the edge of the cliff to ruminate alone. To him, ruminating, had entered Mr Pidgeon.

'Not a word,' Roger repeated now, with some violence.

Mr Pidgeon glanced hastily round, and then his shoulders began to shake. 'You don't, Sheringham? You don't? Well, between you and me, my dear fellow, you're quite right.'

'You and Crystal had it all planned out.'

'We did,' shook Mr Pidgeon.

'The yacht never struck at all. You had it all fixed up with the Captain, and you'd arranged for the stewards to go off. You meant from the very beginning to maroon us all here for a fortnight.'

'For your benefit, my dear fellow,' cackled Mr Pidgeon, carefully keeping his back to the camp. 'Entirely for your benefit.'

'Rats!'

'I assure you. Ask Crystal.'

'What's the idea, anyhow?'

'You don't think it will be amusing to have these people here for a fortnight on an island not half a mile wide, unable to get away from each other, and having to do a great deal of work which will be exceedingly good for them, but which they will no doubt heartily dislike? You don't think that will be interesting?'

'I think you're inhuman,' Roger growled. 'Simply inhuman.'

'Not at all,' Mr Pidgeon protested, pained. 'I may be an experimentalist, but I'm a thoroughly human one – and humanitarian. Think of fat, useless old Sir John Birch. Think of useless Lady Darracott. Think of anyone you like. This fortnight's going to be the making of them.'

'If you get Lady Darracott to take a hand in any of the work, I'll consider your experiment a success. But you won't.'

'There are ways,' murmured Mr Pidgeon modestly. 'Yes, I think there are ways.'

'And for the rest,' Roger continued, grasping another potato, 'it's very kind of you to have arranged this elaborate hoax for my benefit, but I'm afraid we shall all be exceedingly bored with it by the time the fortnight's ended.

I don't think it's a particularly interesting lot that you've collected in any case, and by the end of a fortnight's dull camping they'll all be just bores.'

'It may not be so dull.' Mr Pidgeon's shoulders began to shake again. 'My dear fellow, don't take it for granted that I haven't made arrangements to ensure its not being that, whatever it is. I haven't told you the full beauty of it yet.'

'Are you going to have us attacked by pirates, with machine-guns and an armoured motor-cruiser?' asked Roger, with heavy irony.

'That's an interesting idea,' Mr Pidgeon said, much struck. 'Very interesting. I wonder how Bray would react to an attack by armed pirates. It's a pity I didn't think of something like that. But no, my own small effort will be less elaborate than that.'

'What is it?'

'You'll see,' promised Mr Pidgeon. 'You'll see.'

Roger threw his peeled potato into the saucepan, and gloomily took up another.

3

The first dinner was to be a cold affair, with only Roger's potatoes to be cooked. While they were steaming, cocktails were served in the first marquee.

If Mr Pidgeon had expected quick results from his nefarious plot, he looked like being disappointed. To Roger's surprise the little party appeared more amicable than ever. A misfortune in common was making them positively coo at one another. The disposition, confined at first to the youngest members, to treat the whole thing as great fun, had already spread to everyone except the very oldest, and even Sir John Birch was now grunting with some approach to joviality that they'd dashed well show the dashed fellers.

In this general atmosphere of good-fellowship, with the lamps already lit and twilight beginning to fall outside, Mrs Fayre remembered the mystery of the ruined stone hut and began to press her cousin-in-law for the story. Others supported her, until at last Mr Pidgeon, with an air of great reluctance, consented to tell it.

'Though whether I am wise in doing so,' he added gravely, 'in view of the circumstances, is perhaps open to doubt. However, if you insist, the responsibility must be yours. So far as I have been able to ascertain, by enquiries I made in Lisbon and elsewhere, the story is roughly as follows.

'On the coast of Portugal, very many years ago, there lived a young fisherman named Pedro Lopez, worthy but poor. This young man was engaged to be married to a charming girl, as honest and worthy as himself, but alas, no less poor. A run of bad luck had left the young man in a position in which marriage looked even more remote than before. He was, however, of a sanguine and plucky disposition, and in these straits his thoughts began to turn towards his great-uncle, whose heir he considered himself undoubtedly to be.

'Now this great-uncle was very old and reputed very rich, but he bore a dreadful reputation in the countryside in which Pedro lived. This reputation was not in the least diminished by the fact that no one on the mainland had set eyes on him for at least twenty years; for he lived, all alone, on a small island many leagues out to sea, even the exact position of which was a matter of uncertainty to the good fishermen who muttered his name with bated breath. It was this uncertainty which was, in fact, responsible for the old man's continued existence, which, could he have been apprehended in time, he would certainly have been put to death. The crime was no less than sacrilege, beside which his other evil living, his many thefts, and even the two murders of which he was suspected, paled into insignificance. He had stolen the sacred vessels, the jewelled cross, and actually the sacred relic, the guaranteed genuine mummified right hand of St Anastasius himself with which he wrote his well-known and popular creed, from a neighbouring church which was dedicated to that saint.

'Reports had reached the mainland from time to time of this wicked old man's life on his remote island, but vague and impossible of substantiation. He was reported to have grown exceedingly rich; by means of a few young trees and plants which he had prudently taken with him on his flight, it was stated that he had established a plantation which produced oranges and bananas of a size hitherto beyond the wildest dreams of man; and it was confidently stated that a vessel was despatched each year from Madeira for the particular purpose of purchasing and conveying away this crop, for which each year a fabulous sum was paid. And lastly, it was rumoured that the old wretch was set still firmer in his evil ways, and not a day passed but that he spoke flippantly aloud of the holy saints and, on feast days and Sundays, of the Holy Ghost Himself. The conclusion to the simple fisher-folk was foregone: the old reprobate was not merely the incarnation of all evil, but was actually in league with the Devil.

'Nevertheless, in spite of these appalling tales, the plucky young Pedro Lopez was not deterred. He found another spirit as bold as himself, young Colorado Claro, his closest friend who was engaged to be married to Pedro's sister and to whom he promised a half-share of whatever spoils might accrue; and with a last fond embrace of their respective senoritas, the two foolhardy young men embarked in a felucca, into the purchase of which each had put the last peso of his savings.

'They set their course according to the most reliable of the rumours, and the voyage was uneventful until about a week after leaving their native village, they sighted, far ahead of them, a small island lying low on the horizon. Then the sky grew slowly overcast, the gentle rocking of the waves grew to a threatening swell, and an indescribable feeling of dread seized upon both the hardy young adventurers. They looked at each other questioningly, but neither would be the first to admit to the panic with which their breasts were now filled, or suggest putting the boat about. Instead they pressed on, and beached their vessel on a sandy cove convenient to the purpose.

'It was now nearly evening; the sky was already inky black, and there was barely light for the two to find their way up a winding little path from the beach to the heights above. They spoke little, but each knew by instinct that they had found the goal they sought. Arrived at the top they descried, a bare quarter of a mile away, a plantation of orange trees and banana-palms, and there was just enough light for them to be able to make out, among the trees, a small stone hut, scarcely worthy to be designated a house. To this they directed their steps. The air was now oppressive and stifling, and distant rumblings told of an approaching storm. They reached the hut, and Pedro knocked on the door. There was no reply. He knocked again, and still without result. Then, desperate for shelter, for the rain had suddenly begun to fall in torrents, while jagged flashes of lightning tore the sky open above their heads, Pedro summoned all his courage and lifted the latch. The door refused to open. Pedro pushed, at first gently and then with all his strength, but it was not until his friend joined him that the combined efforts of both caused the door suddenly to give way, precipitating them both into the room.

'At first it seemed to them that the room was empty, for not a sound was to be heard in the pitch darkness which confronted them. The next instant, however, a blinding light illuminated the dreadful scene, as a clap of thunder exploded almost on top of the very roof. What they saw in that moment sent them back, heedless of the storm and the rain – shrieking, stumbling, falling in their mad efforts to get away from that fearful place. One glance had been enough at that blackened face, which had seemed to be grinning at them from its distorted jaws, while it watched them with its sightless eyes: that face framed in a halo of white hair, and those bony hands resting on the table just in front of it.

'Pedro, in his headlong panic, missed the path. With a fearful cry he plunged over the edge of the precipice not a dozen yards from where we are now sitting. Colorado was more fortunate. Reaching the shore he succeeded, by a superhuman effort, in launching the felucca. He sprang into it, and at once the wind and the current seemed to draw him at incredible speed away from the island, as if the very elements knew that it was an island of the Devil and the dead, and that the living had no place there. He reached home: but it was a broken man, with hair as white as that of the apparition in the hut itself, who stepped ashore once more in Portugal. That was forty-three years ago. Since then not a single human being has slept on this island – or would sleep on it, for a king's ransom. For every night, so the story goes, a dreadful scream is heard, and – but no,' concluded Mr Pidgeon somewhat abruptly, 'I won't tell you that part.'

It was a tribute to Mr Pidgeon's powers that for a full minute after he had finished, no one spoke. Then Captain Twyford, with a slight smile, remarked:

'And the old tough's ill-gotten gains?'

'History doesn't relate,' Mr Pidgeon smiled back. 'At any rate I fancy they cannot be there any longer.'

'You've looked?'

'I did have a glance round,' said Mr Pidgeon, with an apologetic air.

'And we're the first people to sleep on the island since...?' Miss St Thomas pretended to shiver. 'Reggie, get me another cocktail. But it's rather glamorous for all that,' she added.

'Then – the island is haunted, Guy?' Mrs Fayre's smile was just a tiny shade unnatural.

'Oh, no,' said Mr Pidgeon quickly.

'But if a dreadful cry is heard...'

'I didn't mean to tell you that bit. It's just nonsense, of course.'

'I adore ghosts,' observed Miss Vincent, with enthusiasm. 'Don't you, Harold?'

Mr Parker smiled feebly.

'It isn't haunted, eh?' put in Mr Bray. 'Well, I can't say it makes much odds to me whether it is or it isn't, but the ladies'll be glad to hear it isn't, I expect. Anyhow, that explains a bit why you got the place so cheap, Pidgeon, I wouldn't mind betting. Eh?'

'It might have something to do with it,' Mr Pidgeon admitted.

'Now then,' said Crystal briskly, 'if Guy's quite finished telling us ghost stories, I must go and see to my potatoes. Are you ready, Enid? Well, if you'll get everyone into the next tent, I'll dish up. Roger, you'd better come and help me.'

Roger followed her out in silence.

In the kitchen-tent she looked at him with twinkling eyes. 'Well, my sweet? What did you think of that naughty old lamb's effort?'

'Rotten,' said Roger sourly. 'I never heard so many clichés in my life. I suppose, by the way, there wasn't a word of truth in it?'

'Not a word. We made it up together. He really did tell it rather well. You'd say so if you weren't jealous.'

'And that's part of the silly plot?'

'Yes, just a teeny-weeny part. Don't let it out that it's not exactly true, will you, love?'

'I make no promises. In fact, I wish you wouldn't take me into your confidence. I don't want to get mixed up in the thing at all. Why do you tell me, you unpleasant woman?'

'Because you *are* mixed up in it,' Crystal giggled. 'You're one of us. And you know perfectly well you're loving it really.'

'I'm not. I'm too old for this silly kind of practical joke. And, by the way, do you really seriously think you're going to cause a panic among a lot of sober-headed, sensible people with a ridiculous story like that?'

'I don't know about a panic,' Crystal said comfortably, tipping the potatoes into a cullender. 'We may, though. But not with that story, of course. That's only just a bit of local colour, thrown in for make-weight.'

'With what, then?'

'You wait.'

Roger made the sound usually spelt: 'Pshaw!'

Crystal looked at him. 'Roger, Guy really has got something up his sleeve,' she said, more seriously. 'I won't tell you yet what it is because that would spoil it, but I will tell you something: it's right in your line. Oh, I can promise you, there's more in all this than meets the eye – even your eye, my pet. Yes, really.'

'In my line?' Roger was puzzled. Crystal had spoken as if there really was some solid purpose behind this foolish joke, and her eyes had not twinkled. For the first time Roger was mildly impressed. Was it possible that...?

'Just wait till after dinner,' said Crystal.

Roger stood by while she twirled the potatoes round in their dry pan with a lump of butter, before putting them in the dish. Then, taking the dish, he conveyed it through the service-flap from the kitchen into the dining-tent and put it on the table.

'Tell Guy dinner's ready,' Crystal called after him.

Roger made his way into the other marquee. Mr Pidgeon was in the act of disengaging himself from one group and walking towards another. Roger followed him. Before he could reach him, however, Captain Twyford had intercepted him. Roger arrived just in time to hear the Captain say, in a very nonchalant voice:

'Oh – er – by the way, Pidgeon, there's nothing in that tale of yours, of course?'

'Nothing in it?'

'I mean, about the island being haunted? I mean, the women...'

'Oh, nothing, of course; just an old wives' tale,' Mr Pidgeon replied blandly.

'Dinner's ready,' said Roger stolidly and refused to encounter Mr Pidgeon's ribald eye.

chapter five

By the time dinner was over, the party seemed to have become quite reconciled to their enforced stay on the island. The meal had been surprisingly good, and not much had had as yet to come out of tins, for a store of fresh provisions had been landed from the yacht, and the far-sighted Mr Pidgeon had included among the camping gear a paraffin-driven refrigerator. It was felt generally that Enid and Crystal had risen to the occasion in no uncertain manner; for though Crystal had been the chief of staff, and so shouldered most of the work, Enid had not for a moment abrogated her post of commander-in-chief. Sir John too, introduced to the really admirable little cellar buried by Mr Pidgeon's foresight on his previous visit in the ground around the little spring, had taken his duties seriously and, given Captain Twyford as his aide-de-camp, kept that languid young man quite busy; with the wines served at dinner no more fault could be found than with the dinner itself.

Over the port Mr Pidgeon, having previously begged the ladies not to absent themselves, rose to his feet; and so altered was the temper of the assembly, mellowed by its excellent food and drink, that his action was actually greeted with applause. Mr Pidgeon, bowing benignly, stood in his place at the end of the long table and surveyed for a moment the rows of faces that receded on either side of him.

'Ladies and gentlemen,' he said, with some solemnity, 'my apologies you have already received for the lamentable contretemps in which we find ourselves; it is my more pleasant duty at this moment to announce to you an amusing and instructive method which I have at my disposal for rendering your sojourn on this island less intolerably tedious than it might otherwise have proved.'

'Hear, hear,' said Miss Vincent loudly, and blushed. Mr Pidgeon bowed gravely in her direction.

'By a strange series of chances,' he continued, 'fate has placed in my hands a secret of astonishing gravity. This secret is known to only one other person in the world besides myself; and that person has no inkling of my own knowledge. The person is, moreover, present among us here this evening.' And Mr Pidgeon allowed his eye to travel benevolently up one row of faces and down the other, without, however, pausing for an instant upon any countenance in particular.

'Ladies and gentlemen, you may have thought that this little group which I invited for the cruise, which has been so unfortunately interrupted, was a fortuitous one. That is not the case. Each individual was carefully chosen, and for the purpose which is now in my mind. Most carefully.'

We're getting the truth at last, thought Roger; and his interest quickened.

'That purpose,' Mr Pidgeon went on, 'is, in point of fact, the unravelling of the secret to which I alluded just now; for this secret is not a private secret, a personal matter into which it would be impertinent to pry; on the contrary, it is a secret against society, a guilty secret, a secret which it is the duty of each one of us to bring out into the open; a secret which must be divulged, in due season, to the authorities themselves of law and order.

'You may ask,' suggested Mr Pidgeon, with some diffidence, twirling the stem of his wine glass, 'why, if this secret is so weighty, I have not communicated it to the authorities already; and if you do so, I have to admit that, strictly speaking, I ought to have done so as soon as it became known to me. It is, however, a secret of some years' standing, and I did not think that a few more weeks would materially affect the course of justice; and I therefore held it up in order to make use of it, if required, to enliven the possible moments of tedium in a four-weeks' cruise. I am glad now that I did so; for, though I do not wish to appear heartless, I do think that the feelings of the original holder of this secret need not be considered very seriously in comparison with the amusement and benefit which I am able to offer you from it, in the circumstances in which we now find ourselves placed.'

Again Mr Pidgeon's eyes passed gently over the assembly. Every face now wore an expression of acute interest. Even Sir John Birch's mouth hung slightly open, while Mrs Bray had so far forgotten herself as frankly to gape. Roger wished that Mr Pidgeon would come to the point.

Mr Pidgeon proceeded to do so.

'You will, however, be wondering what this secret is, and why it occurred to me to make use of my knowledge of it in this way. I will tell you. Some of you may have heard of a game which was popular in certain circles a year or two ago called the Murder Game. In this game a certain person was chosen as the murderer, another as the victim, and another as the detective. A mock-murder was enacted, and the detective was required to discover the identity of the murderer. In the game I now offer you there will, I am glad to say, be no victim, nor will any murder be enacted; moreover, there will be not one detective, but everyone will be a detective. Everyone, that is to say, with the exception of one person, not, of course, including myself. That person will not require to act as a detective, for the identity of the murderer is only too well known to the individual in question.

'Yes, ladies and gentlemen,' said Mr Pidgeon impassively, 'there is, in point of fact, amongst us here tonight a murderer.

'The story of how this piece of knowledge came into my hands is interesting and curious; for so far from this individual having ever come under suspicion, murder itself, in the case of the death in question, was never even suspected. The reason for this was that all the tiny facts, both of the actual deed and of the circumstances which prompted it, were never known at the time to any single person. A truly remarkable series of accidents (if they were accidents) has now placed them in my hands – or at any rate enough of them for me to be able to prove murder beyond the possibility of refutation.

'You will understand now why the personnel of this party has been so carefully chosen. Beyond my cousins, Mr and Mrs Fayre, not a single one of you was known to me six months ago, with the exception of Mr Sheringham, with whom I came into contact when he was an undergraduate in my charge nearly twenty years ago and whom I have not seen or heard of since, and Miss Vincent, whose parents it is true I know well, but with whom herself I don't suppose I had exchanged, before this voyage, as much as half a dozen words. You will consider therefore whether either Mr or Mrs Fayre, whose intimate affairs I have at any rate a better chance of knowing, may be this unknown murderer of ours, or whether the series of accidents which I have already termed extraordinary, a word which I will now amplify into the phrase "almost beyond belief," might not better justify this description if it related to one who was more of a complete stranger to me. With regard to Mr Sheringham and Miss Vincent, here again the chances are slightly more in their favour than in that of the rest of the party; and you will consider whether Miss Vincent, undeterred by her youth, as in the case of the famous Constance Kent, might have gone to this extreme step, or whether Mr Sheringham, relying on his reputation as a hunter of criminals, may have felt tempted ever to exchange the role of avenger for that of villain.

'As for the rest, with one or two I have had a slight acquaintance during the last few months; the others were unknown to me, personally, until the very beginning of this cruise. Do not, however, allow yourselves to be influenced necessarily in favour of the former. I repeat, the tricks of fate which have placed the proofs in my hands are more fantastic than anything I have encountered in the most highly coloured fiction. An author of fiction would, in fact, refuse to employ them, so incredible would they appear to his readers. You may, on the contrary, ask yourselves: would he have invited any complete strangers at all if it were not to lose the needle of one complete stranger in the haystack of a number? That is an argument I commend to you, without, however, in the least promising that it has any validity.

'With regard to Mr Sheringham, assuming for the moment that he is not the person we are seeking, it may prove to his experience a childishly simple exercise that I have set him. I think therefore that Mr Sheringham ought to be handicapped. That is to say, when he has solved the problem, as I make no doubt he will, he shall communicate the result to me privately, and shall only be considered the winner if no other competitor sends in a correct answer. I mention this,' said Mr Pidgeon deprecatingly, 'because in order to stimulate interest in the hunt, I have provided two modest prizes, a ladies' and a gentlemen's, which I hope to be able to award before our fortnight here has expired. The – er – ladies' prize consists of a platinum wrist-watch, set with, I believe – er – diamonds; and the gentlemen's of a – um – gold cigarette-case.

'Well, that, ladies and gentlemen,' beamed Mr Pidgeon, 'is, I think, all. It only remains for me to hope that my little scheme meets with your approval, and that it will help to relieve the monotony to which, I fear, we may be condemned. The chase has always been a fine old English sport, and if we are to believe the apologists of fox-hunting, the fox enjoys the run almost as much as the hounds themselves. I hope that our fox will be equally entertained. To the fox at any rate the fortnight should not be a dull one, for the days will be full of happy stratagems and cunning twists for the avoidance of capture. Ladies and gentlemen, I give you the health of our fox. May he – or, if it turns out to be a vixen, she – give us the run of our lives.'

Mr Pidgeon solemnly drank the toast that he had proposed, but few followed his example. Doubt and something not unlike dismay sat on every brow. To look at the two rows of faces, one would have said that each single one belonged to an undetected murderer.

Miss Crosspatrick was the first to find her voice.

'Of course, you know' she drawled to her host, 'this is quite impossible.'

Mr Pidgeon was all polite attention. 'Impossible?'

'Quite. One simply doesn't do things this way.'

'No?' Mr Pidgeon looked upset. 'You don't think it's a good idea?'

'I do not. If you have information of this sort, you must give it to the authorities.'

'But I'm going to,' Mr Pidgeon replied humbly. 'As soon as we get back to England. I've only held it up for a few weeks; and as it has already been held up for some years, I didn't think that would matter. Do you think it does?'

'I think it's absolutely glamorous,' pronounced Miss St Thomas, in her loud tones. 'I'm all in favour. Personally, I believe it's you, Reggie. You must have murdered dozens of people, haven't you?'

'Too right,' agreed Captain Twyford.

'Reverting to what the last speaker said,' broke in Mr Bray, 'I concur. You can't do things like that, you know, Pidgeon, old man.'

'Can't I?' said Mr Pidgeon innocently.

'No, you can't, take it from me. You'd much better let sleeping dogs lie.'

'Ah, you think that?' Mr Pidgeon fixed Mr Bray with a look so full of sinister meaning that the latter drew back in his chair.

'I agree,' piped Mr Combe, before Mr Bray could utter his indignation. 'If some poor devil was once driven to murder, and you've found it out, let him be. He's probably had a hell of a time since. It's a wicked thing to make a game out of his agony, as you propose to do.'

'You don't hold with bloodsports?' asked Mr Pidgeon pleasantly. Mr Combe hunted regularly.

'That's beside the point. I – '

'Anyone else know what you know, Pidgeon?' interrupted Sir John. 'Told anyone?'

'Not a soul.'

'Put it in writing?'

'Not a word.'

'Then my advice is, leave it alone.'

Mr Pidgeon looked round in a bewildered sort of way. 'Dear me,' he murmured, 'there seems – not a conspiracy, of course, but a surprisingly universal agreement that the ends of justice should be defeated.' He looked round again, questioningly.

'How do you know what justice is?' demanded with some truculence Mr Combe, who appeared to have liked the port just a little too well. 'My God, when I think of the poor devil, whoever it is, living day in, day out with the ghost of – '

'Guy!' said Mrs Fayre plaintively.

'Yes, Enid?'

'Really, you know, I don't think it's a very nice idea. Don't you think you'd better give it up?'

'Well, really, Enid…what do you think, Willie?'

Mr Fayre appeared to shrink, as he always did when someone addressed him in public. 'I don't know, Guy. Just a little – what's the word? – macabre, isn't it?'

'But I *like* macabre things,' said Mr Pidgeon, as plaintively as ever Enid could achieve. 'I thought everyone liked the macabre. Don't they?'

'There are some things, old man,' Mr Bray replied for the assembly, 'which overstep the limits of good taste. Eh? A word to the wise, you know.'

'That certainly does seem the general opinion,' murmured Mr Pidgeon, in a chastened say. 'Certainly I should shrink from overstepping the limits of good taste. Lady Darracott, may I ask what you think? You, after all, take precedence in our small company.'

Lady Darracott, on Mr Pidgeon's right, made a helpless little gesture. 'I should in any case not enter for your competition, Mr Pidgeon. In my younger days, even, I hardly think the idea would have attracted me, though we indulged in plenty of mad pranks then; as it is...no. I agree with Sir John, Mr Pidgeon.'

'Isn't that just a little dim of you, auntie?' complained her niece.

'I'm afraid I am dim, dear, in these days,' sighed Lady Darracott.

Mr Pidgeon bowed to the majority opinion.

'I'm so sorry I said anything at all about it,' he apologised, in deprecating tones. 'Please forget the whole thing.'

2

It was quite dark when Mr Pidgeon took Roger's arm an hour or so later and led him out of the marquee. Dinner had been cleared away by the housemaid squad and the things washed up by the scullion squad; and with two tables of bridge in progress, conversation, and reading, everything in the marquee and outside it was peaceful and harmonious. It was quite plain that not a single person in the assembly remembered the sinister presence in the midst of it of an undetected murderer: quite plain, for not another word had been uttered on the topic.

'It's astonishing how soon a thing like that passes out of the average mind, isn't it, Sheringham?' observed Mr Pidgeon, with innocent surprise, as he piloted his guest down the path towards the beach. 'One would have thought it rather important. But no. No sooner said than forgotten.'

'I don't suppose they've forgotten really,' grunted Roger, who found himself disapproving more and more strongly of his late tutor in *literae humaniores*.

'Ah,' said Mr Pidgeon.

They reached the little beach in silence, and began to pace up and down along the edge of the water.

'Well?' Roger said.

'Yes?'

'What have you brought me down here for?'

'You think I've brought you down for some purpose beyond the sheer pleasure of your companionship?'

'I know you have.'

Mr Pidgeon uttered his sinister chuckle. 'What perspicacity you have, my dear Sheringham. And, of course, you're quite right. I noticed that you did not add your voice to those of the critics of my little scheme, which I still consider quite admirable. I want to hear what you thought.'

'I thought it was abominable.'

Mr Pidgeon chuckled again. 'And I thought it would appeal so readily to the after-dinner atmosphere. *αὐτὰα ἐπεὶ πόσιοζ χαὶ ἐδητύοζ ἐξ ἔαον ἕντο*... But nothing of the sort. A blunder in psychology of which you, I'm sure, would never have been guilty. But really, I'm surprised to find you on the side of the carpers. I should have said that the conception would have pleased you, Sheringham. No? You disappoint me.'

'It isn't often I find myself in agreement with Combe,' said Roger, 'but I really do think the idea was a little too thick. In fact, it's about the cruellest thing I ever heard of.'

'I abandon it. I give it up. *Pono, tristisque recedo*.'

'Do you though?' Roger asked suspiciously. 'I'm not sure that it's possible. You may abandon the manhunt, but you've divulged both too much and not enough. As I said just now, they may be pretending to ignore it, but they haven't forgotten really. I believe we're in for a thoroughly uneasy fortnight.'

'You think that?'

Roger was too occupied in sorting out what he did think to notice the slightly peculiar tone in which Mr Pidgeon had spoken. 'Yes, I do. I shall carry on as if you'd said nothing, of course, and do my best to help other people to do the same; but it's not going to be an exactly pleasant feeling for the weaker spirits and the women, to think that they're shut up for a fortnight here with an unknown murderer, is it?'

'I don't agree that the weaker spirits and the women should be classed together,' returned Mr Pidgeon, mildly argumentative. 'If you imply that the words are synonymous, I agree still less.'

'Don't quibble,' Roger said impatiently. 'It's obvious that you and Crystal and I have got to take charge of this situation that you and Crystal have created between you; in other words, I've got to step in and help you out, now that your preposterous plan's gone astray. Really,' said Roger bitterly, 'I think you must have been insane, both of you. You might have foreseen that this crazy idea of a cooped-up manhunt wouldn't appeal to anyone, and – '

'It was really for you,' Mr Pidgeon pleaded, grinning horribly. 'We both thought you enjoyed detecting. We did really. Crystal thought we'd never be able to bring a real live murderer to your tent door, so to speak, but I told her money can do anything.'

'Rubbish!' Roger was really indignant. 'Don't pretend you did it on my behalf; it was just to satisfy your own abnormal cruelty, both of you. Like the people who rush after a lynching procession. I said it was abominable, and I stick to it. Just think of the feelings of this wretched murderer, with whom you're playing like a cat with a mouse. He's got a fortnight of life, that's all. You've told him so. A fortnight to remain the decent, normal citizen that everyone supposes him. After that you're going to make him an outcast and an outlaw. And you've told him so.'

'My dear Sheringham, I never knew you could be so eloquent,' said Mr Pidgeon, with admiration. 'But I never said it was a "he," you know.'

'I don't care whether it's a he or a she,' Roger retorted violently. 'And what's more, I refuse to gratify you by asking a single question about his or her sex, or identity, or anything else. I'm not going to waggle a little finger to find out anything about her or him, and I'm not in the very slightest degree even interested.'

'Well, well, well,' said Mr Pidgeon mildly, and blinked up at the large, amber, benevolent-looking moon.

There was a little silence, gentle so far as Mr Pidgeon was concerned, somewhat heated on the part of Roger.

Mr Pidgeon broke it. 'You're not even interested in the reactions of the rest to the idea? I thought reactions were part of your stock-in-trade as a novelist?'

'Huh,' grunted Roger, and kicked a small stone unnecessarily out of his path.

'Anyhow, you do admit there is a "situation," owing to my ill-timed divulgation?'

'Of course there's a situation. I'm glad to get to the bottom at last of all the mysterious hints you and Crystal have been dropping, but upon my word I never expected anything so impossible as this.'

'You seem to take it very personally, my dear fellow,' Mr Pidgeon observed, with gentle surprise.

'You make it personal, by trying to drag me into it. I feel like a nursemaid in charge of two monster children.'

Mr Pidgeon's shoulders began to shake. 'You use the word "impossible." What exactly do you find "impossible" in the situation? That we should be cooped up here with a murderer loose among us, or that Crystal and I should have brought it about that we are so cooped up?'

'Both,' Roger said grumpily. 'But chiefly that you and Crystal should have been insane enough to believe for one moment that the rest of us would have the shocking bad taste to join in your preposterous manhunt.'

'Oh, I never really thought they would,' Mr Pidgeon replied genially. 'Even Crystal didn't go so far as that.'

Roger stared at him. 'Then what was the idea?'

'Oh, hadn't you gathered? Why,' explained Mr Pidgeon happily, 'to watch the reactions of a body of apparently quite normal people to the idea of an unknown murderer among them, from whom they couldn't get away. I thought that might interest you too, my dear fellow. I did truly.'

Roger made a noise of disgust. 'Really, I don't believe you're human. What you mean is, you're sacrificing this poor devil on the altar of your fiendish curiosity. Just curiosity! I never heard of anything so cruel in my life.'

'But if the person in question had committed a cold-blooded murder?' Mr Pidgeon pleaded. 'Isn't sympathy rather wasted in such a case? Isn't it allowable that he – or, of course, she – be butchered to make a Sheringham-cum-Pidgeon holiday?'

'No, it isn't,' Roger said shortly. 'In such a case one simply hands over one's knowledge to the police – if one thinks that the circumstances justify the action. One doesn't play with the person like a cat with a bird.'

'Doesn't one?' Mr Pidgeon accepted humbly. 'I'm afraid I'm not very much up in the etiquette of these matters. Then, if I understand you rightly, your only real objection to my and Crystal's scheme is the cruelty involved to the central figure of the piece, the murderer?'

'Yes,' Roger agreed, though not at all sure that he was not being edged into a corner. If so, he had, however, only himself to blame; just as he had only himself to blame for having taken up a position in which it was impossible for him to ask for even the slightest hint as to the identity of the murderer in question, burning with curiosity on that point though he was. Could that old villain Bray possibly have ever...?

'Your accusation of cruelty doesn't cover the other members of the party, whose reactions it is required to study? You don't think it cruel to them to have informed them that there is, in point of fact, a murderer among us? You said we might be in for an uneasy fortnight. You don't consider it cruelty on my part to have inflicted an uneasy fortnight on them, in order to observe what particular forms their individual uneasinesses might assume?'

'Cruel? No, I don't think so,' Roger found himself forced to allow. 'Inhuman perhaps; but actively cruel, no. But in any case, that's quite beside the point. I – '

'No, it isn't; no, it isn't,' Mr Pidgeon interrupted. 'I want to pin you down to this: that the only justification for the charge of cruelty which you brought against me, with an amount of emotion which does you infinite discredit, is the cruelty of the cat-and-bird business with our murderer. You agree to that?'

'Yes, I said I did,' Roger admitted, with some defiance. 'Well?'

Mr Pidgeon's shoulders began to shake once more. 'Then you may make your mind easy, my dear fellow. Perfectly easy. There is no murderer.'

'No murderer?'

'None at all. I invented him. I told you, it was the reactions of the rest of the party I wanted to observe – and to present, incidentally, to you – not the feelings of a trapped murderer; and for that purpose a *bona fide* murderer was, of course, not necessary, only a suggested one. So I invented him. They swallowed him whole, don't you think? Yes, yes, even you did, my dear fellow. I ought to have been on the stage; I see that now quite clearly. Yes, they swallowed him. And at present they're being very British about him, and just pretending to ignore him. But wait a few days. Yes, I shall be very disappointed if we don't have an interesting fortnight here after all. And you'll oblige me by being honest and admitting that you're going to be just as interested in it as Crystal and myself. Yes, you'll oblige me by admitting that, Sheringham, because, of course, you will be. Eh, my dear fellow?' cackled Mr Pidgeon. 'Eh? You admit that?'

'Perhaps.' Roger could not help laughing. The anti-climax was so complete. 'But what on earth gave you this preposterous idea?'

'Sir James Barrie,' replied Mr Pidgeon unctuously.

'Barrie?'

'Certainly. You remember his playlet, *Shall We Join the Ladies?* Really, my dear Sheringham, I'm surprised that you didn't observe the similarity of the situations. I was quite nervous on the point. I fully expected you to rise up at the table and denounce me as a plagiarist.'

'Good gracious, of course.'

'Of course. Precisely. I am only following in the footsteps of the master, you see,' said Mr Pidgeon humbly. 'Merely trying to add, in my own poor way, a second and third act to that ingenious little drama. It is true that my medium is only human nature itself, unsophisticated and unpolished, unlike the written word; but even such a medium is not without its own peculiar interest, don't you think?'

'Barrie's idea of writing a one-act play ending in a huge question-mark, and calling it Act I, was, of course, a brilliant one,' Roger said, somewhat didactically, 'and people fell for the Act I part of it like autumn leaves. But this did unquestionably involve the shirking of the pretty little problem which he presented.'

'Precisely, precisely. And it is a problem which I have always felt ought to be answered, in the interests of psychopathy, psychometry, and al the other strange but no doubt brilliant new mental sciences which America has invented for us. What, after all, would a company of perfectly normal, presumably civilised persons do on learning that their numbers included an undetected murderer? Grave issues of etiquette are surely involved. Do they merely ignore the fact, as our friends above are so gallantly doing at this moment? Do they, in fact, play the ostrich, or do they determine to cut this cancer out of their corporate body and take steps accordingly? Do they scream, or do they sneer? Fascinating questions, my dear fellow, fascinating questions. You agree? Yes, of course. By the way, Crystal thought it inadvisable to tell you the truth. She thought it would be more amusing to watch you spending your fortnight nosing after our non-existent murderer. But I hadn't the heart to withhold the full beauty of our plan from you. No, I hadn't the heart.'

Roger laughed again. 'Well, really, I'd never have believed it. Aren't you and Crystal ever going to begin growing up? You make me feel more like a nursemaid than ever. So Crystal didn't want me told? All right. I'll have it in for her for that.'

'I don't believe she trusted you,' Mr Pidgeon grinned. 'By the way, I am right, am I not? You are to be trusted?'

'Oh, I'll play trains with you,' Roger promised.

'It's funny, I always have liked playing trains,' said Mr Pidgeon, with impish gusto.

3

It was half past eleven before Roger got to bed. Everyone was tired, and the dispersal had been made earlier than usual. Even Miss St Thomas and Captain Twyford, who could usually be relied on to outsit everyone else, talking in low, confidential tones, had joined the exodus.

Roger read for his customary half hour by the excellent little reading-lamp on the table by his bed, then put it out and turned over. He ruminated for a short time on Mr Pidgeon and his strange whims, and decided that on the whole the present one might be rather amusing – so long, of course, as it was kept strictly in hand. It was amusing already to notice how the subject of the supposed murderer had been shunned, by silent, unanimous agreement, the whole evening. Miss Vincent had made one artless reference to it, but the blank looks which had greeted her words had quelled even that irrepressible young woman. It was evident that their host's lapse from taste had pained his guests in their tenderest spot. Roger wondered whether they would keep it up as successfully.

He turned over again, and slept.

As a rule Roger was one of those fortunate people who sleep their full eight hours without a moment's intervening consciousness. On this night, however, he woke up, in a vague indeterminate sort of way, just sufficiently to realise that he was awake but not fully enough to make him open his eyes. He was hardly conscious: certainly not so much so as to wonder whether he had woken of his own volition, or whether some external agent had found himself pushed over to the side of wakefulness by a sudden noise from outside. After a moment's hazy consideration he diagnosed the noise as a yell, faint and distant.

Roger turned over again in some disgust. There was only one explanation of the yell. It was Mr Pidgeon, imitating his young fisherman. No doubt everyone who heard it was supposed to grab his watch, and eagerly compare times the next day. It was really rather childish. Mr Pidgeon was altogether too old to go out imitating ghosts in the middle of the night. Did he really think he was going to alarm people seriously with such childish devices?

'Pooh!' thought Roger, in a superior way.

Two minutes later he was asleep again.

chapter six

Roger was awakened out of a perfect sleep the next morning by Mr Valentine Combe.

'Come along, you lazy hound,' Mr Combe was saying. 'Get up. It's a peach of a morning.'

'Go away,' mumbled Roger crossly, and turned over on his other side.

Mr Combe was doing officious things to the tent door, letting in a flood of horrid light that hurt Roger's eyes through their lids. 'Get up!' he repeated, with loathsome heartiness.

'Go away!' said Roger loudly and firmly.

'I'm not going away. Stop hogging it, and get up. We're taking you down to bathe.'

'Who's "we"? I don't want to bathe.'

'Yes, you do. Twyford and I. Get up.'

'What's the time?'

'Half past seven.'

'Then go away!' roared Roger, who never got up before half past eight.

Mr Combe pulled off the bedclothes for answer, and laughed shrilly. He appeared to think that he had performed a humorous action.

Roger got up, exceedingly annoyed. Mr Combe, in pyjamas and carrying a towel, with his black hair dishevelled, smiled upon him with the maddening superiority of the early riser over the sluggard.

'I dislike you, Combe,' Roger said morosely, feeling for his shoes. 'I always have done. Where's Twyford?'

'Eh?' said a languid voice just outside the tent. 'Got the blighter up? Good man. Let's go.'

Roger blinked at him with malice as he passed out into the sunlight. 'Well, Twyford, how are you this morning?'

Captain Twyford, already in bathing-costume, was hugging his magnificent arms over his broad chest. 'A trifle chilly, just at the moment,' he replied, quite seriously. 'I expect it will pass off in the water.'

'Sleep well?'

'Marvellously, thanks,'

'Ghost didn't worry you?'

'It's rather funny,' said Captain Twyford, still quite seriously, 'I did hear someone walking about quite late.'

'I'm afraid the explanation's probably anything but otherworldly,' Roger said coarsely. 'Very well, if I've got to come and admire you two doing your tricks, let's go.' Mr Combe swam like an otter, and Captain Twyford was a really first-class diver. It usually seemed to happen that they bathed to an audience.

The three made their way down to the beach. The sun was just beginning to warm up the air, and the sea looked inviting. Captain Twyford and Combe edged towards the rocks on the left of the cove to look for a good diving-station; Roger, hugging his arms over his chest, dabbled his toes in the wavelets as they rippled up the sand, and waited for the experts. A few minutes later two clean swoops marked their entry into the water and Roger began leisurely to wade out to join them. He was an average swimmer, but a perverse instinct made him pretend to be much worse than he was in the presence of those who were much better.

Swimming was in any case a little on the risky side, owing to the number of submerged rocks, with their sharp edges, that littered the fairway out to sea; and Roger proceeded cautiously on his way to join the other two, who had climbed up on one that was larger than most and were standing now with the water washing round their knees. When he reached them they were looking out to sea a little to their left, and discussing an object, floating on the waves, which Combe's sharp eyesight had detected.

'A porpoise, is it?' Combe was saying, shading his eyes with his hand, as Roger pulled himself up besides them. 'Are there porpoises in these waters?'

'Oh, yes,' Captain Twyford said carelessly. 'It's a dead porpoise, I expect.'

'It's certainly dead,' agreed Combe.

Roger shook the water out of his hair. 'Warmed up, Twyford?' he asked solicitously.

'Much warmer, thanks.'

'You know, I don't think it is a porpoise,' said Combe, still watching the object as it dipped lazily on its bed of water, now disappearing altogether, now quite visible in its whity-pinkness. 'Let's swim out and see, Twyford.'

'I don't think I will. We don't know what currents there may be outside the lee of that bluff, and we've got no boat.'

Roger, with early-morning cynicism, did not know which to admire least, the Captain's caution or the poet's vainglory.

'Oh, I don't think there are any currents to matter. In any case, I want a swim, and I like an object for it. If I'm drowned, tell my wife I thought of her at the last.' He dived, and made off with a swift, steady crawl stroke.

Roger watched him without love. There had been just enough seriousness in Mr Combe's last remark to grate on Roger's public-school standard of good taste.

'Bit of a crashing little cad,' murmured Captain Twyford impersonally, 'but he can swim.' He dived, and Roger splashed in after him.

When they next caught sight of Combe it was from the ridge of rock that ran out from the easterly bluff. Combe was swimming strongly, and was only thirty or forty yards away from his objective. Twyford began to examine the water at the base of the rock for the possibility of high-diving, and Roger, sitting on a nicely warmed piece of rock, divided an idle attention between the two of them. A shout from the sea, carrying faintly over the water, drew his gaze upon Combe. The poet had turned about and was swimming back towards land, with a flurry of splashing quite unlike his usual smooth progress.

Roger called to his companion. 'Look at Combe. What's the trouble? Surely he's not in difficulties?'

Twyford looked out to sea. 'Seems to be panicking, doesn't he?'

'Perhaps there is a current.'

'Shouldn't be surprised. I warned him there might be.'

Roger was nettled by the other's indifferent tone. 'Well, we must do something.'

'What can we do?'

'Swim out and see if he's in difficulties.'

'Not an idea I take a good view of,' remarked Twyford. 'If there is a current, I don't see the point of all three of us getting drowned instead of one.'

'Well, we can't stop here and do nothing.'

'Why not?'

'Damn it, man – we can't! He may have cramp, or something. Well, if you're not going, I am.' Roger plunged into the water.

If his idea had been to shame Twyford into plunging in after him, it did not succeed. All the other did was to shout lazily:

'Want any help, Combe?'

Roger could see Combe shake his head and, as if steadied by the shout, begin to swim more calmly. He turned back and, not without a sense of anti-climax, pulled himself out of the water again.

'I've seen lots of men drowned to no purpose by trying to help others who never really needed it,' was all that Twyford saw fit to comment.

In some annoyance Roger composed himself to wait for Combe's arrival.

Swimming more strongly now, Combe drew near at a fair speed. It was obvious that he needed no help.

He said nothing until he was grasping a point of the rock on which the others were sitting. Then looking up at them he gasped:

'My God, do you know what that is out there?'

'Of course we don't,' Roger said crossly, disliking this drama. 'What is it?'

'It's Pidgeon,' said Combe, and began to giggle hysterically. 'And I thought it was a dead porpoise.'

2

'Shut up!' said Roger sharply. 'Is he dead?'

'Dead?' Mr Combe stopped giggling. 'As dead as a dead mule – and that's the deadest thing I know.'

'Hell!' said Roger, and instantly into his mind there leapt a huge number of unpleasant possibilities.

'Here, give me a hand, one of you. Can't you see I'm whacked?' called Mr Combe peevishly.

Twyford bent down a hefty arm and hoicked the poet's slender form out of the water.

Roger bent a troubled gaze on the two of them. 'We've got to get him in, you know.'

'Who? Pidgeon?'

'Of course.'

'Have we?' Captain Twyford seemed to be digesting this. 'What exactly is the point?'

'Well, we can't leave him out there,' Roger said impatiently.

'Why not? I mean, isn't that the best thing to do? We can't keep him long here, and we'd only have to put him back again in the sea. I doubt if there's enough earth, you know, to bury him on the island.'

Roger failed to admire the Captain's practical mind. 'Of course we must bring him ashore,' he repeated.

'I agree with Twyford,' piped Mr Combe. 'What's the use? Eh, Sheringham? What's the use? He's dead. We can't bring him back to life. My God, I won't help to bring him in. He – rolled at me. It was beastly.' Mr Combe shivered violently, and then uttered another high-pitched giggle.

'If you make that noise again, I'll have to hit you,' observed Captain Twyford, without emotion.

Mr Combe looked pained, but stopped giggling.

'We've got to get him in,' explained Roger, with patience, 'because we've got to determine the cause of death. There will have to be an enquiry, as soon as we get back to civilisation.'

'Drowned. That's obvious enough.'

'Because he's in the sea now?' Roger looked superior. 'It would hardly do to take that for granted. And I must ask you two to realise just how bad it would look for us to have to admit that, although the body was only a couple of hundred yards out at sea, and although there are two exceptionally strong swimmers here, we simply left it. Can't you see it's out of the question?'

'Sorry, afraid I can't. There's no point in taking unnecessary risks. That's the first thing one has to learn in my job. I'll take the responsibility.'

Roger was beginning to feel angry. Was Twyford merely callous, or was he actually anxious that the body should not be brought in? Roger looked at him steadily.

'Look here, Twyford, I don't want to be officious, or offensive, but you may force me to be both. I'm afraid you're not in a position to take responsibility. The responsible position is mine. I'm sorry, but I can't avoid it. After the way I've occasionally been attached to them, officially, Scotland Yard will certainly hold me responsible for these matters being conducted in an orthodox way; and I'm determined that they shall be.'

'What's Scotland Yard got to do with it? This isn't British territory.'

'In view of what Pidgeon told us last night, I rather think Scotland Yard will have a great deal to do with it,' Roger said grimly. It was bluff, of course, but he did not think that Twyford was in a position to call it.

'Well, what are you proposing? That I should swim out and bring the body in?'

'That all three of us should.'

'I'm not going to,' put in Mr Combe shrilly. 'I don't care a damn for Scotland Yard, or anybody. I won't swim another stroke, and you can do what you like about it.'

Twyford's eyes were fixed on the forlorn pinky-white bundle, still rolling in the swell. 'I rather think your problem's being solved for you, Sheringham,' he drawled. 'The tide's bringing him in.'

3

Roger sat on the beach, waiting for Mr Pidgeon's body to come within wading distance. He had managed to get rid of the other two: Twyford had gone up to the top to stop the unauthorised, or such of them as were yet up, from coming down to the beach, Mr Combe had been sternly sent to his tent to try to pull himself together.

It seemed to Roger hours before he was able to go out into the water and draw the body gently back to the sand; actually it was twenty minutes. He carried the spare form under the lee of some rocks, to give shelter from spying eyes above, and stared at it unhappily. Of all the dead men and women he had ever seen, none had stirred him as this one did. He pushed aside his emotion and, almost mechanically, took note of the facts.

The body was in pyjamas, torn in places into gaping rents. The face was badly damaged, obviously by the rocks, and there was a horrid flattening on one side of the head, the skull bone showing white through the sparse, matted hair; through the torn pyjamas raw body-wounds were visible. It was plain that a severe battering on the sharp rocks must have taken place, to cause such fearful injuries.

Roger had more than a smattering of medical and surgical knowledge. It did not take him three minutes to be quite sure that death was not due to drowning.

He examined the body carefully. The wounds, made presumably by the rocks, were the only marks on it. Mr Pidgeon had not been strangled, or shot, or done to death in any obvious way. So far as Roger could see, the actual cause of death must have been the blow on the side of the head which had splintered the skull; and from such a wound there were only two inferences to be drawn. Either it had been inflicted by another human being, or Mr Pidgeon had fallen from a height onto his head.

Roger looked out to sea at the spot were the body had first been drifting, and then at the cliffs behind him. If Mr Pidgeon had fallen over the cliff in the darkness, his body must have been carried out to sea on the outgoing tide, just as it had been brought back again by the incoming one. In that case, where might he have been expected to fall? Not over the western bluff; probably over the eastern one. In fact, only a little way south of where the camp was pitched.

Roger walked out from the shelter of the rock and looked up in the direction of the camp. No faces were visible, peering down on him. The news apparently had not yet got out. He still had a short time before they would be down on him. Making his calculations, he ran over the sand and began to scramble over the huge rocks that littered the base of the bluff.

It was difficult going, but he had not far to go. A few yards before the actual point of the bluff a patch of dull crimson on a projecting piece of rock about a hundred feet up caught his eye. He hurried towards it. At the foot of the rocky cliff a few boulders stood up above their fellows, their height growing less the nearer they drew to the sea. These higher ones, clustering tight against the rock wall, were not covered at high tide. The smears and patches and fantastic arabesques of dark crimson on the serrated surfaces of those just underneath the projecting rock told quite clearly where Mr Pidgeon had met his death.

Roger turned, and scrambled back to the sand.

It was no longer deserted. Enid Fayre was there, bending over the body. It was her privilege and Roger could not gainsay her.

She stood up as she heard him coming, and clasped her hands.

'Oh, Mr Sheringham!'

Damn it, thought Roger, even when she's up against the real thing she must play-act. And there aren't any tears in her eyes.

'Oh, Mr Sheringham, this is dreadful. *Dreadful!*'

'Shocking,' mumbled Roger.

'How – *how* did it happen?'

'He fell over the cliff. Just there.'

'Oh! How do you know?'

'It's obvious. There's blood.'

'Poor, poor Guy. Mr Sheringham, did you say just *there* – where I'm pointing?'

'Yes, just about.'

Mrs Fayre clasped her hands and stared at him with awed eyes. 'The very spot,' she whispered.

'What spot?'

'Where the poor young fisherman fell over.'

'Oh, I see. There's nothing in that. Your cousin made up the whole story. He told me so.'

'He told you so?'

'Yes.'

'Mr Sheringham,' said Mrs Fayre very earnestly, 'I don't believe he did. He told you that, because he saw he had made a mistake in telling us the story at all. That story is true. And this island is…' Mrs Fayre sank her voice.

'Yes?'

'Accursed.'

Roger groaned.

4

Roger waited until Willie Fayre came down to join his wife. He arrived, unhurried and perfectly calm and stood for a moment or two looking down at the body, apparently as unmoved by it as by his wife's lamentations. The only sign of feeling he showed was a dead-white pallor, patchy through his tan; but Roger noticed that he had to swallow once or twice before he could speak.

'What are we to do, Sheringham?' he asked a little huskily.

'If you'd stay here, while I take Mrs Fayre up to get some breakfast...?'

'Oh, Mr Sheringham, I couldn't eat any breakfast! How could I , with poor Guy...'

Neither of the men took any notice of her. Willie gazed out to sea as if he had hardly heard Roger's question. Then he suddenly nodded.

'Yes, all right,' he said.

'Come along, Mrs Fayre,' said Roger, with such authority that Enid ceased her protests and went.

Roger escorted her to the door of the marquee. He had already sent a message to Crystal by Twyford, breaking the news and asking her to get breakfast on the way at once, and occupy as many people as possible over the serving of it. Roger felt grateful for Crystal in such a situation.

With more tact than he would have expected, the rest of the party, now all up and about, remained out of the way in the marquee. Unhampered, Roger walked round to the bluff and peered cautiously over the edge. Fayre was sitting in the exact middle of the beach, still gazing out to sea. Roger walked along the edge.

When he was able to see the projecting piece of rock in the face below him, he stopped a few yards short of the vertical line above it, dropped onto this hands and knees, and began to advance very slowly, scrutinising the ground. The edge at this particular place was a right angle, with coarse turf and a species of sea-pink growing right to the drop: not chamfered off, with broken spurs of rock, as round most of the island. When he noticed, a few feet ahead of him, a few inches of bare earth showing, just as if a clump of sea-pinks had been detached from the extreme edge, he paused and gazed at it thoughtfully.

He was still gazing when he heard his name spoken behind him, and looked hastily round. Crystal was coming towards him, from the direction of the camp.

'The others are having breakfast. Roger!'

'Yes?' Roger got up.

'This is awful.'

'It is,' Roger agreed grimly.

Crystal, whose eyes hitherto had been dry, began quietly to cry. 'Poor Guy. He really was such a wonderfully good sort. I was terribly fond of him. Roger, *how* did it happen?'

'That's just what I'm trying to make out, Crystal.'

'Did he really just walk over the edge in the dark?'

'Who told you he did?'

'That's what Captain Twyford says he must have done.'

'Oh, does he?' Roger said thoughtfully. 'Well, if he did, this is where he did it.' He pointed towards the tiny dip in the edge, which a cluster of sea-pinks might have filled.

Crystal followed his finger. 'How do you know?'

'There's blood on the rocks below,' Roger said bluntly. He went down on his stomach and wriggled to the edge, to stare down among the rocks at the base. Though the bluff was three hundred feet high, he could distinctly see the smears on the rocks at the bottom. His eyes examined the boulders, and it seemed to him that he could make out a tiny glint of green in a spot almost directly below him. 'Could you get hold of a pair of field-glasses, Crystal?' he asked over his shoulder.

Crystal went, without a question.

When she brought them, he focused them on the speck of green. He had been right. It was a little clump of sea-pinks. Their delicate lavender-pink heads were clearly visible through the glasses.

Roger rolled back from the edge and looked up at Crystal. 'What do you make of it?' he said.

Crystal had stopped crying. She looked from the camp to the bluff and back again, as if considering the line between them. 'Why should he want to come here at all?' she asked.

'That's just what I want to know. One couldn't mistake it even in the dark, for the way down to the beach. And anyhow, why visit the beach in the dark?'

'There's an electric torch in every tent,' Crystal said slowly. 'Surely he'd have had his?'

'We must see if it's missing.'

Crystal was pondering. 'You know what Guy was. That story he made up about the fisherman, for instance... It's just about here that he pretended the man rushed over the cliff, wasn't it?'

'So Enid Fayre has already pointed out. She thinks the island's accursed. I hope she keeps the idea to herself, if we're to be here for a fortnight.'

'Yes, that's what I mean. Guy was trying to make people's flesh creep with that story. I wonder if he could have come out here last night to imitate a ghost or something?'

'Imitate a ghost?'

'Oh, you know what I mean. Help the story out, in some way. Give people a fright. It would have been just like him. And – and then he lost his footing, and fell.'

'It's quite possible,' Roger agreed. But that explanation no longer quite satisfied him. He said nothing of the yell he had heard in the night.

He crept very carefully towards the broken edge, examining every inch of ground on the way. Crystal stood and watched him in silence.

'No footprints,' he said at last. 'I didn't expect any.' He sat back on his heels and scratched his head. 'This is pretty damnable.'

'Yes,' said Crystal slowly. She meditated for a moment. 'Roger!'

'Yes?'

'When you went for that stroll with him last night, on the beach. He told you that speech of his was all spoof?'

'Yes. Why?'

'Oh, nothing. I'm just rather glad he did, that's all. You see, you mightn't have believed it if I'd told you it was, now.'

'I see your point,' said Roger. 'Yes, he told me.'

He wriggled forward again on his stomach, to the place from which the sea-pinks had been torn, and looked down once more. Then he grunted, and applied the field-glasses to his eyes.

'What is it?' Crystal asked anxiously.

Roger hesitated. 'Something that might be rather significant. Or not at all. I don't want to make mountains out of molehills, but...no, damn it all, it's not natural.'

'What isn't?'

'Why, it's quite obvious where he hit the rocks at the bottom, and the place isn't exactly below here. It must be, as near as I can gauge, at least a dozen feet to the left. And those sea-pinks aren't vertically below here. They're about a couple of yards to the right.'

'Well?'

'Well, meaning that he couldn't possibly have walked straight to the edge, and fallen over plumb. Wait a minute, let me sort out the possibilities. It mans, you see, that just as he fell his foot exercised a sharp pressure to the right (the right, that is, as we're facing now), so that his body was thrust out to the left and the sea-pinks to the right. So that – well, he'd hardly have been running full-tilt in a direction parallel to the edge, would he? That might have done it. Or an enormous standing leap, also diagonal to the line of the cliff. Besides, in either of those cases his body would have travelled much farther that it did outwards from the cliff. No...'

'What, then?'

'Just that it's curious,' Roger said, in a shut kind of voice.

Crystal looked at him with an apprehension she did not disguise.

Roger got to his feet. 'Let's see if his torch is in his tent, or not. Now's the opportunity.'

5

Mr Pidgeon's was the farthest tent in the easterly of the two parallel lines. No torch could be discovered in it.

As Crystal and Roger were coming out, they saw Mr Harold Parker hovering uncertainly in the doorway of the tent exactly opposite, across the alleyway.

Mr Parker cleared his throat nervously. 'Oh, Mr Sheringham, in connection with this unfortunate occurrence...'

'Yes?'

'I'm sure you'll think it of no importance, but knowing what you've done in the past,' babbled Mr Parker, 'and having read detective stories, where it always says one should volunteer any information, whether it seems to have any bearing or not...' He paused, and scratched a pimple with a deprecatory air.

'That's absolutely right,' Roger encouraged him kindly. 'Any tiny fact, whether you think it can have any importance or not. What is it?'

'Well, only that I did hear voices last night.' Mr Parker swallowed twice. 'I didn't get to sleep very early last night, what with the excitement, and never having been camping before, and being cast away on a desert island, as you might say. And I heard voices, after everything was quiet.'

'Oh, yes?' Anxious not to alarm his witness by showing too much interest. Roger kept his voice to a note only of mild interest. 'From Mr Pidgeon's tent?'

'Well, that's where they seemed to come from. I didn't attach any importance to it at the time, but in view of this unfortunate accident, I thought perhaps...perhaps...'

'Absolutely,' Roger agreed firmly. 'What sort of voices?'

'Well, one was Mr Pidgeon's.'

'Ah! You're quite sure of that?'

Mr Parker instantly looked doubtful. 'It's not a thing I'd care to swear to in a court of law, but I remember I thought at the time, 'That's Mr Pidgeon's voice,' I thought, and I remember wondering who the other one was; but it's not a thing one would care about taking one's oath on, if you understand me.'

'You didn't recognise the other voice, then?'

'No, I'm afraid I can't say that I did.'

'What sort of a voice was it?'

'Well, it was a sort of high voice. Squeaky, in a manner of speaking. But that might have been excitement, I suppose. Anyhow, it was sort of high.'

'A woman's?'

'I – I'm afraid I couldn't rightly say,' Mr Parker replied unhappily. 'I – I didn't take that much notice, you see. I can't put it stronger than that it might have been a woman's. And then again it might have been a man's, sort of excited. I didn't take all that notice at the time.'

'Of course not; why should you? Anyhow, you think the voice was excited?'

'Well, I couldn't say that. It sounded as if it was in Mr Pidgeon's tent; but it might have been outside, mightn't it? And then they sort of died away.'

'Could you hear any words?'

'Oh, no. They weren't so near as that. Besides, it was kind of muffled, coming through the tents. That's partly why I can't say whether it was a man or a woman.'

'Of course. Well, have you any idea what time it was when you heard these voices?'

'Well, not to the minute, I'm afraid, but I know it must have been soon after one a.m., because I'd switched on my torch to look at my watch, not being able to sleep, and it was three minutes to one a.m. then, and it wasn't long after that that I heard the voices. I fancy I must have gone to sleep after that, almost at once.'

'I see. And that's really all you can tell me?' It was, however, already evident that Mr Parker had heard no yell.

'I'm afraid so, Mr Sheringham. I don't know whether I was right to mention it at all, but...'

'You were absolutely right, and I'm very grateful to you,' said Roger firmly. 'If you happen to remember anything else about it, or think you recognise the voice, let me know instantly. It was very intelligent of you to come forward so promptly.'

'I'm sure it's very good of you to say that, Mr Sheringham,' said Mr Parker, his pimples gleaming with gratification.

Roger and Crystal walked away.

When they were clear of the line of tents, Roger looked at Crystal significantly.

'And then they sort of died away,' he quoted softly.

Crystal twisted her fingers together. 'Oh, Roger,' she muttered, with a little moan.

"Keep your head, Crystal,' Roger said sharply. 'For heaven's sake, keep your head.'

'I'll try,' Crystal promised, and gulped.

6

'There's no proof,' Roger muttered. 'Even if the two voices sort of died away, which can only mean that the two owners of them walked off together, there's no proof that they were still together when Pidgeon reached here.'

Crystal did not answer.

As if drawn to it irresistibly, Roger had led her back to the edge of the cliff. On the beach below Willie Fayre still kept vigil alone, and still sat motionless, gazing out to sea.

'But if there is proof,' he added, 'it's here, or at the base, that it will be. And we've got about three minutes to find it, before the crowd finishes breakfast.' He stared moodily at the few feet of ground which separated him from the edge of the cliff, unwilling for all his previous examination of it to tread on the scanty turf for fear of obliterating some vital trace overlooked before. But no vital trace presented itself to his gaze.

'If I only had some idea of what to look for,' he groaned.

A little patch of a darker brown on the browny-green surface of the scorched grass caught his eye, and he looked at it absently. Then his interest suddenly quickened, and he dropped on his knees beside it. The little place, only three or four inches square, was not between himself and the edge, but almost in a line with where he was standing, perhaps a dozen feet from the drop.

He looked up at Crystal. 'This is interesting, at any rate. You see the indentation? Browny grass at the edges, and going right down into earth? I should say a stone had been lying here, quite recently.'

'It looks like it,' Crystal agreed cautiously. 'And so...?'

'Well, I'd just like to know where that stone is now; that's all.' Roger pored over his find. 'Yes, quite recently. There's no sign yet of green at the edges. Well, of course, someone might have kicked it. In that case...' He got up and began to search the surrounding area, but no stone which might have fitted the contour was to be found.

Nevertheless, his search, conducted this time over a larger area than before, was not without result. Half hidden between two tufts of turf lay a large white pearl button, the size of a half-crown.

Roger drew it out eagerly. 'This is from his pyjamas,' he announced. 'There was a button missing. It's the same pattern. My God, Crystal...' He measured the distance from the edge to the button's lair. It was about ten feet. 'Of course, it might just have dropped off,' he murmured. 'I suppose buttons do drop off.'

'How else could it have got there?' Crystal asked half-fearfully.

Roger shrugged his shoulders, and began to crawl once more to the place on the edge from which the tuft of sea-pinks had been dislodged. Leaning out as far as he dared, he examined the face of the cliff immediately below the top. Crystal, watching him, saw his body go suddenly tense.

His head squirmed back over his shoulder. 'Crystal, I want you to come and look at this.'

'I can't,' Crystal shivered. 'I should get giddy and fall over.'

'Nonsense; I'll hold you. I want a witness.'

Feeling rather sick, Crystal wriggled up beside him, and Roger clamped his arm round her.

'Do you see this mark – just *here?* Look at it carefully, and remember where it is. It's about six inches below the edge, and it's on earth, not rock, because by the providence of heaven there's a rim of earth under the turf and above the rock, absolutely designed to take marks like that. And do you see what the mark is? It's the mark of the heel of a slipper (at least, I think a slipper, not a shoe, or it would be bigger), and it couldn't possibly be the mark of anything else. And not only so, but notice its angle and its direction. Its angle is about forty-five degrees to the face of the cliff, running upwards and inwards; and the round end is at the bottom, that is to say the outside. Look at it very carefully, learn it by heart, and don't ever forget it.'

Crystal, hanging over the edge of the cliff, with the blood running to her head, and very much afraid in spite of the arm around her, forced herself to concentrate on the mark pressed into the dry, hard earth.

'I'll remember it,' she gasped, and Roger let her wriggle back.

They sat on the turf and looked at each other.

'It was his other foot?' Crystal said.

Roger nodded. 'Yes, and a good yard away from the other mark. That's a big gap, sideways. But it's the direction that's most important. You saw which way the foot was pointing?'

'Inwards to the land.'

'Exactly. And that means that the whole body was facing inwards to the land. And *that* means that he went over the cliff backwards. Crystal, I'm afraid this is a pretty damnable business.'

'Roger, you can't think that...'

'I don't merely think: I know. There are the voices that prove he wasn't alone; there's the sideways thrust of the body, and the proof that he was standing with his back to the edge, showing the desperate attempt to recover his balance when he was already toppling; it's true there's no sign of a struggle, but I don't believe there was a struggle. But there was violence. That stone played some part in it, you may be sure. And that pyjama button didn't fall off – it was wrenched off. How? Well, his pyjamas are of the Russian pattern, with a high collar and side pockets. I suggest he had his hands in the pockets when the stone, or the fist, or whatever it was, caught him. Pulling his hands out suddenly, and wide, the button got wrenched off. That's only a suggestion. The point is that the button helps to prove violence. My dear girl, we've got to face it. Poor old Pidgeon never merely fell over this cliff. He was pushed over.'

Crystal bit her knuckles. 'But Roger – *why?*'

'I don't think there's any need to look very far for the motive,' Roger said dryly.

'I can't see one.'

'Then just throw your mind back to that speech he made last night. You remember what he said? That it had come to his knowledge that one of the people here now had committed murder. That this murder had never been even remotely suspected. That he, however, could prove, beyond any doubt, that murder was committed. That he had divulged this knowledge to no one, not written it down, or, apparently, possessed any record of it except what was in his own brain. And finally, that when we got back to civilisation he was going to hand this murderer and the proof over to the police.'

'But that was all nonsense. He made it up. He told you he had.'

'He was wrong.' Roger corrected soberly. 'He thought he'd made it up. In point of fact, he hadn't. By the most damnable of chances he'd hit on the sheer literal truth. There is such a murderer here. And the coincidence cost Pidgeon his life.'

chapter seven

'Your cousin wasn't alone when he fell over the cliff. I've established that someone came to speak to him in his tent, and the two of them walked off together. They must have been strolling dangerously close to the edge, and your cousin actually had his back to it when he fell. I'm a little surprised that the other person hasn't come forward already. If you agree, I think he – or she, for it may just as well have been a woman – ought to be asked to do so, and tell us exactly how the thing happened.'

Roger had called Willie Fayre and Enid into consultation. They must now be considered the host and hostess of the party; and though Roger was ready to pay lip-service to their authority, he was determined that matters should be handled in as orthodox and correct a way as possible. He had said nothing to them about murder, and had, moreover, bound Crystal to silence on that point; for although he was as convinced that murder had been committed as if he had seen it with his own eyesight, his actual proofs were very slender. Nor was there any point in raising the alarm too early. If the murderer could be lulled into believing that no one had any suspicion that the death was anything but an accident, the chances were enormously increased that he might be persuaded into declaring his identity – or she, for there was nothing that Roger had found to eliminate that possibility.

'Oh, I do agree.' Enid Fayre raised swimming eyes to Roger's. 'I should never rest if we neglected the smallest opportunity of finding out how poor, poor Guy came to do this shocking thing. Would you, Willie?'

Willie detached his gaze from the sea. The three were standing at the head of the path from the beach, whither Roger had brought Enid to wait for Willie. During the whole of the interview so far Willie had not spoken a word, nor once detached his gaze from the sea. He seemed to have fallen into a state of trance-like helplessness.

'Would you, Willie?' Enid repeated, not without impatience.

Willie did not turn his head. 'No.' he said shortly. 'But is it the least use, Sheringham?'

'In what way?'

'I mean, if the person hasn't come forward already, is an appeal at all likely to have any result?'

'Of course the person will come forward, Willie.'

'I think at any rate we ought to try,' Roger insisted.

Willie sighed. 'Yes, I suppose so.'

'Willie dear, what's the matter with you? Of course we must try. And I can't believe that the person, whoever it was, would be so cruel as to refuse to come forward and set our minds at rest. This uncertainty is terrible. Terrible!'

'What uncertainty?' Willie asked abruptly.

'Why...' Enid hesitated. 'Why, the uncertainty of not knowing what happened to poor Guy.'

'He's dead. That's what happened to him. I don't see that anything else really matters much, does it?'

'Willie!' Enid emitted a shocked wail. 'Willie, how can you be so – callous?'

'We don't all wear our hearts on our sleeves, Enid,' Willie said, in a weary voice. 'And I can't see anything callous in stating facts.' For the first time he turned round and looked directly at Roger. 'You said you'd established that this mysterious person was with Guy when he fell over, Sheringham. How do you know?'

Roger gave a judicious selection of the facts he had gathered, suppressing the inferences he himself had drawn from them.

'But the fact that Parker heard voices, apparently in Guy's tent, doesn't prove anything. Even though the two did apparently go off together, Guy might only have been taking the other person back to her tent – or his tent, of course. He could have gone on to the cliff alone.'

'He could, of course,' Roger had to admit.

As if he had lost interest in the point, Willie fell back into silence.

'And in that case,' Roger added, 'I can see no earthly reason why the person in question should not come forward.'

'Of course not,' Enid agreed warmly.

Roger glanced at Willie Fayre. Once more he was gazing out to sea.

'By the way, Fayre,' he said casually, 'you've got the tent next to your cousin's, haven't you? Did you hear these voices?'

Willie shook his head. 'I heard nothing,' he said dully. 'I was very tired. I went off to sleep at once. I'm a heavy sleeper.'

His wife's slender eyebrows lifted. 'Willie!' she said reproachfully.

Fayre turned and looked at her, and Roger was astonished at the man's expression. If it meant anything, it meant a dislike amounting to hatred. And yet Willie Fayre was notoriously his lovely wife's most doglike worshipper.

His tone, however, was perfectly even, almost indifferent. 'Ever since this cruise began I've been sleeping like a log, my dear.'

Enid, who herself had appeared a little taken aback by the look which her husband had turned on her, shrugged her shoulders. 'I'm glad to hear it, darling; it must have been a nice change for you,' she said sweetly.

'Well,' Roger put in, 'have I your authority to make this appeal, Fayre?'

'Oh, yes,' Fayre said, like an automaton.

'Of course,' his wife amplified. She twirled the sunshade on her shoulder. 'Can't we do it at once, in the marquee? I simply daren't think what's going to happen to my nose if I stand out here in the sun any longer. This sunshade's just a little bit worse than useless.' She gave Roger a sadly whimsical little smile, that said: Even in affairs of life and death we foolish women must be feminine, you know.

Roger did not give her a whimsical smile back. He was too busy pondering the odd change in Willie Fayre. The man seemed stunned by his cousin's death; and yet he had never known him well. The two were only second cousins after all, and one is not dazed with grief at the death of a second cousin. But Willie was not only dazed. His whole attitude to his wife had altered. He had answered her shortly and abruptly, a thing Roger had never heard before; he had produced opinions of his own in opposition to hers, and maintained them; it was impossible to forget that look he had turned on her for one brief second. Willie was no longer a walking apology for his own existence. The doormat had begun to show its bristles.

As Roger followed the two to the marquee, he was thinking:

And Willie's lying, too. He did hear those voices. And what's more, he recognised the second one.

2

The little gathering, clustered together with odd unanimity at one end of the marquee, stared at Roger with rapt attention. Everyone was standing up except Lady Darracott, whose frail slenderness had been tenderly deposited a moment ago in a chair by Sir John Birch. Roger waited until she was quite settled.

'Mr and Mrs Fayre have asked me to say one thing to you,' he began curtly. 'Mr Pidgeon's unhappy death will, of course, have to be reported to the authorities as soon as we get back to England, and in order to put things on a proper footing Mr Fayre will have to offer the usual detailed account of the circumstances of the accident. And not only those, but an account of Mr Pidgeon's state of mind at the time. I need hardly explain why. You have all read reports of inquests, and know the kind of questions which have to be answered. It's always important, in accidents, to make absolutely certain that it really was an accident, and not suicide. Insurance policies, for instance, usually have a covering clause against suicide, and that sort of thing. That is why the authorities always take a statement from the last person to see the deceased alive, so that they can get evidence, up to the last possible moment, of the state of mind. We all know, of course, that Mr Pidgeon did not commit suicide. Nevertheless, these questions will have to be asked, and answered, and it is much better to look into them now, before anything is forgotten.'

Roger glanced round. The expression on the faces in front of him had altered perhaps a tiny bit. Whereas before he began to speak there had been a tinge of horrified anticipation not unmixed with relish, the composite look now turned on him seemed to include a minute proportion of disappointment.

'It's important, therefore, to make sure who was the last person to see Mr Pidgeon alive. Well, there's not very much doubt about that. It was obviously, I think, the person who was talking to him in his tent round about one o'clock this morning. Now who was that?'

Roger glanced round again, this time with an expression of mild enquiry. Nobody answered him. The profound silence began to grow oppressive. If Roger had hoped to get his result by means of this cat-like approach to his question, he had failed.

He smiled, with a nice blend of incredulity and confidence.

'Oh, come. One mustn't withhold formal evidence of this nature, you know. Please!'

He waited. The silence this time passed from the oppressive to the ominous.

Roger shrugged his shoulders. 'Really, this is rather absurd, isn't it? For the last time I ask the person who was talking to Mr Pidgeon in the small hours of this morning to declare the fact voluntarily.'

People began to shift uneasily. No one spoke.

'Very well. If the person forces me to do so, I must ask each of you in turn, with apologies to twelve out of the thirteen. Lady Darracott, may I ask you first: were you talking to Mr Pidgeon, in or near his tent, at approximately one o'clock this morning?'

'No, Mr Sheringham, I was not.' Lady Darracott's voice was not nearly so faint as usual.

'Thank you. Sir John, were you?'

'Eh? Me? Good Gad, no. Eh? Why should I?'

'Mrs Fayre?'

'I? *No*, Mr Sheringham.'

'Fayre?'

'No.'

'Mrs Vane?'

'No.'

'Miss St Thomas?'

'Nope.'

'Twyford?'

'Not guilty.'

'Mrs Bray?'

'Well, I never! *No!*'

'Bray?'

'Nothing doing.'

'Combe?'

'No! But – '

'Unity?'

'No.'

'Parker?'

'No.'

'Then – Miss Crosspatrick?'

'Oh, no.'

Roger stood his ground for a moment, in a horrid silence. Then he turned to Fayre.

'I'm sorry. For some reason the person seems to want to conceal the fact. I'd like to talk to you alone, if I may.'

'Wait a minute.' Mr Bray's large voice arrested the assembly in the act of turning away. 'Look here, Sheringham, what about coming out in the open? You know as well as I do why the person you say was in Pidgeon's tent last night won't admit to it. And so does everyone else.'

'Yes? In what way?'

'Well, I mean to say, old man, it's no use treating us like kids. We all know poor old Pidgeon never fell into the sea last night without cause. We all know someone pushed him in. Let's face facts.'

'Then you all know more than I do,' Roger retorted. 'I think you're exaggerating, Bray, aren't you? How can you possible *know* any such thing?'

'Oh, I'm not going to split words with you. Suspect, then, if you like, but suspect almost strong enough to know. After all, it stands to reason.'

'You mean, because of what he told us last night?'

'You've hit it. What did he tell us? Why, that – '

'Just a minute. I'm glad you brought that up, Bray, because that's a thing I ought to explain.' Roger had had to take a quick decision, but he could see nothing against telling the truth on this point and at this juncture everything in its favour. 'I don't know if you noticed that Mr Pidgeon and I went for a walk on the beach yesterday evening after dinner. Well, while we were down there – ' Roger paused, and shifted his position so that he could see every face ' – while we were down there he told me that he'd invented the whole thing. The story about a murderer among us, which he told us after dinner last night, was a complete fabrication.' With all the intensity of which he was capable Roger swept his glance over the faces in front of him. It was the psychological instant. This piece of news, if anything could, ought to produce its reaction in the guilty person's face. Who looked taken aback?

Roger could have wept. Everyone looked taken aback. There was hardly anything to choose between the various expressions.

'Eh? What's that?' wheezed Sir John Birch, the first to recover. 'Mean to say the feller was pulling our legs?'

'He was Sir John. He told me that – '

'Stuff!' contradicted Sir John robustly. 'Don't believe a word of it.'

A murmur of assent took Roger by surprise.

'Try something else, Sheringham,' observed Captain Twyford, with languid mockery. 'Bit too thin, that, you know.'

'But you must admit it would have been a glamorous idea if it had been true, Reggie,' shrilled Miss St Thomas.

'Oh, stupefying,' agreed the Captain.

'Now look here, Sheringham,' boomed Mr Bray, in a kindly roar, 'I know you mean well, and all that, but look here, old man, as I said just now, we're not kids. We can face facts. I'm sure I'm speaking for everyone when I say we can look after ourselves. So you needn't try to stuff us up with a yarn like that.'

'But it's perfectly true,' Roger protested. 'Someone else knows it's true.' Roger protested. 'Crystal, for goodness' sake tell them what you know.'

Rather white, Crystal faced the group. 'It's quite true. Guy – Mr Pidgeon did make that story up. He – I think he wanted to frighten you, to – to see what everyone would do. I helped him.' said Crystal bravely. 'We made it up before we left England. It was a sort of joke. It was all planned out, even being left here and the stewards going off and everything. Honestly it was.'

Doubt again made itself apparent. Crystal's obvious sincerity was being weighed against the improbability of her story.

'But good God!' almost shrieked Mr Combe. 'It's – it's inhuman. It's incredible. We might have gone mad. The strain…'

'I realise that now.' Crystal agreed quickly. 'It was only meant to be a joke, but it was a very cruel joke. I can't think why we didn't see how cruel it was.'

Once more there was a doubtful pause.

'I was quite sure, last night, that the story was an invention,' said Miss Crosspatrick gently, almost to herself. Roger could have kissed her.

But the feeling was against credulity. Mr Bray, shouting down the growing whispers, summed it up.

'Ladies and gentlemen, if you'll let me say a word, I'm sure we're very grateful to Mr Sheringham for trying to make us easy in our minds, and to Mrs Vane, too, for taking her cue so prompt and backing him up, even if their story is a bit thin. Anyhow, it won't do to take any chances. There's some of us who believe that our late host was speaking the truth last night and considering what's happened we're likely to go on thinking it. And those of us who do think that, think that the particular party he was referring to pushed the poor old chap over the cliff last night, having inveigled him out there for the purpose, rather than be given away when we got back to England. Very well. We know what to do. Mr and Mrs Fayre are in charge here now, and I'm sure we'll all back them up in whatever they think fit to do. Very well. And we all know who Mr Sheringham is, and what he's done in the past; and I for one don't mind laying the odds that he'll have this dirty dog by the heels before a couple of days are out. Well, what I'd like to say is, he can count on me to help him, just as I'm sure, ladies and gentlemen, that he can count on all of us. So what he'd better do is to get busy, because I've got a sort of hunch that this island isn't going to be worth living on till we know who the swine is who'd done one murder already before he came here, and now he's done another.'

The cries of approbation that greeted Mr Bray's conclusion left no doubt of the general sentiment.

'And as seemingly we're going to be here for a whole blessed fortnight,' added Mr Bray more lugubriously, 'we look like having plenty of time for the job.'

Enid Fayre glided up to Roger with both hands outstretched. She seized his, and spoke in a low, vibrating voice, broken with grief.

'Mr Sheringham, please – *please* help me to avenge my poor Guy's wicked death.'

Roger groaned again.

3

Morosely Roger watched Mr Bray setting the stage. Mr Bray had taken complete charge of the situation. He had invited Roger to get on with the job, and now he was busy seeing that his invitation was accepted. Roger was clearly expected to do his detecting in the way in which Mr Bray considered detecting should be done. At the end of the alleyway between the tents Mr Bray had set a table, with a chair behind it facing the little camp; on the table, with a vague reminiscence of boardrooms, he had arranged, in neat geometrical exactitude, some pens, some ink and some paper, all laid on a large sheet of virgin blotting-paper. Under Mr Bray's directions Harold Parker was already bringing a second chair, for the interviewed.

Roger, leaning against the pole in the doorway of Crystal's tent, eyed these preparations with disfavour and, in a voice whose lowness was an unconscious tribute to Mr Bray, spoke his heart to Crystal inside.

'Damn the man!' he said, with no little bitterness. 'What's the good of trying to get at anything now? He's scared the bird beyond all hope. I was particularly anxious to avoid all talk of murder.'

'Blast him,' agreed Crystal warmly.

'He forced my hand. I was going to keep the truth about Guy's speech up my sleeve, in case I wanted it, but he made me bring it out. Hell's bells! It might have been much more effective if I could have plumped it out at each person separately. I might have had a chance then to see how people took it. In all that crowd it was hopeless.'

'Of course it was. He means well, of course, but...'

'I loathe people who mean well,' Roger said crossly.

By the table Mr Bray flapped a large hand towards Roger. 'All ready for you,' he roared.

Roger looked at him without affection. 'I'd like a plan of the tents, with the names of their occupants.'

'You shall have it, old man,' assented Mr Bray at once, in a kindly bellow. 'Harold, make Mr Sheringham out a plan of the tents, with the names of their occupants.'

Mr Parker jumped nervously to the task.

'Roger,' Crystal asked slowly, 'you don't think it's hopeless, do you?'

'What?'

'To find out who did it.'

'I don't know. In some ways it looks about the worst job I've ever tackled. There's so little real evidence, you see.'

'But you're going to try?'

'Of course I'm going to try,' Roger said, almost angrily. 'I liked Pidgeon. I can promise you, I'm going to do my damnedest.'

'You'll do it,' Crystal said, with the strange confidence that women have in men whom they do not know intimately. As soon as they know a man really well, the confidence disappears.

Mr Bray flapped his hand again.

'OK, old man,' he shouted, with a note in his voice that added: 'Here are your toys. Now detect.'

Roger nodded.

'I'll send 'em up to you in alphabetical order,' announced the master of the ceremonies.

Roger nodded again.

'Oh, well,' he muttered, and withdrew himself from the tent pole. Putting his head inside the tent he added:

'In any case, even if I hadn't liked Guy, I should do my damnedest, because I've an idea that Bray spoke a truer word than he knew in the course of that oration of his. Do you remember, Crystal? He said he'd got a hunch that this island wasn't going to be worth living on till we knew who it was we're looking for. I've got that hunch too. There's something about an unknown murderer that gets people just where their nerves are rawest.'

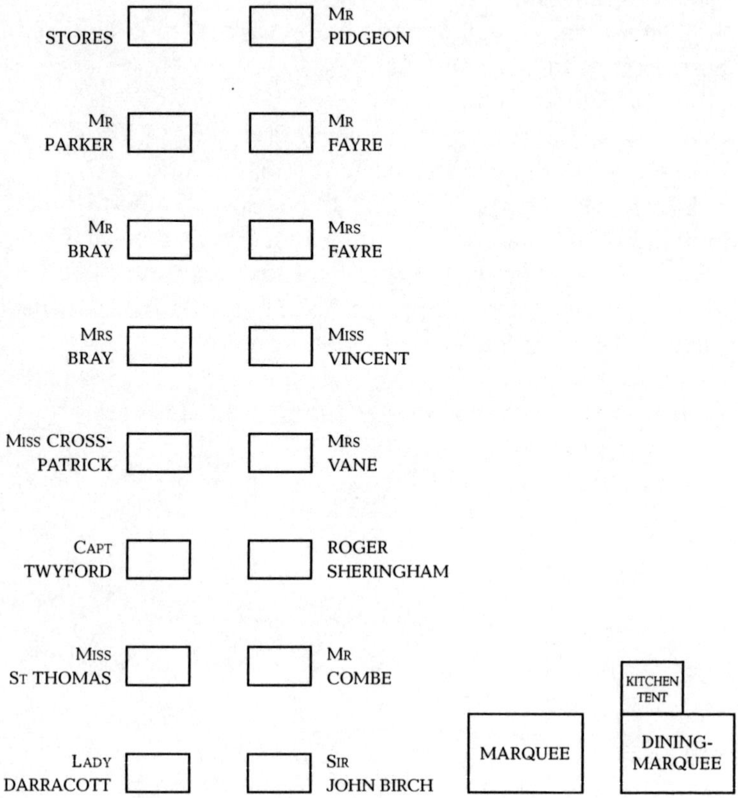

Mr Parker's Plan of the Camp

chapter eight

Seated in state at his neat little table, Roger first studied the plan of the camp, swiftly but competently drawn out for him by Harold.

Beside the two marquees, there were sixteen sleeping-tents, arranged in two parallel rows of eight each. The distance between tents in each line was about twenty feet, to allow a passage clear of the guy-ropes, and the distance across the alleyway between thirty and forty. The little street was thus nearly seventy yards long. The tents, twelve feet long by eight wide, were arranged so that their doors, in the shorter sides, opened into the alley.

Lady Darracott and Sir John Birch faced each other across the alley at the two ends nearest to the cliff; Mr Pidgeon's tent, opposite an unoccupied one containing certain stores, was at the other. Willie Fayre was next to Mr Pidgeon, and Enid next to her husband. Opposite Willie was Harold Parker, and next to the latter Mr and then Mrs Bray.

'Humph!' said Roger

Sir John Birch was the first comer, plainly resenting Mr Bray's attentions.

Roger asked him two questions. Had he heard anything at all during the night – say from midnight onwards? Could he offer any other information which might throw any light on the affair?

To both questions Sir John grunted a negative reply.

'Anything more?' he asked, still resentful.

'Nothing,' said Roger.

Sir John heaved himself out of the chair. Before he went he turned his flaming face on Roger for a moment, and gave him an unexpectedly piercing look from his blue eyes. 'It's murder all right, eh?'

Roger did not dissemble. 'I'm almost sure.'

'Um!' Sir John paused. 'Bloody business. Eh? Yes. Well, count on me, y'know.' He rolled off, with his peculiar lurching gait.

Mr Bray, shining with pride of duty, led up his own Gladys.

Mrs Bray had heard nothing; nor could she find any information to offer. Roger allowed her to get a few ladylike regrets and alarms off her chest, and then dismissed her.

Mr Bray presented himself, in alphabetical order.

Had he heard anything? Not he, he hadn't, worse luck; slept like a log all night, Mr Bray had. And to think of the dirty dog creeping past Mr Bray's tent like that, almost under Mr Bray's nose. Mr Bray was jiggered!

Mr Bray then proceeded to offer Roger a great deal of advice on (*a*) not trying to spin yarns that made grown-up people look like kids, (*b*) the art and craft of crime detection; and with many promises of support for the future dismissed himself.

Roger awaited the advent of Miss Crosspatrick with more interest. She also would almost certainly advise him on the craft of detection, but she might have something of interest to offer as well. Roger did not like Miss Crosspatrick, but he could not forget that she alone had believed him on the matter of Mr Pidgeon's revelation on the beach.

'Miss Crosspatrick, did you hear anything at all last night between, say, midnight and one a.m.?'

'Bearing on the crime, I take it?' Miss Crosspatrick smiled as if mildly correcting a small boy.

'No, I don't. I said, "anything at all." It's my job to determine whether it had any bearing on the crime. If, indeed,' said Roger severely, 'any crime has been committed at all, which is still more than open to doubt.'

'Oh, I see. Let me think, then. I put my light out at exactly midnight, but I was awake for at least twenty minutes after that. Now what did I hear in those twenty minutes? I heard Mrs Bray snoring, and I gladly leave it to you to determine whether that had any bearing on the crime. I heard Angela St Thomas talking to Captain Twyford in his tent. I did not hear Captain Twyford talking back. I don't think he did. I heard her go to her own tent – at, I should think about a quarter past twelve. I heard the sea on the rocks, and that again I leave to you to assess in relation to the crime; personally, I consider there is quite a connection, but that isn't my job. What else did I hear? I heard you coughing a great deal before you went to sleep. Perhaps you were busy drowning the murderer's footsteps. You smoke too much, Mr Sheringham, you know,' said Miss Crosspatrick pleasantly. 'You shouldn't.'

Roger, disregarding this advice, did his best to look official. 'Have you any information you can give me that might throw light on Mr Pidgeon's death?'

'I can tell you who pushed him over the cliff if you like,' Miss Crosspatrick drawled, with her little smile.

'Thank you,' Roger said coldly. 'I won't ask you to be libellous until we can prove that he was pushed over at all.'

'Well, really, there isn't very much doubt of that, is there? I need hardly ask you if you found the print of his heel in the earth just over the edge of the cliff, which shows quite clearly that he had his back to the cliff before he fell.'

Dash this woman, thought Roger. He said aloud, still more coldly:

'You've been doing a little detecting yourself, then?'

'A little,' agreed Miss Crosspatrick imperturbably. 'That is to say, I saw you and Mrs Vane leaning out over the cliff, and it didn't take me long to find what you had been looking at.'

'Perhaps you found something else while you were there?' Roger asked, with sarcasm.

'I did,' Miss Crosspatrick agreed, with the utmost amiability. 'I found this.' Nestling in her bag, wrapped carefully in one of her large, sensible handkerchiefs, she showed him an electric torch.

'Ah,' said Roger eagerly. He was sportsman enough to have the welfare of his side at heart rather than his own prowess; and therefore, in his pleasure that the torch had been found at all, did not grudge Miss Crosspatrick her little triumph. 'I've been looking for that myself. I can't think how I missed it. Where was it?'

'Among the rocks at the bottom of the cliff. I marked the place for you. In the meantime I thought it better to remove this before anyone else found it.'

'Excellent,' Roger said, with more friendliness than he had yet shown. 'I haven't had time to make a proper search down there myself yet, but you're quite right: we mustn't let anyone else get ahead of us.'

He stretched out his hand to take the torch, which Miss Crosspatrick had not yet removed from her bag, but she unhurriedly removed the latter from his reach.

'I've kept it wrapped in my handkerchief,' she said. 'That's the right thing to do, isn't it?'

'If you mean fingerprints,' Roger smiled, 'I don't think we're likely to have very much luck in that line with Mr Pidgeon's torch.'

It was Miss Crosspatrick's turn to smile. 'But this isn't Mr Pidgeon's torch,' she said, with quiet certainty.

'Not his torch? Then whose is it?'

'The murderer's,' smiled Miss Crosspatrick, rather as if instructing a small and not particularly bright boy.

Roger, too surprised to be resentful, could only stare at her. 'How on earth do you know that?'

'It's only we who have these long, black-cased torches,' Miss Crosspatrick explained, with an effect of good-humoured patience. 'Mr Pidgeon had one of those square hand-lamps. Didn't you notice it when he was lighting us out of the marquee last night? Of course he may have had one of these torches too, but I don't think so.'

Roger was quite sure that if Miss Crosspatrick did not think so, that thing could not be. 'There's no torch of that pattern in his tent this morning,' he said, almost humbly. 'I looked.'

'And have you looked in the other tents for Mr Pidgeon's square lamp?'

'No. Have you?'

'Yes. I couldn't find it.'

'No wonder. It's at the bottom of the sea by now.'

'Precisely.' Miss Crosspatrick's tone expressed commendation of this sign of intelligence.

'And from one of the tents a black torch is missing?'

'On the contrary.' Miss Crosspatrick smiled gently. 'There is a black torch in each of the tents.'

'What?'

'I looked into the store tent, too. There is a box containing eleven black torches there. I think one asks oneself, why not a dozen, doesn't one?'

Roger nodded. 'That was clever,' he said appreciatively, but did not add whether on Miss Crosspatrick's part or on that of the murder. 'Did Pidgeon show the contents of the store tent to anyone?'

'I don't know. It's possible. It was open all day yesterday, and people were going in and out, weren't they?'

'Yes. I don't think there's much to be learnt there.'

'And in the meantime, we have the murderer's fingerprints,' Miss Crosspatrick pointed out pleasantly.

'I hope so. I'll have a look at that later. Would you like to keep the torch till I can examine it quietly? We'd better not bring it out here. Anyone may be watching.'

'Precisely what I felt. Then I think that's all for the moment, isn't?'

'Just one thing,' Roger said curiously. 'You were the only person just now who believed me when I told them that the story about the murderer was an invention. Why did you?'

Miss Crosspatrick smiled tolerantly. 'It didn't really need a deep knowledge of psychology to realise that Mr Pidgeon was telling a wish-fulfilment story. Besides, his premises were, practically speaking, impossible weren't they?'

'I thought he made a very good story out of it.' Roger felt constrained to defend Mr Pidgeon.

'Oh, perhaps. But the situation wasn't even original, was it? Isn't there a play called *Shall We Join the Ladies?* that contains precisely the same idea?'

Roger could not withhold his admiration. Irritated victims might term Miss Crosspatrick a know-all, but she certainly did know a great deal; and she always seemed to be right.

He told her of Mr Pidgeon's remarks.

'I thought so,' said Miss Crosspatrick with complacence. 'It was quite obvious.'

'And yet you had no doubt from the beginning that his death was due to murder?'

'Oh, none. That was quite obvious too.'

'Then how do you reconcile the two?'

'In the same way as I'm sure you must be reconciling them, Mr Sheringham,' said Miss Crosspatrick gently. 'There actually was someone listening to him who had committed just such a murder as he described. In a gathering of over a dozen people that is not such an impossible coincidence. The impossibility was, of course, that Mr Pidgeon could have learned of it. But, unfortunately for Mr Pidgeon, the murderer did not wait to realise that.'

'Yes,' beamed Roger, 'that's exactly my own theory.'

'Of course,' said Miss Crosspatrick.

2

Roger was a little preoccupied as he rose to receive Lady Darracott. Miss Crosspatrick's discovery of the torch definitely proved the presence of another person on the top of the cliff last night, and so linked up with the dying voices heard by Mr Parker. Murder itself could not yet be said to be proved as clearly as a court of law would require, but there could no longer be any reasonable doubt about it.

Roger wondered on whom Miss Crosspatrick had fixed her decision as the perpetrator. She was a shrewd woman, and though one kept longing to show her wrong, she always seemed to be maddeningly right. Roger was quite sure that she would be able to defend her case with argument and reason, but he did not want to hear those arguments just yet. He preferred to let his own enquiries lead him, if they turned out to be so obliging, towards a suspect first. Then it would be interesting to see if the name was the same.

Miss St Thomas and Mr Bray between them lowered Lady Darracott into the chair, and circumspectly retired.

'I'm sorry to bother you like this, Lady Darracott,' Roger apologised. 'I won't keep you a minute.'

He put his two questions. To each Lady Darracott returned a faint, bewildered negative. Roger beckoned to Mr Bray, and Lady Darracott was removed, Mr Bray in his solicitous zeal almost carrying her bodily.

Mr Combe, who had been mislaid when his turn was due but had now been run to earth by Mr Harold Parker, was ready to talk a great deal, but Roger cut him short without mercy. He had no information to offer, and Mrs Fayre was swiftly installed in his place.

To her Roger put careful questions about the voices, without, however, mentioning Mr Parker as having actually heard them, but was able to obtain no further help. Enid, sleeping for once soundly (a matter on which she would, apparently, never forgive herself to her dying day), had heard nothing at all. In mere courtesy Roger had to listen to her sad little wails and the surprising depth of her affection for poor Guy, but got rid of her as soon as he decently could.

Willie Fayre was another matter. He still retained the abstracted, shut-in manner which he had adopted ever since learning of his cousin's death, and he had, very definitely, no information to give.

Roger was inclined to bully him a little.

'Look here, Fayre, I don't want to press the point awkwardly, but your cousin was heard talking in his tent quite loudly to some person at about one o'clock. Your tent is next to his. Did you really hear nothing at all?'

'I was asleep.' Willie returned, with a touch of sullenness.

'So far as I gather, the voices were quite loud enough to wake up an ordinary sleeper. They didn't wake you?'

'No.'

'Just try to throw your mind back. Even if they didn't quite wake you, it's very strange if you didn't hear them with at any rate half your mind. Can't you recollect anything at all?'

'No, nothing, I'm afraid. I was asleep.'

Roger played with the pen on the table. 'And yet, according to your wife, you're not a very sound sleeper?'

A slow flush worked its way over Willie's face and neck. 'I used to suffer from insomnia years ago. Women never forget anything. I haven't had it for a long time now. Since this voyage began I've been sleeping like the dead – like a log.'

'Then you've nothing at all to tell me to clear up your cousin's death?'

'Nothing. And – er well, is there any real proof that he was – er – murdered at all?'

'Oh, yes,' said Roger firmly, with quite unwarrantable conviction.

Mr Fayre looked just a little taken aback. 'Oh! I – I thought there was still more than a possibility that it was just an accident?'

'Unfortunately not.'

'I see. And – what is the proof?'

'I'm sorry,' Roger said sternly. 'I'm not at liberty to say.'

Luckily Willie did not press the point, which Roger might have found some difficulty in maintaining. Instead, he merely looked at Roger rather as if he were going to cry, and said nothing.

'All right, Fayre. Thank you. That seems to be all.'

Roger watched the little man's retreating back. Fayre no longer seemed exactly to be apologising to the ground for every step he took on it; but on the other hand his whole aspect was so dejected that apology seemed no longer necessary.

The little miserable! thought Roger, with no small irritation. He knows who did it too, but I'll never get it out of him. Whom can he be shielding? I wonder what the deuce he *did* hear last night.

He passed over Mr Parker, from whom no further information could be expected, and went on to Miss St Thomas.

Miss St Thomas dropped in an angular manner into the chair, and crossed her unstockinged legs.

'Well, this is a crashing piece of bother, isn't it?' she observed chattily. 'Still, I suppose it's no good getting strenuous about it. How's sleuthing?

With some severity Roger put his two questions.

'Not a hope,' returned Miss St Thomas, with unabated cheerfulness.

Roger pretended to consult his notes. 'You were walking about the camp last night between twelve and one, weren't you?'

Miss St Thomas' eyes opened wide. 'I? My dear man, what a perfectly lousy idea.'

'You mean you weren't?'

'I mean I wasn't.'

'But you left Twyford's tent at twelve-fifteen, according to the information I've got.'

'Oh!' Miss St Thomas' still wide eyes narrowed considerably. 'There are some pretty dim cads in this lot, aren't there?'

'No doubt. Anyhow, what I want to know is, when you were outside, did you see anyone else about?'

'No, I didn't. I was bored petrified at going to bed so early, so I went into Reggie's tent to talk about life. I suppose it was about a quarter past twelve when I left. No, I didn't see anyone else.'

'As far as I know, you were the latest person out. Can you give me any idea how many tents were still lighted up then, and whose?'

'This is glamorous,' observed Miss St Thomas, with renewed enthusiasm. 'Scotland Yard isn't in the race. Am I an important witness?'

'Quite,' Roger said dryly. 'Well?'

'Let me think. Naturally I didn't notice much, and I fell over a tent-peg, which didn't help. Still... Well, my aunt's light was out. Sir John's wasn't. Reggie's wasn't, of course; nor was Vallie's.' Vallie was Mr Valentine Combe. 'Yours was out; Crystal's wasn't. Stella Crosspatrick's was. That's all I can tell you.'

Roger glanced at the plan. 'Those tents are all up at this end. You didn't notice the other end at all?'

'Sorry, I didn't.'

'Um.' Roger noted down the meagre information.

'This is all very interesting to me,' Miss St Thomas volunteered.

'Is it?'

'Yeah. I've often thought of writing a detective novel, but I'm weak on plots. No objection to me working in a few ideas from this situation, have you, Roger? I mean, you won't be wanting it yourself?'

'No,' said Roger, who objected to being called by his Christian name by people he did not like.

'I've got a theory too, if you'd care to hear it?'

'Yes?'

'My idea is, keep your eye on Bray.'

'Bray?'

'Yeah. Our Harry. He's a tough.'

'Possibly. But…?'

'Well, I'm only applying your own rules. I read some articles you wrote once for the *Daily Courier*, or some rag. Pot-boilers of course, but I thought quite a lot so sense in them,' said Miss St Thomas kindly. 'Your idea was that murder is only committed by people who are capable of committing murder, or something. And to that I'd add, on my own behalf, people with no imagination. Well, cast your eye round. I don't know how many of us here are capable of committing murder, but I'll lay you a pony to fourpence that Bray is; and I should say he's got just about as much imagination as would leave a bare rim round a pin's head. Also he was one of the few people whom Guy knew before the cruise began. That's all. Think it over, Roger.'

'Thank you,' said Roger. 'I will.'

Miss St Thomas heaved herself out of her chair. 'By the way, talking of pot-boilers, I saw that some American tough described you the other day as a writer of pot-boiling thrillers.'

'Indeed?' Roger said coldly. 'Who was that?'

'Oh, I don't know. One of the usual hangers-on the skirts of literature, you know, who make a living out of writing smart-Alex pars about real authors. Alexander Woollybed, or something.'

'I think you must mean Alexander Woollcott.'

'I dare say. A bit dim, I thought. But perhaps pot-boiling doesn't mean the same over there as it does here.'

'Alexander Woollcott is a distinguished American critic.' Roger said, still more coldly. 'His language is well thought out and his phraseology dignified. He occupies an important position in the near-literary world, and corresponds to Mr Hannen Swaffer in our country. It is quite impossible that he could have used the gratuitously offensive and vulgar phrase you mention.'

A tinge of wistfulness crept into Miss St Thomas' face. 'I should like to be a distinguished critic, and say rude personal things about people who aren't supposed to answer back. Between times, I might even criticise their books instead of the people behind them; though that seems to be against the rules.'

'You speak with a certain bitterness, Angela,' Roger said, not unkindly.

'And so would you if you were me,' Miss St Thomas agreed. 'Just because my father isn't Mr Someone-or-other and lives in Bloomsbury, half the critics scream the most absurd praises of anything I write, I suppose hoping to get asked to dinner; and the other half condemn everything out of hand, knowing, I suppose, that they won't. I could count on the fingers of one hand the genuine criticisms I've had, by people who didn't care a hoot whether I live in Hill Street or Hampstead.'

'I think you're getting libellous,' said Roger, 'You'd better send Twyford along to me.'

'Oke,' said Miss St Thomas.

Captain Twyford appeared much perturbed by the footsteps he had heard during the night. Roger pressed him as to the exact time at which he had heard them, but the Captain could not help on that point. He had been asleep, and the footsteps had woken him up.

'They must have been thudding ones to do that,' Roger opined.

Captain Twyford looked hurt. 'I sleep like a cat,' he explained. 'Have to, in my job, or there wouldn't be much chance of getting through.'

Roger apologised, wondering vaguely how cats sleep. So far as he knew, one may lift up a sleeping cat and bump it on its head before it will consent to wake up if it does not happen to feel that way. Presumably, however, Captain Twyford did not mean that his native bodyguard could pick him up and bump him on his head before he would stop sleeping.

'Well, which way were they going?' he asked.

'South to north,' Twyford replied without hesitation.

'You're sure of that?'

'Absolutely.'

Roger looked at the plan of the tents.

'Um!' he said 'Man or woman?'

'Couldn't say definitely, but of the two a woman.'

'Why?'

'They were very light.'

'Oh!' Roger did not like to say so, but he could not help feeling it odd that the Captain should have been awakened by very light footsteps. 'Fast or slow?' he asked instead.

'Just medium. No, perhaps a bit on the quick side.'

'I see. Did you hear anything else during the night?'

'Well, as a matter of fact, I believe I did.' Captain Twyford leaned across the little table and looked extremely impressive. 'I believe I heard a shout.'

'Ah!' Roger sat up. Here at last was someone else who had heard that shout. He had purposely not mentioned it to any of the others, because he had not wished to suggest it on them; and if they had heard it, they would certainly have said so. 'Why do you say you only believe you heard it?'

'I was asleep, you see; but in my job one learns to register subconscious impressions during sleep. And when the footsteps woke me up later, I'd got the distinct impression in my mind that I'd heard a shout not long before.'

'I see. That's interesting. Then the shout took place before the footsteps?'

'Yes, definitely. I can't say how long, but probably within fifteen minutes or so.'

'And I suppose that's why the footsteps, which you describe as light, woke you up, because you'd already been roused to some extent by the shout?'

'Possibly. But in my job one develops rather an instinct for footsteps, you know. I mean, I might hear a native creeping about on tiptoe, and sleep through an explosion.' Captain Twyford spoke very seriously, as if these were weighty matters to him. Roger supposed they might be, though he could not help wondering whether cats sleep through explosions.

'Anyhow, the footsteps put you quite on the alert?'

'Yes, definitely. As a matter of fact I began wondering whether I oughtn't to turn out and have a look round.' Captain Twyford laughed, a little self-consciously. 'Silly of me, of course, but when one's always been in charge of a camp, it's not easy to shake off the feeling of responsibility.'

'Yes, of course. I wish to goodness you had got out and had a look round.'

'My word yes, so do I, now. At the time – well!' The Captain laughed again. 'You see, I couldn't help remembering that story Pidgeon told us about the young fisherman.'

'Oh, the ghost?'

'Well, the ghost, yes.' Captain Twyford laughed once more, a shade uneasily.

Roger marvelled that great men should have such strange weak spots. 'I should have thought you'd be hardened to ghosts by now,' he said mildly. 'I always understood the jungle is full of them.'

'I wasn't afraid of the ghost,' retorted the Captain, with some warmth, his languid manner quite discarded. 'Hang it all, man, I mean I thought it was someone monkeying about, pretending to be the ghost, and I wasn't going to gratify them by bothering to turn out. And when I remembered the shout, I was sure, so I just went to sleep again.' The Captain had spoken with heat and some earnestness, but Roger did not find himself altogether convinced. Of course, it was absurd to suppose that such a gallant adventurer had been at all alarmed by a silly ghost story, and yet... Anyhow, the point was of no importance.

'That's exactly what I thought,' Roger nodded.

'You heard it too, then?'

'The shout; not the footsteps. And so far as I know we two are the only ones who did hear it. That seems odd, doesn't it? It woke me up.'

'I seem to remember that it was a sizable shout,' the Captain agreed, puzzled.

'Our tents are opposite one another. That may have something to do with it.'

'Trick of the wind, perhaps,' suggested Twyford, though he still sounded puzzle.

'Anyhow, we did, and presumably no one else. Now, you didn't hear any voices, did you?'

'No.'

'And it was only one pair of footsteps that passed your tent?'

'Yes. The – the murderer coming back, I suppose?'

'If there was a murder at all,' Roger said, rather smugly.

'Oh, hang it all, there's no doubt about that, is there?'

'Between ourselves, no, there isn't. But for goodness' sake don't let the women know, or they'll be going into hysterics all over the place. I could have brained Bray when he talked like that. I was trying to gloss it over.'

'I'm absolutely with you. We don't want any hysterics. The situation's bad enough as it is.'

'Quite,' Roger agreed. He had never taken very much to the gallant Captain, with his rather silly pose of languor and boredom; but he would have a chance now of showing his real mettle, and undoubtedly he should be a useful man to have by one in a crisis.

'I mean, this person must be pretty desperate, to push poor old Pidgeon over the cliff as clean as a whistle like that.'

'He thought Pidgeon knew too much. Quite wrongly, as it happened, but he thought so.'

'Yes, that's what I mean. And if it's suspected that he told any of us what he knew – you, for instance, on the beach last night – well, I don't think I'd care about being in that person's shoes.'

'Oh,' said Roger, rather surprised. That possibility had not occurred to him.

'I mean, I hope I'm not a rabbit when it comes to standing up to another man in a fair fight, and all that sort of rot,' said Captain Twyford very seriously, 'but I must say I don't care about stab-in-the-dark methods. Never did. That's what I mean when I say I think we'd better watch our steps.'

'How?'

'Well!' Twyford uttered his rather self-conscious little laugh again. 'I'm sure Bray was right when he said we could look after ourselves, and all that, but supposing one of us did happen to find out who the person was – well, I mean, he'd have to look after himself pretty closely, don't you think? I mean, there aren't any police to look after one here.'

'Oh, perhaps. But that mustn't stop us trying. Besides, I was relying on you to help me.' Roger was puzzled. Was the man suggesting that there should be no investigation at all?

'Oh, of course,' Twyford said quickly. 'I'm your man. Anything I can do, of course. I was only thinking of the women, that's all. Rotten position for them, I mean.'

'Oh, I see. Yes, of course. Still, I don't think it's very likely that one of the women should find out the truth before ourselves.' Roger resolutely refused to entertain the thought that Miss Crosspatrick might falsify this assertion.

'No, and speaking of the women, I'd like to tell you an idea of mine. There may be nothing in it, of course, but I'll give it you for what it's worth. I believe a woman's at the bottom of all this.'

'A woman?'

'Yes. I've been thinking about it, and that's my conclusion. A woman could have pushed Pidgeon over the cliff, if he'd been near enough to the edge; and if he wasn't, she could get him there more easily than a man. And the more I think of it now, the more I think those footsteps I heard last night were a woman's.'

'Well, it's quite possible.' Roger ran his mind through the list of possible candidates. 'And yet, you know, I can't quite see any of these women going quite to those lengths. Mrs Bray, Mrs Fayre, Miss Crosspatrick, Lady Darracott, Unity, Crystal – no, I can't. Can you?'

'I wouldn't trust any of them,' said Twyford, with strange vehemence. 'Not one. Not even Angela herself. You can't ever *know* with a woman. No, no, I wouldn't trust a single one of them.'

'Well, well,' said Roger, mildly astonished.

chapter nine

Lunch was a difficult meal. There were short silences, followed by spasmodic outbursts of meaningless conversation. The presence of their host's body lying on the beach below was very much in everyone's consciousness.

Nor was that the only thing. Roger, trying to watch intently in the intervals of relapse into uneasy meditation, was perturbed by the suspicious glances which he was constantly intercepting between this person and that. It was a dreadful thing, this not knowing whether one's neighbour in the next chair might not be a double murderer, but if people once began giving way to it...

For murder seemed now to be taken quite for granted. The word was never spoken, nor even a single reference made during the whole meal to Mr Pidgeon's death; but the whole atmosphere was vibrating with it. Roger wondered gloomily how much of this was due to Mr Bray's ill-timed outspokenness, or whether the same thing would have happened in any case. He thought that probably it would.

Nor was he happy about the result of the interviews. Apart from the torch that Miss Crosspatrick had found, very little information had accrued. Twyford's was the last of any importance, for Unity had had nothing to offer and Roger had not bothered to subject Crystal to a formal interview.

Well, what it all came down to was that everything depended on the torch. If any luck remained with justice, there would be fingerprints on it; for the torch had lodged between two rocks well above water-level, whence the glint of the sun on its lens had attracted Miss Crosspatrick's attention. And if there were fingerprints, they would be those of the murderer. Roger was perfectly familiar with the very simple science of fingerprints, and had no doubt of this ability to identify any he might find.

And suppose they were the fingerprints of the murderer, and Roger identified him – or her, if Twyford were right. What then? What the deuce were they going to do with a murderer for a whole fortnight, if they really were to be stranded on the island all that time? A desperate murderer, too. Keep him tied up for a fortnight? Knock him on the head with a stone? Push him over the cliff himself? It would certainly be a problem. If Twyford really had been hinting that it might be better to postpone investigation till civilisation was reached, he might not be so wrong after all. Roger felt worried.

It had been arranged between Willie Fayre, Roger, and Twyford that Mr Pidgeon must be buried that afternoon: or rather Roger and Twyford had arranged it, and Fayre had apathetically agreed to anything they decided. Twyford had volunteered to walk over to the plantation and make trial of the soil there with a spade which was believed to be in the Nissen hut. He had set off, and Roger's short-lived spurt of sympathy with Miss St Thomas had died speedily when he saw her setting off, too. Roger was old-fashioned.

On his return just before lunch Twyford had reported, as Roger feared, that the earth was not deep enough. Mr Pidgeon must be buried in the sea. Twyford had brought back with him a length of canvas from the hut, and a book of sail-maker's needles which he had discovered. Somebody would have to sew the body up, together with some pieces of rock, and then it would have to be towed as far as possible out to sea and sunk.

'And I'm afraid it looks like being you and me, Twyford,' Roger said gloomily.

'Not me, I'm afraid,' Twyford said, with decision. 'I'll tow it out for you, if Combe will help me, but I can't undertake to help sew it up.'

'Why not? Someone's got to.'

'Sorry, that sort of thing would turn me up,' Twyford said simply. 'It's bad enough to swim out with him, but I'll do that.'

Roger turned away, annoyed. He did not know whom else to ask. Mr Bray would probably agree, but Roger did not feel that he wanted Mr Bray. Of the other men, the only one Roger thought would be much use at such a job would be Sir John, but somehow he did not care to ask the older man when there were so many younger ones available.

He was still pondering when the party filed out, in somewhat dismal procession, from the dining-tent, envying the scullery squad who had work to do. A gentle voice at his elbow made itself heard.

'Did I hear Captain Twyford refusing to help you sew up the body?'

Roger turned round, to meet Miss Crosspatrick's quizzical smile. 'Yes,' he said, wondering how the deuce Miss Crosspatrick had heard any such thing, for he and Twyford had been apparently quite alone.

'Have you asked anyone else?'

'No, I was just wondering who could.'

'I'll help you if you like,' drawled Miss Crosspatrick.

Roger thanked her, and forgave Twyford. After all, if that kind of thing did turn a man up it was best to say so firmly;

it was a rotten job, anyhow, having to swim out with the body, in the deplorable absence of any sort of boat, but Twyford had voluntarily offered to do that. Twyford was not at all a bad fellow after all. For that matter nor was Miss Crosspatrick, always rising to the occasion when really needed. Nor, of course, was Crystal, who had been so plucky that morning. And if one came to that, Bray had been honestly trying to be helpful. So had Mr Parker. So had Sir John. And Angela. And all the rest of them. Roger began to cheer up as he followed Miss Crosspatrick down the winding little path to the beach. Really, people were behaving very well. The situation might quite well have begun to look ugly that morning in the marquee. As things were, it just seemed to be bringing out the best in everyone. For even Willie presumably thought he was being chivalrous.

Chivalrous!

A sudden thought struck Roger. Willie was obviously shielding someone. When a person in that position acts as a shield at all, the odds are overwhelming that the shielded is a woman. Again Twyford might not have been so far wrong.

'Miss Crosspatrick!' Roger said.

Miss Crosspatrick halted and looked back over her rather square shoulder. 'Yes?'

'You told me this morning you know who the – the person we're looking for, is. I don't want to hear the name yet, because I think it might be more useful for us to talk it over when I've made up my own mind. But I'd like you to tell me this: is it a woman?'

'Oh, no,' said Miss Crosspatrick.

'Oh! – I suppose, by the way that you've got no absolute proof? No evidence, for instance, that I haven't had?'

'Proof, no; certainty, yes. And I've got no more evidence than you have,' said Miss Crosspatrick gently. 'Quite possibly not so much.'

'Um,' said Roger.

He was not impressed. Women, even the most reasonable of them, will jump to conclusions. That the conclusions are so often untenable does not in the least affect the obstinacy with which the jumpers cling to them.

They reached the beach. Roger threw down the roll of canvas, produced the sail-maker's needles and twine, and set about his gruesome job, while Miss Crosspatrick looked on.

Within three minutes Miss Crosspatrick was doing the job, far more efficiently, while Roger looked on. He felt he ought not to be doing any such thing, but he had been given no option.

2

The job had been done. From a selected position off the rocks the horrid bundle had been launched, with Roger, Twyford and Combe supporting it. Roger had swum with them, lending what help he could, for as far as dared; the other two had managed to make progress, pulling on the rope that had been twisted round the canvas, for another twenty yards. Only two really first-class swimmers could have managed to tow a dead weight as far. The body had been in really deep water when it was dropped.

By the time the three had dried and dressed tea was ready, in the near marquee. Roger – contemplating the scene, with the women sitting comfortably in the wicker chairs, the men handing round plates of freshly cut bread and butter and cakes, and Enid sitting beside a tray with two large teapots, while Mr Parker ran eagerly backwards and forwards to the kitchen for hot water – Roger felt his confidence grow. Nerves were normal. People were behaving well. The suspicious looks which had been thrown about at lunch were no longer in evidence. It was as if with the removal of their host's body, everyone felt a weight off his or her own mind. Perfectly illogical; but then the mind is not naturally a logical instrument.

Sir John rolled up to him.

'Buried him?' he grunted, with his usual abruptness.

Roger told him what had been done.

'Bad business. I've been busy myself.'

'Yes?'

'Took young Parker and rigged up a beacon on that knoll north-west of the banana plantation,' wheezed Sir John. 'Hoisted a distress signal, too. Any ships passing will go by on the north. Want to get us out of this bloody hole as soon as possible. Mustn't neglect chances.'

'That was a grand idea,' Roger said warmly. 'Young Parker, eh? Why not Bray? He's stronger.'

'Don't like him,' Sir John replied briefly.

'Or Fayre?'

'Don't trust him.'

'You don't trust Fayre?'

'No.'

The two men then stood side by side in complete silence for five minutes, until Sir John said 'Ah!' and rolled off towards Lady Darracott's chair.

So Sir John, too, did not trust Fayre. That was interesting.

There was, however, another problem worrying Roger, which prevented him from paying due attention to that one. Was it or was it not inadvisable to pursue investigations into Mr Pidgeon's murder at once? Roger was quite sure that the whole party was encamped on a wasps' nest. As things were, the wasps were tucked safely away underground. But once one began stirring things up...

He wished he knew whom to consult on the point. Twyford, with whom he would have been most ready to talk things over, had already given his opinion. Roger knew exactly what would happen if he asked his host and hostess: Enid would clasp her hands and say that her poor Guy must be avenged, at all costs; Willie would mumble better leave things for a bit and see. Bray, having no imagination at all, would not understand why investigation need be held up for a minute; Sir John would probably grunt something about letting sleeping dogs lie, as he had done after dinner the evening before. The whole party's reactions were almost childishly simple to forecast, Roger thought.

In the end he determined to call into consultation Crystal and Miss Crosspatrick. Crystal was a woman of the world, and she had a feeling for psychology too; Miss Crosspatrick was hard, sound sense on legs. Roger unobtrusively called the two of them out, took them for a stroll towards the interior of the island, out of reach of any possible prying ears, and put his case, for and against.

The result rather surprised him. Crystal, whom he would have expected to advise delay in order to preserve the present equanimity, strongly urged an immediate, persevering, and undisguised investigation.

'People are all right now,' she pointed out, 'but who knows how long that's going to last? There's nothing like uncertainty for getting on one's nerves. And if they see that nothing's being done, it won't be long before everyone will be imagining the murderer's hiding under their beds each time they go into their tents in the dark. But if they see that we're trying all we can to find out who the murderer is and draw his sting, that will give them something to bite on.

Besides, they'll all join in the hunt, and that will keep them busy. They must be kept busy, and they must be given as much hope as we can hand out: a ship must always be coming within a few hours, we must always be just on the verge of grabbing the bogey – and confident. Aren't I right, Roger?'

'It's a sound argument,' Roger admitted, unexpectedly impressed. He realised that he had never given credit to Crystal, with her butterfly appearance, her 'pets' and 'sweets,' her seemingly superficiality, for the hard core of shrewdness which had brought her where she was.

'Stella?' said Roger. 'Do you agree?'

'On the contrary,' smiled Stella Crosspatrick, with her air of knowing so much better. 'I think Crystal is quite wrong. We may find out who the murderer is, but are we going to prove it? I don't think so. And what are we going to do if we can't? We can't hold anyone prisoner here on suspicion. In fact, I very much doubt if we could hold anyone prisoner here at all, though I haven't examined that galvanised iron erection over there yet. And if we only suspect and can't prove, are we going to tell people or not? And supposing we never do find out at all? Isn't there a saying about hope deferred? A fortnight is too long a time to play the game Crystal suggests. Everyone would be mad before the end of it.' She smiled again.

'What do you advise, then?' Roger asked.

'That we do nothing. Let it be known that you aren't going to investigate at all, and that the murderer has nothing to fear. When we get back to England, of course you'll report the case to the authorities; but the murderer will know that he's quite safe then; there won't be any evidence left. When people realise that there's no danger, because there's no investigation, they're much more likely to keep calm than they are on Crystal's plan.'

'That's a perfectly sound argument, too,' Roger said judicially.

'But it's nothing short of condoning murder,' Crystal said, with warmth.

'What I'm trying to do is to prevent any more murders,' Miss Crosspatrick drawled.

'We can't let Guy be killed like this and not do anything about it. It's abominable.'

It's no good bringing sentiment into the question. This is simply a problem of expediency, and nothing else. Don't you agree, Mr Sheringham – Roger, I mean?' corrected Miss Crosspatrick, with a tolerant smile.

Roger intervened before Crystal's Irish blood could become too warm. They discussed the matter for a few minutes more, both in its general aspect and, more particularly, in regard to the torch found by Miss Crosspatrick and what was to be done about that.

In the end Roger found a compromise which he urged as being in the truly British tradition. Both systems were to be given their chance. Fingerprints were to be taken, and the torch examined. That would show everyone that something was being done. Then, whatever the result of the examination, the announcement was to be made that there had been no result. After that, investigations were to lapse. In the meantime, with any luck the murderer's identity would be known to Roger, and he, keeping the torch as proof, was to inform Miss Crosspatrick of the name so that, in the event of anything unforeseen, there would be a witness to the fact, and a witness about whom the murderer would know nothing. Crystal was not to learn the name, for, as she said, nothing could induce her to be even civil to the devil, and then the game would be given away.

'Well, let's get back before they've finished tea,' said Roger.

3

The announcement, by himself, that Mr Sheringham wished to take the fingerprints of the company, caused a somewhat excited stir. This, so went the plain but unspoken thought, was the real thing. Roger explained elaborately that it was a measure of precaution only that for the moment it meant really nothing, that permission was an act of courtesy and nothing else, and that if anyone objected there was no more to be said. He looked round questioningly, but no one did object.

Enid Fayre, already consulted and her approval given, appeared, solemnly carrying a sheet of paper containing a tiny pile of lamp-black. Roger shook it out over the surface and, as each person came up to him in turn, pressed their fingertips on it and then on a sheet of clean paper which Enid, as if ministering to a hierarch, handed to him at the appropriate moment. The individual's name was then inscribed by Roger on the sheet and, quite gratuitously, witnessed by Enid. Enid herself had been the first to have her prints taken, followed by Willie, and the rest of the proceedings had been conducted with all the solemnity of a religious service. Hardly anyone spoke, and if Crystal had been right in her plea for impressing the groundlings, the groundlings had certainly been most satisfactorily impressed.

Roger carried off the sheets of paper to his own tent, and there, after a few minutes, Miss Crosspatrick joined him, with the bag containing the torch. Before he left Roger had suggested to Enid that a move might be made of the younger people to the beach, for a bathe a little later before dinner, and that such of the older ones as could be roped in should be given some job to do to keep them occupied.

'We don't want people sitting about idle,' Roger had explained, as Enid's fine eyebrows lifted a little at the idea of frivolous bathing on such a day. 'When people are idle they begin to think. We've got to try and stop them thinking, for the next fortnight.'

'Oh, I do see, Mr Sheringham,' Enid had replied. 'I'll do my very best. After all, it's little enough that a woman can do at a time like this, isn't it?' And with a sad smile she had floated away to her task.

Roger was therefore able to be satisfied that the camp would not be full of loiterers and possible nuisances while he was carrying out his very important task.

This time Miss Crosspatrick had no option but to look on. She therefore did this job as thoroughly as any other and, planting herself in Roger's canvas armchair, made herself quite comfortable before turning as competent an eye on the worker as that of any overseer.

Roger carefully laced up the door of his tent, and extracted with due care the torch from its nest in Miss Crosspatrick's handkerchief. Laying it on the table, he dusted it all over from a box of face-powder brought by Miss Crosspatrick for the purpose. Blowing away the superfluous powder he uttered an exclamation of delight: there were prints, standing boldly out, all over the shiny black body of the torch.

'And a better job I never did see,' said Roger, with almost more admiration of himself than of the job.

Miss Crosspatrick did not appear surprised. It was as if having found the torch herself, and fingerprints being wanted, fingerprints had almost automatically been there.

'That's good,' was all she said. 'I shall be glad to have this uncertainty cleared up. I dislike uncertainty.'

Roger was bending over the prints, studying them intently, counting the ridges, and classifying them according to the Scotland Yard method, into spirals and whorls and the rest. Having completed this task, he sat down on the bed and began to turn through the sheets, examining each and comparing it with his notes.

The last sheet joined its fellows, and Miss Crosspatrick's brows lifted. 'Well?' she asked.

'That's funny,' said Roger, and began to go through them again.

Again the pile of scrutinised sheets was completed, and again a puzzled look appeared in Roger's face.

'This is absurd,' he said.

'What is?'

'I must have made some silly mistake.'

He got up and made another examination of the prints on the torch, checking the results with the notes he had made before. 'That's perfectly correct,' he muttered.

Returning to the bed he began painstakingly to classify each set of prints on the sheets of paper, poring over them with his pocket magnifying-glass just as carefully as he had pored over the torch and writing down the result in a fresh list. The process took a considerable time, but Miss Crosspatrick interrupted with no silly questions as to the difference between a spiral and a whorl, or even with considered observations on sweat-glands.

When his list was at last completed Roger took it doggedly in one hand and the results of the torch-prints in the other, and checked the latter against each entry on the former. Having done that he laid both down on the bed and stared at Miss Crosspatrick with as much intensity as if she had done him wrong.

'This is just impossible,' he said, frowning. 'Plain, blank impossible.'

'You can't identify the prints?'

'No. They're simply not here.'

'Well, the explanation's quite simple really, isn't it?' said Miss Crosspatrick, with her maddening little smile which added so plainly: You poor fish 'I must have been wrong when I said that Mr Pidgeon had no torch of this type. This is obviously his, and the fingerprints are his fingerprints.' Well, well, added Miss Crosspatrick's smile, what a dumb-bell the man is to be sure, to be sure.

'Well, they're not,' Roger retorted, annoyed no less by the smile than by Miss Crosspatrick's assumption that he should have overlooked such an elementary point in the science of detection. 'I've got Pidgeon's prints here, classified already. I went specially down to the beach to get them, before lunch. Of course, I knew, as soon as you told me about the torch, that I must have Pidgeon's prints to check up on.'

'I beg your pardon,' returned Miss Crosspatrick gently, and her lingering smile continued for her: But of course, he is a dumb-bell for all that. 'Then whose prints are they?'

'I *have* got everyone's here, haven't I? Where's that plan of the tents?' Roger found the plan, and checked the sheets off against the names. 'Yes, they're all here. Well, it may seem impossible, but it's the truth: these prints belong to someone apparently not on the island at all.' He crossed his arms, leaned back and gazed at Miss Crosspatrick from under frowning eyebrows, as if she were responsible for the whole thing. After all, she had deserved as much.

For a moment even Miss Crosspatrick looked shaken. 'You – you don't think there's someone hiding on the island?' she almost faltered.

'No, I don't,' Roger said crossly. But he was not at all sure. It would have been quite in keeping with Mr Pidgeon's impish sense of amusement to retain some member of his staff in hiding, for a purpose connected with one of his schemes: perhaps to imitate the ghost, and so increase the alarm and despondency. But if he had done so, he had obviously said nothing about it to Crystal. And again, if he had done so, the man had apparently risen up and killed him. And if so, why? Could it be that Mr Pidgeon's story about the murderer was not really all spoof? That he had been strictly truthful when telling Roger that it was not one of his guests, but that it was in point of fact one of the crew or a steward? And that Mr Pidgeon, with cruel ingenuity, had ensured that the man had been in hearing when he made that speech? The idea seemed almost fantastic; but with Mr Pidgeon the fantastic so often became the actual that no speculation seemed too wild.

Roger and Miss Crosspatrick stared at each other uneasily.

'It's much more likely,' Roger said, 'that the torch was dropped over the cliff yesterday by a steward, when they were getting things ready. No one would have noticed it, because no one looked there till you did.'

'It would be a great coincidence,' Miss Crosspatrick demurred, 'and I don't believe in coincidence.' Miss Crosspatrick was recovering herself. For a split second Roger had the ridiculous conviction that if Miss Crosspatrick did not believe in coincidence, coincidence did not exist. 'Besides,' added this redoubtable young woman challengingly, 'what would any steward be doing over there at all, let alone with a torch in his hand? It would be quite out of his way.'

'He might have run to the edge to look down at the beach for some reason, or call to someone,' Roger said feebly.

Miss Crosspatrick treated this suggestion as it deserved. 'Stuff! It would have been most inconvenient.'

'Well, can you explain the prints on that torch, then?' Roger asked, nettled.

'No, I can't,' Miss Crosspatrick replied frankly. 'I'll admit that when you found prints on the torch, I had not the least doubt whose they would be. It's strange, but I was wrong.'

'I think we've reached a point when you'd better tell me what's in your mind, Stella. Whose prints did you expect to find on that torch?'

Miss Crosspatrick smiled 'Of course Mr Fayre's.'

4

'Willie Fayre's?' Roger sat up.

'It's quite obvious really, isn't it?'

'Yes, that's interesting. I've been watching Fayre myself.'

'Naturally. It's odd about those prints. There must be some ordinary explanation of them. Because really I don't think that there can be any doubt that Mr Fayre was the person who pushed Mr Pidgeon over the cliff.'

'Then you think Fayre's a double murderer?'

'I'm afraid he must be.' Miss Crosspatrick's gentle tone deplored the fact in a mild way, but held very little concern.

'Um!' said Roger. 'Does one altogether see him in the part?'

'Surely. Not except under provocation, or in self-defence, perhaps; but his first murder may have been under provocation, and this one was certainly in self-defence. The rat-type, I should say.'

'You know this is all very speculative,' Roger said, with some disapproval.

'On the contrary, it's the only logical conclusion.'

'When did you begin to suspect Fayre?'

'Almost at once. At first I considered Sir John – '

'Sir John Birch?' Roger said in surprise.

'Certainly. It was he, if you remember, who asked Mr Pidgeon if he had told anyone else about this murderer of his, or had put anything about it in writing. I thought at the time that was rather significant; especially as he followed it up with advice to let the whole thing slide.'

'Two most unfortunate questions,' Roger commented dryly. 'They killed Pidgeon.'

'That, of course, is my own view. But about Mr Fayre, there were two other things that convinced me. First, his extraordinary manner all this morning.'

'Yes. I was prepared to find that consistent with his shielding someone else.'

Miss Crosspatrick considered this. 'Possible; but not, I think, very probable. If that manner of his wasn't a species of daze of remorseful guilt, I should be extremely surprised. Moreover, he is the only one of us whose behaviour has altered.'

'You put it very well. That's exactly what his manner did suggest.'

'Because that is what it was,' said Miss Crosspatrick, with a slightly amused air. 'And the second thing, of course, is that Mr or Mrs Fayre after all are really the only persons here whose guilt at some remote time in the past Mr Pidgeon might be in a position to prove. Nobody else's affairs could possibly have come into his hands in the way he described but those of Mr or Mrs Fayre; and of those two, Mrs Fayre is quite indisputably innocent.'

Into Roger's mind came a faint echo from Captain Twyford. 'No, no, I don't trust a single one of 'em.' He dismissed it.

'Aren't you forgetting,' he said instead, 'that Pidgeon's story was an invention?'

'On the contrary,' Miss Crosspatrick smiled. 'The point is that Mr Fayre didn't know it was an invention – and he had every reason to take it seriously.'

'You don't find that too much of a coincidence?'

'On the contrary, we have the coincidence already that Mr Pidgeon's invented story did actually apply to someone who heard it. His death proves that. It does not increase the coincidence that the person to whom it applied should have been Mr Fayre. Why not he as well as any other?'

'Um!' said Roger, not very brilliantly. He would have liked to point out to Miss Crosspatrick that she did not believe in coincidence at all, but refrained.

He stared instead abstractedly at his toes, and Miss Crosspatrick respected his meditations.

Roger had been particularly interested in the theory that had been offered him, because it was a theory to which he himself had been reluctantly moving. Pleading guilty to the prejudice, Roger admitted to himself now that all the time he had been pretending to look on Fayre as the shielder of somebody else, he had really felt that it was too much of a good thing on another person's behalf; guilty knowledge may worry and perturb, but it does not turn a man inside out as Fayre had been turned inside out all day. Unless of course it is guilty knowledge concerning a person exceedingly near and dear to us; but in Fayre's case the only such person was Enid, and to suspect her of the crime, with Willie as her accessory after the fact, was plainly absurd – though for one brief instant, when Fayre had turned that astonishing look on his wife in the morning, even that possibility had passed across Roger's mind.

No, Fayre had guilty knowledge all right. Not only his refusal to say anything about the voices in his cousin's tent, which if innocent he must have heard, but the very manner of that refusal too, proved that much beyond doubt. If it were guilty knowledge concerning another person, only the fact of that person being his wife could account for such a degree of apathy and dejection. Unless Enid were the most brilliant actress who never went on a stage, she could not be that person. Therefore Fayre's guilty knowledge should concern himself, and no one else. That was sound reasoning.

Moreover, the theory of Fayre as the criminal fitted in with other points. Harold Parker could not say whether the second voice had been a man's or a woman's. Fayre had a somewhat high-pitched voice; in rare moments of excitement he squeaked. Twyford had not been able to assert with confidence whether the footsteps he had heard pass his tent had belonged to a man or a woman. Fayre was small and slight; he had a light tread for a man. Yes, it all fitted in. Roger was sorry, for he liked the little man, for his abject worship of his beautiful, obviously indifferent wife. Still, it was no use being sentimental.

'Yes, Stella,' he sighed. 'I think you're right. There's no proof at all, but I've feared so all along. The odds are on Fayre.'

'Yes, of course. Mr Sheringham, about those fingerprints.'

'Oh, lord,' Roger groaned, 'I'd forgotten them. Really, I don't know what the deuce to make of them. It's uncanny.'

'You can't think of a single person whose prints you didn't take?' asked Miss Crosspatrick, her usual air of faint amusement a little more pronounced.

'No, I told you, I took everyone's.' Roger returned excitedly. 'I checked them.'

'I don't think you did,' Miss Crosspatrick informed him gently.

'You don't think...whose didn't I, then?'

Miss Crosspatrick's insufferable smile broadened.

'Your own.'

Roger gaped at her.

5

Beyond doubt the prints proved to be Roger's.

'He must have changed the torches,' Roger gasped. 'The devil! He's a cunning little beast. Willie!...'

'I suppose,' asked Miss Crosspatrick, with purely academic interest, 'it wasn't you who murdered Mr Pidgeon?'

'It was not,' Roger said firmly. 'Kindly get rid of that idea once and for all, Stella. I've been suspected of one murder before now, and I don't like it. I suppose you know you're responsible for this?'

'I suppose I must be,' Miss Crosspatrick admitted honestly, and Roger could only hope she felt more remorse than she showed.

'You left your bag in your tent all this afternoon, while we were down on the beach?'

'I'm afraid I did. I had no idea anyone knew I'd found the torch at all.'

'Everyone knows everything on this blessed little island,' Roger said bitterly. 'Everyone overhears everything too. If one doesn't want to be overheard, apparently one has to cross to the other side, or swim out to sea. I expect Willie heard every word we said about the torch this morning; after all, there's plenty of cover behind these tents. Someone's probably outside this one now, with his ear fastened to the canvas. Well, I don't care – let him. Of course, Willie must have seen you find the torch this morning.'

'Presumably. I imagined I was quite alone. I left everyone apparently busy up here.'

'When did you go down?'

'After the meeting in the tent. It didn't take me fifteen minutes. I'd seen the sun glinting on something when I was looking over the top of the cliff, and I wanted to see what it was. I can only suppose that Mr Fayre saw me getting it from the same place. You didn't notice where he was just then?'

'I was talking to Crystal, and watching Bray.'

'Well it's a pity,' said Miss Crosspatrick philosophically, 'but it can't be helped. Once he knew, of course the substitution while we were both on the beach was easy. I think it rather an ingenious touch on Mr Fayre's part to have chosen your torch before anyone else's.'

'And that's the end of our only piece of real evidence,' Roger said bitterly. 'Fayre – if it really is he – looks like getting away with this job.'

'In any case, we do nothing now I understand?'

'We do nothing (or at any rate nothing ostentatious), and we say nothing – except that our enquiries have led nowhere, and the murderer has nothing more to fear. And that after all,' said Roger, still more bitterly, 'is nothing more nor less than the truth.'

They looked at each other.

'In any case,' said Roger, 'we've never *proved* it was Fayre at all.'

Miss Crosspatrick smiled.

'Two murders,' Roger meditated. 'A little worm like that. You know I can hardly believe it.'

Miss Crosspatrick's smile broadened.

They looked at each other again.

Miss Crosspatrick's smile wavered, faded, died away.

'I liked Mr Pidgeon,' she said, more simply than Roger had ever heard her speak.

'Oh, *damn*,' said Roger.

chapter ten

Roger was surprised how things settled down.

During the three or four days that followed Mr Pidgeon's death, life on the island fell into such a quiet and settled routine that one might have imagined the camp to be inhabited by Boy Scouts instead of by marooned and nervous pleasure-cruisers. Mr Pidgeon was not forgotten by any means, but it really did seem as if the circumstances attending his death had been.

At first Roger, consulting with Crystal, had been at some pains to organise affairs on the lines of most resistance to jumpy nerves. On his suggestion Captain Twyford had been put in charge of the camp, and a certain routine, ostensibly laid down by Twyford, had been evolved. In fact, the routine originated from Roger; for Twyford, though an admirable figurehead, seemed disinclined to offer more than vague suggestions. Roger, cursing the laziness of his nominal superior, had voted himself into the post of lieutenant and executive officer; and not only transmuted these suggestions into cut-and-dried regulations, but energetically saw that they were carried out. To his surprise he did not appear to encounter the dislike in consequence that he expected.

In this way it came about that an orderly officer (known, inevitably, as the Dogsbody) was appointed for each day;

reveille was sounded, with a walking-stick on a brass tray, every morning at eight o'clock; breakfast was served at nine punctually in the marquee by the kitchen squad, and washed up promptly afterwards by the scullery squad; beds were made, and tents tidied, by their occupants; and Twyford led forcibly round for a formal inspection of the camp at ten o'clock. Roger had considered that by running the camp on mock-military lines, with a humorous pretence of a discipline which should be, under the humour, something more than just a pretence, nerves would be kept steady and backbones stiffened.

Certain it was that everyone, as if glad of the strong stick of organised discipline to lean upon, joined without protest in the game; but after a day or two Roger had to realise that perhaps he had underestimated the power of resistance belonging to sensible, civilised people. The fact that there was, as everyone was still convinced, an undetected murderer amongst them, no longer seemed to perturb them. The fact was just ignored in general conversation, as Mr Pidgeon himself had rather expected it might be; though what people said to each other in private Roger of course was unable to know; certainly they no longer said anything to him officially.

It had not been, however, without protest that all official investigation into Mr Pidgeon's death had been allowed to drop.

'No, I call that just a bit too dim,' Angela St Thomas had remarked, with unusual warmth. 'You can do what you like, Roger, but Reggie and I will carry on. Everyone's absolutely certain that Guy was murdered, whatever you say; and if someone was such a crashing cad as to do it, we ought to find out who it was.'

'You talk it over with Reggie,' Roger had soothed.

Mr Bray too had intimated with his usual force his opinion that it was feeble to let matters slide.

'But what can I do?' Roger had expostulated. 'I can't make evidence, where no evidence is.'

'Something ought to be done,' pronounced Mr Bray.

'I really don't know what. I know you're taking it for granted that it was murder, but I'm not prepared to say even that. There's no evidence to speak of and I see no point in upsetting everyone by poking about any further.'

'Then I'll poke about by myself; because you can take it from me, Sheringham, there's some of us don't think things ought to be left like this. After all,' said Mr Bray bitterly, 'it doesn't matter what I do, because I'm ruined already. Heaven only knows what's been happening to the markets. I've a feeling they're all over the place, just because I'm out of touch. I'm a ruined man all right, thanks to our pal – sorry though I am that he's dead, of course. So if I do find out anything – well, it won't make much difference to Mrs Bray financially whether anyone drops a rock on my head or not, see?'

'You talk it over with Twyford. After all, he's in charge.'

'Thanks for nothing. I will, though, all the same. Twyford's used to responsibility, he is. No need to tell him. He'll know what's the right thing to do,' had retorted the offended Mr Bray.

Presumably, however, Twyford's languid tongue had succeeded where Roger's had failed, for no more was heard of the matter. If any official investigations were taking place, no report of them had come to Roger's ears. He did not think they were.

Everyone on the other hand was agreed that the presence of the explorer, accustomed to tackling unconventional difficulties and dangers, was nothing short of a Godsend.

Roger suspected that the very spectacle of Twyford's nonchalant indifference had in some cases been enough to massage tightened nerves.

'Really, Mr Sheringham,' had sighed Enid Fayre in confidential undertones, 'I can't help thinking it almost a special provision of Providence that we should have Captain Twyford here, with all his experience. It's so wonderful for us poor weak creatures,' said Mrs Fayre, with a helpless little smile, 'to have someone to *rely* on.'

'We're very lucky,' Roger had agreed dryly, and accepted without protest the implied reflection on his own experience and reliability.

For Mrs Fayre, delicately thirsting as it appeared for vengeance on the miscreant in their midst, had only with difficulty been persuaded, and that not until Twyford himself had been brought in to clinch the argument. The plea of the greater good of the greater number had held small appeal for her. 'We must all suffer, till this dreadful doubt is cleared up.' she had said bravely; and Roger had been forced to be exceedingly firm in his determination to reduce any possible suffering to a minimum.

However, that was all over now, Roger was relieved to think; and so far as Mr Pidgeon's death was concerned, the uneasy word 'murder' might never have spoken at all.

'Oh, no, we never mention it,' Roger had remarked, with some sarcasm to Crystal. 'Its name is never heard. Well, I always said people have short memories.'

'Things do seem to be panning out all right after all,' Crystal had been forced to agree, although it had not been her own advice which had been followed.

Roger had been interested too to notice that his own and Miss Crosspatrick's suspicions concerning Willie Fayre did not appear to have spread to anyone else. Certainly Willie was receiving nothing but sympathy, in his rather awkward position. No sign of cold-shouldering from any quarter had been perceptible.

On the contrary, all was harmony.

The island was too small for any kind of expedition. Indeed, barely five minutes were required to walk right across it. Necessarily therefore people were thrown very much into the general company. Some kind of a break was possible between plateau and beach, but all the latter was overlooked from above. To the beach naturally most of the younger members of the party drifted; bathing and sun-bathing was in progress there all day long, and from the gay colours which decorated it no hint of any sinister background was to be gathered. Moreover, for those in search of private conversation some kind of doubtful privacy could be secured here and there behind some of the larger boulders which littered the base of the cliffs on either side of the inlet.

Roger, still a little on tenterhooks during the first day or two, had watched a certain tendency displaying itself. On the yacht people had been inclined to divide themselves into a number of small groups, or even pairs. Here everyone had seemed to want to remain with the herd. Without any suggestion of huddling together, gregariousness had exercised its appeal. Roger had been relieved. In union, he felt, was strength for jumpy nerves; in isolation, suspicion. When, however, first one couple chipped itself off from the herd, and then another, he had felt no uneasiness. Suspicion, when the company met in full strength for meals and so on, was conspicuously not in evidence. The splitting of the herd was merely a sign of the return to the normal.

Roger, himself making a pair with Crystal after tea on the fourth day, said as much to her as they sat, hugging their knees, on the little knoll on the farther side of the island, their backs propped against the logs of Sir John's beacon.

'Well, I hope you're right,' Crystal returned, with a gloominess quite unlike her usual vivacious optimism.

'Why shouldn't I be right?' Roger demanded.

'Oh, I expect you are. But oh, Roger, my pet, I shall be thankful when this ghastly fortnight is over,' Crystal burst out.

'What on earth's the matter with you, Crystal? Everything's going splendidly. Far better than I expected.'

'Is it? Yes, I suppose it is, really. But...oh, I don't know.'

'You're not jumpy yourself, surely?'

'Yes I am,' Crystal said defiantly. 'I hide it from the others, and I don't think anyone's guessed. But I am – horribly! I could just scream sometimes, when I'm alone in my tent. And at night – oh, my goodness, it's a long time since I wanted Lynn back, but I do here. I positively envy the people with husbands. I – I seem to hear all sorts of things going on...people creeping about round my tent...and whispers...'

Roger, glancing at her uneasily, considered it his duty to speak a fatherly word.

He spoke it.

'Yes, I know,' said Crystal meekly. 'I'm wet.'

'I was afraid a couple of days ago,' Roger said more leniently, 'that I might be going to get a little jumpy myself; but that was solely on account of possible jumpiness in other people. Now that everyone's calmed down, there's nothing to be jumpy about.'

'No, my sweet.'

'But one jumpy person can easily start a whole panic.'

'Yes.'

'Very well, then.'

There was a pause.

'I expect you're absolutely correct, Roger,' said Crystal, still in the meek, little-girl voice. 'Everything's bound to be all right now.'

'Of course it is,' said Roger, not without complacence. After all, he had had no small part in making everything all right.

'Yes,' said Crystal.

She paused again.

'Only I just know it isn't, that's all,' she burst out suddenly. 'There's going to be hell to pay on this damned island before long. Don't ask me how I know. I do know. I'm a journalist, and I've got a sixth sense for these things. I can smell trouble here like an open sewer.'

'Don't be coarse, Crystal,' Roger said lightly. 'Anyhow, what trouble can you smell?'

Crystal hesitated, and then said indignantly:

'Well, *look* at Enid!'

Roger laughed. 'I'm very grateful to Enid,' he said.

2

Roger really was very grateful to Enid. She was keeping no less than six people's minds occupied, including her own; and that, in the circumstances, was useful. Enid was doing it quite without effort. It was, in fact, not Enid's fault that she was not keeping six more minds busy, including Roger's; for Roger, after all, was a man. But Roger, having recently had other things for the occupation of his mind, had not been accepting any invitations.

That she was keeping her husband's mind busy was made obvious to Roger on the fifth morning of the fortnight.

Roger and Willie Fayre were sitting on a nice warm rock, drying themselves in the sun after a not very strenuous bathe. Fayre seemed to have become a little less dejected during the last few days, but was still plainly dispirited. Roger had felt it his duty to be in the little man's company as much as possible, for various reasons. Nobody else seemed to seek him out, for one thing. Certainly his wife did not, though always ready to coo amiably over him when they happened to meet. Roger was afraid that, left alone, Fayre might get too moody; and in any case dejection in any single individual might be bad for the general morale. Besides, Roger was always hoping for some unguarded remark from Fayre which might give him the clue or proof he needed, or might, on the other hand, quite remove such suspicion as still remained on him. Not that this suspicion was still as heavy as it had been. Roger, with some effort, could imagine Fayre perhaps committing a single, desperate murder; he could not see him doing it twice.

Slapping his wet flanks, Roger had glanced round the little cove, gay with the vivid colours of bathing-suits and wraps, among the former of which Unity Vincent's crimson specimen stood out conspicuously in spite of its exiguity.

'Where's Enid?' he asked idly. 'I thought she was down here.'

Willie looked at his toes. 'I think she is.'

'I don't see her.'

'If you looked behind that big rock over there, you'd probably find her,' said Willie, in a flat voice. 'With Bray.'

'Oh. Yes,' said Roger chattily, 'she and Bray seem to get on quite well, don't they? It's curious, in a way. I shouldn't have thought that a woman like Enid would have found anything at all in common with a man of Bray's type.'

'He's rich.'

'Oh, yes, of course he's that.'

Willie was still looking at his toes. 'Women always respect money, don't you think?' he said, almost indifferently.

'That's rather a categorical assertion.'

'I think it's true,' Willie said, without, however, appearing to care very much whether it were or not. 'After all, why not? Money-winning in our times takes the place of knight-errantry in the Middle Ages. It's achievement that women admire, and quite rightly; and when there doesn't happen to be a war on, money-making is the most spectacular achievement, outside sport, open to a man.'

'I wouldn't go so far as to say that, at all,' Roger began argumentatively.

Willie, however, was evidently not inclined for argument. 'No?' was all he would say. 'Well, you may be right. But I don't think I'm wrong in saying that women respect money,' he added. 'They quite obviously do.'

'You mean, that's what Enid and Bray have in common: respect for money?'

'I suppose so. After all, this is Enid's and my first contact with wealth on a big scale. We've always been quite quiet, you know. Not hard up by any means. Comfortable enough for a provincial town like Ficester. But certainly not wealthy.'

Roger nodded. Willie was a wine-merchant, with a small but appallingly respectable family business handed down to him by his forefathers from the days when a wine-merchant was considered a professional man, and the profession itself a perfectly feasible one for a gentleman. Left to himself, Willie would have made no secret of his livelihood, nor indeed did he if he could help it; but Enid (so Mr Pidgeon had wickedly informed Roger) was deadly ashamed of the whole thing, and concealed the gruesome truth whenever possible. She had also tried to persuade her husband to alter his name to Featherstone-Fayre, Featherstone being his second baptismal name; but this, Willie, unexpectedly resistant for once, had refused to do. Mr Pidgeon had taken an unkind pleasure in appealing to Willie or Enid whenever a question arose during the cruise on the matter of wine, with jocular references to his professional capacity.

Suspecting that Willie might be in confidential mood, Roger ventured one blunt question.

'You're worried about Enid, aren't you?' he asked deliberately.

Willie looked up at him in a startled way. 'Worried? No. Why should I be?'

'That I can't say. But you've certainly given the impression of being worried, these last few days.'

'Have I?' Willie said, a little stiffly. 'I really can't imagine why. I'm not worried in the least.'

'Sure there's nothing you'd like to get off your chest?' Roger persisted, still deliberately ignoring all the requirement of good taste.

'Quite sure, thank you,' Willie replied, not without dignity. 'Nothing at all.'

Roger said nothing.

The silence lengthened.

'Well, I suppose I am worried, in a way,' Willie volunteered. 'Not about Enid, of course. That's absurd. But considering the responsibility I feel about Guy...'

'Responsibility?'

'Of course. If there really is any doubt about his death, I am the person responsible for seeing that it is cleared up. You – er – you still really think that there was something unsatisfactory, Sheringham?'

'There's no evidence,' Roger said guardedly, 'one way or the other.'

'No, no. Evidence, no; but...you're not satisfied?'

'At first, candidly, I wasn't. But now I don't know. And in any case, things are settling down so quietly, and people are behaving so well that it's much better to leave things as they are.'

'I suppose so,' Willie sighed. 'And yet if something isn't done now, there's very little chance that it ever will be done.'

'I went into all this with you and Enid,' Roger said gently, recognising the voice of the lady in question. 'You know we decided to leave things well alone.'

'Yes, I know, but – well, it is rather unsatisfactory, I feel. And yet I don't know what I can do.'

'Nothing,' Roger said firmly. 'There's nothing you can do, or any of us.'

'I'm afraid you're right,' Willie said dispiritedly, and returned to his toes.

Roger pondered the conversation.

He did not think he had learned very much from it, except one thing: Willie was acutely worried about his wife.

Was that enough to account for the alteration in him lately? Well, no doubt it might be.

But Roger still suspected that Willie, though he might have had no hand in it himself, knew more about his cousin's death than he had yet divulged. Would he ever divulge it? Roger regretfully considered it in the highest degree unlikely.

And yet somehow he had got from Willie the impression that though he would never willingly divulge what he might know, he would not be at all sorry if it were found out through some other agency.

Roger gave himself a little shake. It was no good indulging in these very impalpable fantasies. Besides, the question of Mr Pidgeon's death was shelved now, definitely shelved, for the good of the community, so it was not the least use speculating about it any more.

3

Mrs Fayre was going to bathe, after her siesta. Mr Parker, who had been sitting outside his tent for the last half-hour with his eyes glued on Mrs Fayre's jumped joyfully to his feet. Mrs Fayre, standing rather helplessly in her doorway, a parasol in one hand, a cushion in the other, and light rug hugged against her pale yellow bathing-robe, sent him a gentle smile of anticipatory gratitude.

'Allow me, Mrs Fayre,' said Mr Parker, possessing himself in a manly way of the cushion and the rug.

Mrs Fayre opened her parasol and drooped it gracefully over one shoulder, as she glanced round the deserted camp. 'How lucky I am,' she said graciously. 'Everyone seems to have disappeared.'

'I'm the lucky one,' returned Mr Parker gallantly. 'I thought perhaps – er – would you care for me to take a chair down to the beach for you?'

'Oh, but that would be far too much trouble.'

'Not in the least, I assure you,' said Mr Parker earnestly, and grabbed up the two chairs which he had placed in readiness half an hour ago.

He walked beside her to the cliffs, swelling with pride. It was the first time that he had not been forestalled, either by Mr Bray himself or by that gloomy Mr Combe, in his attempts to escort Mrs Fayre. And it had been a job to get rid of Unity after lunch too. But he had done it, and here he was. That was what patience and determination could do for a chap.

'What a perfect afternoon,' sighed Mrs Fayre.

'Perfect now you've come out,' mumbled Mr Parker, and instantly turned a brilliant mauve at his own temerity.

But Mrs Fayre did not seem annoyed. On the contrary, she smiled. 'I see Unity's been teaching you how to make pretty speeches, Mr Parker.'

Mr Parker stammered incoherently.

Fortunately at this point the beginning of the path down to the beach threw them into single file, and Mr Parker had a chance to regain his composure and normal colouring. Following on air behind his goddess, he took pride in refusing to let his eyes be so earthy as to linger on the callipygian undulations in front of him, unbelted and free, which the tightly drawn bathrobe enhanced rather than concealed. Mr Parker, thank heaven, was not a Bray or a Combe. No, no.

On the beach Mr Parker led a cunning path as far as possible from the other prone figures which littered the sands, and there dealt manfully with the deck-chairs. Not the most determinedly malicious deck-chair would have had a chance against Mr Parker in that mood.

'I think you'll find that quite satisfactory, Mrs Fayre.'

'Thank you *so* much. That *is* nice.'

Mr Parker seated himself too, and glanced round the cove with shining triumph. He had done it.

'Would you have any objection to my smoking, Mrs Fayre?'

'Of course not. Please do. I like to see men smoking.'

Mr Parker drew cigarettes and matches from the pocket of his bathrobe, and smoked like a man.

'And how is it that you're wasting time on me,' asked Mrs Fayre archly, 'instead of looking after Unity?'

To his own annoyance, Mr Parker at once turned mauve again. 'Not wasting time,' he mumbled. 'Great privilege.'

'Oh, come, Mr Parker! I do believe you're trying to flirt with me.'

Mr Parker was horrified into composure. 'No, really, Mrs Fayre, I assure you. I – oh, no. I wouldn't presume.'

Mrs Fayre's smile changed into a sigh. 'How nice of you. Men are often so funny, you know. They won't let a woman forget that – well, that she *is* a woman. It's very peaceful to be with someone like you, with whom one isn't having to spar all the time.'

'Delighted, I'm sure,' mumbled the intoxicated Mr Parker, beaming with delight.

'But it's absurd for me to go on calling you "Mr Parker," ' Mrs Fayre rallied. 'I shall call you "Harold." After all, we've known each other quite a long time. And besides, I'm almost old enough to be your mother, aren't I?'

'No, no,' cried Mr Parker, outraged. 'You – you look young enough to be – to be anyone.'

'But not so young as Unity? Ah,' sighed Mrs Fayre, 'youth, youth. We don't appreciate it when we have it, and when we do it's too late.'

'You look as young as any girl,' said Mr Parker violently. 'Younger! Besides,' he added recklessly, 'I don't care about young girls. Only old men do. Unity's awfully boring at times.'

'Really, Harold,' said Mrs Fayre, in gentle reproof, 'aren't you being rather unkind? Unity's a sweet girl.'

'She's awfully crude,' said Mr Parker earnestly. 'Crude,' he repeated, pleased with the word. 'Compared with you, that is, if I may say so.'

'You mustn't flatter me, Harold, you know. That isn't fair, between – friends.'

'But I'm not flattering you. Honestly I'm not. It's – I can't tell you what a privilege it is to me to associate with a lady like you. I – I appreciate it very much. You're so beautiful, and – and so *good*. I – it's – shall never forget all this. Never. If – if you'll forgive me saying so.'

'It's very wonderful for me to hear you say it, Harold,' said Mrs Fayre softly. 'Very wonderful.' She gazed in a dreamy way out to sea, apparently heedless of the fact that, perhaps under stress of emotion in the air, her bathrobe had fallen open.

This time it was a very great effort for Mr Parker to keep his eyes fixed on the sea too. But he did it.

Mrs Fayre could not, however, have been quite in ignorance of the candid behaviour on the part of her bathrobe, for she clasped it suddenly round her while her dreamy look turned in a flash to a smile of welcome. Mr Parker, looking round, saw with disgust the figure of Mr Combe slouching across the sand towards them in his faded blue bathing-dress.

Mrs Fayre turned a brilliant smile on him.

'Harold, will you do something for me?'

'Of course, Mrs Fayre,' replied Mr Parker devoutly. 'You have only to name it.'

'Then will you please leave me alone with Mr Combe? It's a terrible bore, but there's something I have to talk about to him quite, quite privately. It's so difficult for me,' added Mrs Fayre, with a sigh, 'for I'm afraid I'm not really a very tactful person. I try, but when people aren't being very nice about something, it's my instinct to speak quite plainly. But then that doesn't always do, does it? You do understand, Harold, don't you?' said Mrs Fayre, in pleading tones.

'Of course,' Mr Parker replied stoutly, but not altogether with truth, as he rose. 'It's a dreadful position for you, I quite realise. If there's anything I can do ever, I assure you there's no trouble that...'

'That's very sweet of you, Harold. We must have another talk some time,' said Mrs Fayre brightly.

With noble altruism in every step, Mr Parker strode away.

Mr Combe in his turn dropped into the vacant chair.

'You got rid of him very smartly,' he said, in a grudging way.

'Really, Valentine!' returned Mrs Fayre coquettishly. 'How do you know I got rid of him at all?'

Mr Combe contemplated her morosely. 'Take your wrap off, Enid. You're far too beautiful to go about draped when it isn't necessary.'

4

'I suppose you know I love you,' said Mr Combe.

Enid gazed out to sea. 'Ought you to say that kind of thing to me *now?*' she asked in a low voice.

'What do you mean, *"now"?*'

'I mean, considering how we're situated here.'

'I don't care a damn how we're situated. I say what I think.'

'Life is very difficult,' sighed Mrs Fayre.

'You're right,' agreed Mr Combe violently. 'It is. Damned difficult.'

'My husband...your wife...'

'Oh, I'm not proposing marriage. Marriage with you would be impossible.'

'Indeed? Why?'

'You're too beautiful,' said Mr Combe simply.

Mrs Fayre nodded slowly twice. 'I understand,' she said softly.

'Well, if you do, you're the first person who ever has. My God, Enid, the agonies I've gone through just on account of lack of understanding in the other person.'

'I know.' Mrs Fayre's voice was sweet and low, and very understanding. 'Life hasn't been too – easy, for me either.' If Mrs Fayre was thinking of the wine-merchant's business, she did not say so.

'You're wasted on that little nincompoop, you know.'

'Please, Valentine! I'm very fond of Willie. Besides...'

'What?'

'One has one's duty, hasn't one?' sighed Mrs Fayre.

'Duty!' Mr Combe snorted so violently that his deck-chair only just bore the strain. 'There's more cant talked in the name of duty than anything else. Duty! You're as bad as Sheringham.'

'Don't you like Mr Sheringham, Valentine?'

'No, I don't. I think he's the most offensive, bouncing bounder I've ever met. And I don't consider he's shown up at all well over your cousin's death.'

'Oh, I am glad you think that, Valentine. You can see how dreadful it is for me to know that one of my guests here is a – a murderer. I never forget it for a moment. The strain is terrible, trying to keep a normal face to the world. But Mr Sheringham wouldn't even listen when I said that our first duty must be to avenge poor, poor Guy.'

'I can't forget it either,' yelped Mr Combe. 'Of course you and I – we're different, more highly strung. We naturally feel a strain more than these insensitive brutes. My God, I wish sometimes that I wasn't so sensitive. We poor devils do get the thin end of life.'

'But then you wouldn't have been able to write your poetry,' Mrs Fayre reminded him gently.

'Would that have been such a very great loss to the world?' demanded Mr Combe, with bitterness.

'Valentine!'

'My God, Enid, it's really wonderful to come across someone like you. If you could only guess what we poor devils of poets suffer through lack of appreciation. Of course one doesn't expect to *sell*, not in this benighted country. But just to know that one's thoughts have got home somewhere – that one reader at any rate has appreciated the naked soul one's torn in half to offer them. And yet I suppose one would go on, just the same, in any case. If the poetry's there, it's got to come out, however agonising its birth. One can't control that sort of thing.'

'But Valentine, there must be hundreds of people who appreciate your beautiful work. Thousands.'

'Are there? You evidently don't realise the mental level against which an artist – any kind of artist in our country – has to contend.'

'But your wife?'

'My wife!' This time Mr Combe's snort was so violent that it provoked response, as it were, from the very winds.

'Got a cold?' asked a languidly solicitous voice behind the pair. 'I thought myself the water was a shade parky this morning. I wondered afterwards if we hadn't stayed in too long. I'm not going to bathe again today, just in case.'

'Oh, hullo, Twyford,' growled Mr Combe.

5

'Got rid of him very neatly,' drawled Captain Twyford, with lazy appreciation. He stretched himself comfortably in the chair just vacated by Mr Combe.

'Really, Captain Twyford! How do you know I got rid of him at all?'

Captain Twyford regarded her from under half-closed eyelids. 'About time we made it Reggie and Enid, isn't it?'

'If you really want to,' said Mrs Fayre demurely.

Captain Twyford's eyelids closed altogether.

'I don't think you ought to be wasting your time on me, Reggie, ought you?' suggested Mrs Fayre. 'Where's Angela?'

'Don't know. Don't care.'

'I expect she's looking for you.'

'I expect she is.'

'I shall be getting into trouble, you know,' persevered Mrs Fayre brightly.

'I'll back you up.'

'That might make it worse.'

'There are times,' pronounced Captain Twyford, with unusual animation, 'when I want a rest from Angela.'

Mrs Fayre nodded sympathetically. 'Yes, one does feel like that sometimes. Even with the people one – loves.'

'I don't love Angela,' said Captain Twyford, with candour, and added somewhat inconsequentially: 'You look stupefying in a bathing-dress, Enid. Know that?'

'Reggie, you *will* get me into trouble. I believe in a minute you'll be trying to flirt with me.'

'Trying now,' yawned Captain Twyford.

6

Mr Bray dropped into the chair vacated by Captain Twyford. 'Managed that all right,' he said with complacence. 'I knew she'd haul him off double-quick, if someone tipped her off.'

'That was very naughty of you.'

'Perhaps you don't mind so much, though, eh?'

'Well – perhaps.'

Mr Bray disposed his large limbs more comfortably.

'Well, how have things been lately?'

'It's very, very beautiful here.'

You know what I mean. Willie.'

'One always has one's – difficulties, hasn't one?'

'Poor little woman! It's a damned shame.'

Mrs Fayre uttered a short, brave laugh. 'It's life, isn't it?'

'He still won't back you up?'

'He says he spoke to Mr Sheringham again this morning, and Mr Sheringham refused to do anything. Willie says he must support him.'

'Huh! Something fishy there, if you ask me.'

'Oh, please...'

'I mean, Sheringham shutting things down like that.'

'Mr Sheringham is just a little bit trying, perhaps. But we mustn't be unfair, must we? No doubt he really does think he is acting for the best. He just doesn't realise what this suspense means to – some of us.'

'You know, I think it's fine of you to be so upset about your cousin – considering, I mean, that you don't come in for a bean from him.' It was common knowledge now that to Mr and Mrs Fayre the death of their wealthy relative made not a ha'-porth of difference. Mrs Fayre had seen that it should be.

'But really, what has that to do with it?' Enid asked now, with innocent surprise.

'Well, I think it's a damned shame. Not that I'd say anything against our dear old pal for the world now he's dead, but on my word, when he's got a fine girl like you in the family to leave his money to, why on earth did he want to go and leave it to the Cats' Home or wherever it is? A damned shame, I call it.'

Mrs Fayre sighed, and then smiled wistfully. 'After all, it was his money. If he thought the nation was more important than his own cousin, why shouldn't he? I dare say it didn't seem as grotesque to him as – well, as it may do to others.'

'Well, I must say you're being pretty wonderful about it. And about everything else too, come to that.'

'One tries to do one's best. One tries to show a brave face to the world. Luckily the world seldom understands.'

'Poor little woman! Well, I understand you all right, don't I?'

'I sometimes wonder whether I even understand myself. I'm – it's silly, I suppose, but I really am so terribly reserved, even with myself.'

'I bet you are. Think I haven't noticed it? But they say travel broadens one a lot.'

'That isn't quite what I meant.'

'Well, anyhow, let's hope it doesn't broaden Gladys any more, eh?'

'Ah, your wife. She's a very, very lucky woman, isn't she? I wonder if she realises.'

Mr Bray smiled complacently. 'There's not much she's got to complain about, I fancy.'

'No, indeed. She's wonderful. But I think you're wonderful too.'

'Well, I don't know about that. Perhaps I have got on a bit more than most. But that isn't saying I might have got on further still, if...'

'If what?' prompted Mrs Fayre gently.

'Well, if I'd had the right wife. Not that I'm saying a word against Gladys, mind. She's a good girl, in her way. But...'

'Yes?'

'Well, what mightn't I have done if I'd had a wife like you.'

Mrs Fayre sighed. 'Life is very, very difficult.'

'Perhaps it isn't too late, even now, eh?'

'What do you mean?'

'Well, look here, here's a proposition,' suggested Mr Bray, somewhat thickly. 'What about us joining up? I can tell you, I've been thinking about it. You're the woman for me. You're wasted on that little worm of a husband of yours. Gladys'd do the right thing, if I put it to her straight. And it's the least

Willie could do for you. What do you say about it? I can give you money, clothes, a good time, anything you like. And you know as well as I do what you could give me. Tone! That's what I want in my wife. And, of course, between you and I, Gladys hasn't got it. Eh? What do you say?'

'Mr Bray!' said Enid faintly.

'Harry.'

'Harry!'

'Well?'

'This is very, very sweet of you, but...'

'But what? What's the odds?'

'I feel we oughtn't to be talking of such things, *now*.'

'What do you mean, "*now*"?'

'I mean, considering how we're situated here.'

'How's that?'

'Well, with poor, poor Guy...'

'But that hasn't anything to do with us two.'

'Oh, Harry, can you forget for one minute? I can't. And can you forget that one of us here – it might be you, it might be me – is a *murderer?* I can't. Oh, I only wish I could. And yet nobody will do anything. Oh, it's dreadful, dreadful.'

'Don't cry, little woman. Don't cry.'

'One tries to be brave, but this dreadful, dreadful suspense...'

'Look here, if I can get things cleared up, will you consider that proposition I put to you?'

'Oh, but really, Harry, I didn't mean...'

'No, of course not. But will you?'

'I – I...'

'They'll get no change out of yours truly. I'll fix it for you. And then, you'll give me your answer to that proposition?'

Mr Bray eyed the beautiful figure in the chair next to him with the gratification of anticipatory proprietorship.

Mrs Fayre wriggled modestly.

'Harry, I can't promise anything. One is so dreadfully torn. After all, one has one's duty. Willie...'

'Damn Willie,' replied Mr Bray heartily.

'And Gladys...'

'And damn Gladys too!'

chapter eleven

Mrs Fayre, gracefully manipulating the articles on the tea-tray, looked across the marquee with a hostess-like smile.

'Mrs Bray? Let me see, you take two lumps, don't you?'

'Yes, please.'

Miss Crosspatrick gave her a glance which seemed to slide over the whole of Mrs Bray's tight compactness. 'Well, you shouldn't,' she observed indifferently. She took off her spectacles and polished them with the air of one who has just performed a helpful act.

Mrs Bray breathed a little rapidly, but managed to say nothing. She liked sugar, yes, and cream too (though she did not much like the condensed milk to which the party was now reduced), just as she liked the other good things of life in which she had been able to indulge since Harry got so rich; and she did not see why she should not have them. Not for all the Stella Crosspatricks in the world she didn't. Organiser, indeed! It was a pity Miss Crosspatrick could not organise herself into a lady, in the presence of ladies. What ever could Lady Darracott think of her?

Mrs Fayre produced some nicely calculated tact.

'Dear me, I wonder where Unity is. Do you happen to know, Harold?'

Mr Parker, thus publicly addressed for the first time, hurriedly swallowed a large piece of tinned cake the wrong way. 'Sorry, I don't,' he mumbled, between coughs.

'I believe I saw her near the beacon,' said Crystal, coming to Mrs Fayre's support. She went to the open side of the marquee and looked vaguely out. 'Unity! Unity!'

Mr Bray had risen efficiently, with a smile of tender helpfulness towards his hostess.

'Unity!' called Crystal. 'Tea!'

'Unity!' bawled Mr Bray.

'Unity!' squeaked Mr Combe.

'Coming,' answered a distant voice and everyone sat down again.

A few minutes later Miss Vincent sauntered in, still in the scanty scarlet bathing-dress.

'Sorry I'm late,' she said, with great airiness, and throwing a single glance of contempt at Mr Parker's now elegantly white-flannelled form. 'I was sun-bathing near the banana patch. Excuse the bathing-dress, Mrs Fayre.'

'Of course,' said Mrs Fayre graciously.

'It's too gorgeous, being able to live in a bathing-dress all day,' pursued Miss Vincent to the company at large, as she sprawled into a chair. '(Is that my tea? Oh, thanks awfully, Mrs Fayre.) Yes, why don't you, Stella?'

'I'm afraid,' enunciated Miss Crosspatrick, with a gentle smile, 'that I haven't got the musical-comedy mind.'

'It isn't a musical-comedy mind you want for a bathing-dress,' retorted Miss Vincent. 'It's musical-comedy legs.' She stretched out her own two slim specimens in example.

Miss St Thomas produced her little black notebook. 'That's quite good, Unity,' she approved. 'Mind if I use it?'

'Oh, delighted. Don't mind me.'

Mr Bray guffawed. 'Yes, one up to you, Unity. Hear that, Lady Darracott? Musical-comedy mind, and musical-comedy legs. See? Yes, had you there, Miss Crosspatrick.'

Miss Crosspatrick raised her thick eyebrows and smiled patiently, as one bearing with a moron.

'Fancy me saying something worth hearing,' observed Miss Vincent.

There was an edge in her voice which mildly surprised Roger. Unity was normally an amiable young colt. He wondered what had happened to upset her.

'What do you think of doing after tea, Lady Darracott?' enquired Enid politely.

'Thank you, I have quite an interesting book. I shall sit in the doorway of my tent. Sir John and I are lucky in having the view of the sea from our tents.'

'Huh,' confirmed Sir John, applying himself to his second whisky-and-soda.

'I'm *sick* of reading,' observed Unity, with some force. 'And bathing. And talking. Can't anyone suggest something new? Not even a wireless…'

Angela St Thomas threw a knowing glance at Roger. 'The confinement's beginning to tell,' she remarked clearly. 'I thought it would, soon.'

'Something's beginning to tell,' said Unity, in a disgruntled voice. 'I'm bored stiff.'

'That's not a very nice thing to say, Unity,' reproved Crystal, though with a smile, 'in the presence of your hostess.'

'Oh, my hostess doesn't have to be bored. She can always find something to amuse her. Or someone.' The edge in Miss Vincent's voice showed so jaggedly that one could not mistake it.

'It's no good beginning to grouse, Unity,' Roger soothed hastily. 'We're all in the same boat.'

'Are we?' said Miss Vincent nastily.

'I wish to goodness we were, ' added Mr Combe. 'Why on earth didn't we put in at Madeira when we had the chance? We might never have got to this benighted hole at all, then.'

'Because Miss Crosspatrick didn't want to, that's why,' supplied Mrs Bray.

Miss Crosspatrick cocked a quizzical eye. 'I was under the impression that you were opposed to the idea too, at the time.'

'Well?' demanded Mrs Bray truculently. 'And what if I was?'

'Are you ready for some more tea, Mrs Bray?' enquired Enid, in a voice just too dulcet.

Mrs Bray turned a hostile look on her. 'No, I thank you. And what I want to know is, what if I didn't want to stop at Madeira? There's others who didn't want eether. You didn't want yourself, Harry, till you found out that Mrs Fayre did.'

'Now then, stop that, Gladys.'

'Why should I? I didn't want to stop at Madeira, and I don't care who knows it.'

'Yes, but that hardly matters now, does it?' said Roger, with a somewhat forced smile.

'Doesn't it? There's some, apparently, as seems to think it does. And maybe I do myself.' Mrs Bray knew that her manner was getting a little unrefined; but no wonder, thought Mrs Bray to herself, breathing rather rapidly. It was difficult to remember that one was a lady, watching Harry making eyes at Mrs Fayre like that, and with all the others looking on too.

'That'll do, Gladys,' frowned Mr Bray.

'Why?' It was Miss Crosspatrick herself who had come to Mrs Bray's rescue. 'Why shouldn't your wife say what she thinks, Mr Bray? This isn't the Victorian age, you know. I expect,' said Miss Crosspatrick kindly, 'that you thought as I did, Mrs Bray, that Madeira was altogether too stereotyped. What I wanted to do was to get off the beaten track: genuine natives in an unsophisticated environment. Don't you agree?'

'Genuine natives?' Mrs Bray turned the words over doubtfully.

'Not oysters. Human beings,' explained Miss Crosspatrick languidly.

'Oysters!' guffawed Mr Bray loudly. 'Ho! That's good, that is. Hear that, Lady Darracott? Oysters or human beings – natives.' Mr Bray was always careful to explain jokes to Lady Darracott. In the drab life of a semi-invalid, Mr Bray appeared to think, a joke is as good as a tonic; and it was not going to be his fault if she did not see the humour of them.

'Very amusing,' agreed Lady Darracott, with the slightly bewildered air which Mr Bray always seemed to induce in her. She glanced, with her usual effect of appealing for help, at Sir John Birch in the chair next to her.

'Huh!' observed Sir John Birch shortly, by way of appreciation, and applied himself to his third whisky-and-soda.

'Oysters!' repeated Mr Bray, with gusto.

'I'm sure,' Crystal said gently, 'that Mrs Bray didn't mean oysters.'

'Well, of course not,' said the flushing Mrs Bray, with all the natural indignation of one who had been wondering why on earth Miss Crosspatrick should want to go and look at unsophisticated oyster-beds near the Canary Islands.

'I once thought of writing a prose-poem on an oyster,' gloomily confided Mr Combe to Roger. 'A kind of subaqueous parallel to *The Life of the Bee*, ending with its reactions to being swallowed alive.'

'I don't suppose an oyster has many reactions,' Roger said politely, 'but if it did, no doubt they would be quite sensational. You could draw a comparison with Jonah, couldn't you?'

'*Jonah!*' snorted Mr Combe, with such remarkable scorn that Roger wondered what literary *gaffe* he had committed to Mr Combe's sensitive mind.

Mrs Bray, sipping her tea, glanced in an unwifely manner at her still guffawing husband. Then she glanced, with a look positively unladylike, at Miss Crosspatrick herself. It was the limit, the way that Miss Crosspatrick was always interfering. A regular busybody, that's what she was, with her silly drawl and her la-di-dah talk; and not a real aristocrat, either, like Miss St Thomas; just a stuck-up busybody. Trying to come between husband and wife, indeed. What with Miss Crosspatrick and that Mrs Fayre – well, what next, Mrs Bray wondered.

'And I didn't want to look at natives, eether,' she said crossly, 'genuine or not. *I* wanted to go to – ' She racked her brains for a town on the coast of Spain. 'Valparaiso!'

A strange sound emerged from Crystal, hastily converted into a cough. Roger avoided her eye.

'Valparaiso?' repeated Willie Fayre. 'Indeed?'

'How romantic,' sighed Mrs Fayre. 'Valparaiso...' She caught Mr Parker's eye, and smiled wistfully. Mr Parker instantly turned a brilliant mauve.

Captain Twyford uncorked one of the eyes which he had kept closed since he had finished his tea. 'Bit of a long trek,' he yawned.

Beside him, Miss St Thomas produced her little black book and looked over Mrs Bray with fresh interest. 'I do think geography's terribly dim,' she said, as she made her note. 'Don't you?'

'I think Mrs Bray means Barcelona.' It was a bore, Miss Crosspatrick's tone implied, to have to be constantly putting the fools of this world right, but one has one's duty.

'I don't mean Barcelona – I mean Valparaiso. Why not, I should like to know?' Mrs Bray's tone was shrill, her eyes defiant. She did wish she knew where Valparaiso was, but wherever it might be it was nailed now to Mrs Bray's mast.

'A connection of mine was sent once to Valparaiso on a diplomatic mission,' said Lady Darracott firmly and clearly. 'He came back saying that he never wished to visit South America again. I'm sure I don't know why.'

There was a dead silence. Then Sir John said briefly:

'Dagoes. Never cared for 'em myself. You ever been to South America, Twyford?'

Roger looked at Lady Darracott with respect. It was just as if that frail lady had taken the heads of the company and banged them together, and then stood their owners in the corner. Moreover, Sir John had known precisely what was required of him, and done it.

But it had been a nasty ten minutes. And all provoked by that little fool, Unity. Roger made up his mind to speak to Unity very straightly; after tea.

2

'Well, what do you expect?' Crystal snapped in the kitchen-tent later. 'People are bound to get on each other's nerves, without anything else. What you'd better do is to speak straight to Enid, not Unity. If the fool can't see the volcano she's stirring up, someone had better tell her.'

'Then you'd better,' Roger snapped back. 'You're responsible for us being cooped up here.'

Crystal made a woebegone grimace. 'Darling, *don't* speak to me like that. I just can't bear it.'

'Well, don't snap at me,' said Roger morosely.

'Roger, my *lamb!*'

Roger smiled, rather one-sidedly. 'Sorry, Crystal. No, it's no use us going on like that. Somehow or other we've got to hold the reins between us. People are getting restive. I wonder if we could get some games of some kind going? That might help, with Unity and so on. I'll speak to Twyford about it. And what's more,' said Roger firmly, 'I'll speak to him straight.'

3

At the same moment, in Miss Crosspatrick's tent, a strange alliance was being formed.

'Mind you,' said Mr Combe, 'it's not my business, but I happen to know the man's annoying her with his attentions, and if we aren't careful that ghastly wife of his is going to make a row in public. Not that one can altogether blame her. The man's making a perfect exhibition of himself.'

'I quite agree. I try not to dislike Mrs Fayre, because I try not to dislike anyone, and – "

'Mrs Fayre's all right,' interposed Mr Combe hotly. 'It's Bray.'

' – and I'm quite indifferent to the moral aspect. But this is a matter affecting the community because, as you rightly suggest, Mrs Bray may make an impossible situation for all of us.'

'My God, why can't people behave themselves? Here we are, cooped up here. Why can't people behave decently? *I* don't want to make trouble for other people. Why should anyone else? The situation's bad enough as it is, with a murderer loose among us.'

'Precisely. So you want me to speak to Mr Bray?'

'I'd do it myself, like a shot, but he might misunderstand. I mean, I think it would come better from you, Stella.'

'I understand. Very well, I'll speak to Mr Bray quite straight.'

4

'Angela.'

'Yes, auntie?'

'I'm a little worried, dear.'

'Well, I'm not surprised. I thought there was going to be a real blaze at tea.'

'Oh, I don't mean that.'

'Oh, I see. Well, it certainly is a bit lousy for you. I'm not saying I'm not a bit panicky myself sometimes, especially at night, though I have got Reggie on the spot. I try not to get strenuous about it, but it really is a bit dim. Personally, I think it's that crashing cad Bray, but Reggie's got hold of the idea that it's a woman.'

'Who is a woman, dear?'

'Why, our pet murderer.'

'Oh, I see. Oh, no, that isn't what's worrying me.'

'You mean, you're not even a tiny bit panicky?'

'No, dear. Why should I be? No one could want to murder a helpless old woman like me.'

'You're not old, auntie. Well, I wish some of the others felt like that. Reggie says everyone's got the wind up really, though they're not showing it. He admits he's got the wind up himself. That's what I like about Reggie: he's too big to hide the fact that he's afraid.'

'Really, dear? Well, I suppose that's very honest of him; though I must admit I'm a little surprised. I should have thought the situation here was very tame to Reggie, after the adventures he's had.'

'He says it's quite different somehow. He says – '

'Yes, dear. But I was telling you that I'm rather worried. Not about our pet murderer, as you call him, in the least, but about Johnnie Birch.'

'Sir John?'

'Yes. Really, Angela, it wasn't a kind thing on Mr Pidgeon's part to put him in charge of the drinks.'

'He can lap it up, certainly.'

'He can, and he does. He's drinking far too much, Angela.'

'Well I don't see what we can do about it. Would you like me to tell Reggie to put someone else in charge of the drinks?'

'I'm afraid that might not be any good. You see, it's very foolish of Johnnie, but I don't think he very much cares for Reggie. There might be a quarrel.'

'Well, what else can we do?'

'I'm afraid someone will have to speak to Johnnie.'

'He wouldn't take that from anyone but you.'

'No, I'm afraid he wouldn't. And very probably not from me. But still, I must try,' sighed Lady Darracott. 'And I shan't mince my words. I shall speak to him quite straight.'

5

There was a great deal of straight speaking on the island between tea and dinner that day.

Roger came in for his share of it. Summoned, as if by royal command, to Mr Bray's tent, he was made acquainted with that gentleman's orders.

'I'm sorry,' said Roger, a little white but managing to control his temper. 'I can't take the responsibility.'

'You can't?' Mr Bray approached his face very close to Roger's. 'But I'm telling you.'

'I'm sorry.'

'You refuse, do you?'

'I refuse. And if you don't take your face away,' said Roger, as equably as he could, 'I shall probably hit it. And perhaps I ought to warn you that I very nearly got my half-blue for boxing.'

'Then get out!' roared Mr Bray, removing his face. 'Get out of my tent, you...'

'Yes?'

'Get out,' said Mr Bray more temperately.

Roger got somewhat perturbed. Things seemed suddenly to be boiling up, and for no apparent reason.

'Sheringham!'

Roger paused, and turned round. 'Well?'

'No good losing our tempers. Sorry if I was a bit strong. I'm used to giving orders, and having 'em obeyed.'

'Oh, that's all right.' Roger made as if to go on.

'No, wait a minute. I'd like you to come and speak to Mrs Fayre. It's her who wants the investigation, after all. Come and talk it over with her.'

'But we've discussed it all once. I can't see any point in going over the same arguments again.'

'That's right. Still, just come along and let's hear what she's got to say.'

Tucking his arm through Roger's, now in the most friendly way, Mr Bray propelled that unwilling gentleman across the alleyway to the tent of their hostess.

'Very well, I'll speak to Mrs Fayre,' Roger said suddenly, 'but it must be alone.'

'Alone, eh?' Mr Bray repeated doubtfully. 'All right, have it your own way. Enid, here's Mr Sheringham wants to talk to you – alone.'

Enid appeared in the opening of her tent. 'Of course. Come inside, Mr Sheringham.'

'Thanks, this will do.' Roger leant against the tent-pole, whence he could make sure that nobody was loitering around to overhear. He looked at Enid without love.

Enid's eyes were swimming; she held out her hands. 'Mr Sheringham, surely, surely you'll do this little thing for me. We know how wonderful you are. Surely you won't refuse to put your great gifts at our disposal.'

'We had it settled. Why do you want to alter it?' Roger asked, disregarding this appeal equally with the outstretched hands.

'Need you ask that?' said Enid, in a low voice.

'Yes.'

'You know I never agreed with what was settled. It was against all my feelings. You imposed your will on me then, Mr Sheringham, but I can't rest, I can't – '

'Just tell me quite plainly *why* you want the investigation to proceed, Mrs Fayre,' Roger interrupted. 'Just that. Why?'

'Mr Sheringham! You don't seem to realise that Guy was my cousin – that I was very , very fond of him – that... Oh, surely you can see why my conscience won't let me rest with his death unavenged.'

'It's just that, then? that you want his death avenged?'

'Isn't that enough?' asked Enid reproachfully.

'Frankly, no, it isn't. You don't seem to realise, Mrs Fayre, that we're sitting on a volcano here: a volcano of nerves. And it may go up at any minute. I absolutely refuse to take any hand in helping to send it off.'

'And you think that an investigation would do that?'

'I do.'

A faint relief made itself apparent on Mrs Fayre's face, somewhat to Roger's surprise. Mrs Fayre had had, in point of fact, some difficulty in explaining the precise reason for her urgency that the investigation should continue. Mrs Fayre never admitted even to herself unworthy thoughts; she had therefore refused to recognise that her distress over Guy dead, about whom in life she had before he came into his fortune known very little and cared less, was due simply to her sense of what is fitting. Relations mourn over dead relations; a victim's kin swear to leave no stone unturned to avenge him on his murder; beautiful ladies of high sensibility are extremely distressed when brought into contact with violence and sudden death – perhaps even more so when they regrettably do not benefit by it. Naturally therefore Enid was distressed; naturally she mourned her dead; naturally she was urgent that vengeance must be pursued at all costs. But if Mr Sheringham had not the wit to recognise high sensibility when he was up against it, Enid could not very well explain further.

She therefore looked her relief at the glimpse of a loophole thus offered her.

'Then you think I ought to sacrifice my own feelings, and let poor, poor Guy's death go unavenged?'

'Temporarily. Yes, I do.'

'It will be very, very difficult,' sighed Mrs Fayre.

'It would be a noble renunciation on your part, Mrs Fayre,' said Roger, leaping swiftly for his cue.

'But then that's life, isn't it?' Mrs Fayre smiled sadly.

'That is life,' Roger agreed, with due gravity.

'Then I will.' Mrs Fayre held out a hand at arm's length.

Roger, not quite sure what he was expected to do with it, shook it heartily. He turned to go.

Then, thinking the moment propitious, he made a fatal error. He turned back.

'Oh, and by the way, Mrs Fayre, about that volcano.'

'Yes?'

'I should lay off Bray,' Roger said bluntly, making up his mind almost as he spoke that blunt methods would serve him best. 'Mrs Bray's not only capable of making trouble; she will make it. Even Unity had better not be provoked. We've all got to be uncommonly circumspect, you know, if we're to get through the rest of this fortnight without squalls, and the tiniest quick-match can fire the biggest mine.' Roger smiled pleasantly.

Mrs Fayre, however, was not smiling. She had drawn herself up to the full of her not inconsiderable height, and her eyes were blazing.

'Mr Sheringham, do you *dare* to suggest that...*oh!* Leave my tent at once, please.'

Roger left it.

She couldn't have done that better if she'd been really innocent – not so well, he thought with appreciation. Of course; she had to do it. But that's all right. She's not such a fool as not to recognise sense when she hears it.

6

It appeared that Roger had overestimated Mrs Fayre's capabilities for recognising sense when she heard it.

'The little idiot went straight across to Bray,' he told Crystal, in some perturbation. 'The only inference is that she told him. Now what's going to happen?'

'The fat's in the fire, of course. You seem to have messed things up nicely, my pet.'

'It was you who told me to speak to Enid straight.'

'Don't blame it on me.'

'Anyhow, what's going to happen? I don't want a stand-up fight with Bray. I think I could knock him out easily enough, but it would make things awkward.'

'And how. Awkward, my lamb, is the word. Well, I suppose I'd better see what I can do to smoothe her down.'

'I wish you would.'

'Is she with Bray now?'

'No. I saw Stella disappear into Bray's tent, and the next minute Enid came out. He's holding a regular reception.'

'What did Stella want?'

'Heaven knows. Oh, and Crystal – when you've smoothed Enid down, you might do the same to Unity. She's feeling sore, and I don't want her and Harold slinging saucepans at each other while we're getting dinner ready.'

'All right. I'll ask her to do the dinner tonight because I'm too occupied, though she's really off duty this evening. That'll keep her busy. And I'll give Harold special leave off. Can you and she manage?'

'I should think so.'

'It's quite an easy dinner tonight. And by the way, I'll say a word to our Gladys too. She's sorer still.'

'We're going to have a lovely dinner-party,' Roger groaned.

7

The various squads had been organised as follows: Kitchen: Crystal, Unity, Harold Parker and Roger. Scullery: Mrs Bray, Miss Crosspatrick, Willie Fayre and Combe. Parlour: Enid, Angela St Thomas, Twyford and Bray.

Roger performed his duties that evening in a continued state of uneasiness, which the obvious gloom of Miss Vincent did nothing to relieve. He opened a large quantity of tins, including seven of kippers, changed a refractory wick on the oil-cooker, fetched water for saucepans and kettles, almost without a word on either side.

Once Angela St Thomas poked her head in from the dining-marquee to make a complaint.

'I say, it's a bit dim, you know. Enid hasn't shown up. Doesn't she know she's supposed to be on duty this evening?'

'Which duty?' asked Miss Vincent unpleasantly. 'She's got so many.'

'Shut up, Unity. I think she's busy, Angela. Are you short-handed?'

'Oh, I've got Reggie here, but he's about as much use as an ear-trumpet to a blind man. Well, I suppose I can manage.'

She disappeared again.

'It's funny,' Roger remarked idly. 'Twyford doesn't really seem to shine at any of the things which you'd expect from a man who's had to fend for himself in all sorts of impenetrable jungles.'

'He doesn't like camping,' Unity said darkly. 'I know he was as sick as mud when the boat went off. I'm not at all sure it wasn't he who pushed Mr Pidgeon over the cliff, out of revenge for bringing us here at all.'

'Oh, for heaven's sake leave that topic alone,' Roger said crossly.

'That's easy enough, isn't it?' retorted Miss Vincent. 'Considering no one ever seems to talk of anything else.'

Roger looked at her. 'Do they talk about it?'

'Don't they just! Not to you, because everyone's been told they're not to mention it to you, but – '

'Who said they weren't to mention it to me?'

'Reggie Twyford.'

'But why not?'

'Oh, I don't know. He said something about you not wanting to discuss it, or some rot. Seriously, Roger, didn't you ask him to put that round? I wonder if he did do it, you know. I wouldn't put it past him for a minute.'

'So everyone's talking about it still, are they?' said Roger thoughtfully.

'Yes, and I wish to goodness they'd shut up,' Unity burst out, with sudden violence. 'I can tell you, I'm getting about fed up.'

8

Since the first evening, when Sir John Birch and Twyford had turned up for dinner in boiled shirts and the other men had not, everyone had tacitly undertaken the Englishman's privilege and duty of putting on a dinner-jacket in the wilder places of the earth.

As Roger, having finished with his tins and left the rest of the preparations to Unity, was fitting studs into a clean shirt, he heard voices raised in altercation from the farther end of the camp. He looked out of his tent, and was aware of other heads protruding tortoise-wise. Miss St Thomas caught his eye across the alleyway, and shrugged her shoulders.

'Sounds like a crashing row,' she observed.

'Who is it?'

'Coming from Enid's tent, isn't it?'

Mr Combe interposed: 'No, Fayre's, I think.'

'Fayre's?' Roger whistled, and wondered whether he ought to do anything about it. After all, why on earth should he? 'Who's with him? It sounds like a woman.'

'It's only Mr and Mrs Fayre,' supplied Miss Crosspatrick, and disappeared back into her tent.

'My God,' said Mr Combe shrilly, 'if he's beating her up...'

'Much more likely she's beating him, don't you think?' drawled Captain Twyford. 'Better keep out of it, Combe.'

At that instant the flap of Mr Fayre's tent was flung violently open, and Mrs Fayre stalked out.

Instantly every tortoise-head shot back into its shell.

Roger, resuming his studs, pondered on the two very obvious facts that (*a*) decently civilised married couples do not quarrel shrilly within earshot of a dozen other people, (*b*) decently civilised other people do not crane their heads towards a marital broil: they pretend not to hear it. What Roger wanted to know was whether the claims of decent civilisation were beginning to lose their grip.

chapter twelve

Contrary to Roger's fears, dinner passed off quite peacefully. There was a good deal of stiff politeness in evidence, but nothing more.

The trouble began when dinner was over.

The two decanters of port, placed with some ceremony on the table by Sir John's own hands, had hardly begun to circulate, when Mr Bray rose to his feet and, to Roger's dismay, faced the assembly with frowning portentousness. The thing was evidently concerted, for Mrs Fayre herself rapped delicately on the table for silence.

'Ladies and gentlemen,' boomed Mr Bray, 'I'm sorry to have to ask you to give me your attention for a few moments, but there's something that's got to be said, and the sooner the better.' Mr Bray glared round in a truculent way.

'Now, first of all, there's two people here who've seen fit to take exception to the conduct of certain of us here. For all I know there may be more, but there's two at any rate who've come out in the open.' Mr Bray turned his glare deliberately first upon Roger, and then upon Miss Crosspatrick. Miss Crosspatrick smiled.

The smile seemed to goad Mr Bray, for his florid face took on a deeper tinge in the lamplight. It was also regrettably evident that Mr Bray had been priming himself for the ordeal of a public speech.

'Well, I'll say here and now,' roared Mr Bray, clutching the back of his chair, 'that that's a thing I won't stand, reflections on my conduct isn't. Never have, and never will, and what's more, if anyone else doesn't like it, I'll knock his block off. Yes, or hers either. All right, you may grin: you'll see. And what's more – '

'Bray!' Sir John's wheezy grunt brought Mr Bray up in mid-sentence.

'Well?'

'Sit down.'

'Were you addressing me, Sir John?'

'Yes, I was. Sit down, you bloody man.'

Mr Bray gaped, swallowed and deflated. 'But I've got an announcement to make,' he said tamely.

'Sit down. We don't want to hear you, or your announcements. Not interested. Combe, the port's by you.'

Mr Bray hung as it were suspended. 'See here, Sir John,' he almost pleaded, 'I've got an announcement to make on behalf of Mrs Fayre. She's asked me to make it.'

'Then make it, but keep yourself and your conduct out of it. No one's interested. Combe, I asked you to pass the port.'

Mr Bray gulped. Roger felt quite sorry for him. Even his dinner-jacket, as if sharing the general reaction, did not seem to fit him so well as it had done three minutes ago.

'Mrs Fayre has asked me to say a few words to you,' proceeded Mr Bray, in somewhat stifled tones. 'It's about Mr Pidgeon. Mrs Fayre thinks we oughtn't to let things drop, and the guilty party get away with it. That's what I think too. In fact, it seems to me a bit thick, if I may use the expression. We all liked our late lamented friend and host. All of us, that is, bar one person. Mrs Fayre isn't satisfied to leave things as they are. Nor am I. Mrs Fayre thinks – '

'Thank you, Mr Bray.' Mrs Fayre was on her feet, and bowing with great dignity to her champion. 'It was kind of you to speak for me. But I think I mustn't shirk the responsibility, after all, of speaking for myself – and, of course, for my husband too, in the (shall I say?) rather anomalous position in which we find ourselves.'

She paused, while Mr Bray, returning the bow with what dignity he might, lowered himself into his chair again.

Enid looked round the table with limpid eyes. Then she spoke in low thrilling tones.

'Dear friends... I may call you friends, mayn't I?'

Roger hid his face in his hands and stifled a groan.

2

The upshot of it all was that Enid wanted the investigation to continue. She was, however prepared to sacrifice her own feelings if those of the rest of the party were against her. She did feel, however, that this very, very important question ought not to be decided, as apparently it had been held to be decided, by just one or two persons on their own responsibility. It was a terrible, terrible question, after all, and it affected everybody; and it should therefore be properly discussed by the whole company, and a vote taken.

Enid looked round once more slowly, in sorrowful appeal and then drooped gracefully into her chair.

'I concur,' said Miss Crosspatrick efficiently, before anyone else could speak.

Roger saw Crystal looking at him with a question in her face, and shrugged his shoulders. He intended to take no part in the discussion, any more than he intended to take a part in any further investigations, if the vote went that way. And he was extremely annoyed with Enid Fayre.

'You think we ought to go on detecting, Stella?' Unity was asking.

'On the contrary. I'm strongly opposed to anything further of that nature. I merely agree that a vote should be taken. No one will be satisfied until it has been. And I see no other way of convincing Mrs Fayre that she is in a hopeless minority.' And Miss Crosspatrick having got this off her chest, removed her glasses, polished them gently, and then sent a pitying smile through them in the direction of Mrs Fayre.

'Here, not so fast.' Mr Bray, with the help of another glass of port, was becoming his own man again. 'Not so much of the hopeless minority. In my opinion there's a good many more would like to see our poor old pal's death straightened out than not.'

'Undoubtedly. But not at the risk of further nerve-racking investigations and cross-questioning on this island.'

'I don't concur.'

'Then put it to the vote now,' suggested Miss Crosspatrick, with a confident little smile.

'Not so fast again. We've got to discuss it first properly, haven't we?'

'Then discuss it. I'm quite ready to listen.' And with an air which no doubt she considered helpful, Miss Crosspatrick leaned back in her chair and assumed an intelligent expression.

Perhaps deterred by Miss Crosspatrick's expression, no one spoke.

Then Mrs Bray plunged, like a suddenly agitated hen, squawking into the breach.

'Well, what I'd like to say is, we've heard a lot about why we ought to go on investigating, I'd like to hear something on the other side. Mrs Fayre's found out all of a sudden she can't go to sleep at night because – '

'Stop that, Gladys.'

'Why shouldn't I say what I think? This is a free country, isn't it?'

In the interests of peace, Roger leaned forward.

'No, Mrs Bray, unfortunately that's just what it isn't. We're dependent entirely on each other here, not on the police, or the law, or anything like that. So we've all got to keep our heads, for the general good.'

'I'm quite capable of keeping my head, I assure you,' returned Mrs Bray, tossing the head in question.

'I really believe you are, I'm glad to say. Very glad,' said Roger, with such gravity that Mrs Bray looked quite gratified and relapsed into silence.

'Well, supposing one of you who thinks things ought to be dropped lets us hear what the idea is,' observed Mr Bray, not without truculence.

'It's been explained to you so many times,' remarked Miss Crosspatrick wearily.

'But perhaps not very clearly,' suggested Mrs Fayre.

'On the contrary, quite clearly. I've explained it to you myself.'

'Then shall I say, perhaps not very convincingly.'

'On the contrary, quite convincingly.'

'Nevertheless, a great many people still remain unconvinced.'

'On the contrary, very few do, as a vote will show you.'

Mrs Fayre flushed delicately. 'Well, really! I don't know why you should be taking this line, Miss Crosspatrick, but really, how can you say that very few people are opposed to my poor cousin's death being hushed up? Mr Bray, as you've heard; Mr Combe, I think...?' Mrs Fayre's eyebrows lifted enquiringly.

'Certainly I agree.'

'Of course. Then my husband – '

'On the contrary, Mr Fayre doesn't really mind at all either way.'

'Well, really! I think you might let *me* be the best judge of what my own husband wants.'

'On the contrary, the best judge of what Mr Fayre wants is Mr Fayre. What do you want, Mr Fayre?'

Willie Fayre, who had been gazing abstractedly at the tablecloth, glanced up. 'I support my wife,' he said tonelessly.

Miss Crosspatrick nodded. 'Well? Who else?'

'Then there's Mr Parker, and – '

'Harold, is that what you're voting?' interposed Unity sharply.

Mr Parker squirmed miserably, and glanced first at Mrs Fayre and then at his employer. 'Well, you see, I think if Mrs Fayre... I mean, it *ought* to be settled, oughtn't it? And if Mrs Fayre wants...well, it ought to be settled, if you see what I mean.'

Unity made a strange noise compounded of many emotions, but derision was plainly uppermost. Mr Parker squirmed again.

'Thank you, Harold,' said Enid, with emphasis. She turned back to Miss Crosspatrick. 'You see? I'm afraid I haven't counted, but that's not exactly a few, is it? And in addition there's Captain Twyford, Mrs – '

'On the contrary, Captain Twyford is strongly opposed to the idea.'

'Well, really, Miss Crosspatrick!'

'Absolutely,' confirmed Twyford. 'Sorry, Enid. I am.'

'Oh, you're too dim, Reggie,' said Miss St Thomas indulgently. 'What does it matter, either way? I'll vote for you, Enid.'

'Thank you, Angela. And Mrs Vane, I believe...'

'On the contrary, Mrs Vane agrees with Mr Sheringham and me,' pronounced Miss Crosspatrick.

Crystal nodded.

'In any case, I think you'll find that a majority, for voting purposes.'

'On the contrary. I counted. It isn't even half.'

Mrs Fayre's delicate flush became a little more rosy, but she managed to produce a particularly sweet smile.

'Miss Crosspatrick, do you mind being so very, very kind as not to say "on the contrary," to me again?'

'On the contrary,' returned Miss Crosspatrick coldly, 'I shall say it precisely as often as I wish.'

The two ladies, breathing now a little rapidly, looked at each other, and looked.

'Enid really is *stupid*,' whispered Crystal to Roger.

'End of Round One,' whispered Roger to Crystal.

3

Crystal leaned towards Roger. 'What's the matter with Valentine?' she asked, under cover of the argument now proceeding between Mr Bray and Unity.

Roger glanced across the table to where Mr Combe was sitting, a few places down. He was tapping, softly but unceasingly, on the table in front of him with the handle of a knife, and staring at the spot with a fixed intensity.

'Getting the rhythm of Bray's periods for an epic on the occasion,' Roger said facetiously. He was not particularly interested in Mr Combe, whom he suspected at the moment of trying to be consciously interesting.

Crystal smiled.

The discussion had lasted now for nearly half an hour, and was still in progress. Everyone had already had their say, with the exception of Sir John Birch and Lady Darracott at one end of the table who, almost turning their backs on the rest of the party, were exchanging desultory remarks about the crops and what had happened to that nice Fortcheviot gairl who had married one of the Tympicestors – was it Dick or Harry? The standard of politeness, though smeared, was still maintaining itself above the mud, but only just above it. No vote had yet been taken, almost as if neither side felt quite sure enough of its numbers to risk the result.

Mr Bray turned from Unity with a noise expressive of exasperation. 'Oh, what's the use of trying to argue with a woman? I ought to know that by now, seeing I'm married.'

'You've no call to say that, Harry, I'm sure,' returned Mrs Bray truculently.

Her husband ignored her, and looked about with a belligerent light in his eye. The eye fell upon Roger.

'Well, look here,' he shouted above the din, 'let's get down to brass tacks. That's what I like: brass tacks. Seems to me that Sheringham there is the chap who's really at the bottom of it all, and yet it's funny but I don't seem to have heard him give us his reasons, like others have. Miss Crosspatrick – well, she's come out in the open, at any rate. So I'm going to put a straight question to Sheringham. I'm going to ask him why he's so anxious for our pal's death to be hushed up, like he wants.'

Mr Bray's words would have produced silence, if his large voice had not already done so. A hush of fearful expectation cut off the noise at one slice.

'That,' said Roger steadily, 'is a highly offensive suggestion.'

'I don't care what it is. Just you come on and answer it.'

'I've absolutely nothing to add to what I said on the subject five days ago.'

'Oh, you haven't, eh? Well, let me tell you that it's about time you found something, because I wouldn't say if you don't that some of us mightn't think there's something pretty fishy about – come on then, I'll fight you, if that's what you want. I'm not afraid of any ruddy half-ruddy-blue from ruddy Oxford.'

Roger had half-risen, with Crystal clinging to him on one side and Angela St Thomas not by any means clinging on the other. Enid and Unity respectively restrained Mr Bray.

'If there is going to be brawling, I think I'll go to my tent.' remarked Lady Darracott quite impassively.

The two men dropped back into their chairs.

'Please, Lady Darracott,' pleased Enid, 'couldn't you stay just a little longer? You see, we haven't voted yet. I'm sure everyone will keep quite, quite calm.'

Lady Darracott bowed, and turned back to Sir John.

'Is there any reason why we shouldn't vote at once?' enquired Miss Crosspatrick.

'I don't think we've really discussed it fully yet, have we?'

'On the contrary, I think we've discussed it *ad nauseam*.'

'Well, there's one thing I want to say before we vote.' observed Mr Bray irrepressibly, 'and one thing I will say; and if anyone wants to take exception to it he can, and perhaps the cap'll fit. It's this. Those of us who vote for getting our pal's death cleared up will be entitled to think what we like about any of those who don't. That's all.'

'Hadn't you better say straight out exactly what you mean, Mr Bray?' drawled Miss Crosspatrick. 'Or shall I say it for you? You mean that the murderer, if there is one, will be among those who vote against the motion.'

'Well, if you think that's what I mean, well and good. It's sense after all, isn't it?'

'Is it? I should have said that only a moderate amount of cunning would be needed to make the murderer vote in favour of the motion, in order to disarm suspicion.'

Mr Bray's face darkened. 'Look here, if you're trying to throw suspicion on our lot...'

'Well, that's only what you're trying to do on our lot, isn't it?' Miss Crosspatrick asked sweetly. 'And if it comes to that, we're quite entitled to say that that in itself is suspicious.'

'Look here, are you trying to insinuate...?' Mr Bray was so furious that he could hardly speak.

'Oh, no. I insinuate nothing.'

'Stella isn't one of the people who think you did it, if that's what you want to know,' put in Unity, with the crude savagery of youth.

Roger, watching anxiously, was afraid for a moment that Bray was going to hurl himself on the child in the next chair to him, but Enid laid a hand on his arm on the other side, and after a moment Bray seemed to shrink inside himself.

'I didn't know anyone thought that,' he muttered.

'Well, they do.' Unity said fiercely. 'And other people think Mrs Fayre did it. So now you know!'

'Unity!' gasped Crystal across the table.

Enid had gone very white, but she held herself together with a really notable effort.

'I think – aren't we getting just a little grotesque?' she said.

'Well, it's about time some things were said straight out, instead of being muttered behind people's backs,' Unity said sulkily.

The theory concerning Enid was news to Roger, but enlightenment as to its origin was not delayed. Happening to glance at Twyford, he saw on that usually indifferent gentleman's face an expression of such acute horror and apprehension as could leave no doubt.

On a sudden impulse Roger rapped sharply on the table.

'Mrs Fayre's quite right,' he said in brusque tones. 'We are getting absurd. We'll have everyone offering defences and alibis for themselves in a minute. I'm sorry this subject was ever brought up tonight at all. We seemed to be getting on very well before. However, as we are in the middle of it, I think I'd better say a word. It's this. Most of you seem to have been taking it for granted that murder was committed here that night. There's been a lot of talk and talk of that sort's unhealthy. I want to give you my own real opinion. It's this. I'm more than doubtful whether murder was committed at all. In fact, I strongly incline to the belief that it was not. There isn't the slightest proof of murder. The confusion in some minds is owing to the fact that there is proof that someone was on the cliff-top with Mr Pidgeon when he fell over. But that has nothing to do with murder. It's my belief that Mr Pidgeon fell over by sheer accident, but that this other person has kept silent through fear of being disbelieved in stating that it was only an accident: a regrettable, but really quite understandable feeling. That is the conclusion I have come to, and in consequence I tell you here and now that whatever the result of the voting, I shall take no part in any further investigations. I believe them to be not only unfortunate in their possible consequences on our morale during the rest of our stay here, but totally unnecessary at that. That's all, and I suggest, Mrs Fayre, that you put the question to the vote now if you really think it advisable, and close the discussion.'

'Well done, Roger,' Crystal whispered.

Roger's words had without doubt had their effect. The sanity and good sense was refreshing after the hectic atmosphere of the last half-hour, and a distinct feeling of relief was perceptible.

Enid Fayre rose to her feet.

'I hope – oh, how I hope, that Mr Sheringham is right. I'm sure he is. But for some of us nevertheless even a little uncertainty on such a dreadful question is so very, very hard to bear. For those, hope is not enough. One feels that one must leave no stone unturned to *know* – to be quite, quite certain. So I think that for the benefit of those who feel like that, I ought to put the question to the vote. Mr Sheringham will understand, I'm sure, and so will those who think as he does. Will those in favour...?'

The voting resulted in the motion for further investigation being lost, six voting in favour and eight against. Both Lady Darracott and Sir John Birch voted against.

'Well, that settles it, doesn't it?' said Enid, with a brave, but wistful smile. 'Shall we go to the other tent?'

Suddenly Mr Combe leapt to his feet, his eyes wild.

'Look here, we can't leave it like this. That's grotesque, if you like. It's impossible. We can't, I tell you.'

Everyone was staring at Mr Combe. His voice had been shrill, with a curious little break on the high notes.

'What the devil's the matter with the feller?' grunted Sir John.

'Murder!' screamed Mr Combe, making absurd passes in the air with his hands. 'That's what's the matter with all of us, you old fool, except clods like yourself. Murder! Do you realise that one of us here is a *murderer?* One of us here, I tell you. Yes, you – or you – or you!' He jabbed a forefinger in turn at Sir John, Crystal, and Bray. 'How are we to know who it is? I know Sheringham's trying to pretend it wasn't murder at all really, but that isn't true. He knows it was, I tell you – he knows it was, and he won't do anything about it. My God, which one of us will be the next? I can't bear it, I can't bear it.' Mr Combe burst into tears and slumped back into his chair, his face buried in his hands, his body shaking.

'Oh, my heavens, it's hysteria,' muttered Crystal, in the dead silence which followed.

Roger pushed her aside, sprawled over the table, and smacked Mr Combe hard on the side of the cheek with the flat of his hand. 'Stop that, Combe!' he said sharply.

Mrs Bray, sitting next to Combe, returned the smack on Roger's face as he still leaned over the table. 'Don't do that to him, you great big bully, you.'

'It's hysteria, Mrs Bray,' Crystal cried.

'I don't care what it is – it doesn't give a big 'un the right to hit a little 'un.'

'Mind your own business, Gladys, my girl,' roared Mr Bray. 'You keep – '

'I shan't! I've kept quiet long enough, I have. You and that Enid of yours! Now perhaps you can see what you've done, the pair of you. I – '

'Shut up, I tell you!'

'It's true!' Roger could hardly recognise Miss Crosspatrick's gentle tones in the sudden burst of fury that had come from her chair. He stared at her in growing amazement. 'It's absolutely true. You and that fool of a woman are responsible for this. I did my best. I tried to stop you. I heard your husband trying to stop you in your own tent. It was madness, bringing it all up now – madness, I tell you. Just to gratify that damned vanity of yours. Do you think our nerves are made of steel, you little idiot? Do you?'

Although she was at the other end of the table, Enid shrank back in her chair as if terrified that Miss Crosspatrick was going actually to attack her.

'Oh, please…' she whispered faintly.

'Yes, and it's true, too, what Combe said,' suddenly shouted Twyford. 'There *is* a murderer among us. Who is it? We must find out, or none of us will be safe. None of us!'

'I thought you didn't want to find out who it is?' sneered Mr Bray.

'I didn't. But things have gone too far now. We must find out, or none of us will be safe. It isn't me. Angela knows that. She was in my tent at the time. She – '

'Reggie – it's Bray!' Angela St Thomas, clinging to Twyford's arm, had joined her voice to the general din: not hysterically, but with a kind of horrid exultation. 'It's Bray. Look at him!'

'Oh, I want to get away from this island.' wailed Unity. 'I'm frightened. Can't we possibly get away?'

'No, we can't,' retorted Miss Crosspatrick, still shaking with anger. 'We've got to stay here to – '

'To be murdered!' screamed Mr Combe. 'Oh, my God, I can't bear it – I can't bear it!'

'Will you keep quiet, damn you?' interposed Willie Fayre for the first time, and struck a feeble blow across the table at Combe, as if imitating Roger.

'Silence, please – silence!'

Lady Darracott was standing, a quiet, dignified figure, in front of her chair. Very gradually, as people became aware of her, the noise died down.

When everything was quiet, she raised her hand.

'Listen.'

Everybody listened.

Lady Darracott looked slowly round the table. 'Are we all here? Mr Fayre, are we all here?...eleven, twelve, thirteen and myself fourteen...yes, we are.'

Lady Darracott looked round again.

'Then who,' she said calmly, 'is that outside the tent?'

4

'There is someone outside the tent.' repeated Lady Darracott firmly. There was little sign left of the invalid about her now. She stood quite straight, without even leaning on the table, and her voice was stronger than Roger had ever heard it. 'I heard footsteps, and then I saw the tent bulge, *there*, as if someone was leaning against it, and then he seemed to trip over one of the ropes. Will somebody see who it is, please?'

No one moved.

'Then I'll look myself,' Lady Darracott said, and turned to do so.

Sir John and Roger were in front of her in an instant. 'I'll look, Lady Darracott.'

'Don't be a fool, Ann,' wheezed Sir John simultaneously. 'Sit down. I'll scout round.'

Roger glanced back. 'All men come, please,' he said sharply.

There was a shuffling of chairs on the dry turf.

'Er – Sheringham, I suppose someone had better stay here and look after the women. Perhaps I'd better do that.'

'All right,' said Roger, at the tent-door. He was not sorry to get Twyford out of the way. He glanced back again. 'Bray, bring Combe with you.' He was not going to spare Mr Combe.

To Roger's surprise, however, Mr Combe was almost the first to join him outside, unassisted by Bray. 'I'm pretty good in the dark,' he remarked, almost jauntily.

'Then you go round the tent this way, with Parker. Sir John will you go round the other way, with Bray? Fayre, come with me round the other tents. If anyone finds the chap, shout. If not, make for the edge of the cliff and try and cut him off – Combe and Parker to the path, Bray and Sir John to the east bluff. If we've still drawn a blank, we'll go straight across to the plantation, in couples as we clear the other places. That's the most likely place for him to have a cubby-hole. All clear, everyone? Move off, then.'

The six moved.

5

It was nearly three-quarters of an hour before they got back to the marquee, and then with nothing to report beyond a certain physical exhaustion. Roger was relieved to find an atmosphere that was almost amicable, with Miss Crosspatrick and Mrs Fayre outdoing each other in sweetness, and Mrs Bray no less on her mettle. The storm had passed; sunshine was again the official state.

At his ease in the middle of them, Captain Twyford was a fine figure of a man.

Speculation was naturally excited concerning the identity of the stranger, and Roger gathered that it was this new fear from without which had brought together those recently thrown apart by the fear within.

As Roger was helping himself to a whisky-and-soda, Angela St Thomas lounged over to him.

'Hist!' she said. 'The aunt wants a word with you in her tent, but no one else is to know. We all washed up in a body. Isn't this glamorous?'

'Stupefying,' Roger agreed politely, lapped up his whisky-and-soda, and slipped out of the marquee.

He announced himself at Lady Darracott's tent, and was bidden to enter.

Lady Darracott looked up from her chair with a smile. She was wrapped in shawls, and was evidently a total invalid.

'You're alone?' Roger frowned. 'Isn't that a little risky?'

'I don't think so. Well, Mr Sheringham, what did you think of my intruder?'

'Obviously it was someone from the boat, acting I should say under Mr Pidgeon's orders, or else you imagined him. I'm inclined to think the latter, I'm afraid. In any case, we found no trace of anyone.'

Lady Darracott smiled. 'You do me an injustice. It was neither. I'm telling you, because I really think you're the only reliable person on the island, Mr Sheringham. I invented him.'

'Oh!' Roger stared, and then laughed. 'Well, you certainly saved what looked like becoming an ugly situation.'

'That was my idea. I'm not sure though, now, whether I acted altogether wisely. Perhaps we may have still more hysteria if they think there's a mysterious person in hiding on the island?'

Roger considered, leaning against the tent-pole. 'It's brought them together, at all events. They're all falling on each other's necks in there now. On the whole I'm inclined to think it's better that they should be frightened of someone outside the party than of someone in it.'

'I think you may be right. If not, it will be quite simple to tell them that I invented the diversion in order to bring them to their senses. It might even be a lesson to them, for really I've never seen people who call themselves civilised behaving in such a childish manner. It was quite embarrassing to see them, like catching somebody unawares in a disgraceful act.'

'I rather think most of them have been working up for it for some days. Now they've let off steam, they may be better. In either case, I'm most grateful to you for coming to the rescue like that.'

'If you would allow me to make a suggestion,' said Lady Darracott, with something of her old helpless air, 'I think it might be very much better if you took charge here for the future: decisive and authoritative charge.'

'I intend to,' Roger said, somewhat grimly. 'I may have a bit of trouble, but I'm ready for that. Though it may be a little awkward for Twyford...'

'Reggie Twyford?' Lady Darracott uttered a sudden harsh cackle which reminded Roger, as nothing else about Lady Darracott ever had reminded him, of her niece. 'If you want to know, Reggie Twyford will be the most grateful creature on the island.'

chapter thirteen

'No, we have not,' Crystal repeated firmly. 'If you think we've seen the end of it, you're all wrong. That was just a little warming up. Wait till we get going with the real thing. Hysterics? Hysterics won't be in it.'

'You depress me, Crystal,' Roger said gloomily.

'I'm sorry, my pet, but you'd better be forewarned. You see, I *know*.'

'Hell's bells,' muttered Roger. 'I don't believe you, but I do wish this fortnight was over.'

He and Crystal were lying on the beach, sunbathing. It was the morning after the evening before, and to all appearances it was like every other morning that had been passed on the island: peaceful, carefree, and peopled with perfect amiable people. But Roger had learned to distrust appearances.

The night had passed better than he expected. On an admirable suggestion of Crystal's, after each woman had expressed at least thirty times her extreme terror of going to bed that night at all, the men had been set to bringing the beds into the marquee for the women, while the other marquee had been allotted to the men. Angela, Roger, Lady Darracott and Sir John had slept in their own tents; the rest had fallen in with Crystal's idea, including Crystal herself.

Twyford had explained to Roger a little elaborately that he was sleeping with the other men in order to keep an eye on them.

'The eye that stays open while you're asleep?' Roger had said flippantly. 'Yes, I understand every explorer has one of them.'

Twyford had looked pained.

The night, both for those sleeping in a body and those alone, had passed without incident.

After breakfast, Roger had asked Crystal to go sunbathing with him after the chores were done, and on the beach he had told her of Lady Darracott's ruse. From that, they had gone on to talk over the general situation, and expectations for the future, of which Crystal took a gloomy view.

'Well, whom can we rely on, to keep sensible?' Roger asked now, digging his toes in the sand. 'Twyford, of course, although he seems to be turning out such an old woman and won't take responsibility; at any rate, he'll keep his head. So will Sir John, Lady Darracott, and Stella.'

'Stella lost her temper last night,' Crystal remarked. 'I was astonished.'

'So was I, for the moment, but after all, it was natural enough. She was very annoyed. So was I. By the way, can I rely on you, Crystal?'

'I shouldn't think so. I always was a coward.'

'So was I. But we can't afford to be on this trip. Who else? Bray may lose his temper, but he won't lose his head; he hasn't enough imagination. Nor, I think, will Mrs Bray. Fayre seems to be all right. Enid, of course, will go to pieces, and so will Unity, and probably Parker. Angela will probably be all right. And the real danger-spot is Combe. My goodness, I wish we could keep him muzzled for the rest of the fortnight.'

'You know, he quite frightened me last night.'

'Of course he did. He frightened everyone, curse him.'

'And you're not going to tell the others that Lady Darracott invented the stranger?'

'No,' said Roger. 'I've thought it out, and on the whole it seems better not.'

'Everyone's still talking about it. Bray says we ought to organise a search-party.'

'I'll encourage that. It'll keep them busy. And let them talk about it. I don't mind that a bit. What I don't like is when they talk about each other.'

2

The day passed so normally that Roger began to hope that Crystal was mistaken. Mr Bray organised his search-party, and kept them busy (to Roger's relief) till nearly dinner-time, when they returned, puzzled but still not quite despairing. As if to make up for the regrettable incidents of the evening before, dinner was almost hilariously cheerful; and after it they all sat in the big marquee and sang old songs, to the accompaniment of Roger, Crystal, Unity and Twyford on combs.

So successful had been the evening, that everyone felt sufficiently restored to go to bed in his or her own tent; and spirits were kept up right to the last moment by hilarities and cheerful insults shouted from tent to tent. Roger felt satisfied and relieved.

He had actually got into bed, when he heard a subdued scratching on the flap and called out a cautions invitation to enter. It was Crystal, in her dressing-gown.

'Really, Crystal,' said Roger facetiously.

Crystal did not smile. 'Roger,' she said, in a low voice. 'I'm worried.'

'Good heavens, why? I never saw such a marvellous recovery.'

Crystal sat down on the end of Roger's bed. 'You don't' think it's too marvellous? You don't think people were *too* cheerful?'

'No, I don't. Why?'

'I don't know. It sounded very forced, to me.'

'I don't think so. You're a Jonah, Crystal.'

'I hope I am. But I had to come and speak to you, because I really do think, Roger, that someone ought to keep watch tonight.'

'Keep watch? What on earth for?'

'I don't know,' Crystal confessed. 'But I've got a feeling that – well, anything might happen.'

'Go back to your tent, my dear girl, and go to sleep. The trouble with you is, you're too Irish.'

Crystal hesitated. Then she went.

Roger began to read.

He read for his statutory fifteen minutes, then blew out his lamp, settled down, and went almost instantly to sleep.

He had been asleep for about three-quarters of an hour when a piercing shriek jerked him abruptly back into consciousness. It was followed, almost immediately, by another, not quite so loud.

3

Roger leapt out of bed, snatched up his dressing-gown and ran out, huddling on the dressing-gown as he went. Out of other tents other people were hurrying, while some were content merely to thrust out their heads with expressions of alarm. The moon was nearly full, and the little camp tolerably illuminated.

Mrs Bray was standing in the opening of her tent, half inside and half out. Shrieks were coming from her with almost monotonous persistence, at intervals of about five seconds.

Roger reached her first and shook her fiercely. 'What's the matter?' he demanded, half angrily and half in alarm himself, for panic is unpleasantly infectious. 'What on earth's the matter, Mrs Bray?'

Mrs Bray, a grotesque figure in bright purple pyjamas, strained, like everything else Mrs Bray ever wore, across the more unruly portions of her anatomy, allowed her tight little mouth, opening just like a fish's for another ear-splitting scream to remain for a moment poised, then she slowly closed it.

'Pull yourself together,' Roger repeated impatiently. 'What's the matter?'

Mrs Bray's mouth was now opening and shutting, still like a fish's, while she stared, in a kind of daze, at the little semicircle of anxious faces by which she and Roger were now hemmed in.

'I heard 'im,' she gasped. 'He come between my tent and Mr Bray's. Oh, my Gawd! I thought he was coming for one of us – straight I did.'

'Who?'

'Why, the man Lady Darracott 'eard last night. Coo!' Mrs Bray was gradually ceasing to tremble. 'Gave me a proper turn, it did.'

'Well, you're all right now, aren't you?' Roger soothed.

'No, I'm not, young man,' retorted Mrs Bray with decision. 'If you think I'm going back to that tent of mine alone, you're wrong. Why, I might be murdered in me bed! Any of us might.'

'That's nonsense,' Roger said loudly, as he heard murmurs of frightened assent rising behind him. 'It's my belief you imagined it, Mrs Bray.'

'Well, that I did not,' Mrs Bray returned in high indignation. 'Imagine my grandmother! Think I can't tell footsteps when I hear 'em , and me lying awake not able to close an eye the last blessed hour? Creepy, they was, I tell you – creepy and quiet, like as if he didn't want to be heard. Coo, it didn't half give me a turn.'

'It was the wind or something. Because I'd better tell you, if this sort of thing's likely to go on, that – '

'No, it's true, Roger,' Unity, with a little gasp, had broken forward from the semicircle. 'Because I heard them too, near my tent. I thought... I thought...' Unity suddenly slumped at the knees.

Roger just caught her, and laid her on the ground. 'It's all right,' he said loudly. 'She's only fainted. Stand back. Crystal!'

Mrs Bray bent on her knees over the girl. 'All right, all right. I can see to her. I'm all right when there's something to be done. It's lying about and waiting I can't stomach. Get some water, someone – Harold.'

She fussed in what seemed to Roger a competent manner with the unconscious girl.

Crystal plucked at Roger's sleeve. 'She screamed too,' she said in a low voice, with a jerk of her head towards Unity. 'I heard her. Just after Mrs Bray began.'

'Set her off, I expect,' Roger muttered. 'No wonder.'

'I happened to see her as she tumbled out of her tent, as soon as you began to speak. She was as white as a sheet.'

'Did you hear anything?'

'Not a sound. And I was awake, too.'

'I suppose we'd better find out who it was moving about, or we shan't get any peace for the rest of the night.'

Crystal nodded. 'And for the same reason I think I should tell them, after all, that there isn't anyone else on the island.'

'Yes, I'm going to.'

They stood in silence, watching Mrs Bray flicking the water which Harold Parker had brought, into Unity's white face.

'Do you really think she's all right?' Willie Fayre asked Crystal anxiously.'

Mrs Bray looked up. 'Course she's all right. There! See? She's coming round. Don't you fret yourself, dearie. No, lay quiet. You're all right.'

Unity stared round. Then she caught Roger's eye. 'I say, awfully sorry,' she muttered. 'Made a ghastly idiot of myself.'

'Not such an idiot as I made of meself,' interposed Mrs Bray cheerfully. 'And all for nothing, Mr Sheringham says. Well, there!' Mrs Bray, now quite restored, happened to catch sight of her own attire. 'Coo!' she said, with a little scream. 'Look at me. Clean forgot to put on a dressing-gown, I did. Lucky Mr Bray isn't here to see. I'd never hear the end of it.' She dived, in matronly confusion, into the shelter of her tent.

'Where is Mr Bray, by the way?' said Crystal, looking round the little group.

There was no answer.

'That hog would sleep through anything,' Mr Combe was heard to mutter.

'Well, I want him,' Roger said briskly. 'Twyford, haul him out, there's a good fellow. I want everyone.'

'Oke,' said Twyford amiably, and went. Roger was both a trifled surprised, and relieved. It was the first direct order he had given to Twyford, and he had not anticipated quite so prompt an obedience. Evidently there was going to be no trouble from Twyford.

Angela St Thomas, who had left the group a few minutes ago, was slouching back again.

'Auntie's compliments, Roger, and are there likely to be any more disturbance, because she wants to go to sleep?'

Roger grinned. 'My compliments to your aunt, and there aren't likely to be any more disturbances.'

'Bit of an optimist, aren't you?' said Miss St Thomas, and slouched away again.

A wheezy grunt announced to Roger that Sir John Birch was about to address him. 'Nothing I can do, Sheringham?'

'No, I don't think so, Sir John.'

'Very well, I'll turn in then.'

Sir John walked back to his tent. Roger watched him. Sir John's voice had given no indication that Sir John was not strictly sober; but his walk was lurching, with alternating periods of extremely slow dignity.

'The old chap's drinking too much,' Roger thought. 'Looks as if he'd got a bottle of whisky in his tent. I hope to goodness he doesn't get awkward. I wonder if Lady Darracott would go all aristocratic and prickle-backed if I asked her to say a word to him; because he certainly wouldn't take one from me.'

Twyford wandered back. 'Sorry, the bird's not there.'

'Not in his tent?'

'Nope.'

'Then there's our mysterious walker-by-night,' said Roger, with relief. 'Do you hear that, Mrs Bray? It was your own husband's footsteps you heard. That's why they seemed to be between your tent and his.'

Mrs Bray appeared at her tent-door, decorously swathed now in a quilted satin dressing-gown in black ornamented with crimson dragons picked out with gold stitching.

'Well, fancy that!' she remarked, with a giggle. 'I'll have a word to say to Mr Bray, you can take it from me. Frightening the life out of me and Unity like that. Well, where is he?'

'Oh, I don't know,' Roger said airily. 'Gone for a stroll, I expect.'

'That doesn't sound like Mr Bray,' said his wife doubtfully. 'Well, I wonder where he can have got to?'

'For that matter,' remarked Captain Twyford lazily, 'where's Mrs Fayre?'

A dead silence fell on the little group. Everyone did not look at Willie Fayre except Roger, who saw that the little man had gone a fiery red.

Willie hesitated, took a tentative step or two towards his wife's tent, and then called:

'Enid! Enid!'

Mrs Fayre's voice floated back, sweet and faintly surprised. 'Yes, darling?'

'Come out here, please. Sheringham wants to speak to everyone.'

4

In the profound silence which continued Roger said to Fayre, as easily as he could:

'It didn't matter a bit. You could have passed it on to Mrs Fayre tomorrow morning.'

Willie did not answer.

Mrs Fayre, tall and graceful in the bright moonlight, floated out from her tent. Roger noticed that she pulled the flap over the opening behind her, with an apparently careless movement. She wore a quizzical little smile as she approached the group.

'Dear me, what has been happening?' She looked at Roger, not at her husband.

'Nothing very dreadful,' Roger replied. 'Mrs Bray heard someone moving about, that was all.'

Did someone scream? I *thought* I heard someone scream,' Mrs Fayre said serenely. 'But I was so dead asleep...' Mrs Fayre shrugged her charming shoulders.

She's overdoing it, thought Roger.

'It's a pity,' smiled Miss Crosspatrick, 'that we don't all sleep as soundly as Mrs Fayre.'

'Yes,' said Roger discouragingly. 'Well, Mrs Fayre, this may not be a very good time to make announcements, in the small hours of the morning, but I think it may give people a better night – or what remains of a better night – if I tell you all that – '

'Sorry to interrupt,' murmured Captain Twyford, 'but before you get going, oughtn't we to see what's happened to Bray?'

'Oh, I expect he's all right,' Roger demurred.

'Never know.' Twyford glanced at Mrs Fayre. 'You haven't seen him anywhere, Enid, I suppose?' he asked, his voice apparently as faintly bored as ever.

'I?' Enid was innocently astonished. 'Of course not. I've only just arrived.'

'Ah, yes. So you have.' Twyford yawned.

Roger hurried on. 'Listen, please, everyone. I was going to tell you that – '

'Well, I'll just stroll over to the edge of the cliff, Sheringham, and make sure,' nodded Twyford, and turned away.

'Make sure of what?' demanded Mrs Bray shrilly.

'That your husband's all right.'

'Why, you don't think?… Mr Sheringham…'

Roger took a sudden decision. 'Yes, perhaps you're right, Twyford. No, of course, your husband's quite all right, Mrs Bray. We'll just make sure, that's all. Scatter, everyone, please, and look around.' Roger clapped his hands, as if shooing fowls. 'Scatter, all of you.'

'Bray! Bray!' shrilled Mr Combe.

'Mr Bray!' cried Harold Parker.

'Harry! Har-ree!'

'Stop shouting!' Roger raised his own voice above the rest. 'Obviously he can't hear you. Scatter, I said, and look for him.'

Twyford smiled again at Roger.

'If you try to shout again, I'll knock you out.' Roger said, in a fierce undertone. 'Do you want to make more trouble than we've got already?'

'I never could stand people who don't play fair,' drawled Twyford.

'Then play fair yourself, and leave the coast clear. Off with you, man.'

Twyford grinned once more and then strolled away, his hands deep in the pockets of his dressing-gown.

'Get everyone else out of the way,' muttered Roger to Crystal.

Crystal nodded understandingly, and shepherded off the few who remained. Mrs Bray and Willie Fayre had already gone. Only Enid remained, her eyebrows just a little raised, the picture of amused perplexity.

'Really, Mr Sheringham. Wouldn't it have been better to make your announcement, which I'm sure would have been very interesting, and send everyone off to bed? I should think that Mr Bray, wherever he may be, is quite capable of looking after himself.'

Roger looked at her without affection. 'Yes?' he said coldly. 'I think Mr Bray might be in the kitchen-tent. Go and see.'

Enid drew herself up. 'Really, I don't think you – '

'Listen to me.' Roger was far too angry to remember that he was that quaint survival which some people still call a gentleman. 'I've got no time to waste. Go and see if Bray's in the kitchen, you little idiot, while I get him out of your tent.'

'Oh!' Enid's hand flew to her mouth. 'He...it's not anything...he just couldn't sleep, and came across to ask me if I'd like to go for a walk in the moonlight...and then that ridiculous woman began screaming, and he had to slip inside my tent...you mustn't think...'

'I don't think anything. I'm not interested enough. Will you kindly go now and see if Bray is in the kitchen-tent?'

Enid went.

Roger walked quickly over to the tent and tried the flap. It was fastened on the inside.

'Come out, Bray,' he said, in a low tone. 'The coast's clear.'

There was the sound of the flap being untied, and Mr Bray edged into the world once more.

'Thanks, old man,' he said effusively. 'I won't forget that in a hurry. I take back,' said Mr Bray handsomely, 'all I said after dinner last night.'

'Oh, that's all right,' Roger returned impatiently. 'For heaven's sake let's get farther away from this tent.'

Mr Bray cleared his throat. 'I shouldn't like for you to be under any wrong impression, old man, you know. I just happened to be strolling about – couldn't sleep, and that's a fact – when all of a sudden Gladys let out a screech, and I dived into the nearest tent to me. By a bit of real bad luck it was – '

'Yes, yes. I don't mind. It's no concern of mine. Now then, before the others get back where did I find you?'

Before Mr Bray could answer this important question, a hurricane appeared to precipitate itself upon him, quite without warning. Clap, clop! Before he could stagger back or raise a hand to defend himself, both Mr Bray's jowls were soundly smacked.

'You beast – you brute, you,' shrieked Mrs Bray, bedside herself. 'I saw you! I saw you sneak out of that —'s tent. You dirty 'ound, you – I'll 'ave the law on you for this, see if I don't. I knew what your game was. Yes, and Mr Fayre saw too. And for why? Because I took him be'ind me own tent, I did, to see. I knew where you were. Gawd, you swine!'

'Here, Gladys, old girl, draw it mild,' pleaded Mr Bray. 'It wasn't what you think. I only – '

'Ho, wasn't it? I know what I saw. And don't you, Gladys *me*, if you please.'

'Well, be a bit quieter, can't you? Don't want to let everyone know, do you? Specially as you'll be kicking yourself in the morning, over making such a silly mistake.'

'Ho, I shall, shall I? Kicking meself, eh? Damn that for a tale. Think I 'aven't been watching your goings-on with that — little — of a — ?' Here Mrs Bray regrettably used three expressions which caused her hearers first to start violently, and then to look with complete unconvincingness, as if they had not heard them. 'Begging Mr Faye's pardon, I'm sure, who's a reel gentleman, which you'll never be, Harry Bray, not so long as you live, in spite of your dirty money, got by – "

'Gladys, Gladys, for goodness' sake. Remember where you are,' groaned Mr Bray.

Roger, who had retreated before the storm, had been trying since in a dazed way to identify this vulgar termagant, wild of hair and dangerous of nail, shrieking obscenities as shrilly as any fishwife, with the extremely refined, tightly white-clad Mrs Bray. Giving it up, he took his courage in both hands and intervened. He felt safer in doing so since several other members of the party, attracted by the screaming, had come hurrying back.

'Mrs Bray.'

'Well, and what do you want?' demanded Mrs Bray truculently. 'You get busy and find that murderer of yours, and don't come interfering between husband and wife. Yus!' Mrs Bray did not quite say 'yus,' but the word she used came as near to it as makes no difference. 'Yus! You get busy and find that murderer, 'cos we'll not have another minute's peace on this bloody island till you have. See? I know. That's what drove my Harry to this. Nerves – that's what it is, nerves. Think I don't know? Harry always was one of the nervy ones, though you mightn't think it to look at him.'

'That's right, Glad,' Mr Bray said humbly. 'It wasn't anything really.' He laid a hand on a plump shoulder. 'I promise you – '

'Here, don't you come pawing me, Harry Bray. You go and paw that fancy piece of yours – begging your pardon again, Mr Fayre, but that's what she is and ever more will be. I know her sort. Yes, and where is she, I'd like to know? Skulking somewhere, I'll be bound, and leaving my Harry to take her blame as well as his own. Never mind, I'll find her, wherever she's hidden her dirty little self. I'll find her, and give her a bit o' my mind. Just let me catch her, that's all.' Mrs Bray, who just now had shown signs of calming down, was working herself up afresh.

Roger looked round helplessly, but no one seemed likely to be of much use. Undoubtedly, Mrs Bray, after much provocation it was true, was in a dangerous temper, and Roger would not have liked to be in Enid's shoes if Mrs Bray got hold of her just then. He was just about to risk interfering again in person, when Harold Parker stepped forward.

'Mrs Bray,' he said courteously, 'permit me to offer you my arm.'

'Eh?' Mrs Bray gaped.

'Let me escort you back to your tent. It is getting late,' observed Mr Parker, with grave courtesy. 'If we don't get to bed soon, we shall get no sleep at all tonight and I'm sure you must be tired.' And possessing himself of the lady's round arm, Mr Parker tucked it under his own with an air and led her off in the direction of her tent.

Mr Bray stared after the couple. 'Well, I'll be jiggered,' he muttered. 'Went like a lamb, she did. Never known Gladys do that before, not in one of her tantrums.'

'It's Harold you've got to thank,' Unity told him fiercely. 'Now perhaps you won't swear and shout at him any more. He's worth six of you.'

'Yes, the least you can do is to double Harold's salary,' Roger agreed, not a little impressed. 'Do you know, I think that was one of the most efficient actions I've ever seen? Well, that's that. I should give her ten minutes, and then go in and make your peace. And for heaven's sake, man,' added Roger, 'try not to provoke any more scenes till we get off this island.'

'You're right, old man,' agreed Mr Bray, with humility. 'I'll watch my step.'

Nobody seemed to have taken any notice of Willie Fayre. He might almost not have been present at all.

'By the way,' remarked Miss Crosspatrick, 'before we disperse, Roger, perhaps you'll tell us what it was you were trying to say before all this burst on us.'

'Oh, yes. Are most of us here?'

'Call the roll,' suggested Miss St Thomas. 'I don't want to go back to bed at all. Do you, Reggie? I call this an absolutely stupefying night.'

'Too right,' agreed Captain Twyford, not stifling a yawn.

With the exception of Lady Darracott, Sir John, Mrs Bray, and a probably chastened Enid, everyone was once more reassembled.

In a few words Roger told them of Lady Darracott's ruse.

'So you see there isn't anyone prowling about the island, and if you hear someone going for a stroll under the stars, don't raise the roof. That's all. Good night, everyone. Kitchen squad, breakfast at the usual time. No: no allowance for lost sleep. So make the most of what you can get now. Good night.'

'With the exception of the Bray Regional, all stations will now be closing down,' observed Miss St Thomas, just not *sotto voce* enough.

Thirteen minutes later Roger was once more asleep. He was very tired.

He was allowed to sleep for eight minutes. Then he was woken up once more.

5

It was Unity who woke Roger up this time, and she did it by shaking him vigorously.

'Roger! Roger!'

Roger slowly recovered his senses. 'What the blazes...oh, it's you, Unity.' Unity had already lit the lamp. 'My dear girl, what on earth is it now?'

'Oh, Roger, do come. I'm absolutely petrified. There's a simply ghastly row going on in Enid's tent.'

'If it's Willie telling her off, for heaven's sake leave them to it. It's the best thing for both of them if he does.'

'Yes, but they're shouting at each other. They're – I think they're saying awful things to each other.'

'It's about time someone said awful things to Enid,' said Roger, swallowing a tremendous yawn. 'Anyhow, I'm not going to interfere. Good night, Unity.'

'But I can't go back to my tent,' Unity wailed. 'It's next to theirs. I tell you, they frightened me, Roger. I can't go back.'

'Well, you can't stay here,' Roger retorted, not without satisfaction. 'Go in to Crystal.'

'Oh, Roger, won't you really come and make them shut up?'

'No, I won't.'

Unity was listening. 'Roger – hark!'

Roger listened. There were cries coming from other tents now. 'Shut up!' 'Lie down, you two.' 'Park it till the morning.' 'Be quiet!'

Roger groaned. 'I won't butt in. Why should I? Let someone else do it for a change.'

There was a fumbling at the tent-flap, and Crystal came in. 'Roger, you must...hullo, Unity. Oh, of course, you're next to them.'

'He says he won't go. Crystal, do tell him he's got to.'

'Really, I think you must, my pet.'

'I won't!' Roger shouted. 'Go back to bed, you two pestering females, and leave me alone. There you are, you see. It's dying down. Now are you satisfied?'

Certainly the shouts had died away. Nothing now was to be heard at all. Even the quarrelling must have ceased.

The next instant a loud scream startled even Roger into action.

'Oh, damn,' he said, and tumbled out of bed.

'Listen!' said Crystal intensely.

A voice in the distance had risen, clear and shrill:

'I killed him. Now you know. *I* killed him.'

6

'Who the devil is that?' Roger whispered, frozen for the moment into inaction. The anonymous voice had chilled him with an odd, altruistic fear.

Before either of the women could answer there was the sound of scurrying footsteps outside, and Enid Fayre precipitated herself into the tent.

'Mr Sheringham – Mr Sheringham, please, please come.' She did not appear to notice Crystal and Unity at all. 'My husband – Willie – he's gone mad.'

'He has, has he?' Roger said grimly, tying the sash of his dressing-gown. 'What's his trouble? You?'

'No, no. He – he says it was he who pushed Guy over the cliff!' wailed Mrs Fayre. 'He's shouting it out in front of everyone.'

'The devil he is,' Roger stared.

'And – and he swears he's going to push me over next. Oh, Crystal...' Graceful even in this extremity, Enid drooped onto Crystal.

Roger hurried out. Were things coming to a head at last?

7

Rather a horrible spectacle met Roger's eyes, and ears, as he emerged once more into the moonlight. At the other end of the camp Willie Fayre was standing in the middle of the alleyway opposite his wife's tent, shouting almost incoherently, while the tears streamed down his face.

'I killed him, do you hear? I did. Now perhaps you can have some peace. I killed him. I killed him. – And I'll kill anyone else,' sobbed Mr Fayre, 'who says I didn't. *I* killed him.'

Before Roger could reach him, a figure had slipped out of Mr Parker's tent and advanced confidently towards the raving little man.

'Mr Fayre, permit me to escort you back to your tent. I expect you're very tired, and – ouch!'

This time Mr Parker's courtesy had not been so successful. Mr Fayre, without for a moment ceasing his refrain, had hit him fiercely in the eye.

Not without uneasiness, and very conscious of the numerous heads protruded once more from each tent, not one of whose owners offered for a moment to help him, Roger went up to the little man.

'Come alone, Fayre,' he said, in as matter-of-fact a tone as he could summon up. 'You're disturbing people, you know. Come to bed.'

Fayre clung to him with both hands. 'I killed him, Sheringham. I did it for Enid's sake. It's been terrible. And she doesn't care, that's the awful thing.'

'Yes, yes. I understand. Come along now.'

'Mrs Bray said there wouldn't be a moment's peace till they knew who'd done it. Everybody's been saying that all the time. Bray and Enid themselves said so last night. You remember? Bray and Enid...'

'Yes, that's all right now.'

'So I thought I'd confess. It wasn't fair to the others if I didn't, was it?'

'No, it's very decent of you. We'll go into it together in the morning. It's too late now.'

Fayre allowed himself to be led into his tent and put in bed like a small child.

'All right now?' Roger asked heartily.

'Yes, thank you. Much better. I shall sleep tonight, I think, now. Do you think the others will be able to sleep too?'

'I'm sure they will. Good night, Fayre.'

'Good night, Sheringham.'

To Roger's astonishment Willie closed his eyes, and almost in the same action began to snore.

Nerves absolutely dead-beat, Roger thought. He ought to be safe to sleep the clock round.

Anxious questions were flung at him as he made his way back to his own tent.

'Hush!' Roger answered them collectively. 'He's asleep. Don't wake him.'

'Yes, but did he really do it? Really? Was it him?'

'Of course it was. Didn't you hear him confessing? Yes, of course we know where we are now.'

From the shuddering sighs of relief, Roger realised that people's nerves had been stretched even more tightly than he had realised.

The three women were waiting outside Roger's tent.

'He's gone to bed?' Enid asked anxiously.

'He's asleep. Almost immediately.'

'Mr Sheringham – he didn't really do it, did he? He's just gone mad for the moment. He can't really have done it. Can he?'

'He's confessed, quite circumstantially,' Roger answered dryly. 'Anyhow, he's asleep now. I think you're quite safe for the rest of the night.'

'Enid's coming into my tent for the night,' Crystal said. 'You can come along and help with her bed.'

'And mine,' Unity added firmly. 'I'm going in to Stella, whether she wants me or not.'

Crystal made a little grimace at Roger over Enid's shoulder; but Roger did not think she regretted her hostess' company, or any company, for the rest of that night as much as she would wish it thought.

chapter fourteen

Roger sat on Willie Fayre's bed. Willie seemed quite normal and sensible this morning, but Roger thought that he was running a small temperature and had better be kept in bed. In any case, he wanted him kept in bed, out of the way. Roger had been sitting there for nearly half an hour now, but did not seem to be getting much further; and Willie was becoming sulky.

'I've told you I did it,' Willie grumbled. 'Why do you want to keep bothering me with all these details? They don't matter.'

'No, of course they don't *matter*. But it interests me to get them cleared up. For instance, what about the stone? Who threw that?'

Willie paused, looking at Roger suspiciously. 'Guy threw it,' he said, and then paused again. 'That's what made me lose my temper.'

'He picked it up from the very edge of the cliff, and threw it at you when you were standing a few paces inland?'

'Yes. What on earth does it matter?'

'Not a bit. It's just curiosity. And the torch?'

'Whose torch?'

'Well, both torches, if you like.'

'Oh. Well...what about them?'

'I mean, what happened to them?'

'Good gracious, I don't know,' Willie said crossly. 'I expect they fell in the sea.'

'One was found at the foot of the rocks, you know.'

'Was it? No, I didn't know.'

'I kept it quiet. But that's why I wanted the fingerprints taken.'

'Oh! Because of what you might find on the torch?' There was no mistaking Willie's interest now.

'Exactly.'

'And – you didn't find mine?'

'Well, no one ought to know that better than you,' Roger laughed. 'I mean, considering what you did.'

Willie smiled faintly. 'Yes, that was – that was rather clever, wasn't it.'

'I should think it was. Certainly I never expected you to find the torch where I'd hidden it under my bed, and wipe it clean before I could test it at all.'

'No,' said Willie, more firmly. 'No, I had you there, Sheringham.'

'You certainly did. By the way, have you any idea how Pidgeon found out about that other murder of yours?'

Willie looked startled. 'What other murder?'

'I mean, the one he told us about. That was why you killed him, wasn't it? Because he'd found out about the other murder?'

'Oh, I see. Yes, that's why I killed him. No, I haven't any idea how he found out.'

'You said last night,' Roger remarked in a casual tone, 'that you killed him because of Enid. What did you mean by that?'

'Did I?' Willie looked puzzled. 'I don't know what I meant, then. I was a little – distraught.'

'Naturally. By the way, which way did you come back to your tent from the cliff?'

'Which way? Well, straight.'

'That would take you behind the marquee and the mess-tent. That way, do you mean?'

'I expect so. Really,' Willie said peevishly, 'you can't expect me to remember all these details. I was – I was very worked up.'

'Of course you were. But just tell me – '

'No, I won't. I – I don't care to talk about it any more. Besides, I can't possibly understand why you should want to ask me all this. I killed Guy. I pushed him over the cliff. That's all that matters, isn't it?'

'Yes,' said Roger, getting up, 'that's all that matters. Well, I should stay in bed for a day or two, Fayre. You've had a trying experience, and your nerves are bound to be on edge.'

'Yes, I think I will. By the way,' Willie added, a little diffidently, 'are you going to – to put a guard on the tent?'

'Oh, dear, no; nothing like that. I suppose,' Roger said, with a slight smile, 'that I have your word not to murder anyone else?'

'Good gracious me, yes,' said Willie, looking taken aback.

Roger sought Crystal. She was in her tent, talking to Miss Crosspatrick. Both of them looked up eagerly as Roger appeared.

'Well?'

Roger spread out his hands, palms upwards. 'Well, we're no nearer a solution, I'm afraid. I asked him a few test questions, and he got every single answer wrong. We only know one more thing, and that is that Willie at any rate didn't do it.'

'Well, I never thought he did,' said Crystal.

2

'Are you quite sure of that?' Miss Crosspatrick asked, somewhat uneasily.

'Absolutely. He did his best to satisfy me, but it was hopeless.'

'Then why did he confess?'

'I think,' Roger said thoughtfully, 'for a mixture of two reasons. Willie is quite possibly of the type that does confess to murders which it hasn't committed; but chiefly, I imagine, he confessed, worked up as he was last night, to put the general nerves at rest. You remember he said last night that there would be no peace till it was known who did it. So Willie, throwing himself altruistically into the breach, up and made the noble gesture: which will deceive everyone, presumably, except the real murderer. And we shan't hear any contradictions from him – or her.'

'You intend to keep it a secret, then, that Mr Fayre's confession is false?' asked Miss Crosspatrick.

'Most emphatically. They're quiet now. If they know the confession isn't the truth, they'll get restive again at once.'

'And the fact remains that there's still a real murderer among us?'

'If murder was ever committed,' Roger said, with a rather rueful little smile. 'You heard my views on that the night before last.'

'Yes, and didn't believe a word of them,' Crystal retorted. 'But, Roger, if it isn't Willie Fayre, who is it? Have you thought? Really, there's hardly a candidate for the post. Everyone's so absolutely ordinary. I suppose Bray could fit the bill, but somehow I don't see him as a double murderer. Do you?'

'Heavens knows,' Roger said helplessly. 'No, I don't really. But there isn't anyone else. Combe? Twyford? The St Thomas lot? Stella here? Mrs – '

'Oh, don't,' shuddered Miss Crosspatrick.

Roger looked mildly surprised, and changed the subject.

'Anyhow,' he said, 'I am more than ever convinced of one thing. Willie didn't do it himself, but he has a very shrewd idea who did. And that's a third reason why he confessed to it himself.'

'You mean, he's protecting someone?' asked Crystal.

'I do. That was my first idea, and I've come back to it.'

'That means a woman.'

'Yes.'

'And whom,' asked Crystal thoughtfully, 'would Willie protect to such lengths but his own dearly beloved Enid?'

'Late dearly beloved Enid,' Roger corrected dryly. 'And can you really see Enid pushing people over cliffs?'

'No,' Crystal admitted. 'I can't.'

'And neither can I,' said Roger.

Miss Crosspatrick said nothing.

3

The rest of the day passed quietly. Only one new development occurred to perturb Roger. In spite of his precautions, the news travelled round the camp with surprising rapidity that Willie's confession was false. Nor did people seem very much surprised. The concept of Willie as a cold-blooded murderer, and a double murderer at that, was, in the reasonable light of day, almost untenable.

Roger traced the story in one or two instances back to Enid, and remonstrated with her not without emotion.

Enid opened her eyes very wide. 'But why shouldn't I defend my husband's character, Mr Sheringham? Perhaps you don't quite realise how very, very difficult things are for me already, without it being thought that my husband is a murderer.'

'It didn't occur to you, I suppose, that your husband's idea in confessing at all was to set people's minds at rest? That by contradicting him you are making them uneasy once more, to say nothing of stultifying a very sporting gesture?'

Enid fluttered her eyelids. 'People must be brave,' she murmured. 'One tries to be brave oneself. I couldn't let poor Willie's good name suffer because a few people have behaved foolishly. Sure, surely, Mr Sheringham, truth is the most important thing, after all?'

Roger swallowed a bad word. 'And how do you know that what your husband told us isn't the truth? He hasn't denied it.'

'Oh, Mr Sheringham, I think I know my own husband better than that. Besides,' added Enid, with a little smile, 'someone told me.'

'Who?'

'Oh, I couldn't possibly tell you that, if you look so fierce. You might push him over the cliff too. Really, Mr Sheringham, you quite frighten me sometimes,' said Enid, not without pleasure.

Banking on the most likely possibility, Roger sought out Mr Combe. Mr Combe's tent was next to his own.

'Look here, Combe, why did you tell Enid that Fayre's confession wasn't true?'

'Why not? I knew what she was suffering. Her nerves are all to pieces after the way that brute Bray forced his way into her tent last night. It was abominable.'

Roger mentally gave Enid full marks for ingenuity, and returned to the subject in hand. 'You overheard what I said in my tent this morning?'

'Well, and what if I did?' demanded Mr Combe shrilly. 'You shouldn't talk so loud if you don't want to be overheard.'

Roger looked at him. 'Well, if we have trouble – real trouble, you'll be responsible. Remember that. And if I have any interference from you again, I'll deal with you roughly. Don't forget.'

'A hell of a he-man, aren't you?' sneered Mr Combe.

'I try not to get hysterical, if that's what you mean,' retorted Roger childishly.

'Damn you, stop that, you swine!' shouted Mr Combe furiously. 'Just because you're a great insensitive brute yourself, you think other people have no nerves either. Well, let me tell you, there's a great deal of dissatisfaction with the way you've been butting in. Twyford's in charge of this camp, and – '

'No, he isn't. He's abdicated. I am.'

'You? And who the blazes put you in charge, eh?'

'I did,' Roger said calmly. 'And in future discipline's going to be tightened up, do you understand? Anyone who interferes with me, or makes scenes, or upsets the general peace, is going to be dealt with so drastically that he won't be able to make a nuisance of himself again for a long, long time. And if it's you, Combe,' Roger added fiercely, 'I'll pitch you into the sea with my own hands. That's all.'

Roger had taken a firm line because he expected Mr Combe to be intimidated. But Mr Combe did not appear intimidated. He stepped back a pace and glared at Roger with such malice and fury that for a second Roger was startled.

'Do you know something, Combe?' he remarked, recovering himself. 'There is, in the cant phrase, "murder in your eyes." I should watch myself a bit more carefully, if I were you.'

Without waiting to see the effect of this final shot on Mr Combe, Roger turned on his heel and almost bumped into Sir John Birch, who appeared to have been an interested onlooker of the little scene.

'That's it,' grunted Sir John quite affable. 'That's the only way to deal with those fellers. Kick 'em. They understand that. Poet, or some nonsense, isn't he? Bloody man. Always kick poets. They understand that. Don't understand anything else. You found that, Sheringham? Eh? You found that?'

'Yes, rather,' Roger agreed, absently. He was concerned with the thought that he had just made an enemy – perhaps a nasty little enemy; and was it tactful to make enemies just at present? Yet he hardly saw what else he could have done. And without doubt Mr Combe's bark was worse than his bite; when he calmed down he would take the hint to heart. 'Yes, rather,' said Roger. 'There are some poets I should very much like to kick.'

'*All* poets ought to be kicked,' said Sir John firmly. 'Only way to treat the fellers. By the way, Sheringham, heard you mention a word just now. "Abdicate." Reminded me of what I'd been thinking myself. Pass the idea on to you. Know what this island wants, Sheringham? A king. Eh? Yes. Fellers respect a king. No more bother if we had a king. Eh?'

'That's a very good idea, Sir John,' Roger agreed warmly. He had realised now that Sir John was already a little drunk, although it still wanted half an hour to lunch-time.

'Well, sh'll I see about it, or will you?'

'Oh, I think you'd better. It's your idea. Yes, you see about it. Well, I must go off now and peel potatoes, I suppose.'

'Be a glass of sherry in the big tent, before lunch,' Sir John called after him, evidently not be outdone in duty.

4

In the afternoon Roger organised a game of rounders, with a ball of squeezed paper wound tightly with string and a spare section of tent-pole. Nearly everyone joined in, the moderately unwilling ones being persuaded on a plea of helping the weaker spirits. Sides were chosen, and quite an amount of enthusiasm worked up. The game lasted an hour and a half, ending in a general stampede for the beach and a bathe before tea, and a return match had been arranged on the spot, to take place the next morning.

Roger was pleased. Everyone had enjoyed the game, and it had seemed to be what people really wanted: there had been a more normal atmosphere than at any time for days. The only absentee had been Mr Bray, who had disappeared, with a somewhat chastened air, directly after lunch and did not return till tea-time. Roger would not have believed that anyone could disappear on the tiny island, but certainly Mr Bray, wherever he was, had not been visible. After tea Roger noticed him sidle gently out of the mess-room, and wondered, a little uneasy, what the man might be up to.

Unity echoed his thoughts almost exactly. 'I say, what's the Bray's little game, Roger? He's gone off again.'

'I don't know Unity. It's no business of mine. Or yours.'

'Isn't it, though?' Unity said indignantly. 'It's your business to know what everyone's doing. I don't trust Mr Bray. I'll put Harold on to find out. He can think up some excuse for going to look for him.'

'I'd much rather you didn't meddle, Unity,' Roger said mildly. 'Mr Bray might not want to be disturbed.'

Unity gave him a look of scorn, and went off in search of Harold. Roger did not press the point. It seemed quite unimportant.

He was sitting in a chair outside his tent, resolutely reading, when Unity strolled up to him half an hour later.

'Come for a scrumble, Roger, you lazy hound,' she said loudly. 'Do you good to work up an appetite for dinner.'

'Oh, bother you, Unity. All right.' Roger got up.

When they were out of earshot from the camp, Unity turned to him. 'I did that rather well, didn't I?'

'Very well. What's a scrumble?'

'A cross between a scramble and a tumble. Harold invented it. It just describes what happens on this foul island, doesn't it?'

'Exactly. Well, and is that all you wanted me for – a scrumble?'

'No, of course it isn't. Listen, Roger. Do you know what the Bray's doing, all by his lonesome? No, all right; I know you don't. Well, he's digging. He must have found a spade in the stores-hut, and he's digging.'

'Well, what's the excitement? That seems harmless enough.'

'Does it? Well, do you know what I think? I think he's digging a grave.'

'A grave? My dear girl, what on earth for?'

'For the next person he murders, of course.'

'Oh, for heaven's sake, Unity, leave that subject alone,' Roger groaned.

'That's all very well,' said Unity, with some indignation, 'but you know perfectly well that you think he did it yourself, and if he's done it once – well, twice, that would make – why on earth shouldn't he do it again?'

'And how do you know what I think?'

'Well, I happened to be in Crystal's tent this morning,' Unity said, without shame, 'when – '

'Eavesdroppers to right of us, eavesdroppers to left of us. If I had any nerves myself – and it's lucky for the rest of you that I haven't – what would get on them is this continuous, infernal eavesdropping.'

'Don't swear, please,' Unity said primly. 'I've given up swearing since we left England, so there's no reason why you shouldn't too. Besides, you're in the presence of a lady.'

'I'm not,' Roger retorted, with violence. 'I'm in the presence of a nasty little sneaky eavesdropper. And let me tell you, if I catch you at it again, I'll give you a public spanking.'

'Shouldn't mind if you did,' said Miss Vincent airily.

'Oh, you wouldn't, wouldn't you, you hussy? Well, perhaps Harold Parker might.'

'I wonder if he would,' said Miss Vincent, with interest.

'In any case I'm not interested in you or your concerns. So as you've brought me this distance, you may as well tell me what all this nonsense is about Bray digging.'

'Oh, you are interested, after all? Well, I'm not at all sure that I'll tell you, after you've been so horrid. – All right, all right, I will. – Well, I sent Harold off to find him with some excuse about the accounts he's supposed to be getting on with here, and Harold says the Bray was tucked away behind the banana grove, digging away like mad. And he wasn't best pleased to see Harold either, Harold says, but of course, he couldn't say anything. But Harold says it's very suspicious that he wasn't interested a bit in the accounts, but began a long explanation of why he was digging.' Unity paused dramatically.

'Well, why was he digging?' Roger asked, with patience.

'For exercise, *he* said. Well, I mean, can you see the Bray digging for exercise? Harold says he went into long explanations why rounders weren't any good to him: he wanted his exercise hard and tough: putting on weight lately, so thought he'd sneak away where the others couldn't see him and make fun of him, and really get busy. Can you beat it? And listen, Roger, he made Harold promise not to tell anyone he'd been digging, because the others would only laugh at him. So what,' concluded Unity, with triumph, 'do you say now?'

'And Harold came straight back and told you?'

'Well, of course he did.'

'And you tell me, and I tell someone else, and in half an hour the whole camp knows that Bray's been digging behind the banana grove?'

'Oh, no, it won't,' replied Miss Vincent serenely, 'because you won't be such a cad as to give Harold away. Anyhow, Roger, what do you think about it?'

'That Bray is telling the truth, if that's what you mean, young woman,' Roger replied coldly. 'And I strongly advise you not to meddle with the concerns of grown-up people.'

'Oh, Roger,' cried Miss Vincent, 'you really are *dim*.'

They turned and walked back towards the camp.

Roger replied only absently to his companion's chatter. Although he could see no reason at all for feeling worried, he did feel worried. Bray's explanation sounded perfectly plausible. It was exactly the kind of thing about which bulky middle-age is sensitive. Besides, if Bray had been lying, what on earth could be the real reason for his digging operations? For the life of him Roger could not find any other.

5

It was, in fact, Crystal who found the other explanation.

When Roger told her of the episode, in strict confidence for the protection of Mr Parker, Crystal began to giggle.

'Behind the banana grove? Oh, Roger, that's awfully funny.'

'Is it? Then I miss the joke.'

'Why, that's where the remains of that little stone hut are.'

'Yes? I'm afraid I'm very dense.'

'Why, don't you see what the man's digging for? The buried treasure that Guy said ought to be there,' giggled Crystal.

'Oh, of course.' Roger grinned. 'Well, that's fine. I hope he keeps it up.'

Crystal exploded. 'He's found the jewelled cross – that's what he's done. Oh, Roger, how marvellous.'

'What jewelled cross?'

'Not a real one, silly.' Crystal wiped her eyes. 'A fake thing from some theatrical shop. It's worked beautifully. Oh, poor Guy, how he would have enjoyed it.'

'That looks like a long job,' Roger said, with satisfaction. 'It ought to keep Bray nicely out of mischief. He's the persevering sort, too.'

Crystal suddenly sobered. 'Roger – you don't think Bray can have killed Guy to get hold that treasure, do you? He did try to buy the island off him, you remember, and Guy wouldn't sell.'

'Yes, but that was before he'd heard about the treasure.'

'Guy might have dropped a hint. We made up that story about the fisherman weeks ago.'

'Well, I suppose it's possible,' Roger said doubtfully. 'Bray was certainly very much upset that day, over losing touch with his business.'

'He said Guy had ruined him,' Crystal said fearfully. 'Roger, I believe he did it to get hold of the treasure. Oh, why, *why* were Guy and I so mad? Talk about playing with fire. Oh, I wish someone would murder me. I deserve it just as much as he did.'

'Now then, pull yourself together, Crystal,' said Roger sharply.

6

Things seemed to have quietened down. Nothing disturbed the serenity of the evening. Whether it was that even a false confession had served something of a purpose, or that people had really determined to take themselves in hand, the whole atmosphere was appreciably easier. Against hope, Roger began to hope.

Mr Bray remained in the big marquee all the evening, jovial once more, though in rather a subdued way, and took his part in the comb concert which Roger insisted upon again. There was not quite the same rather hectic hilarity of the evening before, but to Roger's sensitive observation the cheerful note was more genuine: it rang truer than it had twenty-four hours ago.

When a move was made to bed there was not the same calling from tent to tent, except for a time between Unity and anyone whom she could get to answer her, and the camp quickly settled into quietness.

Nevertheless, the night was not to be without its event. Roger was still reading, and just beginning to think about putting out his light, when a loud bellow, like that of an ox in pain, dispelled in one sickening second the faint but persistent hope which had been slowly forming in him once more.

With a despairing curse he jumped out of bed.

He was still fumbling with the last hook of his tent's fastening, when the flap was torn out of his grasp and Mr

Bray staggered in, blood pouring from a very nasty-looking wound on his right temple.

'Here, Sheringham,' panted Mr Bray, 'you've got to do something about this, see? They're trying to lay *me* out now.'

7

'"They?"' repeated Roger stupidly, staring at Mr Bray's encrimsoned temple, from which the blood was streaming down onto the front of his mauve silk pyjamas. 'Who's "they?"'

'Who?' Mr Bray's voice had become absurdly high for such a large man. 'Why, this swine of a murderer we've got here, of course. Who else do you think?'

'Half a minute, then, while I do something to that forehead of yours.'

'Not on your life. Now's the time to catch the swine. He's out of his tent. We've only got to find out who isn't in bed, see?'

'Well, come and stand outside, where we can watch the fronts of the tents, and tell me what's happened. That's perfectly safe. He can't get back under our noses. I'd rather know the facts first.'

Grumbling a little, Mr Bray consented to this course, and the two took up a position in the middle of the alleyway, where not a fly could wriggle through the flap of any tent without being seen in the clear moonlight.

Mr Bray flapped a large, impatient hand at the usual array of alarmed faces. 'Nothing, nothing. Get back to bed. Just tripped over a tent-peg, that's all. It's all right, Glad, I tell you.'

'But your face is bloody,' squeaked Mr Combe.

'So's yours,' growled Mr Bray. 'Caught my forehead on another tent-peg,' he said more loudly.

Looking a little dissatisfied with such an unexciting explanation, Mr Combe withdrew.

'Sorry to disappoint you,' Mr Bray called after him.

'Now then,' Roger murmured, when no head remained. 'I'll watch that side, you watch this. What happened? Keep your voice low.'

Mr Bray's story was brief. He had emerged from his tent to have a sniff of fresh air before getting into bed, and almost the instant his head appeared outside it had received a violent blow from what felt like some sort of cudgel. Mr Bray had staggered, and caught at the sides of the tent to steady himself, and during that couple of seconds his assailant must have disappeared; for when Mr Bray had recovered himself enough to dash round the tent in pursuit, there was no sign of him.

'So you never caught a glimpse even of what he was wearing?' Roger asked.

'Not a glimpse. He must have been right at the side of the tent when he lammed me. If I catch the swine…'

'But you're sure it's a man?'

'I'd like to see the woman,' said Mr Bray ruefully, 'who could hit like that.'

'Well, I think we've got him this time,' Roger said, with some elation, feeling quite grateful to Mr Bray for having been hit in such favourable circumstances. 'No one's been into any of these tents since you came to me. You stop here and keep watch, while I go the round.'

Mr Bray nodded, and Roger made the circuit of the camp, stopping in front of each tent and asking the occupant by name whether all was well. As he did so, he wondered whether a sniff of fresh air had really been all that Mr Bray had been seeking.

Conscientious to a degree, Roger even made his stereotyped enquiry of Lady Darracott and Sir John; and needless to say, both answered him. The trouble was that everyone else did so too. Roger returned to Mr Bray a disappointed man. From each tent had come a response, indubitably that of its legitimate occupant.

'He's got back somehow,' he reported.

Mr Bray swore horridly. 'Well, I don't know how he managed it, but I'll get the swine before I've done with him.'

'It's annoying. The fellow must be cunning. Well, I really don't see what else we can do. It's no good inspecting each man in person: we shouldn't learn anything. So you'd better come along and let me do something with that forehead of yours.'

'Oh, that's all right, old man, thanks all the same. I'll get the missus to have a go at it. She won't faint at the sight of a bit of blood.'

Mr Bray made off towards his wife's tent, and Roger went back to his own, to ponder there at some length. There were no further disturbances that night.

chapter fifteen

Almost before breakfast-time the next morning the news was round the camp that Mr Bray had not bumped his forehead on a tent-peg at all: he had been attacked. Roger, too full of despair to be angry, did not even trouble to find out how the leakage had occurred, though Mrs Bray was the obvious suspect. The situation, without ever quite slipping out of his control, kept on producing fresh tentacles for him to tie down; and he was beginning to wonder if the time would arrive when the production of new tentacles might outgrow his powers of tethering them.

Breakfast therefore, in unpleasant contrast with dinner the evening before, was an uneasy affair, with suspicious looks once more in evidence, and people edging surreptitiously away from their neighbours. Even Crystal could not produce an imitation of Irish high spirits, and Mr Combe was frankly jumpy, eyeing Mr Bray's bandaged forehead with a kind of repelled fascination. He would hardly speak to Roger.

It was heavy work, when the chores had been done, to get the game of rounders going. People seemed much more inclined to stand in little knots of two and three, and talk, sometimes feverishly; but by alternate bullying and persuasion Roger did it. There was, however, no spirit in the game, and finally it fizzled out in a dismal way as the players simply strolled off the ground in ones and twos, to leave the organiser in disconsolate solitude with Crystal.

'Well,' said Crystal, 'that's that. I think I'll go back and wash out some stockings.'

Roger walked back to the camp with her.

She had hardly disappeared into her tent when Mr Bray approached Roger and, linking arms in a somewhat effusive way, led him away from the camp again.

'Look here, old man,' said Mr Bray, with great geniality, 'I don't want you to take this wrong – no offence meant, you know, and I hope none taken – but I can't say I like the way things are going, and neither does Mrs Bray. When it comes to getting bashed on the head, it makes you think a bit. Now you and me haven't seen eye to eye before now as to how things ought to be tackled, but you got your way and I'm not one to bear a grudge. But I can still think for myself, can't I? So I'll tell you what I'm going to do. Mrs Bray and me don't care about stopping in the camp here any longer, and that's a fact. We may feel safe here among others, or we may not; that's not the point. The point is, we don't care about stopping here.'

'No?' said Roger, in some surprise. 'But you can't get away. That's everyone's trouble.'

'Oh, yes we can, if you don't mind me contradicting you, old man. And that's just what we're going to do. We're going to take a tent and up camping for ourselves, on the north side, near the stores-hut.'

'Near the banana plantation, you mean?'

'That's right, on the other side of the banana plantation. Out of sight, out of mind, let's hope. Now what I wanted to ask you, old man – well, you've no objection, I take it?'

'No,' Roger said slowly. 'Why should I have? You're quite free to act as you like, so long as you don't upset other people. You don't think this – this flight is likely to do that?'

'Why, no; frankly, old man, I don't. After all, it's no good beating about the bush, and I know some of our pals here seem to think it was me pushed our poor old late lamented over the cliff – though why I should want to do a thing like that for a man I admired and respected like him, well, it just beats me. Still, there are some who think it, and they're entitled to their own silly opinions. So you can see, it's not very likely to upset other people if I get out of their way, is it? More likely to relieve 'm, I'd say.'

'There may be something in that,' Roger agreed. 'All right. And when do you propose to make the move?'

'As soon as ever is. Young Harold can give me a hand with the tents and things.'

'But what are you going to do about food?'

'Oh, there's plenty in the hut. Tinned stuff, but what's the odds? There's another little oil-stove there too. Our pal certainly did things in style: two of everything as you might say. And the missus used to be a tidy hand at cooking in the old days. Take it from me, she won't half mind the chance of getting among the stew-pans again. 'Course at home she doesn't ever go into the kitchen now; it wouldn't do.'

'All right,' Roger nodded. 'You do as you think best.'

During the rest of the morning in consequence, Mr Parker made many weary journeys from side to side of the island, and Mr Bray even carried a few things across himself; while Roger had to answer a great many questions, and listen to a great many comments, some of the frankest relief and some of an unreasonable, formless apprehension.

To Roger himself the reason for Mr Bray's withdrawal was obvious, and it was not the reason which that gentleman had given. Mr Bray had, in fact, found an admirable excuse for staking out a squatter's claim on the site of the non-existent buried treasure. Roger did not, however, inform anyone of this interesting point, for he did not wish Mr Bray to learn that the treasure was non-existent. A Bray busily occupied in harmless digging operations was better than a Bray hanging round Enid Fayre and attracting trouble. Mr Bray was very well out of the way.

2

Roger recognised that he too had caught something of the general uneasiness. Lunch was a moody meal, eaten for the most part in a silence broken only by grumbles over the tinned food to which the catering was now reduced and the lack of fresh vegetables. After it, Roger drove such as he could down to the beach, to laze on the warm sand, but did not follow them. He wanted to get away from them for a breathing space. It was terribly hot, with a closeness in the air that promised a storm within a few hours, but Roger could not rest, or read, or do anything peaceful. He began to pace the alleyway, trying not to wish that a boat would pass within hailing distance of the island, and that very soon. The two gaps left by the Brays' tents made a break in the symmetry of the camp which annoyed him in a vague way.

When he saw Mrs Bray walk in, he regarded her sourly.

'Hullo, Mrs Bray. I thought you'd left us?'

'Well, not quate yet, Mr Sheringham, as you see, though perhaps this might be a good opportunity to say goodbaye, and thenk you for all you've done; I'm shaw you've been wonderful. But reahly I walked over to get a few things I'd forgotten from the cook-tent. Would you believe it, I'd quate overlooked the salt. One gets so out of the way of cooking, doesn't one, when one hasn't touched a saucepan or anything for yahs?' Mrs Bray was more refined than Roger had ever heard her before. She positively oozed lady-likelihood. But then she had something to live down now.

'I suppose one does.'

'You've no objection, I presume?'

'Oh, no: take anything you like.'

'Thenks so much.'

Mrs Bray walked mincingly towards the cook-tent, and Roger, for lack of anything better to do, strolled moodily after her.

Mrs Bray was still making her choice, when Angela and Twyford passed by. Seeing Mrs Bray, they stopped and spoke to her. Roger did not hear the beginning of the conversation, but he heard Angela say:

'Come on, Reggie. Let's go and pay a call on him.'

'I don't rahly think Mr Bray wants anyone to call on him,' Mrs Bray put in, rather doubtfully.

'Oh? Why not?'

'Well, I don't rahly know, but that's my fancy. I wouldn't advise it – rahly I wouldn't.'

'Well, he's not likely to throw a fit if we walk in on him, is he?'

'One doesn't know,' said Mrs Bray darkly, 'what might happen on this 'orrid – *h*orrid little island, and that's a fact.'

Angela laughed. 'Come on, Reggie. Thanks for the warning, Mrs Bray, but I think we'll risk it.' Miss St Thomas could not have been out of earshot of Mrs Bray before she added in her strident peacock tones: 'Of course I'm just dying to know what that tough's up to over there. I'll bet he's got some game on. Don't you think so, Reggie?'

'Too right,' said Captain Twyford.

Roger watched them on their way across the plateau, and turned to find Sir John at his side.

Sir John was still a little drunk.

'About that king business, Shengham,' he began, swaying gently backwards and forwards. 'Thought you'd like to know what I've decided.'

'I should like to hear that.'

'Going to take on the job myself.'

'What job?'

'King of this island,' replied Sir John testily. 'Annex it. Independent kingdom. It's the only way. Thought it all out very carefully. You agree?'

'Oh, certainly,' Roger was wondering how best to break it to Sir John that the charge of drinks must be removed from him. The man would be finding pink elephants about the place soon if this went on much longer. In the meantime, presumably he must be humoured.

'Glad you agree,' grunted Sir John. 'Otherwise have to have you executed. Powers life and death now, y'know. Tell you what I'll do instead. Make you my Prime Minister.'

'Thank you very much, Sir John. That's very gratifying.'

'Ought to be calling me "your majesty" now, eh? Not Sir John any longer. Your majesty – my majesty – everyone's majesty now. eh?'

Before Roger could reply to this difficult question, there came a sharp interruption from the north side of the island. It was the report of a shot, that was followed instantly by a loud shout – whether of alarm or pain Roger could not say.

'Ah,' said Sir John, in warm approval, 'that's better. Shooting some of these cads down, eh? That's the best thing to do with 'em – shoot 'em. Said so all along, if you remember.'

But Roger had hurried off in the direction of the shot.

3

The only thing to be seen on the plateau was Twyford, running at top speed for the camp, with Angela St Thomas strolling after him.

Roger met him just beyond the tents.

'In a hurry, Twyford, aren't you?' he asked acidly.

Twyford seemed to have some difficulty in recognising him. 'Oh, it's you, Sheringham. Thank God! Look here, this – this has got to be stopped. Bray fired at us – *fired* at us.' Captain Twyford was undoubtedly agitated.

'So I heard.'

'But you don't seem to understand, man. He tried to kill us.'

'Did he?'

'Well, aren't you going to do anything about it?' shouted Twyford.

'Aren't you?'

'Me? No. Why should I? You would be in charge here. You've got to take responsibility.'

'That's perfectly true.'

'Then do something, man!' Twyford almost screamed. 'You don't seem to realise. He tried to kill us!'

'Oh, I don't think he did really, Reggie,' Angela said, arriving at that moment. 'He simply said that if we went on any further he'd fire, and we did, so he did. But I don't think the bullet went anywhere near us.'

'Don't be a fool, Angela,' Twyford said loudly. 'I don't know about you, but let me tell you it nearly hit me.'

'Poor darling,' Angela said fondly.

'Yes, that's all very well,' Twyford muttered. 'Anyhow, it's no good pretending you weren't frightened.'

'Oh, I was. Petrified. But I didn't want the Bray to see that I was, that's all.'

Twyford turned from her impatiently. 'Well, aren't you going, Sheringham?'

'And what exactly is it you want me to do?'

'Good God, man, get that gun away from him, of course. Don't you understand? He'll murder the whole lot of us.'

'I don't think he will. And please stop shouting, Twyford. You'll frighten the whole camp.'

'What's it matter if I do? Perhaps somebody might do something then, if you won't. Good God, man, can't you see that gun has to be got away from him? I don't care what you say. He'll come over one night and shoot the whole lot of us in our beds.'

'I said stop shouting,' Roger replied sharply. 'What's the matter with you? You're behaving like a hysterical girl. Only girls seem to have more courage nowadays than men.'

'No, he isn't,' Angela interposed hotly. 'Don't be such a crashing beast. Can't you see Reggie's had a shock?'

'I don't care whether he's had a shock or not. He's got to control himself. I won't have the rest of the camp frightened to death.'

'Damn you, Sheringham,' said Twyford shrilly, 'who do you think you are? You think you can come along and give your damned orders to anyone you like. Well, you can go to hell. You're not going to give any damned orders to me. So you – "

'Oh, yes, I am.' Roger interrupted fiercely. 'I told you to stop shouting, and I'll see you obey.' He hit Twyford as hard as he could on the point of the jaw, knocking him straight over backwards. 'Now perhaps you'll obey next time?'

Twyford did not answer. He was rolling on the ground, holding his jaw with both hands.

Angela threw herself on Roger, beside herself with fury. 'You cad, you swine, you beast!' she screamed, beating at his face with both hands. 'How dare you touch him? If you do anything like that again, I'll kill you. Do you hear? I'll kill you.'

Roger caught her wrists, and looked at her suffused face, grimacing with rage.

'And I'll have no insubordination from you either, Angela,' he said, as calmly as he could. 'You'd better realise we've come down to a pretty primitive state here now, and there's no room for more than one person in charge, and that's me.'

'Who put you in charge?' Angela asked shrilly, writhing to free her wrists. 'Who put you in charge? Oh, let me go, you beast.'

'I put myself in charge, because no one else seemed ready or fit to take responsibility, and I'll have no disobedience now I am in charge, from man or woman. Do you understand? If I think you're being a public menace, I'll knock you down just as I knocked Reggie.'

Angela stopped struggling. 'You wouldn't knock me down?'

'Indeed I would – and will. And if you've any sense, as I think you have, you'd thank me for it later.'

Roger had spoken with such menacing conviction, that Angela really believed him. And now that the first fury of her rage had passed, she realised that she did not want to be knocked down at all.

'All right,' she said sulkily. 'One isn't used to dealing with such cads as you. You can let me go.'

Roger released her wrists, and she stood back from him, breathing quickly. Roger regarded her with a frown. 'And if you're wise again, you'll keep that Reggie of yours in order for me yourself.'

Angela had dropped on her knees beside Twyford's still prostrate body. She looked up at Roger with a frown as formidable as his own.

'Will you shut up?' she shrieked.

Roger glanced back at the camp. Half a dozen people were standing among the tents, looking on at the scene with fearful interest.

'Would I have knocked her down?' Roger mused, as he set off across the plateau. 'If I'd seen those people there, and realise that it was touch and go for keeping the whole camp in order, I should know I ought to. And I think,' added Roger to himself, with some surprise, 'that I should have done it. Well, well, we are getting primitive.'

4

'Sorry, old man,' came Mr Bray's bellow from among the thin trees. 'I mean it. You can't come any farther.'

'But you can't entrench yourself like this, and keep people off with a gun.'

'Sorry, old man, Mrs Bray and me aren't taking any more chances.'

'Well, I'm coming to have a talk with you,' Roger shouted back, 'so put that weapon away.'

'Don't do it, old man,' pleaded Mr Bray's bawl. 'Same rule for all. If you come another step, I'll have to shoot.'

Roger advanced three steps. He did not advance a fourth, because a bullet pinged quite close enough to him to be unpleasant. It did not crack, so that Roger was able to deduce that Mr Bray was purposely shooting wide. The warning, however, was quite clear.

'Aren't you being rather childish, Bray?' he shouted, a little angrily.

'Dare say I am, old man, but I can't help that. Mrs Bray and me are going to keep ourselves to ourselves the rest of the time we're here. No exceptions.'

Roger paused. Then he shouted:

'Where did you get the rifle?'

'Found it in the stores-hut, and ammunition. It's a .22. Nice little gun.'

'Is there another?'

'Sorry, old man, there isn't.'

'But I want that one myself: there's a bit of trouble going on in the camp.'

'Sorry, old man, you'll have to manage without it.'

'I suppose you know,' Roger shouted, 'that you're frightening people badly.'

'No need for 'em to be frightened, if they don't come poking their noses in here.'

'They're saying that you intend to come over and murder the lot of us.'

It was Mr Bray's turn to pause.

'Well, they're entitled to say what they like,' bawled Mr Bray. 'You know I'm not. All Mrs Bray and me want is to be left alone.'

'And that's all you've got to say?'

'Sorry, old man, that's all.'

'Very well. But don't be surprised,' shouted Roger, with what dignity he might, 'if they won't leave you alone after all. I can't be responsible for your and Mrs Bray's safety, if you persist in staying out here on your own.'

'That's all right, old man. We'll look after ourselves.'

Roger turned on his heel, and walked with extreme dignity back towards the camp.

Before he was quite halfway, the sound of a shot from that direction quickened his steps considerably.

'Oh, my heavens,' he groaned. 'There *is* another rifle. And if it's Twyford who's got it...'

5

On the outskirts of the camp Roger was met by a highly agitated Mr Parker, with no dignity at all.

'Oh, Mr Sheringham, please come quickly. I was waiting for you, when...it's Sir John.' Mr Parker paused to swallow.

'What is?' Roger asked sharply.

'He – I think he must have gone mad. And now,' gasped Mr Parker, 'he's started shooting.'

Pink elephants! thought Roger.

The two began to walk rapidly. In his agitation Mr Parker has grasped Roger's sleeve and was leading him, like an intelligent dog, in the direction of the big marquee.

'Is he – seeing things?' Roger asked guardedly.

'I don't know,' said Mr Parker, with a little gasp. 'But he's got Unity – Miss Vincent in there. And the other ladies, of course. And – and I don't know what's happening.'

'Well, why didn't you go in and see?'

'Oh, I did try, Mr Sheringham. At least, I just got to the entrance. Sir John was standing on a table. He had the gun then. He – he said something quite inexplicable about – about it being his throne room now, and no one could come in without his permission. So... I hope I'm not a coward, Mr Sheringham, but I did judge it better to withdraw.'

'Distinctly better,' Roger agreed. 'In fact, I've just been doing the same thing myself.'

Mr Parker looked relieved.

'Was he shooting at anyone just now?' Roger asked, as they hurried along.

'I don't really know. I'd come away to look for you.'

'Who's in there with him?'

'There's Mrs Fayre, Mrs Bray, Miss Crosspatrick, Mrs Vane, and – and Unity. And I,' added Mr Parker, with a sob, 'sent them there.'

'You sent them there?'

'Yes. Sir John issued an order to me to find all the ladies, and tell them Sir John wished to see them in the marquee. Lady Darracott requested me to inform Sir John that he was behaving foolishly, and Miss St Thomas was absent from the camp, but all the others went. Mrs Vane and Unity came all the way up from the beach.'

'I see.'

The conversation had been rapid, and the two had almost reached the marquee when a voice was raised behind them:

'Mr Sheringham! Roger!'

Roger looked back. At the door of her tent Angela St Thomas was beckoning frantically.

'Sorry,' Roger called. 'I'm busy.'

'Oh, just wait a second,' Angela implored, and began to run towards them.

'You'd better move off a bit,' Roger said to Harold.

Mr Parker moved.

'Oh, Roger, what are you going to do?'

'Do? See what Sir John's up to, of course.'

'Well, do be careful. Yes, all right, I apologise for making a scene just now. It was pretty dim of me. Only you mustn't knock Reggie about, you know; he's not used to that sort of thing. Anyhow, I just wanted to warn you that if you show yourself in front of the marquee, Sir John will shoot.'

'I see. Thanks for the warning. You don't happen to know who was the target just now, do you?'

'Yes, I do. It was Reggie!' said Miss St Thomas indignantly.

Roger suppressed a smile. 'Did he hit him?'

'No, thank heaven. He's all right – at least, he's not wounded.'

'Where is he?'

'In my tent. Please don't go in. He – he's rather upset.'

'Naturally,' Roger agreed gravely, 'being shot at twice in one afternoon. You weren't with him this time?'

'Oh, yes.'

'But didn't he try to get into the marquee?'

'Yes, we were strolling in together.'

'And Sir John fired at Twyford, not at you.'

'Well, I suppose in a way he fired at both of us,' said Miss St Thomas doubtfully.

'But you're not upset?'

'Oh, I've got Reggie to look after.'

'Did you happen to see what Sir John was doing?'

'Yes, he was sitting in a chair on the big table. Crystal and Unity were standing on the table too, and Mrs Bray, Miss Crosspatrick and Mrs Fayre seemed to be standing in a row in front of him. I think he was speaking to them when we crashed in, but I didn't hear what he was saying. It's DTs, I expect: Auntie's been afraid of it for the last day or two. And perhaps you'd better know that Sir John had a sister who went batty and used to bite people in the neck when they thought she was going to kiss them. They had to have her shut up.'

'I see. Thanks.'

'And Roger – I really do apologise, you know. And I hope you would have knocked me down too. I've told Reggie he's simply got to be sporting and do what you tell him in future.'

'Thanks, Angela,' Roger said hurriedly, 'I thought you were sensible. I don't care a bit personally, you know, but I simply can't have the rest of the community upset..'

'No, I suppose not. But damn the rest of the community, for all that. I never saw such a lot of feeble little funks in my life.'

Roger, turning away, paused to look at her curiously. 'Certainly the presence of our murderer doesn't seem to have worried you, Angela.'

'Of course not. Why should it? I thought at first it was going to be quite amusing, tracking him down and all that; but when people began getting so strenuous about it, I just lost interest.'

'Having Reggie to look after?' Roger smiled maliciously.

'Now, Roger, don't be a cad, please.'

Still smiling, Roger waved Mr Parker to keep well behind him, and approached the marquee.

He approached it cautiously, from the side, and listened. Not a sound was to be heard. Roger wondered what on earth they were up to, inside.

'Sir John!' he called gently. 'Your majesty! Have I permission to enter?'

'Eh? Who's that? Who's that?'

'Your Prime Minister.'

'My what?'

'Don't you remember? You made me your Prime Minister this afternoon.' Roger saw Mr Parker staring with open mouth, and winked at him.

'Eh? Ah, yes, so I did; so I did. No, you can't enter just now. I'm busy. Training my harem, if you want to know.'

'Oh, I see, then of course I can't enter.'

'No,' grunted Sir John. 'You can't.' And to emphasise his words he fired his gun in the direction from which his Prime Minister's voice had come.

Roger ducked, and then stared at a little round hole in the canvas not six inches from his head. Unlike Mr Bray,

Sir John had fired to hit: or rather, did not care if he hit or not. Someone inside the tent uttered a faint scream.

'No need to be alarmed, my dear,' Roger heard Sir John wheeze affably. 'I expect you'll see me shoot down dozens of 'em before I've finished with 'em. Only thing to do. Cup-bearer,' added Sir John sternly, 'my glass is empty. See it doesn't occur again.'

Roger crept away. He had had a nasty fright. This affair was more serious than he had thought.

Mr Parker was still gazing on him as men gaze on heroes, though that anyone could feel less heroic than he did just then, Roger gravely doubted.

'I must get into that tent somehow,' he muttered causing Mr Parker's gaze to grow richer and deeper. If he had known just how frightened Roger was feeling he would, had he appreciated the difference between foolhardiness and real bravery, have looked at him more admiringly still.

There was, though neither of them knew of it, another act of bravery being performed at that same moment which even transcended Roger's. Shaking with fear, Mr Combe was driving himself up the path from the beach, to see if his help were needed in the fracas that was obviously taking place in the camp.

'Well, if I can't get in, at any rate I can see in,' Roger added. 'Got a knife on you, Parker?'

Speechlessly Mr Parker produced a penknife and handed it over.

Treading very delicately, Roger crept towards the side of the marquee and very gently ripped a line two or three inches long in the canvas. Pulling the edges apart, he applied his eye to the little gap.

What he saw was surprising.

Wearing now a crude cardboard crown on his head, Sir John was still sitting in an armchair on the table, nursing the rifle on his knees and holding a glass in one hand. Behind his left shoulder Unity, still in her bathing-dress and very white in the face, waved slowly over Sir John's head a contraption which was evidently doing duty as a fan, but which Roger suspected of being in reality a broom with two dusters hanging from its head. By his right side knelt Crystal, holding a whisky bottle, while Sir John's hand rested affably on her head.

Sir John was wearing an expression of extreme complacency, as well he might, thought Roger, not knowing whether to laugh or not. For in a row on their hands and knees before the table, crouched Mrs Fayre, Miss Crosspatrick, and Mrs Bray, bumping their foreheads rhythmically on the ground in front of them to the conducting of the glass in Sir John's left hand.

6

'There are four of us,' Roger said, looking at his allies. 'Surely we can think up a plan to equalise us with one small .22 rifle?'

Mr Combe had now arrived from the beach and Willie Fayre, throwing off his role of semi-invalid, had also presented himself. Standing in a little knot at a prudent distance from the marquee the four were working out a plan of attack.

'I've told you,' Willie said indifferently. 'I'll walk in and push him off the table, if someone will attract his attention elsewhere for a minute.'

'And I've told you, that's too risky. After all, there's no need for anyone to walk in. I still think my own plan is the best, to crawl under the back wall if you three will create that same diversion towards the front.'

'Better for two of us to crawl in, on opposite sides,' said Mr Combe, with a scowl at Roger to make it quite clear that he was not doing anything to oblige him personally, but only his duty to the community. 'I'll be the other one.'

Roger looked doubtful, thereby causing Mr Combe's scowl to increase, then suddenly changed his mind. 'All right, Combe. That's sporting of you. You shall be the other one.' Perhaps the man wanted to rehabilitate himself; and if so, he must certainly be allowed to do so; though so far as actual physical help went, Mr Combe was likely to be about as much use as an enthusiastic daddy-long-legs.

'Well, you two can do as you like,' Willie said, with sudden obstinacy, 'but I'm going to try from the front. Or, if you like,' he added, with a mirthless smile, 'you can regard me as the diversion.'

'But you'll get shot, man!'

'I don't think so,' Willie said calmly. 'Besides, Sheringham, this is really my affair, you know. It's I who am in the unfortunate position of host here, now.'

Roger shrugged his shoulders. 'Well, if you must commit suicide, I suppose I can't stop you.'

'I don't think it's likely. Sir John may have given you a close shave, because he couldn't see you. I'm quite sure he won't fire at anyone deliberately. I shall make him talk to me if I can. That will give you more chance.'

'And what shall I do, Mr Sheringham, please?' Mr Parker asked excitedly. 'I can do anything you fancy would be useful.'

'Well, I don't quite see what you can do, Parker, though it's sporting of you to offer.'

'Suppose I ran across the front while Mr Fayre was slipping in? I could create a diversion from him, then, perhaps.'

'You might get hit,' Roger said disapprovingly. 'We don't want the whole camp full of wounded heroes, you know.'

'I think it's very unlikely I should get hit if I ran as fast as I could. I've never handled firearms myself, but I've always understood that a moving target is extremely difficult to hit. Please let me, Mr Sheringham. I should appreciate the honour very much.'

'All right,' Roger laughed, 'if it is an honour. But please understand, both you and Fayre, I don't approve of either of your proposals and I can't take any responsibility for either of you.'

'Oh, that's *quite* all right, Mr Sheringham,' beamed Mr Parker.

In this way it was settled, and Roger moved quietly towards the marquee to make, with as little noise as he might, entrance places for himself and Combe by unhooking the rope loops at the bottom of the back wall from the dithering tent-pegs. It was not an easy job, for the canvas was tightly strained, and Roger, whose nerves had grown in the last fifteen years unused to rifle bullets, jumped agilely as the sharp crack of another shot came from inside the tent. He ran hurriedly to the side of the marquee, just in time to see Mr Parker pelting into sight at top speed from a trial trip across the front.

'Missed me by yards,' he shouted to Roger in high exhilaration. 'I said he would.'

Roger shook his fist at him, and motioned for silence. Then grinned broad encouragement and praise, and went back to his task.

This accomplished at last, he rejoined Combe and Willie, just as another shot cracked from the tent, to be followed instantly by the appearance of Mr Parker, pelting as before.

Mr Parker swerved round the angle of the marquee, and added himself to the little group.

'Believe me, Mr Sheringham,' he beamed, 'there is a surprising kick to be gained out of doing that. I feel quite – quite exultant.'

'Ever played "last cross"?' Roger laughed.

'No, I can't say I've ever actually indulged in the game itself. They don't play it in Golders Green, I think. But I've heard of it, and I imagine the sensation must be quite similar,' replied Mr Parker in all seriousness.

'Well, are we ready?' Fayre said brusquely.

Roger nodded. 'Harold, lead off the ball. Fayre, you're acting on your own responsibility, but I do suggest that you wait till Parker has run across three times – with irregular intervals between them, of course, Parker – before you try to get in yourself. In the meantime, Combe and I will begin edging our way under the canvas at once, as we shall probably take some time over doing it in silence. Right you are. Come on, Combe. I think we've got the old chap stiff.'

Mr Combe followed in stern silence, and both men began at once very cautiously to work their heads and shoulders through into the tent. Roger heard Combe gasp when he first caught sight of the spectacle inside and held his breath for a moment in case Sir John had heard. Sir John had not, but Crystal had. She stared at them so fixedly that Roger was alarmed again. If Sir John did happen to turn round and see them, their situation, pinned down as they were by the heavy canvas, would be desperate. Unable to wriggle out with any speed, Sir John would be able to take pot-shots at them like sitting rabbits. Roger waved frantically to Crystal to take no notice of them. Fortunately she understood, and looked away.

In the meantime, Mr Parker was doing his part valiantly. Twice already he had run across, dodging and twisting, and twice Sir John had fired at him, and reloaded immediately. Each time too, Mr Parker had called out mocking: 'Missed me! Rotten shot, sir, rotten shot.' Without doubt he had been successful in engaging Sir John's whole attention.

Then Roger, over halfway through now, was seized with a horrible wish to cough. His throat began to tickle unbearably. It was like balm to hear Crystal say, during an inactive pause:

'Would you like me to sing to you, your majesty?'

Without waiting for an answer she began to sing, so shrilly and so loud that Roger was emboldened to take the risk of coughing gently into the crook of his arm, and with success.

Crystal had tried too to engage Unity's attention and sign to her to sing too; but Unity's eyes were fixed in horror on the open front across which Mr Parker was darting so nimbly; she was evidently too petrified with fear for him even to scream faintly at each shot as it was fired.

A third time Mr Parker darted, and escaped unscathed; and Roger recklessly hastened his progress. He was, in point of fact, thoroughly alarmed on behalf of Willie Fayre. Seen from the inside, the open front of the tent looked so large that it seemed impossible for anyone to run in through it and reach Sir John with even the smallest hope of not getting hit.

It was impossible.

Hardly had Mr Parker disappeared for the third time than Willie came running round the corner post. Roger groaned to see that he was making straight for Sir John, without even trying to dodge or confuse the older man, half-drunk as he was. Sir John did not even trouble to lift the rifle. He fired from the hip: and Willie dropped.

Two of the women screamed.

'Well, that's one of 'em,' Sir John remarked with satisfaction, as he reloaded. 'Don't waste your breath on him, my dears. It's going to happen to all of 'em, except you.'

Roger had struggled to get through before Sir John could reload, but one of his feet caught in a rope outside and he could not free it. Wrenching it clear just a couple of seconds too late, the force of his struggle launched him fully inside the tent just as Sir John snapped home the bolt. Nor was the launching a quiet one. This time Sir John could not fail to hear him, and did not fail. Crystal did her best to keep her body in the line of sight, but Sir John brushed her carelessly aside off the table to the ground.

'Another of 'em, eh?' grunted Sir John with pleasure, and lifted the rifle.

7

Roger never knew quite what happened next. He had come to a dead halt as he saw the rifle swing round upon him; and he even saw Sir John's finger tightening on the trigger, just as he saw the women, stopping in their absurd antics, staring with horror, too frozen even to scream. The next instant Sir John's chair was violently upset, and Sir John himself flung off the edge of the table. Crystal, getting there just in time, had gripped the chair's legs with all her strength and succeeded in overturning it.

'Well *done*, Crystal!' Roger cried, bounding forward. 'Come on, Combe. We've got him now.'

But Sir John was not finished yet. Picking himself up with surprising agility, he thrust the muzzle of the rifle against

Unity's side. With a sick feeling Roger realised that it had not yet been fired.

'Stand still,' Sir John panted. 'If either of you moves an inch, I'll shoot her. I really cannot have disturbances of this kind.'

Roger and Combe stood still: there was nothing else to do. Still feeling sick, Roger watched the gun poked against Unity. The girl stood like a statue, too terrified to shift a muscle.

'Get out, both of you,' grunted Sir John.

'If – if we go, will you promise not to shoot her?' Roger asked, controlling his voice as well as he could.

'What's it got to do with you, whether I shoot one of my own concubines or not?' demanded Sir John peevishly. 'Dammit, sir, it's no business of yours.' As Roger did not move, he suddenly roared: 'Get out, I said.'

Roger tried to make the look he sent Unity a reassuring one, as he said: 'Come on, Combe. We mustn't disobey his majesty, you know.'

With tread as delicate as Agag's he walked out of the tent, with Combe trailing on his heels.

As soon as they were clear, Combe burst out.

'Don't be a fool, man,' Roger said wearily. 'He certainly would have shot Unity if we'd gone for him. There was nothing else to do but get out.'

Mr Combe sneered.

'Mr Fayre was hit?' asked Mr Parker breathlessly. 'I saw through your spy-hole, Mr Sheringham. Can't we rescue him?'

'If you'd tell me how, Harold, I'd be grateful.'

'Couldn't we cut the tent-ropes?' Mr Parker suggested excitedly. 'And while Sir John was looking round, I could run in and carry Mr Fayre out on my back.'

Roger shook his head. 'I'd thought of cutting the ropes and letting the tent down on the lot of them, so that we could smother Sir John in the folds while the women crawled out. But I'm afraid it would be too dangerous. Sir John would almost certainly take a pot-shot at one of them before the tent came down.'

He looked round at the sound of voices behind him, and saw Lady Darracott and Angela approaching. Lady Darracott was not leaning on her niece, as she usually did; she was walking quickly and very upright, her white hair uncovered.

'Auntie, don't,' Angela was pleading. 'You know what your heart is. Please come back to your tent.'

'Nonsense, Angela,' Lady Darracott retorted briskly. 'Please be quiet. Mr Sheringham, what's this I hear? Johnnie's gone mad? Well, I can't say I'm surprised. Has he hit anybody with that gun?'

'Yes, Fayre. I don't know how badly. Fayre made a rush at him. We told him it was suicide.'

'That's true. Johnnie use to be a good shot at a running target when he was younger,' Lady Darracott said, causing Mr Parker to look a little uneasy. 'Please tell me exactly what has happened.'

Roger told her.

'I see. I'll go in and speak to him.'

'You'll go in and... Lady Darracott!'

'Auntie!'

'But Lady Darracott...'

'Well?' Lady Darracott looked serenely at the objectors.

'But Lady Darracott, you can't,' Roger said feebly.

'Indeed? And why not, young man?'

'You know you can't, auntie.'

'Don't be so absurd, child. You know quite well that Johnnie Birch would never shoot at me.'

'But, auntie, your heart. The strain. You'd be in bed for weeks.'

'I think my heart will stand the strain of sending Johnnie back to his tent.'

The discussion grew. Everyone did their best to dissuade Lady Darracott from such a rash idea. Lady Darracott merely smiled.

'It's no good,' she said finally, with no trace at all of her old helplessness. 'I am the only person to whom Johnnie is in the least likely to listen; and I can assure you I shall not run the slightest risk.' She began to move towards the front of the marquee, the others still expostulating as they followed her.

'Then if you're really determined, Lady Darracott,' said Mr Parker, 'you must please allow me to escort you.'

'Escort me, Mr Parker?'

'Yes. I couldn't possibly allow you,' said Mr Parker, with great firmness, 'to enter the tent alone.'

'And I am afraid that I could not possibly allow you to accompany me. You don't seem to realise, young man, that Sir John won't in the least mind shooting at you.'

'I don't think he will, if you'll agree to a little idea of mine, Lady Darracott,' Mr Parker said modestly. 'If you will agree to be called – just for the moment, of course – the queen-consort, and permit me to enact the part of your train-bearer, I think Sir John might be so flattered that he will not shoot either of us.'

Lady Darracott stared; then she smiled grimly. 'Very well, Mr Parker; you shall be my train-bearer. But kindly do not carry my train too high.'

Roger and Angela exchanged glances. Roger shrugged his shoulders, and Angela shrugged hers. This was a new Lady Darracott, whom not even her own niece knew.

Lady Darracott and her escort halted just before the angle of the tent, where Mr Parker very gingerly possessed himself of the extreme hem of Lady Darracott's dress. Then they disappeared.

The others held their breath.

'Her majesty, the queen-consort.' Mr Parker's voice rose from inside, a little shaky but quite clear, 'and her majesty's train-bearer.'

No shot followed.

Lady Darracott, hardly looking at the absurd figure on the table, eyed the scene with considerable interest. Sir John, re-throned and re-crowned, was once more seated in state; on the ground in front of him Miss Crosspatrick, Mrs Fayre, and Mrs Bray were once again monotonously beating their foreheads, now wearily and sadly out of time.

Having taken in the scene, Lady Darracott bent a formidable frown on his majesty. 'Johnnie, what is the meaning of this?'

'Forgot to tell you, Ann,' replied Sir John, in a shamefaced way. 'Annexed this island this afternoon. First king. This is my harem.'

'You appointed yourself king of the island, without even asking me to share your throne?' Mrs Darracott said severely. 'That was not at all nice of you. However, I've appointed myself queen-consort, so perhaps I'll overlook it.'

'Meant to, Ann,' mumbled Sir John. 'Quite inadvertent. 'Pon my soul, I did.'

'I hope so. Well, perhaps you'll be good enough to get me a drink.'

'Send one of my slaves. Those are my slaves salaaming. These two are my concubines,' pointed out Sir John, not without pride.

'Indeed? But I'm afraid I never accept drinks from slaves. None but his majesty himself shall serve me. Give me that thing you have in your lap, whatever it is, while you get down from your throne.'

Sir John hesitated, then handed over the gun. Lady Darracott gave it to Mr Parker, who ran out of the tent with it.

And that was the end of the reign of King Johnnie Birch.

chapter sixteen

Willie was not dead.

He seemed, however, very seriously wounded. The bullet had entered the right side of his chest and had probably pierced the lung, in which, Roger thought, it might even be lodged. Roger's first care was to get him carried, as gently as possible, to his tent and put to bed. No one in the party had any surgical knowledge, and nothing could be done except to make him as comfortable as possible and hope for the best. Willie was quite conscious and seemed indifferent alike to his paint and the possibilities.

In his short interview with Enid it was Roger who seemed the most agitated of the two. 'I implored him not to do it,' he said. 'I warned him that it was suicidal. We all did. But he wouldn't listen. I've never seen anything braver – but I've never seen anything more foolhardy, either.'

Enid nodded. She was not weeping, but she was trembling all over. It was obviously an effort to her to control her lips enough to allow her to speak. She had just been through a dreadful ordeal, culminating in the wounding of her husband, and it might have been forgiven her if she had broken down; but though plainly distressed, she appeared to be a long way from that.

'He did very well in the war,' she said, a little shakily. 'Did you know he had the Military Cross? He was recommended for the VC.'

'No, I didn't know that,' Roger said, impressed. He was surprised too. Willie Fayre had never struck him as a possible hero.

'And, of course, when he saw what had happened, he just saw red,' Enid went on, even in such circumstances preening herself just a little. 'Willie's so terribly fond of me,' she added, with a sigh.

'Of course he is,' Roger said heartily, and did not append his private opinion that whatever the sojourn on the island might or might not have done in the case of other people, it had worn Willie's fondness a little thin.

He left the patient in Enid's care, and hurried off to see after the other women. As he went he marvelled slightly. The words 'One must be brave' were often on Enid's lips, and there was no doubt that Enid herself was brave. And yet Roger would not have expected Enid to shine for bravery in a crisis any more than he would have expected Willie. The fact is, he mused as he hurried along, her bravery is really a pose: brave is what she would like the world to think her: and she poses so damned hard that brave she actually is. The pose had become the woman.

The other victims of ex-King Johnny Birch were also doing their best to be brave about it, but not with quite the same amount of success. Seeing how shaken they all were, Roger had asked Combe to give them a stiff dose of brandy before tea, and when Roger arrived they were sipping it. Roger noticed that they huddled a little together, and there was a good deal of rather shrill laughter. He noticed too that most of the laughter came from Crystal and Unity.

Roger was interested to observe the effect their ordeal had had on each individual. Mrs Bray, for instance, appeared to be highly indignant.

'And what Mr Bray will say about it,' she was observing as Roger arrived, 'I wouldn't like to think. He won't care about it at all, me being dragged into a thing like that.' She fixed an accusing eye on Roger. 'Why, this camp isn't safe, it isn't. A very good thing Mr Bray and I've moved out of it. I wouldn't care to spend another night here, and that's a fact.'

'Oh, the camp's all right,' Roger affirmed. 'Sir John's been drinking too much, that's all. And that might have happened anywhere.'

'Huh,' replied Mrs Bray, and tossed her head, as much as to ask what was the good of Roger if he couldn't stop that sort of thing.

'Oh, by the way,' Roger said lightly, 'I was almost forgetting. What's happened to your husband, Mrs Bray? He really mustn't begin shooting at friendly visitors. What's his idea?'

Mrs Bray's face took on a shut expression. 'Mr Bray doesn't want any visitors.'

'But why not?'

'Mr Bray and me, we've decided to keep ourselves to ourselves.'

'But he can't shoot at people like that.'

'Mr Bray says he doesn't want anyone interfering with him any more. He doesn't know who gave him that crack on the head, and he says it's safer if we don't have anyone over there at all.'

'But there must be exceptions, surely?'

'Mr Bray says there can't be any exceptions.'

Roger shrugged his shoulders, and then laughed. 'Well, warn him for me that if he gets into trouble over it, he'll have to take responsibility. I wash my hands of him.'

'Mr Bray's shoulders are quite broad enough to take any responsibility,' replied Mrs Bray stiffly. 'And if that's all, I think I'll be going.'

No one gainsaying her, Mrs Bray went.

'Oh dear, I've never...it was awful.' Unity shivered, and then laughed on a high note. 'Awful!'

'I didn't mind it till he began – shooting,' Crystal said shakily. She caught Roger's eye and then laughed too. 'We must have looked a scream to you, Roger, didn't we?'

'You saved my life,' Roger said, lightly enough. 'I never saw such presence of mind in my life. Have another drink.'

'Lots more,' Crystal replied, with another shrill little laugh. 'I feel I need it.'

Mr Combe manipulated the bottle with grace.

'And as for Parker,' Roger continued, 'you were a regular Douglas Fairbanks, Parker.'

Mr Parker giggled modestly. 'Very kind of you to say so, Mr Sheringham, but it wasn't anything really.'

'It was,' Unity said emphatically. 'You were marvellous, Harold.'

'Then stop shaking, Unity,' Roger said, with mock severity. 'It's all over now, with the greatest credit to all concerned.'

'I know it's over, but...it might happen again, mightn't it? Sorry to be such a funk, but I can't help it. Roger, can't you possibly get us off this ghastly island? Are you sure you've thought of everything?'

'Quite sure,' Roger said gently. 'We've just got to stick it out till the yacht comes back.'

'Oh dear, what a bore.'

'Unity.' Mr Parker put his arm boldly round the trembling girl, and then blushed as no Douglas Fairbanks ever blushed.

'And we're all in the same boat, remember, ' added Roger.

'Oh, no, we're not,' Mr Combe put in gloomily. '*One* of us isn't in any danger.'

'Nobody's in any danger,' Roger said sharply.

'No?' sneered Mr Combe. 'Well, I'm glad to hear it.'

'Oh, don't *talk* about it!' suddenly burst out Miss Crosspatrick. Her face was the colour of whey, and the hand that held her glass was shaking violently. 'For heaven's sake stop *talking* about it!' she almost screamed, and turned violently away.

Roger looked at her uneasily, but before he could speak Angela St Thomas, strolling towards the little group and just in time to raise her eyebrows at Miss Crosspatrick's back, had spoken to him instead:

'Roger, could you come over and speak to Reggie? He wants a word with you.'

'Yes, of course.' With another uneasy glance at Miss Crosspatrick's shaking shoulders, Roger muttered to Crystal: 'Come and tell me if she gets out of hand,' and accompanied Miss St Thomas.

On the way over he said to her: 'That was an extraordinarily plucky action of your aunt's.'

'It was absolutely marvellous,' Angela agreed. 'I can't think how she did it. She's always seemed to think that the least exertion or excitement would make her just drop down dear. Now she's taken Sir John completely in hand, won't let me do a thing, and is feeding him aspirin by the dozen; and what's more, he's taking them like a lamb.' Just outside her tent she halted and added in a lower voice: 'Don't be harsh with Reggie, Roger. The poor darling really is terribly upset.'

Roger nodded, and they went inside.

Captain Twyford was sitting on Angela's bed, holding his head in both hands, his elbows on his knees. He looked up with a violent jerk as the two entered.

'Well, Twyford?'

'Yes? Oh, yes. Er – where's Sir John, Sheringham?'

'In his tent. He's quite quiet.'

'But you can't leave him there?'

'Oh, I thinks so.'

'But he might break out again at any minute. You must shut him up somewhere.'

'Where? It's not much good trying to shut him up in a canvas tent, is it?'

'You could shut him in the stores-hut.'

'Bray might have other views. Besides, Sir John might find another gun there.'

Twyford shivered. 'Did he get the rifle from there?'

'I told you, Reggie. He told auntie he took it days ago, to see if he could find anything to shoot.'

Twyford looked at her dully. 'He found me,' he said, without a smile. 'Are you sure the gun's safe now, Sheringham? Where is it?'

'In my tent.'

'Unguarded?' Twyford's voice rose to a higher note. 'You mustn't leave it unguarded, man. He – he might get hold of it again.'

Roger smiled. 'I think Lady Darracott has him in hand. Is that all you wanted?'

'No, no. Don't go. Sheringham, I've been thinking. We must collect everything that could serve as a weapon. Razors, pocket knives, sticks, tent-mallets. I'm very worried. The place isn't safe, you know. Nobody's safe. We must take precautions. It would be an awful thing if...' He broke off with a shudder.

'If what?'

'If anything more happens. And it will. I know it will. Don't you think the Brays were wise to clear out, Sheringham?' Captain Twyford asked earnestly.

'I think it was a little – what shall I say? – lacking in the communal spirit.'

'No, no. It was just a precaution. I – I suppose we couldn't all separate, could we? Don't you think that would be a good idea? All separate to different parts of the island?'

'I think most people feel safer together.'

'I don't,' Twyford groaned.

'Well, I don't see what else we can do. Is that all?'

Twyford nodded. 'I just wanted to ask you. You will see that all weapons are collected, won't you? Even – frying pans, I think, don't you?'

'I'll see to it,' Roger said soothingly, and made his escape.

Angela followed him out. 'I think it's quite a scheme, don't you?' she said, without very much conviction.

Roger could no longer keep the contempt out of his voice. 'I'm afraid Twyford's lost his nerve, Angela.'

Angela was on the defensive at once. 'Well, it's hardly surprising, is it? Reggie isn't used to this sort of thing.'

'No? I should have thought that this sort of strain was exactly the kind of thing he was used to.'

Angela looked at him in a curious way, as if she were about to say something; then she evidently changed her mind and kept silent.

'Anyhow, I leave him in your charge, Angela,' Roger concluded. 'Keep a tight hand on him, please. The others are quite jumpy enough already.'

He walked back to the little group, which was still as he had left it.

Just as he was reaching it he saw Stella swing round on Unity, her hand raised as if to strike the girl.

'Don't *talk* about it!' she screamed.

Unity shrank back, her face white.

'Oh, Stella,' said Roger, 'you're in the scullery squad, aren't you? Did you know the teacups haven't been washed up? I wish you'd see to it. I want my tea.'

Stella looked at him vacantly for a moment, then nodded and turned away.

2

In the kitchen-tent Stella was sitting on a chair, staring at the ground. She had a dishcloth in her hand, but no teacup.

Roger smiled at her. 'Feeling better, Stella?'

She did not answer. Roger was perturbed to see that she was shaking all over, far more violently than before. He erased the forced smile from his face and spoke sternly.

'Now, Stella, this won't do, you know. Pull yourself together. You mustn't give way like that, especially in front of the others. You know I'm relying on you to help keep people calm. You – '

Stella jumped to her feet.

'I can't help it. And I don't care. I tell you, Roger, I can't stand it much longer. I'm not brave at all. I've pretended not to mind all this time, but I can't keep it up. I can't, I tell you!' Miss Crosspatrick's voice rose more and more shrill. 'You seem to think everyone ought to be made of iron. Don't you understand? I'm terrified – terrified!' Miss Crosspatrick's teeth were chattering: her eyes stared at Roger wildly. 'I've got a feeling I shall be the next one. I *know* I shall be the next one!' she suddenly screamed.

'Stop that nonsense, Stella.' Roger hoped fervently that no one had heard the scream. Screams are infectious.

'It isn't nonsense. Why the hell don't you *do* something, instead of standing about and showing how brave you are? Get us off this island, you fool. Oh, get us off this island,' Miss Crosspatrick sobbed. 'Get us off this island. You could if you wanted to.'

'Stella, you're being absurd. Stop making this exhibition of yourself.'

'I won't. I'm not used to this sort of thing. I haven't slept for nights. Don't you understand? For nights I haven't slept a wink. And – and I always have been afraid of the dark. Oh, my God, *do* something! I can't stand the strain any longer.' Miss Crosspatrick began to cry, hiccoughingly and unbeautifully.

Roger was at a loss. He knew the girl was overwrought. She had had a nerve-breaking experience, and if it was true that she had not slept for nights her nerves would have been in tatters without that. But the complete breakdown of pride which made her not even care any longer what sort of a figure she cut, showed that she really had reached the end of her tether. And what Roger was to do with or about her, he did not know.

What he did do was to pat her clumsily and mutter something about keeping up appearances in front of the others, which caused Miss Crosspatrick to cling to him with both hands and weep against his shoulder.

'You're the only person I trust,' she sobbed. 'I only feel safe when you're with me.'

'There, there,' said Roger.

'You will look after me, won't you, Roger?'

'Of course I will.'

'Can't we really get away from the island? Couldn't we make some sort of a boat out of the tents, or something like that?'

'I'm afraid it wouldn't be practical. Anyhow, there's less than a week.'

Miss Crosspatrick lifted a tear-stained face. 'A week. I can't stand it. I shall go mad. I shall go mad!' she shrieked. 'Roger, I shall go *mad!*'

Roger disengaged himself from her.

'Stella, you'll do nothing of the sort,' he said firmly. 'You'll help me set an example to the others, that's what you'll do. You and Crystal and Lady Darracott – we four have got the responsibility of keeping the rest of them calm. You're not going to let us down, surely – you of all people?'

Miss Crosspatrick was silent for a moment, except for the occasional hiccoughing sobs that still came from her. Then she spoke in something like her normal voice.

'All right. I'll try. Sorry – made a fool of myself. Go away, Roger. Where are those teacups? I'll...'

Roger slipped out.

3

The little knot in the alleyway had now disappeared, but Crystal ran out from her tent as Roger came into view.

'Is she all right?' she asked anxiously.

Roger nodded. 'I think she'll do.'

'Oh, Roger. Stella, of all people. Had I better go to her?'

Roger hesitated. They had moved instinctively away from the camp towards the cliff, out of earshot. 'I don't know,' he said. 'She may be better alone, if she keeps busy.'

'Here comes Lady Darracott,' warned Crystal, glancing back.

Roger turned back. Crystal waited.

Lady Darracott was advancing with a firm stride. 'Did that scream I heard come from Miss Crosspatrick?' she asked grimly.

'It did,' Roger answered, raising his shoulders helplessly. 'But I think she's better now.' He glanced apprehensively towards the cook-tent.

As if in direct reply a piercing wail at once came from it.

'Roger – Roger! Don't leave me, Roger!'

'Oh, my goodness,' Roger groaned, and took a step or two towards the tent.

Lady Darracott stopped him. 'I will see to Miss Crosspatrick,' she said serenely. She paused for a moment and fixed on Roger a look so piercing that he instantly felt guiltily responsible for every single thing that had happened on the island.

'And let me tell you this, young man,' Lady Darracott followed up her look. 'What you had better do is to concentrate your energies on unearthing this murderer we hear so much about, and putting him under safe restraint. Because if you don't, I shall soon be the only sane person left on this island.'

'Hell's bells,' Roger muttered to himself, as he rejoined Crystal, 'I believe she's right.' He looked gloomily at his companion.

Crystal uttered a nervous little laugh. 'I don't think Stella will scream any more. I wouldn't dare, with Lady Darracott helping me to get tea. Oof, I wish tea was ready: I want mine.' She dropped onto the warm turf. 'Oh, my goodness, it's hot. I wish the storm would burst. I feel stifled. Sit down, Roger. I can't bear you frowning down on me. That's better. Roger, what will you do to me if I go all gaga like Stella did? I can't help feeling I might, you know, at any minute.'

'Nonsense,' Roger said stoutly, but with an uneasy remembrance of Lady Darracott's words. 'You wouldn't Crystal. You've got outlets.'

'Outlets?'

'Yes. That's why Stella cracked. Suppression. Or perhaps she doesn't pretend hard enough. There's the contrast with Enid. Enid pretends so hard to be brave that she ends up actually being brave. But she has a safety-valve in pretending simultaneously to be more of a coward by nature than she really is, so that her bravery shall be all the more remarkable. Stella never let out that she was really frightened at all. She had the harder pose, and it broke her down.'

'And Harold!'

'Harold was truly magnificent. It was a film gesture, of course, but what a gesture. Who said the films never did anyone any good? And incidentally, thank you, Crystal, my dear for saving my life.' Roger leaned forward and kissed Crystal on the cheek.

'Oh, that's quite all right, my pet.' Crystal was recovering something of her normal manner. 'I'd do it whenever I could, but life in London's so lacking in opportunities.'

'Life here seems to be bringing people's real natures out,' Roger said, a little grimly. 'Bray, not caring anything so long as he gets hold of that treasure; Twyford....well, who could have foreseen the magnificent Twyford reduced to this contemptible creature? And Lady Darracott. I don't think that Angela even now can see her as a *malade imaginaire*, she played her part so well: a selfish old creature, but rising to the occasion magnificently when necessary. And I really can't think why Angela herself should have been at such pains to hide the good stuff that must have been always in her, underneath the sillinesses and affectations. As for

Combe, I can't quite make him out; he's got so many poses, one doesn't really know which is the man. I think he's the sort of person who goes to pieces under anticipation or strain, but can be really brave when physical courage is wanted. And who would have thought that Willie all but won the VC?'

'Yes, and who of them all,' asked Crystal sombrely, 'pushed Guy over the cliff? Or if not pushed, was with him when he fell over? Roger, you see what this uncertainty is doing to people. Stella herself has collapsed under the results of her own plan. No, I was right. Roger, you *must* find out who it was.'

'Lady Darracott said much the same thing,' Roger said gloomily. 'I think you're right. But what can I do? Now Willie's out of it, I can't get a line on anyone.'

'Can't you get anything from the attack on Bray?'

'You think that was necessarily made by the same person?'

'Well, I should think obviously. Don't you?'

'I don't know. It seems likely. But what was the motive?'

'You don't think that perhaps Bray had got somewhere near the truth, and the person tried to kill him, just like he killed Guy?'

'Bray seemed to think the person tried to kill him, but I don't know. It was a nasty crack, but a very long way off a fatal one. And how did the unknown get back to his tent? Or to hers, for there's nothing yet to show that it wasn't a woman. I suppose he or she must have dodged round like lightning and crawled in at the back. There was time.'

'That sounds like someone in the opposite row. It... I suppose it couldn't have been Stella, could it? She's got the next tent to Bray's.'

'Why on earth should Stella want to biff Bray?'

'I don't know,' said Crystal helplessly. 'Unless for the reason I mentioned.'

'It all seems very far-fetched,' Roger muttered. 'And yet by this time I'm almost ready to believe anything of anybody. Under acute stress civilised people evidently revert to the primitive a great deal more quickly than one would ever have imagined.'

'They do,' Crystal said, with feeling. 'I can't tell you how primitive I feel myself.'

Roger pulled at his cigarette. 'The attack on Bray,' he said thoughtfully. 'That should be a pointer, of course; it seems only reasonable that it was made by the same person. But the trouble is that there's no more evidence in that case than in the other.' He groaned. 'Can't you think of one little point we could follow up, Crystal? Not a single one?'

Crystal sat up with an Irish noise of impatience. 'Do you know what I should do, Roger? Bother your pointers and your evidence! I should take each person aside in turn and ask them why they attacked Bray. And if you can't spot the liar among them, what's the use of you?'

Roger looked at her with admiration. 'Do you know, Crystal, that's a very interesting suggestion. Most unorthodox, but very interesting. I'll try it at once.'

He jumped to his feet. Angela St Thomas had just appeared at the top of the little path coming from the cove.

'Angela!'

Angela hurried towards them. 'Oh, I say, have you seen Reggie anywhere? He was going to join me on the beach, but he hasn't turned up, and – '

'Yes. One minute, Angela. I want to ask you something first.' Roger fixed her with a stern eye. 'Why did you attack Bray the night before last?'

Angela stared at him. 'Me?'

'Well, Twyford then, if you like.'

'What the hell are you talking about?'

'Nothing,' Roger said quickly. 'What were you asking? Twyford? No, I haven't seen him. I expect he's still in his tent.'

With a somewhat puzzled expression Miss St Thomas nodded and walked away.

'Well, it wasn't either of them,' said Roger to Crystal.

'I should try Stella,' Crystal advised.

Roger looked a little doubtful, but began to walk towards the cook-tent. Crystal followed him. As they approached, Stella appeared in the opening.

'Tea's ready,' she called.

'Stella!' Roger called back.

Stella waited for him to reach her.

'Feeling better?' Roger asked abruptly.

'Yes,' said Stella abruptly.

'Then perhaps you'll tell me now,' Roger barked, 'why you attacked Bray the night before last?'

'Have you gone quite mad?' Stella asked, with something of her old gentle superiority.

'No,' said Roger, 'but I soon shall be.'

He went back to Crystal.

'It wasn't Stella, he said, 'and tea's ready.'

'Thank heaven.'

Just outside the marquee Unity and Mr Parker were talking.

'Unity!' Roger summoned.

Unity came over to him. Crystal strolled towards Mr Parker.

Roger took Unity's arm. 'Unity,' he said fiercely, 'why did you hit Bray on the head the other evening?'

'What?'

'You know what I mean. Why did Harold attack him?'

'What on earth are you talking about, Roger? You know perfectly well Harold didn't.'

'No?' sneered Roger. 'Then I suppose neither of you did?'

'Of course we didn't, curse you!'

'I never thought you did,' said Roger. 'Run away.'

'Oh, Roger, are you trying to trap – '

'Run *away*.'

Unity ran, giggling.

Crystal strolled back, lifting her eyebrows. Roger shook his head.

'Crystal,' he said, 'why did you hit Bray over the head the other night?'

'Because I don't like those suede shoes he wears, my pet. Why did you?'

'I believe it was Mrs Bray, after all,' Roger said gloomily.

'Or Lady Darracott.'

'I expect really it was Twyford all the time.'

'Reggie hasn't the guts.'

'It doesn't require much guts to hit an unsuspecting man on the head as he comes out of a tent,' Roger pointed out. 'In fact, the whole attack surely shows that it was carried out by someone without guts.'

'Well, what about Valentine?'

'Combe? It's not unlikely.'

Unity scampered up to them, grinning. With the exuberance of puppyhood she seemed now to have shaken off most of the effects of that terrifying half-hour in the marquee that afternoon.

'Come on, you two. Tea's ready. I say, is Stella all right? She still looks a bit groggy. I suppose you know the latest? Angela can't find her darling Reggie. I say, have you found out who bashed the Bray yet, Roger? Have you asked Lady Darracott if she did?'

'Go away, Unity,' Roger said sourly. 'I dislike children.'

'Oh, crumbs,' observed Miss Vincent, 'here comes the Darracott. Come on, Crystal.' She disappeared into the marquee.

Crystal followed her. Roger waited politely for Lady Darracott, who was coming from the direction of her tent.

Lady Darracott glanced round in an apparently casual way, then slowed her pace and beckoned. Roger hurried towards her.

'Mr Sheringham,' she said, 'there is something I think you ought to know. Mr Parker told me he had put the rifle Sir John had on your bed. I looked myself about a quarter of an hour ago. It was there, and I put the ammunition I took out of Sir John's pockets beside it. I've just looked in again to make sure that they were still there, and they're not. Have you put them away somewhere?'

'Put them away?' Roger echoed stupidly. 'No. I haven't even seen them.'

'Then it looks,' Lady Darracott said calmly, 'as if someone has taken them.'

4

It was a depleted party for tea, and an uneasy one. The Brays, Willie Fayre, and Sir John were all absent, and Twyford did not turn up; and the various reasons for their empty places evidently weighed on the others. Stella and Combe were both moodily silent; Angela St Thomas was restless; Unity's laughter and chatter, as well as Mr Parker's effort to respond, were still a little feverish; and it was obviously an effort for Crystal herself to appear normal. Only two of the party appeared to advantage.

Roger, depressed himself, noted with wonder and relief the firmness with which Lady Darracott took charge. Having accounted at the beginning that Sir John was sleeping soundly, she proceeded to carry the conversation on her own shoulders. Discussion after discussion was inaugurated upon such totally impersonal matters as the theatre, foreign travel and the political situation in Germany; and no one was allowed to remain uneasily outside its orbit. Roger did his best to back up Lady Darracott, as did Crystal; but both were easily outshone by Enid who, every inch the charming hostess, continued to smile round with imperturbable graciousness, to all appearances quite untouched either by her recent experiences or by the fact that her husband, for all that anyone knew, might be at the point of death.

During the meal Roger meditated the information that Lady Darracott had given him. The twin facts that Twyford, as well as the rifle and ammunition, had vanished, appeared to him to be obviously linked. That Twyford should disappear by himself would not have worried Roger at all; but Twyford with a loaded rifle in his hands was a different matter. As soon as he thought it advisable Roger slipped unobtrusively out of the marquee.

His exit, however, had not been unobtrusive enough. Immediately he got outside the tent, Angela was at his heels.

'Roger,' she said at once, 'I'm worried about Reggie. I think we ought to have a look round.'

'Just what I was going to do,' Roger nodded. 'You go back to the others, Angela. I'll look for Twyford.'

'No, I'm coming, too.'

'I'd rather you didn't.' Roger hesitated. 'You see, I have an idea that he may have taken the rifle Sir John had. It may be a little dangerous to look for him.'

'Not if I'm with you,' Angela said firmly.

Roger, unable to dissuade her, had to agree. They started on a circuit of the island.

'I'm worried,' Angela said again, as they passed the head of the path to the beach. 'You see, Reggie really was rather – upset.'

'Do you mean you're afraid that he may have done something foolish?' Roger asked bluntly.

'Yes,' Angela muttered. 'I am.'

'Well, it isn't suicide, or he wouldn't have taken the gun,' Roger pointed out, grimly kind. 'Still, we'd better try the tops of these cliffs. He doesn't seem to be on the beach. He got rid of you, did he?'

'I suppose so,' Angela admitted reluctantly.

Roger forebore to remind her that she should not have left Twyford to follow alone, and they trudged on.

As he walked, Roger's resentment grew. Why must he always be called in to look after every hysterical nuisance, male or female? Why did people appeal only to him to get them off the island? Why did Lady Darracott assume that only he could clear up the mystery of Pidgeon's death? Why couldn't anyone else have some feeling of responsibility? He almost began to hope that Twyford had fallen over the cliff and broken his neck. That at any rate would be one danger spot eradicated.

His meditation had reached this point when there was a sharp little crack ahead of them, and a splinter of rock flew off a boulder beside them with a high-pitched hum.

'The devil,' said Roger, and halted sharply.

5

They had reached a point on the cliffs almost due west from the centre of the island, peering down among the jagged edges of rock as they went. The shot brought all their attention ahead.

Angela had not stopped as Roger had done. She continued to walk on, calling loudly:

'Reggie! Reggie!'

'Go away,' came a distant voice.

'But it's me, Reggie.'

'I don't care who it is. No one's coming here.'

'I'm coming.'

'Then I'll shoot you.'

'All right – shoot!'

Angela was still advancing. A bullet pinged into the turf just in front of her. She did not stop.

Roger ran forward and grabbed her arm. 'Come back, you little fool. He means it.'

'If auntie can do it, I can,' Angela said defiantly.

'Not while I'm here, you can't. I don't want to be shot, if you do.' He pulled her back by main strength.

'Anyone else who tries to get at me I'll shoot,' came Twyford's voice, raised to a hysterical pitch. 'Tell them that. I'm going to look after myself now.'

The two walked quickly back towards the camp.

'We've got Bray to thank for this,' Roger said angrily.

'Reggie didn't really mean it,' Angela remarked, in a dull voice.

'What I can't understand,' Roger burst out, 'is what's happened to the man. What's broken his nerve like this? He was the man I was relying on to take command and keep us all under discipline. A famous explorer like him to be as scared as an old woman with a mouse! He isn't drinking, is he?'

'No,' said Angela, in the same dull tone. 'But he isn't an explorer either.'

'What?'

'Don't tell anyone, but Reggie's never been more than fifty miles from Johannesburg. Haven't you ever noticed that he's only shown in the tame jungle bits? The really wild jungle – well, Reggie isn't there. They bring the animals down from up-country for him to put his foot on for the photographs.'

'I don't understand.'

'Why, an English company wanted to do explorer pictures like the American ones, and they hired Reggie because he looks the part. His films are just fakes. He let it out to me by mistake. Nobody knows. So you see, he...' Angela laughed dismally. 'Well, he can't help not being a hero, poor old Reggie.'

'Are you fond of him, Angela?' Roger asked sympathetically.

'Damn it, I can't help it if you think it's dim of me, but I am,' replied Miss St Thomas, not without resentment.

Roger was about to reply suitably, when a howl ahead of them brought him up with an anxious curse. But this time it was a howl of joy. Mr Parker, dancing as madly as any dervish, was shouting in all directions through megaphoned hands:

'A ship! There's a ship!'

6

The little group stood on the top of the cliff, watching the boat as it crawled along, at least two miles out to sea.

The Brays and Twyford could not have seen it, for none of them had appeared; while Miss Crosspatrick, in her frenzied anxiety, had gone right down to the beach, as if to get a few yards nearer to the objects of their hopes. Mr Combe, after one long gaze, had disappeared abruptly – probably, Roger thought uncharitably, to have an attack of hysteria in his tent.

Unity took her eyes off the boat for a second to look down at Miss Crosspatrick.

'Roger,' she said, 'what on earth is Stella doing?'

Roger looked down. Miss Crosspatrick had taken off her dress, and was walking down to the sea.

'She certainly means to be the first aboard,' Roger said, with a little laugh. 'My goodness, she's going to wade out.'

Miss Crosspatrick was indeed wading out. All eyes watched her with growing astonishment while she waded farther and farther, and then began to swim, strongly and purposefully, in the direction of the boat.

'Roger!' Crystal turned to him in horror. 'Don't you see what she's doing? She's going to try and swim out to it. She's mad! She'll be drowned under our eyes.'

'Combe's the only one who can overtake her,' Roger muttered, and began to call: 'Combe! Combe!'

'Allow me – have a try too,' gasped Mr Parker, and set off heading down the path, tearing off his coat as he went.

'No, no! Harold, you're not to!' shrieked Unity in anguish. Miss Crosspatrick was a tolerably strong swimmer: Mr Parker was an exceedingly weak one. 'Harold – come *back!* Oh...'

But Mr Parker did not come back. Instead, he paused on the path a hundred feet or so above the beach and shouted as loudly as he could:

'Stella! Stella! Wait for me – I'm coming too.'

Miss Crosspatrick, now some little distance out, seemed to hear him, for she turned her head.

'Wait for me! Coming too!' howled Mr Parker, and sped on.

The little group watched him with breathless fear as he crossed the beach and ran into the water, in his shirt and trousers. Miss Crosspatrick had evidently heard him, for she was waiting. Roger continued to shout for Mr Combe, but that gentleman remained invisible.

'Oh, hell,' said Roger, and began to run down the path himself; though he knew quite well that he was not a strong enough swimmer to rescue Mr Parker when he began to sink, as undoubtedly he would. As he ran Roger was vaguely conscious of a couple of shots from the island behind him. The Brays or Twyford, he thought, must be trying to attract the attention of the boat too.

Not that Mr Parker appeared to be anywhere near sinking yet, though his little dabbing strokes did not carry him along very fast. Miss Crosspatrick was showing signs of impatience too, and the onlookers could hear her calling to her pursuer, though they could not distinguish her words.

'Oh, I can't bear it,' Unity moaned. 'He'll be drowned. I know he'll be drowned.'

Mr Parker had almost reached his quarry now, and Miss Crosspatrick had already turned and begun to swim on, when the audience heard a faint scream of unmistakable terror. The next instant Mr Parker threw up his hands and disappeared under the water.

Unity uttered a strangled little shriek and threw herself on the ground, her face in her arms.

'Oh, the poor, the poor boy,' murmured Enid through white lips.

But it appeared that Mr Parker was not drowned yet, for he bobbed up again, maintained his position for a few seconds, and then, with another but feebler scream, disappeared once more.

'No!' said Crystal eagerly. 'Look – she's going back for him. Oh, well *done*, Stella! She's got him up – she's holding him – she's...yes, she's bringing him in. Oh, Stella...'

'She's bringing him back?' asked Unity, jumping up.

It was true. Slowly and very laboriously Stella was making her way to the shore, swimming on her back, with Mr Parker an inert weight upon her. Roger met them just over halfway, and was able to help her to support the weight.

Unity flew down to the beach. Mr Parker may not have been quite drowned, but he had come very near it. He was quite unconscious and, while Stella lay panting on the sand a little distance away, tended by Crystal, Unity helped Roger to administer artificial respiration.

At last his eyes opened, he sat up, and was at once extremely sick.

When Unity had fussed over him for a minute or two, Roger asked, with some severity:

'Well, and now perhaps you'll tell me, young Harold what you thought you were going to do before you nearly committed suicide? I suppose you know we nearly had two corpses on our hands then instead of one?'

'Well, you see, Mr Sheringham,' Mr Parker explained modestly between gulps, 'I thought if she saw I was sinking, she'd have to make an effort to rescue me. And then of course she'd have to come back to land. Well, I mean, it stood to reason really, didn't it?'

Roger looked at him. 'Do you mean to tell me, young Harold, that you deliberately swam out there, knowing you wouldn't be able to swim back, with the intention of drowning under her eyes if she didn't rescue you?'

Mr Parker wriggled. 'Well, Mr Sheringham, that isn't quite a fair way of putting it. I mean, not really. Because I knew that Miss Crosspatrick – well, she'd feel she had to rescue me, wouldn't she?'

'It's not a chance I should have cared to bank on,' Roger said grimly.

'Harold!' Unity's eyes were shining. 'Harold, do you know that you're the bravest man I know?'

'Oh, come now, Unity.' Mr Parker positively squirmed. 'It's awfully decent of you to say a thing like that, but I'm not a bit brave really. I wish I was. I was awfully frightened just now. Well, quite terrified, you might say.'

'Don't contradict the girl,' shouted Roger. 'You are the bravest man she knows. And the bravest man I know too.'

'But oh, Harold,' Unity sighed, 'I do wish it had been me you rescued.'

A scream of despair from Stella cut short his exchange.

'The ship!' she shrieked, shading her eyes as she stared uselessly into the west. 'It's – gone.'

As if in farewell salute, a positive fusillade of shots burst out from the island behind them.

chapter seventeen

'He fired at me!' shouted Mr Combe hysterically. 'I told him I only wanted to light the beacon, but he wouldn't take any notice of me. He fired at me. It's his fault we're still here, I tell you – Bray's fault.'

'Perhaps he didn't hear what you said,' intercepted Roger tactfully.

'Of course, he heard,' Twyford supported Mr Combe in a below of fury. He waved his rifle threateningly at the circle of intent faces which surrounded the two, as if offering to shoot the head off anyone who disagreed with him. 'I heard, didn't I? I came out to help Combe fire the beacon. It was – it was my duty. He fired again, at both of us.'

'And you fired back?'

'Of course I did,' shouted Twyford, almost incoherently. 'I fired every cartridge I'd got at the swine. But I couldn't see where he was. You heard what Combe said, Angela?'

'Of course I did,' Angela replied shrilly. 'Anyone could have. Bray must have heard.'

'Where were you, Angela?' Roger asked.

'Just past the tents here. I'd thought of the beacon too, but Vally was ahead of me.' Angela was shaking with anger. 'Bray deliberately stopped anyone getting to the beacon. It's my belief he didn't want us to be rescued.'

'Of course he didn't, you fools!' suddenly screamed Stella. 'Don't you see why? He killed Guy Pidgeon, and he knows we know it. He wants to keep us here, to save himself.'

An ugly murmur of assent followed Stella's words: a kind of inarticulate growl which sounded indescribably menacing.

Roger, a little alarmed, stepped forward.

'Stella, shut up. Listen to me, everyone. We don't know that Bray killed Pidgeon any more than we know that anyone else did. After all, he – '

'Then why does he shut himself up there, and shoot everyone who goes near him?' demanded Unity.

Something like a shout approved her interruption.

'I'll tell you, if you'll only listen,' Roger shouted it down. 'He thinks there's buried treasure there. Pidgeon laid a trap – a joke. He planted a jewelled cross near the hut. Bray dug it up, and – '

'Rot! Lies – just lies!' shrieked Mr Combe, beside himself. 'Don't try to shield him like that, Sheringham, or we'll believe that you've got an interest in keeping us here too. You haven't seemed so damned keen to get us off, have you?'

'Don't make a fool of yourself, Combe,' Roger returned curtly. 'Crystal, you know about Pidgeon planting the cross. Tell them.' Everyone stared at Crystal.

'Yes, that's true enough, but...' She paused.

'But what?' Roger prompted impatiently.

'He shouldn't have stopped Valentine firing the beacon, should he? We might have been off the island by now if he hadn't done that.'

'Oh, my God,' sobbed Stella. 'Off this island...'

'Stop that, Stella,' Roger said sharply. He was becoming angry himself. It was foolish of Crystal to have added that rider.

'Stop that yourself, Sheringham,' Mr Combe cried. 'I tell you, we're tired of you trying to boss things here. Aren't we, everyone? Enid, aren't we?'

Enid gave a sweetly long-suffering smile. 'I've never pretended to think that Mr Sheringham has done as much as he might have done since...since...'

Roger went across the circle to her. 'Do you want a riot?' he asked, in a savage undertone. 'Because if you don't, back me up.' He looked round for one supporter at least, but even Crystal avoided his eye. Lady Darracott he had seen a few minutes ago, look out of Sir John's tent, shrug her shoulders, and go back again.

As the looks thrown on him became more hostile, his anger grew. He strode across to Twyford.

'Give me that gun, Twyford,' he ordered curtly.

'I'll do nothing of the sort,' Twyford replied in a high voice. 'I want it. And do you know why? To shoot Bray. You'd never do anything like that, but someone's got to. Otherwise he'll shoot all of us. He murdered Pidgeon, and he'll murder all of us if he gets a chance.'

'Reggie's right, Roger,' put in Angela unexpectedly. 'You'd better keep out of this from now on.' Between them the two defeated Roger's effort to grab the rifle.

'Lynch him!' suddenly screamed Mr Combe. 'Lynch the murderer! Lynch Bray!'

Roger looked round helplessly. The faces surrounding him were almost unrecognisable, distorted all of a sudden with hate and terror and a dreadful anticipation.

'Stop, everyone!' he shouted above the din. 'I think you're going mad. Bray didn't murder anyone. Use your sense. Bray was attacked himself. If there is a murderer at all, it's only reasonable to suppose that it's the man who attacked Bray, isn't it?' He paused to glare round, and then made his gesture. Pointing a dramatic finger at Combe, he thundered: 'Combe, you're the man. You attacked Bray. Why?'

'Because I know he was the murderer, and I was afraid he was going to murder Enid in her tent, under our noses!' screamed Mr Combe.

Roger found the wind taken out of his sails. He looked at Combe helplessly.

'I've always said it was Bray, Roger,' Crystal put in, almost pleadingly. 'We must do something. Things can't go on like this. Won't you...?'

There was a moment's tense pause.

'Have you all gone mad?'

Lady Darracott's tone of cold disgust brought every head round.

'Auntie,' Angela cried, in peremptory anxiety, 'keep out of this, for your own sake. Your heart...'

'If you think I am going to stand aside, Angela, and watch you take part in an attempt at mass murder,' Lady Darracott said, with spirit, 'you are indeed wrong.'

Roger, seizing his chance, jumped forward, twitched the rifle from Twyford's hand, and, exerting all his strength, snapped the stock across his knee, tossing the broken pieces aside. A howl of anger went up.

'Perhaps that will bring you to your senses,' Roger shouted. 'There'll be no shooting of Bray while I'm on this island.'

Above the clamour a lazily interested voice made itself heard from the fringe of the circle.

'No need to shoot the bloody man. String him up. Perfectly in order.' Sir John nodded sagely, as though he had been meditating the problem all this time in his tent.

'Lynch him! Lynch Bray!'

'Twyford, get a rope. One of the tent-ropes will do.'

'Here's a knife, Twyford.'

'We ought to have done this at the beginning.'

'But I say – what about his gun?'

'He can't shoot the lot of us, can he?'

'I don't care if he does. Anything's better than what we've been through.'

'Lynching… I never expected to see anyone lynched.'

'Angela, I insist…'

'Auntie, *do* keep out of this.'

Roger, completely disregarded, looked round for Combe. There was nothing to do but knock him and Twyford out. The others would be more manageable. Combe had disappeared. Twyford was already cutting the guy-ropes from one of the tents. Roger marched up to him.

Before he could reach him, there was the patter of swift footsteps behind him and a stunning bow on the back of the head. But Roger never felt the blow.

2

The first thing of which Roger really became aware, as his senses oozed back to him was a thundering headache. He tried vaguely to put his hands up to it, but found something impeded them and groaned instead.

The voice of Lady Darracott, surprisingly close, said sharply: 'Mr Sheringham!'

Although the effort hurt him considerably, Roger succeeded in opening his eyes. He found them looking at a face, for the moment unrecognisable, only an inch or two from his own. The face drew itself back a further inch or two, and resolved itself into that of Lady Darracott.

Roger swallowed. 'Where's – the others?' he asked thickly.

'Are you sensible now?'

'No,' groaned Roger, and shut his eyes again.

In a moment or two he felt himself shaken violently, and his head rocked. He protested incoherently.

'Pull yourself together, Mr Sheringham, please. Don't you understand? There's murder being done.'

Roger opened his eyes again. 'What the devil...?' he muttered. 'All right – half a minute. Let me pull myself together.' He pinned his still swimming senses into their proper places.

Quite suddenly everything became clear.

He and Lady Darracott were lying on the ground, facing each other. They were tied together. That is to say, Roger's wrists were fastened together behind Lady Darracott's back, and hers behind his, and the right ankle of each was tied firmly to the left ankle of the other. Neither could move.

'Tell me what's happened,' Roger asked, in a steady voice.

Lady Darracott told him. When Roger had been struck down from behind by Combe, she had tried to stem the rising hysteria alone. But the sight of the man who had held them back all this time lying helpless on the ground had seemed to drive them still further into insanity. Even Unity, and Crystal herself after a second's compunction, had found no more thought for Roger. Led on by Twyford, Combe, and a dementedly howling Stella, the one idea had been to get at Bray. They were all taking his guilt as indisputable. Lady Darracott herself had received summary treatment. While Twyford held Angela back from interfering, three or four of them fell on her. Enid Fayre had suggested tying her and Roger together, to keep the pair of them immobile, and had herself helped to do so.

'Enid!' exclaimed Roger.

His blood began to boil.

'I was lucky to escape serious injury,' said Lady Darracott calmly. 'They didn't hurt me much, in spite of the *mêlée*.'

'Enid!' Roger repeated. His brain was not working properly yet, but part of it was functioning automatically. '*Enid!*' said Roger.

A plaintive note came into Lady Darracott's voice. 'Do you realise that one of my arms is underneath you, Mr Sheringham? It's getting rather painful. Could we roll over?'

'How long have I been unconscious?' Roger demanded, when they had succeeded in transferring his weight to Lady Darracott's other arm.

'About five minutes.'

'And the others?'

'They went off at top-speed across the island. There was a good deal of shouting, and – listen!' There was the sound of shots.

'My goodness,' Roger fumed, 'if they catch him. And her. I must get there.'

He began to tug frantically at his wrists, using Lady Darracott's sides without ceremony as fulcrums for the levers of his arms. But the knots had been tied too well.

'Can't we even get apart from each other?' he panted. His head was throbbing painfully, but he was master of himself now.

'I can assure you, I've done my best,' Lady Darracott said, with a grim humour. 'I have the highest respect for you, Mr Sheringham, but I prefer to air it at a little greater distance from its object.'

Really, Roger thought as he twisted and wriggled, she's been wonderful. If Lady Darracott's heart was genuinely unsound, she ought to have been dead by now.

'It's no good,' he groaned. Their arms were too inextricably mixed up, and the tethering of their ankles prevented any possibility of sliding out that way.

Roger thought desperately, the faint shouts and shooting from the other side of the island driving him nearly frantic.

'Look here, Lady Darracott – I *must* get there. I must!'

'Then we shall have to go together.'

'I'm afraid we shall. Look here, can you stick it?'

'Do you intend that we should roll across the island?'

'No, no. If we can only get to our feet, I think we might be able to get along. Though one of us will have to go backwards. But with your heart...'

'My heart,' said Lady Darracott briskly, 'must take its chance. If you can get us to our feet, I'll follow where you lead. In fact, I shall hardly be able to do anything else.'

'Lady Darracott,' said Roger, with emotion, 'you're grand!'

'Wait till you've got me to the other side of the island,' retorted that lady dryly. 'One minute before we get up. Do you see the remains of Reggie's rifle over there? You only broke the stock, you know. Luckily they didn't appear to realise that it's perfectly capable of firing.'

'But we haven't got any ammunition.'

'We have one cartridge. I saw it on the ground. It must have fallen out of Reggie's pocket. It was just out of my reach, and I amused myself in getting possession of it while I was waiting for you to come round. I'm afraid I can't hand it to you, but if I leave it on the ground here behind your back, you ought to be able to get it with a little complicated rolling.'

In spite of the situation Roger could not help laughing. 'And after that I'm afraid we shall have to roll over to the rifle. I wish now I hadn't thrown it so far.'

'Well, I'm ready, when you are,' said Lady Darracott, in a resigned voice.

They began to roll.

Roger was glad there was no one to observe them.

Lady Darracott must have been gladder still.

By dint of complicated manoeuvres Roger succeeded in getting hold of the business-part of the rifle and the single precious cartridge.

'And now,' he said, 'we've got to get to our feet.'

Somewhat breathlessly Lady Darracott acquiesced.

They struggled to do so, first calmly, then frantically, then calmly again. Then they rested.

'Once more,' Roger panted.

But it was impossible. Their bonds were too tight, and it was impossible to retain enough balance. They were exhausting themselves fruitlessly.

'Oh, my goodness,' Roger groaned, 'we can't do it.'

Lady Darracott had no breath left even to groan. They lay, gasping helplessly.

'Roger!' said a voice. 'Oh, thank goodness you're all right.'

The next moment Crystal was cutting the ropes that tied them.

3

Crystal hurriedly explained. She had seen that even though she supported Roger against the others, her help would be useless; so she had pretended to acquiesce in the hope of being useful later. Now she had slipped back to see what she could do.

'But the others?' Roger asked breathlessly, rubbing his chafed ankles and wrists. 'What are they doing? Bray's firing at them?'

'Yes. And they're split up. Combe and Twyford have gone round by the beacon to try and get him in the rear, while the rest keep him busy in front. They hardly seem afraid of his rifle.'

'They're mad. I must go along. Lady Darracott, you stay here, please. If they see you, they'll know I'm free. Look after Fayre, will you? Are you all right, by the way?'

'Tolerably,' replied Lady Darracott, though looking now somewhat shaken.

'But what are you going to do, Roger?' Crystal asked.

'I don't know.' Roger looked doubtfully at the broken piece of rifle as he picked it up. He had no plan.

'It's no good trying to stop them. They really are mad. You'd only get killed next time.'

'I must wait for the right moment, that's all,' Roger nodded. 'And I only hope I shall recognise it when it comes.' He glanced round. The twilight was falling fast now, and the hovering storm made the light murkier than usual. 'I ought to be able to creep up through the plantation without being seen. You must join the others again, Crystal, to avoid suspicion. And when the time comes, back me up as best you can. It will be when I fire this shot – I've only got the one. But I shall hold my hand till the last possible moment, in case some of them come to their senses in time. Hullo – what's that?'

There had been perhaps half a dozen shots in quick succession, followed by a minute's silence; and then one huge, prolonged shout, in which the triumph was unmistakable.

'They've got him,' Roger said grimly. 'Come along, Crystal.'

He set off at a run across the island, followed by Crystal. When he was halfway across a burst of flame, and more cheering, showed that the beacon had been fired.

'A lot of use that is, now.' Roger muttered angrily.

He reached the edge of the plantation unseen, and slipped into the greater darkness inside it, while Crystal ran round the flank to join the others as unobtrusively as possible. The trees in the plantation were not very close together, but Roger, advancing with rapid caution from one to another, had little fear of being seen. He gripped the broken rifle anxiously as he approached the farther edge and took cover behind a sturdy trunk from which a view of the clear ground beyond could be obtained, with Mr Bray's recent digging operations in full evidence.

At first it was difficult to see what was happening. A great deal of noise was in progress, shouts and cries and high-pitched squeals. Then the flames from the beacon, growing fiercer, lit up the scene with an appropriately red glow.

The squeals, Roger now saw, were coming from Mrs Bray, who struggling frantically, was being tied to a tree only twenty yards away by Combe and Twyford. The rest of the party seemed to be clustered round something that was lying on the ground. Roger strained his eyes. Had they killed Bray already?

Apparently not, for Twyford and Combe, having secured Mrs Bray, made their way over to the other group and got busy again. Roger could not see what they were doing, but he thought that Bray was unconscious and that the two were trying to revive him. Roger's hands itched on his rifle, but the man's danger was not, it seemed, immediate, and the one cartridge was precious.

He started violently, and swung the barrel of this rifle round. Someone had appeared beside him. It was Crystal, and she was thrusting something into his hands.

'Bray's rifle,' she whispered. 'Better than your broken one. It was lying on the ground. No one saw me.' And she was gone.

Roger extracted his cartridge from the breech of the other, dropped the broken gun gratefully on the ground, and cuddled the undamaged one into the crook of his arm.

As he did so there was another outburst from the group in front of him, an upheaval of some kind, and then Roger found himself staring at Bray himself.

The man, having apparently been revived, had been dragged to his feet and was now standing there, swaying slightly and looking round in a dazed way at the frantically gesticulating figures round him. Darkness had quite fallen by now, but the leaping flames of the beacon illuminated the scene. Bray's face was running with blood, his clothing torn and his collar missing. His hands appeared to be tied behind him.

Suddenly Stella Crosspatrick darted forward and tried to shake him. 'You killed him!' she screamed. 'Say you did – admit it.'

'Yes, confess you did it!' Unity joined in shrilly, shaking her fists under Bray's nose.

Bray gazed at them in bewilderment. 'Here, what's this?' he suddenly bellowed. 'What the hell's all this about? Killed who?'

Mr Parker stepped forward. 'They want you to admit you killed Mr Pidgeon.'

'But I never did.'

Stella slapped him with all her strength on the face. 'Liar!' she screamed.

'Here, stop this tommy-rot,' Bray roared. 'Undo my 'ands. What the 'ell's up with you all? By cripes, I'll...' He lowered his head, and charged forward.

Twyford swung a fist to the side of his head, and knocked him down, and Roger saw Combe kick him as he lay there. Once again the unfortunate man was jerked to his feet, amid renewed howls that he should confess.

Mrs Bray, still struggling with her bonds, was moaning to herself. 'My Gawd, they'll kill 'im – my Gawd, they'll kill 'im.

And he never did a thing. 'Elp – 'elp!' No one took any notice of her.

'All right,' bellowed Twyford above the din, 'if he won't confess, we know what to do with him. Come on, Combe.'

Evidently they had a prearranged plan, for both moved at once. Roger lifted his gun, and then lowered it again; they did not mean to kill him yet. He saw now that a long rope had been tied round Bray's body just under his arms. Pulling on this, Twyford and Combe dragged him over in the direction of the iron hut. Bray tried to pull against them, but Stella, following behind him, battered her fists on his head and Unity helped to push him. He stumbled to his knees, and the pull on the rope brought him full-length to the ground bellowing and cursing. Stella and Unity both joined the men and dragged him along thus. Angela walked with them. Parker hung back, as if still a little uncertain, and so did Crystal. Sir John stood by with his hands in his pockets, looking on in silence.

Someone else was looking on in silence too.

Enid Fayre had taken no part in the scrummage. She was standing alone, watching the proceedings with a rapt expression that chilled Roger even more than the naked blood-lust of the others. For some reason he obtained the impression that this was the culminating hour of Enid's life, and that Enid knew it. Dramatising herself as usual, she was yet able for once to stand outside herself and watch others as well as herself; for the others were all a part of herself at that moment. Standing aside, she saw nevertheless Combe pulling on the rope, and Stella raining blows on Bray's head. Roger felt a rising nausea as he watched her. A great many things were clear to him now.

They had got Bray to the hut, and were doing something complicated with the rope. Roger moved a little away from the tree. If they were really going to hang him... As Bray's body rose suddenly from the ground into the air Roger took a step or two forward and lifted his rifle.

But they were not hanging him yet after all. Kicking and roaring, Bray appeared now to be stuck, a few feet above the ground, on the side of the iron hut. Twyford and Combe were both out of sight, the former to reappear a minute later round the hut. Roger realised what had been done. The rope, passed right over the roof of the hut, had been pulled on and fastened the other side. Bray was suspended right enough, but not by the neck.

The rising of his great body had been the signal for a further uproar, which Twyford now did nothing to abate. With hootings and jeers Bray was again being urged to confess, Twyford was asking shrilly why, if there was nothing to hide, he had prevented the beacon being fired, and Angela St Thomas, herself carried away by the general hysteria, was frenziedly demanding to know why he had fired on Reggie.

'I didn't know there was a boat in,' shouted Bray, his voice now a little less robust. 'Catch me stopping you if I'd known. I didn't try to hit 'im, Angela. Honest to goodness I didn't. Ask 'im – he knows I didn't.'

'Liar!' yelled Twyford. 'Damned liar! You did!'

'Hang him!' screamed Stella, flecks of froth at the corners of her mouth. She executed some absurd little steps, like a grotesque dance. 'Hang the murderer!'

'Hang him! Hang him!'

'You can't hang me – I say you can't!' Unmistakable fear was showing in Bray's voice now. 'I never done anything. It'd be murder. Oh, come on – be sports. Let me down. It's past a joke, this is. This rope's cutting me into – '

His words were drowned in a shrill roar. Combe had appeared on the roof of the hut, a coil of rope and an axe in his hands.

Amid shouts of encouragement he slithered down the side of the roof to where Bray's head almost reached it, and slipped a noose of rope round the wretched man's neck. Then with a shout of triumph he tossed the slack back over the roof. Twyford darted round out of sight. The rope tautened enough to make Bray let out a shout of fear and protest. Twyford was evidently securing it on the other side of the hut.

Combe brandished his axe, and Roger's rifle lifted.

But apparently Combe's action had had unexpected results. When it came to the point, perhaps nerves which had been too tightly stretched drew back a little towards normality. Unity, screaming incoherently a moment ago, suddenly shrieked out a shuddering protest. Crystal instantly took her up. Twyford appearing round the corner of the hut, called out to Combe to cut the rope that was holding Bray up, but Crystal shouted him down.

'No – no, wait a minute, Valentine! Wait a minute!'

Combe lowered his axe and peered down. 'What's the matter?'

'He – he may not have done it after all,' Crystal called desperately. 'Give him the benefit of the doubt. Keep him tied up till the yacht comes back.'

'Oh, bravo, Crystal!' Roger, whipping round as nervously as any cat, found Lady Darracott beside him. She lifted one eyebrow quizzically and shrugged her shoulders by way of explanation.

A howl had greeted Crystal's words. But it was not all disapproval. Mr Parker's voice had been unmistakably for delay; though Sir John, surveying the scene benignly as he rocked gently backwards and forwards, seemed to be grunting in a detached way that Mr Bray was a bloody man and had better be strung up for everyone's sake. But the dissension was enough to make itself felt.

Shouts and counter-shouts began to arise. Crystal ran forward and tried to offer herself as a support for Bray's swinging feet, but was knocked out of the way by Twyford, who was loudly calling for Combe to cut the rope.

Combe lifted his hatchet again.

'Shoot, Mr Sheringham – shoot!' urged Lady Darracott.

'Remember I've only one cartridge,' Roger whispered tensely, as he drew a steady bead on Combe.

But Mr Combe had lowered his axe again.

'Wait!' he shouted into the din. 'If we're not all in agreement, let Mrs Fayre decide, one way or the other. She won't be afraid to take the responsibility, and we'll abide by what she says, whatever it is. Enid!'

Again a dead silence fell on the shrieking group. Even Stella restrained herself, to stare at Enid.

Enid surveyed them as they waited for her word, and a tiny little smile curled the extreme corners of her exquisite mouth.

'Enid!' implored Mr Bray, in a choked and desperate appeal. 'You know I didn't do it. You know I wouldn't do a thing like that. For God's sake tell them so.'

Enid prolonged the pause almost unbearably.

At last she spoke, thrillingly and clear.

'Friends, this man has killed someone who was very dear to me. For that he must die himself. It is the law.'

For a moment everyone stood stock-still and silent, except for a scream from Mrs Bray and a last groaning 'Enid!' from the doomed man. Then there was a shout of such exultation that Roger felt Lady Darracott herself shiver against him.

Combe lifted his axe for the last time.

Roger stepped out from the tree.

'Combe!' he bellowed. 'Get off that roof, or I'll shoot you.'

Every head swung in his direction. Combe arrested his action for an instant and then, with a shrill, unnatural laugh, swung the axe up.

Roger pressed the trigger.

There was no report. Bray's capture was explained. His rifle had jammed.

Combe's axe descended, and the aim was true. With a snap the rope parted. Mrs Bray's scream sounded like that of a trapped rabbit, and Bray's body leapt downwards.

4

Bray's body reached the ground with a thud, and for a moment everyone, including Roger himself, stared at it stupidly. It ought to have remained in the air, jerking and twisting and clutching at a rope round its neck, but it had done nothing of the sort. For the instant nobody seemed to know why.

It was Twyford who found the explanation. 'The knot!' he shouted. 'It slipped.'

'You fool!' Combe stamped with insane rage on the roof. 'You didn't tie it properly.'

'I thought I'd tied it.'

'Well, you hadn't. Go on – don't stand there! Go round and pull the other rope.'

They stared at each other.

Crystal came running towards Mrs Bray. She had a knife in her hand, and began rapidly to cut the cords binding the frantic woman.

'I cut the other rope,' she called exultantly to Roger.

'Well done!' Roger was thinking rapidly. If Bray could recover himself, there was a chance. Two men against two –

that was better than equal, so long as Parker remained neutral. And as for the women... His eye fell on the broken rifle he had brought with him. Automatically he extracted the cartridge from the jammed one, threw the useless rifle aside and, picking up the other, slipped the cartridge into the breech. Combe and Twyford were still arguing, Twyford pointing out that he could not unaided haul Bray up. Bray was still lying on the ground, with Mrs Bray already on her way to him.

Combe jumped down suddenly from the roof.

'All right,' he said furiously, 'if you can't, you can't. So I'd better finish the job myself.' He swung the axe over the prostrate man's head.

Roger took what aim he could, and shot. This time the luck was better. Combe dropped where he stood.

There was a petrified silence.

Roger walked forward.

'And I'll shoot the next person who disobeys me, man or woman. Twyford, go back to the camp. Angela, you stay here.'

Without a word Twyford slouched away. Angela hesitated, looked at the rifle in Roger's hands, and stood her ground.

Bray struggled slowly to his feet.

Still the silence persisted.

An unexpected voice broke it: a large, hearty, rough voice that spoke in a jovial kind of shout.

'Ah, here you are. What's the idea? Marooned, are you? Saw your light, so we put a landing-party ashore, and – hullo, what's this? Accident of some kind?'

Roger made the hardest effort of his life and kept his voice calm as he turned to a little party of seamen, headed by the mate who had spoken.

'Yes,' he said, 'we were marooned. 'I'm delighted to see you. An accident? Yes, I'm afraid we have.'

'Not serious, I hope, hey?'

'It very nearly was,' said Roger.

epilogue one

Roger, walking down Jeremy Street one day, ran into Willie Fayre. Willie tried to pass with a nod, but Roger took his arm.

'How are you, Fayre, after all this time?'

'Very fit, thanks, very fit.' Fayre looked round him as if seeking a way of escape, but Roger held firm.

'Come along to my rooms in the Albany. I've got some rather pleasant sherry.'

'Oh, no, thanks. Really, I must be getting along.'

'Or there's a cask of XXXX, if you prefer it.'

'No, really, I...'

'Come along,' said Roger firmly. 'I want to hear all about your good fortune.' He marched the other along the pavement.

In Roger's sitting-room Willie, perched on the extreme edge of a chair as if ready to spring away at any moment, sipped his sherry.

'The old wound quite all right now?' Roger asked chattily.

'Yes, quite, thanks. Quite.'

'You were lucky it wasn't more serious.'

'Er – yes.'

'Have you seen Combe at all?'

'Er – no.'

'He's all right, of course. He only got it through the flesh of the thigh, but you'd have thought it was through the tummy from the fuss he made while we were getting him on the boat.'

'Really?'

'Yes. Like this sherry?'

'Very nice indeed.'

'Well, you ought to be a judge. But I suppose you have nothing to do with the wine business nowadays?'

'Er – no. I've retired from that.'

'Well, I should think so. Quite a romance, your coming into all Pidgeon's money so unexpectedly, wasn't it?'

'Er – I suppose it was, yes.'

'And so long afterwards. How long was it before the will turned up, or was sent for probate, or whatever it was?'

'Nearly a year, I think.'

'Nearly a year, yes. Very odd. And in the meantime, I was very sorry to see you'd lost…' Roger looked grave.

Willie shifted uncomfortably on the edge of the chair. 'Yes. Er – yes.'

'I see she married again very shortly afterwards.'

'Yes, I – I believe she did.'

'Poor Enid.' Roger sighed sententiously. 'I hope she's happy now, at all events. Is he a nice kind of fellow?'

'Very, I believe.'

'But considerably younger?'

'Yes, oh, yes.'

'Well off?'

'Er – fairly, I believe.'

'But nothing like so well off as you?'

'Well – I suppose not.'

Roger grinned. 'It gives me quite a warm feeling, to be talking to such a rich man.'

'Really?' Willie smiled nervously. 'I mean, how absurd.'

'Not at all. Of course, you knew about this secret will before you knocked your cousin over that cliff?'

Willie bounded in his chair, and his face went as white as a ceiling.

Roger took the glass from his shaking hand and refilled it.

'At least,' he remarked chattily, 'when I say "knocked" I'm consciously exaggerating. I know perfectly well you wouldn't knock anyone over a cliff. I suppose really he just fell over during the quarrel?'

Willie stared at him with huge eyes.

'It's quite all right,' Roger said reassuringly. 'There are no concealed witnesses or dictaphones.'

Willie continued to stare.

'Don't you think,' Roger said more gently, 'that you'd like to get it off your chest?'

There was a long silence.

Gradually the colour came back into Willie's cheeks.

'Take another drink,' Roger advised.

Willie took one.

'One can talk about Enid now that she hasn't anything to do with you,' Roger pursued. 'It was she who was at the bottom of it, wasn't she?'

Willie hesitated. 'Only – indirectly.'

'I meant indirectly.'

'Yes.' Willie stared into his glass. 'Enid had always been dissatisfied,' he said, in a low voice. 'She had, in the cant phrase, expensive tastes. I wasn't making an expensive income. Enid was always heavily in debt, and blamed me for the fact. She seemed to consider it her right to have anything she wanted – I don't know why.' Willie looked as if this old problem of his still puzzled him.

'Beautiful women with no intelligence often do,' suggested Roger.

'Enid had no intelligence, of course.' Roger noticed that Willie spoke of her as if she were dead, though quite without emotion. 'I can't imagine, now, why I ever fell in love with her. Still less why, having fallen, I remained in love with her for so many years. But I did. I knew really all the time that Enid could never feel any love, even any unselfish affection, for anyone except herself, but I suppose I persuaded myself that there was always hope. A man is exceedingly foolish, when a beautiful woman is concerned.'

'Exceedingly,' Roger agreed, not without bitterness.

'She was always taunting me,' Willie pursued, in a mournful, deprecating voice. 'She had a habit of referring to the wives of our richer friends and the things they had, as if I was wilfully withholding something from her which I could quite well have given. She used to talk about what "other people" did for their wives, and how "other people" could make money for their wives to spend. She despised me very thoroughly for not being able to make money. The making of money was her only criterion of a husband's worth.'

'She possibly wasn't unique.' Roger interjected dryly.

'Possibly not. But it used to worry me a great deal. It seems hardly credible now, but her taunts used really to upset me very deeply. She actually made me *feel* guilty. I lived in a constant dread that she would leave me one day for a richer man. As, in fact, she did in the end.'

Willie paused, drank a little sherry, and then seemed to relapse into brooding reminiscence.

Roger coughed. 'And that's what you quarrelled with Pidgeon about?'

'Well, yes. At least, that was the cause of it. During the time we were on the sea she had driven me almost crazy.

She was always holding Bray up to me as the type of man she admired. She said he was attracted by her, and would go off with her at any minute if she only raised her little finger. I – I was acutely distressed. Really, I was hardly responsible for my actions. And I went to Guy's tent that night to say that the position was intolerable. He must get us off the island somehow, or I wouldn't answer for the consequences. Somehow or other Guy got the whole story out of me.

'He was not at all sympathetic. He was – er – extremely outspoken about Enid, and naturally I resented this. He then informed me that he had planned the whole cruise with the idea of freeing me from Enid. He said something about her and Bray that – that made me almost see red. Then he grinned in that exasperating way of his, and said that I was getting too rowdy for a respectable camp and we had better continue the discussion away from it. We went off together and strolled along the cliffs.

'There Guy told me something which surprised me very much. He said he had not left his money to the nation at all. He had only given that out in order to prevent Enid stopping with me; for he was asserting that it was only a question of time in any case before she left me. Actually, he said, he had left it all to me, and I remember how he chuckled as he pointed out how that would serve Enid right, when she found she had run away from the richest man in England. I asserted just as firmly that Enid was an honourable woman, and not at all what he thought her. And then he began taunting me.

'He stood on the edge of the cliff, and actually dared me to push him over. That was all I had to do, he said, to obtain an enormous fortune: and I hadn't got the guts to do it. No wonder Enid despised me. He asked me how I would face her in the morning, not having had the courage to do a little think like that for a wife who liked money so much. It wasn't even, he said, as if there would be any danger. No one had seen us leave the camp together. His death would be put down at once to an accident.

'And then he called Enid a really most unpleasant name. I was incensed to the point of frenzy. I picked up a stone that was lying near my foot and flung it at him. It hit him in the chest. He uttered one dreadful shout, and disappeared over the edge.

'And to this moment,' said Willie very solemnly, 'I am unable to say whether I flung the stone in rage at hearing Enid called a – that is, in rage, and without thought of the consequences, or whether I really did hope that it would do what in point of fact it did do – er – knock him over the cliff. But this I do know. While I was in the very act of throwing, the thought did flash through my mind that if murder ever was suspected, there was a murderer on the island already and the affair would naturally be put down to his account.

'We now know that there was nothing of the sort. But whether I am to consider myself a murderer, or merely unfortunately reckless, I cannot to this day determine; and it has caused me a great deal of distress.' Willie looked extremely distressed.

'The same distress, I suppose,' Roger suggested, 'having been responsible for your public confession that day?'

'Precisely,' nodded Willie. 'It was a genuine sentiment. I was not only very worried at what I had done, but I saw that the consequences might be serious if the mystery were not promptly cleared up. Nevertheless, I am ashamed to say that, having acted on the spur of the moment, I had repented by the next morning and was cowardly enough to be exceedingly frightened of what might be the consequences. I therefore, by pretending ignorance and misleading you on certain vital points, was able to make you think that the confession was a bogus one.'

'You took me in completely,' Roger admitted. 'Completely.'

'Nevertheless, you realised the truth later?'

'Only after we got back to England. And then only by elimination. I decided that it must lie between you and Enid, and I eliminated Enid. It was only a guess.'

'It was a perfectly correct one. I'm glad someone knows. You see, you can give me advice. I am still worried. Do you think I ought to go to the authorities and make a statement, or would no good purpose really be served? You see, I cannot make up my mind whether I am a murderer or not.'

'How long ago was it?' Roger meditated. 'Nearly three years. No, I think on the whole, Fayre, no good purpose would be served.'

'You really think that?' Willie asked anxiously. 'That certainly is a great relief to me. You're quite sure?'

'Quite. Besides,' Roger added with a smile, 'it would be a pity, after you'd held the will so long to give Enid her chance of escaping from you in ignorance, to spoil Guy's plan by not living yourself to enjoy the fruits, wouldn't it?'

epilogue two

Roger lunched that day at his club. He was glad to have met Fayre. He liked tidy ends.

In the smoking-room a large man with a moon-like face greeted him eagerly.

'Ah, Sheringham, just the fellow I wanted to see. Look here, you know Jocelyn Dammers, don't you? Pots of money and doesn't know what to do with it. He's just bought a yacht, and we're making up a party for its maiden cruise. About a dozen, you know; assorted sexes. We shall be away for about a month. It'll be a great time. We can count on you, can't we?'

'Give my thanks to Jocelyn,' Roger said steadily, 'but I'm afraid I shall be too busy that month.'

Anthony Berkeley

Death in the House

When Lord Wellacombe, the Secretary of State for India, collapses in the House of Commons and dies, everyone suspects a stroke. His death causes political waves as a successor is sought and there is the question of a bill to be put through. But then tests show Wellacombe to have been poisoned and not by any conventional method – a thorn covered in South American poison is discovered under the dead man's coat collar. Is this the work of an international terrorist or someone closer to home?

'Anthony Berkeley is the supreme master not of the "twist" but of the "double-twist"!' – *The Sunday Times*

Jumping Jenny

A Roger Sheringham case.

Gentleman sleuth Roger Sheringham is at a fancy-dress party where the theme is murderers and victims. The fun takes a sinister turn however when a real victim is discovered hanging on the roof. Is it suicide – or a perfect murder?

ANTHONY BERKELEY

THE LAYTON COURT MYSTERY

A Roger Sheringham case.

Mr Victor Stanworth, an apparently carefree sixty-year-old, is entertaining a party of friends at his summer residence, Layton Court. When one morning he is found shot dead in the library it is hard to believe it is either suicide or murder. As one of the country-house guests, gentleman sleuth Roger Sheringham resolves to solve the murder. As he pursues the truth he does not conceal any of the evidence, and the reader is able to follow his detection work to the conclusion of this original mystery story.

MURDER IN THE BASEMENT

A Roger Sheringham case.

'Don't come down, Molly. There – there's something pretty beastly here. I must get a policeman.'

When Reginald and Molly Dane return from their honeymoon to a new house, they are curious to explore the cellar. Reginald notices a corner where the bricks have been inexpertly put back to cover a hole dug in the floor. Convinced he will find treasure he takes a pickaxe to it – but discovers a body of a woman in a shallow grave, not treasure in a chest. Chief Inspector Moresby and gentleman sleuth Roger Sheringham are soon on the case. What was the vicitm's identity? Why was she shot through the back of the head and why was she buried naked except for a pair of gloves?

ANTHONY BERKELEY

THE POISONED CHOCOLATES CASE

Roger Sheringham's most famous case.

In this, the best-known of Anthony Berkeley's novels, amateur detective Roger Sheringham investigates his most famous case. When Joan Bendix makes a bet with her husband for a box of chocolates, no one imagines that winning will cost her her life. The seven she eats poison her, and the two her husband eats nearly kill him. The Sheringham Crime Circle find the unusual case baffling, but eventually come up with some very interesting theories – which they then proceed to disprove one by one. Due to a series of false clues the identity – and motive – of the killer appears to be out of reach...

THE SILK STOCKING MURDERS

A Roger Sheringham case.

Gentleman sleuth and novelist Roger Sheringham would not have ordinarily been curious about the suicide of chorus girl Miss Unity Ransome. However when he receives a cry for help from a country parson attempting to trace his missing daughter Janet in London he finds himself involved. And when three other young women are found hanged dead by silk stockings, Sheringham realises that what he is investigating is actually murder.

PAYMENT

Please tick currency you wish to use:

☐ £ (Sterling) ☐ $ (US) ☐ $ (CAN) ☐ € (Euros)

Allow for shipping costs charged per order plus an amount per book as set out in the tables below:

CURRENCY/DESTINATION

	£(Sterling)	$(US)	$(CAN)	€(Euros)
Cost per order				
UK	1.50	2.25	3.50	2.50
Europe	3.00	4.50	6.75	5.00
North America	3.00	3.50	5.25	5.00
Rest of World	3.00	4.50	6.75	5.00
Additional cost per book				
UK	0.50	0.75	1.15	0.85
Europe	1.00	1.50	2.25	1.70
North America	1.00	1.00	1.50	1.70
Rest of World	1.50	2.25	3.50	3.00

PLEASE SEND CHEQUE OR INTERNATIONAL MONEY ORDER
payable to: HOUSE OF STRATUS LTD or HOUSE OF STRATUS INC. or card payment as indicated

STERLING EXAMPLE

Cost of book(s):...................... Example: 3 x books at £6.99 each: £20.97
Cost of order: .... Example: £1.50 (Delivery to UK address)
Additional cost per book:............... Example: 3 x £0.50: £1.50
Order total including shipping:........... Example: £23.97

VISA, MASTERCARD, SWITCH, AMEX:

☐☐☐☐☐☐☐☐☐☐☐☐☐☐☐☐☐☐☐☐

Issue number (Switch only):

☐☐☐

Start Date: ☐☐/☐☐ **Expiry Date:** ☐☐/☐☐

Signature: ____________________

NAME: ____________________

ADDRESS: ____________________

COUNTRY: ____________________

ZIP/POSTCODE: ____________________

Please allow 28 days for delivery. Despatch normally within 48 hours.

Prices subject to change without notice.
Please tick box if you do not wish to receive any additional information. ☐

House of Stratus publishes many other titles in this genre; please check our website (**www.houseofstratus.com**) for more details.